THE WATCHING

Michael Donovan was born in Yorkshire and now lives in Cumbria. A consultant engineer by profession, his first novel *Behind Closed Doors* won the 2012 Northern Crime competition.

By the same author

THE WATCHING

MICHAEL DONOVAN

HOUSE
ON THE
HILL
Publishing

First Published 2018 by **House On The Hill.**

ISBN-10: 1 986676 13 7
ISBN-13: 978 1 986676 13 7

Cover design by **House On The Hill** from Shutterstock images.

p0004

Published by Human Vertex Publications, UK.

For the victims we've failed

PART 1

Curiosities

1

It's eleven fifteen, Thursday morning, and Kate Walker is swimming through treacle. The approaching weekend is a distant concept on the far side of a hopeless appointments list and tomorrow's nightmare court hearing whose subject is fidgeting infuriatingly across her desk as her receptionist hisses in her ear. Violet has called twice now against strict orders, the first time to request an update on Kate's schedule and the second to insist that she talks to a pushy client and not hide behind "do not disturb" admonitions. Violet's an astute woman. She sees no connection between her interruptions and the waiting room backlog simply because she chooses not to.

'Just a moment...' Kate says.

'Talk to him.'

'Just a moment... Excuse me, Jerome: those are confidential.' Kate reaches to take back a folder her client's fingers have lifted off her desk. Off to the side her laptop chimes with another email and somewhere amongst the mess is a coffee she hasn't touched and a Post-it note to call Rache to cancel their lunch date which is now dead in the water.

The front corners of Kate's desk are guarded by two Dracaenas in urgent need of re-pot and which are destined for either a new home or the bin so that she can once again talk to her clients without feeling like an exhibit in a Punch and Judy show. Between the Dracaenas, Jerome Welland is inspecting a sheet he's freed from the folder. Kate calls his name again and Jerome hands the paper back then crosses his arms and turns his head in his particular way, hunching his underdeveloped shoulders to broadcast his irritation.

Kate works the sheet back into place and moves the folder out of reach then pulls the phone back to her mouth.

'What does he want?'

'He wants us to act for him.'

Kate's eyes roll at this absurdity. The caller is Wesley Leach, a former client she's steered previously through two marginal escapes from criminal convictions but who three weeks ago dismissed their firm after deciding that Kate's latest efforts weren't up to scratch.

'Leach is no longer our client,' Kate therefore points out.

'He's changed his mind. Wants to know when you can see him.'

'I can't see him.' Kate shakes her head in frustration. She'd told Violet no interruptions and this is her response: a call in the middle of a client briefing whose purpose is to load her unmanageable list even further, this time with a client who's previously walked out along with his dire prospects. The walkout was a stupid move but one that Kate had supported wholeheartedly on the basis that Wesley is not only a disastermonger but an unpleasant and possibly dangerous one. He's the last client Kate wants back.

'Tell him we're not available,' she tells Violet.

'He won't listen. I'll put him through.'

'No! Call Arthur.'

'Arthur's left.'

'Then try Hartley. I didn't notice a queue outside *his* door.'

Violet's voice drops. Stuck between Kate's unwillingness and a caller who won't take no for an answer, she's trying to act business as normal in front of her waiting room audience.

'You know Hartley. Leach is your client,' she says.

Kate bites down anger. 'Leach is not my client,' she says.

'Just talk to him.'

Kate closes her eyes.

'Okay. Tell him I'll call him back in twenty minutes.'

But the line has already clicked and Leach's voice is in her ear.

'Kate? What's going on?'

'Wesley. Good morning.'

'Good morning, hell! I've been on hold for ten minutes.'

'We're a little snowed under. I wasn't expecting your call.'

'I'm a paying client. I'll call when I need to.'

Across the desk Jerome is inspecting his watch, something he'd failed to do in the forty-five minutes they've wasted dancing round his problem. He catches her eye and taps his wrist.

Kate holds up her palm. 'Wesley, I'm going to make this short.' She grabs her organiser, flipping pages and spotting a single blank space right after tomorrow morning's court appearance. The space is a slot known in other professions as "lunch".

4

'I can fit you in at twelve thirty tomorrow,' she says.

'What's wrong with today?'

'...and I must warn you that I'm not sure we can represent you. You've probably left it too late.'

'So that's why you're delaying our appointment?'

'Remind me: when is your pre-trial review?'

'Monday.'

God almighty! Two working days! Leach's case was hopeless even three weeks ago, at which time Parfitt and Quinn had at least a certain *obligation*. And Kate had explained to him then that there was no miracle escape from the consequences of his misdemeanours this time. Leach had disagreed, and when he couldn't convince her he'd walked out to seek more competent legal representation. And now he's back because every firm he's talked to has shaken its head and slammed its door. But it's too late now even for Parfitt and Quinn. Solicitors routinely lose cases but they don't throw their reputations to the wind by arriving at court unprepared. Kate should simply tell Leach that she's not available. She should not be scribbling in her damn diary.

'Tomorrow,' she says. 'Twelve thirty.'

'No good.'

'It's that or nothing,' she says. Please, she thinks, say no. Just slam down the phone and get off our backs. But Leach breathes heavily in her ear and promises to show up tomorrow and then gives Kate at least half her wish by slamming the phone down. She replaces her own handset and presses Violet's button.

'No more calls,' she says. 'No matter what.'

Violet promises nothing. Kate takes a slow breath then looks brightly at Jerome.

'To recap,' she says.

But Jerome is continuing the head shake he'd commenced before the interruption. Denial of truth. Actions and consequences. Jerome is up on a criminal damages prosecution consequent on his wrecking his ex lover's flat in a rage that had stretched way beyond the usual ornament flinging and furniture slashing. Why are gays the worst at break-ups? Kate has seen the photos: smashed ceilings, ripped electrics, shattered bathroom fittings, flooded rooms and damage to the fabric of the building that's spawned repair costs right up there in custodial territory.

And Jerome isn't the person to survive time inside. So Kate needs to keep him out of jail, which miracle might be pulled from the fantasy hat only via a guilty plea and the twin mitigating factors of an abject apology and a meaningful reparation. And the only route to the latter, in the light of Jerome's financial means, is via an equally abject reconciliation with his long-rejected parents and an appeal to them to dig into their savings for the ten thousand pounds Kate estimates as an acceptable minimum. If they work it right they might even stave off a civil action from both the insurance company and the landlord as they take the teeth out of the criminal hearing. If they work it *very* right they might get Jerome down to a community order in the latter. But if they go into court tomorrow with this head-shaking attitude then Jerome is in for the drop.

'We need to agree,' Kate says. 'We plead guilty and ask for adjournment of sentencing pending the organising of reparation payments. And your partner may even speak in your favour if you approach him.'

'Ex partner,' Jerome says. He's still squirming like a kid on a bouncer. Actions and consequences. But consequences of a likely custodial nature mean that he needs to eject from his self martyrdom capsule and step into the real world of alienated lovers and disowned family and use the word "sorry".

'Think about it,' she says. 'There's really no choice here.'

Jerome stops shaking his head and looks at the ceiling. 'I'll die before I grovel to that snake,' he says. He's talking about his ex lover. 'And my parents never gave me shit when I was home. Why would they start now?'

Kate pulls papers together. She'll not be drawn further. If Jerome's not fully on board tomorrow then she'll not raise the adjournment motion. The hearing will find Jerome guilty of criminal damage way in excess of a magistrates' ceiling and he'll be sent for Crown Court sentencing. And he can pack his bags for jail.

Then the door opens and the yoke of Kate's burden digs deeper. It's another client, Donna Jordan. Donna's a pretty girl who recently celebrated her twenty-first birthday in the cells of the local nick after being dragged from the streets of Hackney where she was plying her trade. More accurately, dragged from a car where she was holding her punter, punched, slashed and bleeding, at knifepoint. And even as the police were easing the guy from the vehicle they heard from Donna's own lips, with her wonderful scouse turn of phrase, that all she'd needed was another minute and the guy's balls would have been off. This is Donna's second arrest in six months and some astute argument will be called for to fend off the charge of grievous bodily harm. To look at the five-one waif you'd never imagine her capable of such things. But Kate's a solicitor. She knows anything's possible.

'Donna,' she smiles, 'I'll be with you in a sec. Could you wait outside?'

But Donna ignores her and strides over to stand between Jerome and the desk.

'I've been out there an hour and a friggin' half,' she says. 'I've got me hairdresser's in twenty minutes.'

The hair salon is the least of Donna's concerns. If her prosecution prevails she's looking at eighteen months in a place where salons rarely open their doors. Kate again asks the girl to return to the waiting room and promises to get to her in a few minutes.

'An hour and a half,' Donna repeats in her sandpaper-shrill voice. 'It's friggin' ridiculous.'

'Our appointment was forty-five minutes ago. You turned up early, Donna.'

'You said nine thirty.'

'The book says ten thirty.'

'No way. They got it wrong.'

Kate sighs and rises to escort Donna out but she's barely up from her chair when Jerome enters the discussion with his own advice.

'Sweetie, listen to the lady and get the fuck *out*. This is a confidential meeting.'

Donna turns and tells Jerome to go fuck yourself you little bog brush, at which epithet Kate almost smiles. The phrase triggers what's been in her own subconscious since she first met Jerome. Donna has pinned it perfectly. Street life tunes perception. For Jerome, though, such perception is entirely lacking. He jumps up, eyes blazing, and pushes his face in hers, but Donna has seen a thousand like him and she steps back and cracks her palm across his face hard enough to send him backwards over his chair. Donna follows and drops on him like a cat.

Kate's round the desk in a flash, grabbing the girl's arm and feeling steel, the furious vibrations of her rage. It takes real strength to pull her off.

'Donna!'

Kate yanks hard until her intervention registers and the girl rises with eyes blazing from the infinite depths of a life in free fall.

'It's okay,' Kate says. She maintains her grip until the girl's eyes refocus.

'That friggin' jerkoff can watch his gob,' Donna says. 'This is my appointment he's taking.'

But at least she's listening.

'Five minutes,' Kate says. 'Let's sit you down.'

She guides Donna back to the waiting area where she catches Violet's eye and makes a question. Violet answers with a shrug. The place is Bedlam. They know it. But if clients are going to run through willy nilly then the firm needs to invest in a security door. Kate schedules a talk with Arthur as she gets Donna settled then rushes back to her room where Jerome has pulled himself up off the floor. Kate rights his chair and invites him to sit but Jerome stands his ground in fury.

'I could sue you...' The eyes glisten and he's shaking but it's anger on both counts. 'It's your responsibility to keep crazy clients under control.'

'I apologise, Jerome. But I think you're okay.'

Jerome shakes his head. 'My leg's twisted,' he says, 'and that bitch kneed me in the gut. You call that okay?' He straightens himself and glares.

Bog Brush. The image is hard to shake now that Donna's planted it.

'I'm taking advice,' he warns. His finger stabs the air.

'I'm truly sorry,' Kate repeats. 'That lady should not have come in but there's no real harm done. I'll get Violet to make you a coffee.'

'Forget the coffee. I've just been assaulted right here in your office.'

Now they're fifty-eight minutes over time and Kate's patience is finally up.

'You fell off a chair, Jerome. And you've got bigger things to worry about than a slap in the face.' She fixes him with a look of steel until he sits. Then, as she walks back round her desk, her damn phone starts ringing again and triggers something inside her. She reaches and stabs the Hold button. Sod you, Violet. If the waiting room's on fire piss it out yourself! She glares at Jerome. If he wants immolation tomorrow then so be it. But in two minutes he's out of her door.

And in two minutes she'll be precisely one hour behind, and Donna Jordan's delayed appointment isn't likely to recover any of that.

~~~~~

It's two p.m. and Kate is eating a sandwich brought in by Violet. There's a tap on the door and Hartley Tasker's razor cut head appears and hangs uncertainly. After a few moments the rest of him slides in.

'Everything okay? Heard there was a fracas with your clients.'

Your clients. There's the key phrase. In his concern for her welfare Hartley never considers the impact of his efforts to keep his own portfolio trim and slim. If the client list was shared equally then either Jerome or Donna would have been *his* client, and since Hartley's door is tucked away at the back then the two would have never have met and the *fracas* wouldn't have occurred.

'Just a misunderstanding,' Kate says. 'No harm done.'

'This business!' Hartley shakes his head. 'How did we get into it?'

He walks across to gaze out of her window with the calm demeanour of one who isn't quite as far *into it* as she, one whose clientele are well behaved and whose ordered world is an impressive achievement for a solicitor swimming the treacherous waters of the lower court system. His fuzzy head gleams as it catches the winter sun and his navy pinstripe is razor creased like he's back from a month's vacation. His gaunt smile is sympathetic.

'If only we were all driven like you, Katie. You put the rest of us to shame.'

If goddamn only, Kate thinks. But forget the shame, Hartley. Just *drive* yourself to take five of my clients and I'll have a life back. But it's not going to happen, is it? She holds her attention on her brief. 'I try to keep up,' she says. 'It's what Arthur pays me for.'

'Of course. But frankly, no one could handle the schedule he sets you. I just hope he recognises your contribution.'

'Was there something you wanted?'

Kate's due in court in sixty minutes and is rapidly running out of time to prepare her best shot for a client caught in a stolen car and asking for seven other offences to be taken into consideration. Kate is aiming for a community order but might be looking through the wrong end of the telescope.

She senses Hartley still hovering and looks up. He stands debonair in his press-perfect suit and forty-eight hour stubble, hands in pockets.

'Just thought I'd touch base,' he says. 'Let you know I'm here any time. Some of these people can be a little unpredictable.' Now he's patronising her from the dizzy heights of his five years' seniority at the firm. But if Hartley did the maths, totted up the case tally those extra five years have brought him, he'd find that Kate is way ahead. So Kate knows about *unpredictability,* thank you. And now she's lost another sixty seconds for her preparation unless she abandons the rest of her two minute lunch. Tell me about two minute lunches, Hart, she thinks. She pulls her paperwork closer.

Hartley broadens his grin. 'Okay, Katie. I got it. Get the hell out.' He heads for the door.

Katie. It's Hartley's little familiarity that sets the two of them apart as such good buddies. Kate's eyes are back on her paperwork before the door closes, so she's at least spared the annoying touch of a non existent forelock that is Hartley's sign off.

She tosses the rest of the sandwich into her bin and pushes the cold coffee to the edge of her desk, then grabs her pad and roots for her Waterman to sketch out the key points in her client's favour, which aren't many. The pen eludes her under the mess and she sighs and lifts paperwork but it's not there, nor under the file folders stacking up on the right of the desk nor in the penholder on the left, and it's not hiding behind her laptop or in the Dracaena saucers. For a moment Kate wonders if one of her clients has stolen it and the joys of her work aren't enhanced by the realisation that this is a credible explanation and that she's now two more minutes down on her prep time. She grabs a biro and sets to work, dispirited by her mitigation plea even as it appears on the page in smears and blots. In an hour she'll be reading this back in the tiny courtroom before a stony-eyed police prosecutor and three magistrates whose minds are on the recess, trying to convince them, as well as herself, that the mitigation plea is more than it appears on the paper, more than just cheap biro marks that spell FAILURE.

2

By the time Kate gets home it's too late to eat before going out to meet Rache, whom she's allowed, from the weak position of her lunch no-show, to talk her into a night out. Midweek dates are never a good idea, vulnerable as they are to the vagaries of her working day. That this afternoon's hearing had ended an hour behind schedule was no surprise, but then Kate had run into Barry Chisholm, the solicitor of record for Donna Jordan's assault victim, and the opportunity had been too good to pass up. Barry was running late himself, but Kate's blend of charm and bullying had diverted him into one of the interview rooms for a twenty minute chat.

Barry has had no involvement in the Donna Jordan affair beyond the supervision of his client's statement the night of his misadventure. His client is merely a witness for the prosecution, which is why it had taken all of Kate's charm to get Barry to view an unsolicited approach to him as a goodwill opportunity. What Kate proposed was that Barry offer advice that might save his client no small embarrassment should Donna's prosecution go ahead on the basis of his police statement. Such advice – witness tampering by another name – can't come from Kate without all kinds of ethical complications. But from Barry the advice would be just that. Barry had listened with an air of weariness but had agreed to talk to the man, giving Kate some hope of a way out for Donna. But the only certain thing from the chat was a further slippage to her schedule and a further delay getting home.

Kate showers fast, and the last vestiges of her fantasy of a slow bath and evening in front of the TV are extinguished by the clammy feel of the towel as she steps out. She checks the rail. Stone cold. Kate jiggles the thermostat and sets it fully on then grits her teeth and leaves the warmth of the bathroom to grab a dry towel from the airing cupboard.

She dresses in an elegant rather than sexy jacket and skirt that are sure to raise a smile from Rache, for whom being out is synonymous with being seen. "You are how you dress" is her endearingly meaningless take on life. And although it's a line that Kate can step up to any time she simply can't be bothered tonight with a temperature below five degrees. If she's to go out she'll wear practical clothing.

When she enters Liberace's she spots Rache sitting at the bar with a tousle-haired guy at her shoulder. A woman like Rache doesn't sustain vacuum, and the guy has spotted opportunity and moved in. Rache is wearing a pink and black skater dress that shows off her long legs, and her wash of perfume greets Kate as she leans to peck her cheek. If Rache wasn't her best friend she'd say she was a tart. Has said it, in fact, many times, but Rache always laughs it off. A *classy* tart, she always insists, and she's right. Whether she's wearing her workout gear or high fashion Rache always has class. At thirty-two she fits into Liberace's quasi debutante crowd better than any five-year divorcee should. Rache has *class*, too, in the way she picks and discards her male company. She smiles sweetly now at the guy beside her and throws a few last words before turning away to pat a stool for Kate. Company dismissed. She flicks her chin, and the bartender gets busy producing Kate's rosé.

'I'd almost given up,' Rache says.

Kate apologises for both now and lunch, puts it down to the damn job and tells her friend for the thousandth time that she's in the wrong business. Rache replies for the thousandth time that she's in the right business but at the wrong end of the market. Kate can't dispute that. She *is* at the wrong end of the market, and probably at the wrong firm. She'd joined Parfitt and Quinn straight from LPC, planning to find her feet in the legal jungle whilst she made up her mind about whether she had the commitment for a career amongst the viscera of criminal law. Then at the end of her training Arthur Parfitt had surprised her with a job offer and followed up with his strategy for fast-tracking her via the simple expedient of working her until she either sank or swam. And if that strategy has brought her three times the lower court criminal defences of most of her peers it's still not clear whether the experience is building her up or killing her. Kate's astonished now to compute that she's been nearly nine years at the Parfitt and Quinn treadmill and doesn't know whether the thought impresses or dismays her.

Her rosé arrives and she sips carefully and smiles over Rache's shoulder at the late admirer who's still there, calculating whether it's worth the potential loss of face to pursue either of these two women in the face of Rache's brush-off. The guy is about forty, and his bohemian look is accentuated by his mop of tawny hair which complements his boyish good looks. Kate holds his eye and sweetens her smile then shrugs slowly before pointedly turning her gaze and her body away so that the message is clear.

'How's the fashion business?' she asks, apropos of a conversation she's not entirely up to. Rache manufactures upmarket costume jewellery in a tiny workshop off Carnaby Street and makes around fifty K, which even a solicitor might envy and is more than respectable for a college drop out.

Kate's invitation draws Rache into an update on her business affairs which currently revolve around consideration of a potential partnership with a French guy who promises to deliver her work to the Parisian markets if she cuts him in. Rache is floundering in a tizzy of indecision, as she has been for months, and Kate can help only with sound legal advice, which is to get a good lawyer and see that any partnership remains unequal.

Behind Rache the prospective suitor has slipped away.

It's all just chat. They've talked about Paris before. But the script doesn't matter. They can talk about anything or nothing whilst they enjoy what they're really here for, which is each other's company. It's the attraction of opposites. Rache navigates her frivolous world of trinketry with the common sense and serious outlook that will always steer her from wrong turns whilst Kate traverses the solemnity of the legal world with what feels too often like juggling skills.

'At least,' Rache says, 'I get lunch hours the way I am.' The poke is an opener for Kate to explain her no-show. She's intrigued by a throwaway line Kate delivered this morning about a "damn war" in her office.

'Just my high-strung clients,' Kate explains. She describes the fracas – to borrow Hartley's word – the raised voices and the toppled chair, and Rache listens intently, though there have been toppled chairs and raised voices before. Parfitt and Quinn don't cater to the genteel. Kate's clients fall into two classes, neither genteel. One is the habitual court fodder, criminalised by either their own petty and fruitless misdemeanours or by statute that disapproves of their lifestyle. The other class is the landed fish, the habitual law-abider, dragged thrashing and gasping from the pond by the unanticipated consequences of an over-the-limit breathalyser or a careless hand in the till. The common denominator for both types – those hardened by overfamiliarity and those fearful of the ripples – is the uncertainty of their fates. Parfitt and Quinn's waiting room invokes the fear of a dentist's but without any presumption that things will get better.

'You say the girl's a hooker?'

'A scouse firecracker. All scrawn and bad attitude.'

'I guess I'd have attitude if I was walking the streets,' Rache concurs.

'She's got cause,' Kate agrees. 'But the law doesn't gift her the world for working out grudges with a knife.'

'Not cool. Maybe she should retrain as a banker.'

Rache says "banker" not "lawyer" in deference to her friend's profession. Kate herself would choose "lawyer" every time.

'The sad thing,' she says, 'is that the girl's sweet, deep down. She could have had a life.'

'If she could only kick that knife habit.'

'The knife was defence. Not that I'm condoning it. I'm grasping at mitigation straws.'

'Her client was attacking her?'

'He was demanding services he hadn't paid for. Rape, in legalese.'

'So why didn't she just run?'

A refill arrives in front of Rache. She disassembles the decorative junk and swallows the cherry, places the pick on the bar.

'The guy had her in the back of his Merc with central locking activated,' Kate explains.

Rache laughs. 'Then it serves the bastard right. Why's the girl not just pleading self-defence?'

'It's not so simple. The knife shows premeditation.'

'I see. Not such a sweet girl...'

'A damaged girl. Too far gone for the sweet to surface. Barely surviving. I'll give her ten years before she's pulled cold from some junkie dive with her last customer's juice inside her.'

'Meantime, you'll keep her out of jail.'

'That's my job. I keep telling myself it's worthwhile.' Kate takes another sip. One rosé will be insufficient tonight. The image of her couch keeps infiltrating Liberace's din.

Rache pats her hand: 'Cheer up, girl. You're a life-saver to these people. What do I do? Hang bling round their necks.'

'At least you see results. Your customers feel good with what you create. Half my clients don't even understand what I'm doing for them. All I can do is fail against their ridiculous expectations. What most of them want is for me to turn back the clock.'

The space at Kate's elbow has been taken by a brash preppy type and her bass-voiced male companion. The two have just met and are at the stage of exchanging let-slip-to-impress urbanities at a volume that ensures collateral damage. Kate is regretting more than ever coming out. She's going to have to disappoint Rache and abandon the evening. Preppy's screeching grates across her consciousness...

'Penny for your thoughts.'

Rache's voice has broken into a rerun of Kate's chat with Barry Chisholm. Kate is replaying his words, trying to sense the level of sincerity in his promise to talk to his client. But what she didn't hear this afternoon she can't hear now above Preppy's braying. She grins at Rache and finishes her drink. 'Sorry,' she says. 'I'm lousy company.'

'You've been better,' Rache concurs. 'I see a girl whose heart's back home.'

The mind reading of a friend.

'I guess this wasn't a good idea,' Kate admits.

'You calling time?'

'Better had. I'm driving so I can't even call on Auntie Rosé to mellow me. Need a lift?'

Rache, unsurprisingly, declines.

'I'll hang on here,' she says.

Rache is wide awake, fresh as a new day. How she does it Kate can't fathom. Rache works twelve hours a day producing and selling her jewellery, six days a week, and there's no way Kate would be in Liberace's right now if she was in her shoes. She slips off her stool and plants a kiss and as she moves away the crowd flows in to fill the space round her friend. Rache won't be alone for long.

3

Kate's breath frosts as she exits Liberace's. The temperature's down below freezing, bringing the anticipation of five minutes scraping at her windscreen. But as she approaches her Mazda, fifty metres down a side street, she's relieved to see that the screen is clear. The relief, though, is short lived. It looks like she might have another problem.

The car is down at the near side. Is it the camber of the road or has she parked the front wheel in a grid? Please God don't let it be a puncture. Kate can, in theory, change a wheel, but wheels are not the things to get intimate with when you're togged up in a six hundred quid woollen outfit, and her ability to get the car jacked up on this dark street is far from certain. She squats and reaches a tentative finger to test the tyre, but before she's even touched it her eyes have confirmed the worst case scenario. The wheel is rim-down on the road, the tyre too flat even to drive to the nearest all-night station to pump air to get her home. Kate curses. This is just what she needs.

The fact that she has the ability to change the wheel will bug her all the more when she faces the breakdown guy with his tacit understanding that she's just another girl in charge of a machine she doesn't understand and for which she's lacking the aptitude for even the most rudimentary maintenance. But that's not Kate's main problem. The main problem will be the hour's wait while he turns up. She curses and scrolls her phone, now truly wishing she'd stayed home.

Then she hears footsteps behind her coming down from the main road. She turns and sees a man's silhouette striding purposefully towards her. Kate has never felt threatened on London streets. Her natural caution has kept her from places and isolation that pose risks, and familiarity takes any threat from the territory she considers her own. But she senses threat now on this dark street as the stranger approaches. She steps into the road to let him pass but as he reaches her he stops. And she recognises him.

It's the guy who was chatting up Rache. He's silhouetted against the glow of the main street but Kate recognises the cord jacket and unruly hair scattering the light. His shadowed smile floats down from his four inch advantage.

'Having problems?' he asks.

'No,' Kate says. 'Just a flat.' Nonchalantly. As if fixing a flat is routine. But the contradiction of her denial by the reference to the puncture has come out before common sense could stop her. In revealing her problem she's issued an implicit invitation to help. And she doesn't want help. She wants this guy gone and the breakdown service on their way.

The shadows take definition out of his grin but it's there, the superior smile of the male contemplating the damsel in distress.

'Damn,' he says. 'I was afraid it would be that.'

'Afraid?' She keeps her distance.

'Mucky but easy,' he says. 'No excuse not to help.'

'I'm just calling the breakdown service,' Kate says. 'The muck put me off too. I can't ask you to get filthy on my behalf.'

He laughs quietly. 'It'll be a cold wait,' he says and squats to inspect the wheel. Then without asking approval he walks to the rear and gestures for her to unlock the boot.

Kate grips her remote, undecided. She doesn't want to let this stranger dig through her boot. And even a genuine good Samaritan might have an expectation that they'll stay chatting afterwards and that maybe Kate will offer him a lift home. Kate's instincts want to reject his offer. She'll wait up on the main road for thirty minutes – an hour max – and let her breakdown service sort things out. But the guy is signalling and her display of paranoia seems foolish so she presses the remote. The car chirps and he lifts the boot and roots for the jack and spare wheel. Brings them round. He opens the door and slips into the driver's seat to ratchet the handbrake then he's out again, loosening the wheel nuts, and the moment for declining his help has passed. But even as she grasps that fact she's wondering why he's loosening the wheel before the car is even jacked up.

'The jack...' she hints, gesturing futilely behind his back, but he ignores her and works at the wheel before finally reaching for the brace and sliding it under the car. He turns, still squatting.

'Loosen the wheel first,' he says. 'I once saw a guy fight to get the nuts loose and pull the car right off the jack.'

'Ah,' she says, as if it's obvious. But is that correct? Can you really pull a car off a jack? Or is he covering his mistake? But the guy is spinning the handle and the car's rising, and when the wheel clears the road he goes back to work and seems to know what he's doing. If she was changing the wheel she'd not have the stuff out of the boot yet.

And he does know what he's doing. Precisely four minutes later he's lowered the jack and the car's ready to go. He slams the boot and Kate searches for polite but brief conversation to bring their encounter to an end.

'Do you know my friend?' she asks, banality being preferable to silence.

'Never met her before,' he says. His grin reflects the light from the main road and Kate relaxes a little. This is not the face of a serial killer. Just a guy from Liberace's on his way home. A guy with a cute smile.

'I've met *you* though,' he says.

'Oh?' Kate takes an instinctive step back. The two of them have never met. Of this she's sure, and his claim shatters the illusion of normality brought by the completion of the wheel change. Kate doesn't query his assertion, just nods and thanks him and opens the car door, favouring a hasty exit over curiosity satisfied.

'Camden,' he clarifies. 'I run a boutique. You bought some stuff.'

Camden has many boutiques but Kate has bought little there over the years. She tries to recall when she's ever handed money to this guy and fails. And even if she has, his recollection of her own face from amongst his multitude of customers would be a real feat of memory. Kate drops into her seat.

'I don't recall,' she says. 'But thanks again.'

'Wackyjack's. In the Stables. I call it a boutique but that's a fancy name for a curiosities shop.'

Suddenly she does recall. She did once pick up a Christmas present from the Stables. Was that his boutique? Well, any other time, any other place, she'd be curious about this guy's phenomenal memory. But it's nearly midnight on a dark street, and someone who claims to recognise her from just the briefest encounter only strengthens her desire to be back home. And it really *is* time to hit the sack. Kate has a mountain of paperwork to shift before her court appearance with

Jerome tomorrow. She needs to be in the office by seven, which means that she needs to be *in her bed* and not talking to this stranger on a freezing street.

'I can't thank you enough,' she says, praying he's not the kind to imagine that she should.

Now that she's down in her seat she feels vulnerable. All she wants to do is pull the door closed. But he's blocking it.

'No problem,' he says. His smile is traced by the distant sodium glow. 'Glad to help. Drop by the boutique sometime.'

'I will,' she assures him. She waits to pull the door closed but he's still blocking it. Then he reaches into his jacket and hands her a card and she thanks him again. And now she really needs to go. She pulls on the door and he steps aside to let it slam. In her haste she dispenses with seatbelts and lights and she's already in gear and turning the wheel before catching up. As she drives slowly up the road she sees him in her mirror, watching, and feels a flush of embarrassment at her stampede. All he did was help and she didn't even offer him a couple of wipes to clean his hands. At the junction she completes her flurry of light switching and seatbelt tugging and, feeling like an idiot, turns the corner. When she glances back the pavement is empty.

~~~~~

It's gone midnight but now Kate craves food and a mindless half hour of TV. She flicks the switch in the lounge and when both wall lights stay dark she curses. The damn bulbs have blown again! She replaced them only two weeks ago with long-life lamps that cost five times the price. Kate curses the manufacturer, realising that her failure to keep the receipt rules out a refund. She circles the lounge and switches on standing lamps, pulling their cords with a force bordering on the violent. Chill out, woman, she tells herself.

She whips up a snack of cottage cheese and tuna on crispbread, pours a glass of white and returns to the lounge to kick off her shoes. Then she roots for the TV remote but the thing eludes her. It should be on the nested tables by the sofa but though she searches everywhere nearby there's no sign of it. She curses again and walks over to access the TV's manual buttons. Goes with the first channel that comes up and retreats to the sofa with the opening jingles of a panel show bouncing around her. She's already settled, crispbread in hand, before she realises that she's seen the episode. She curses the BBC for their consistent non delivery against her licence fee. Kate watches at most five hours of TV a week and it's infuriating that every other programme she tunes in is a repeat. Is she just statistically unlucky or is the audience being ripped off? She again tells herself to chill. She wanted something mindless to ease her into sleep mode, and what's more mindless than the glassy-eyed absorption of a previously-watched panel game? So she eats her snack and sips her wine and relaxes, and soon the only remaining thoughts of the outside world are the memory of Rache's warm company and the surprisingly intriguing impression of the big, untidy stranger on a dark street.

As soon as her snack is finished she hits the sack. Pictures Rache, the night bird, still chatting at Liberace's. But Rache doesn't have a nine thirty court hearing. Rache doesn't have Jerome Welland nor a bench of magistrates.

Downstairs the house phone rings. Kate tenses in her bed and half sits but then stops herself. Leave it! If the caller knew her they'd be ringing her Samsung. She's not breaking her neck for a marketing call. After thirteen rings the phone quits and the house is silent. She waits for her Samsung to chime but it stays quiet, which is good because she doesn't want to talk to anyone. Kate closes her eyes and is asleep within sixty seconds.

4

Kate escorts Jerome from the courtroom after a hearing that started an hour late but lasted only twenty minutes. Jerome's guilty plea helped move things along and instilled in the court a disposition to grant a sentencing adjournment pending implementation of his newly announced reparation plans.

And even the hour's delay was productive. Kate had seized the opportunity to collar the insurance company's rep. and sound him out as he sipped weak tea in the court's foyer. The man was a worker ant in an off-the-peg suit, here solely to support the criminal prosecution with details of the damage inflicted on the underwritten property, and more interested in next year's retirement package than this year's financial recoveries, but this morning's delay had emphasised the time-saving benefits of settlements. By the time they were summoned he'd agreed to acknowledge the defendant's intention of seeking such a settlement, bolstering Kate's motion to adjourn sentencing, even if his worker ant's reticence did not permit him to postulate on the likelihood of such an arrangement being accepted by his recoveries people, civil suits not being his area any more than they are Kate's. But Kate must be an optimist. A voluntary reparation even without settlement might persuade the magistrates of Jerome's genuine remorse and elicit perhaps a sentence lighter than he deserves.

Jerome bobs alongside her now towards the exit in an ill-fitting suit that doesn't work.

'What a dump,' he says. He sniffs, as if magistrates' courts are the city's social nuclei and the layabouts occupying the annexe's plastic chairs don't make the grade. Although Jerome is perhaps the last person to point a finger he does so with wanton ease. 'We had to sit in this shit hole all morning,' he complains, 'for just two words with the judges.'

'That's the law,' Kate says. She's not about to educate Jerome on how those "two words" were critical in nudging the bench towards a more favourable outcome. All she needs from him right now is that he's clear about his next move, which is to get hold of the ten K reparation cash from his parents and to produce a letter of apology for his ex that might persuade the latter to appear as a character witness in Jerome's support. Jerome had refused to apologise directly but is willing to work on the letter. But first step: the purchase of a Tube ticket for Lambeth where Jerome will honour his parents with a surprise visit. As they come out onto the steps Kate stops him.

'Let's be clear what we're doing,' she says.

Jerome rolls his eyes. The ill-fitting suit flags him as a surly teenager, to which tribe he undoubtedly belongs. 'Don't worry,' he says, but Kate does worry.

'You need to see your parents today. I want to talk to both London Century and your ex partner's solicitor as soon as possible.'

'Today's out. I've got arrangements.'

A chill breeze gusts off Holloway Road. Kate shivers.

'You've nothing that's more important than the ten thousand,' she says. 'If we're back next month without any settlements then things won't go well.'

'Okay, lady. Stay cool.' Jerome smiles condescendingly, as if he's doing her some kind of favour, and for the briefest moment Kate just wants to walk away. But she's an optimist. She reminds herself of that fact and tells Jerome to go buy that ticket then descends the steps into the teeth of the breeze.

~~~~~

By twelve fifteen, back behind her desk, any sense of optimism is long gone as Kate fights the oppression that invariably accompanies a discussion with Wesley Leach. That Wesley's return to Parfitt and Quinn is entirely her doing doesn't lift her mood. Would it have been too hard yesterday to insist that the firm could no longer act for him? Wesley is her genuine bad-guy client, a career criminal whose business is thievery, violence and extortion and to whom the services of the legal profession are indistinguishable from a car wash: pay and forget; drive out shining.

Leach is projecting his eternal puzzlement as Kate speaks. He gives no sign that he's heard this advice before or that he's walked out after hearing it. Kate senses her words reflecting from his obduracy just as they did three weeks ago. Wesley's immobile face, though, is delivering the simple message that he's here to stay this time. He's here until the right words break through his selective hearing. And his colourless eyes, drilling into Kate's, actually frighten her. She bites back anger at her weakness in letting Leach back in.

And weakness is the only reason that this one-sided conversation is still continuing instead of Kate showing Wesley the door on the simple basis that it's impossible to get his affairs in order for the pre-trial review scheduled for Monday. A review that will not be the standard administrative affair but rather a tightrope walk, with a busy magistrate pulled from his schedule to hear a plea for a delay to trial so that she *might* get Wesley's affairs in order. Kate still has Wesley's preliminary CPS pack but it's now three weeks out of date and the prosecutor has without doubt used that time to assemble a watertight case of which Kate knows nothing. So all the delay will guarantee is a further overloading of her work schedule, more headaches and stress.

'Being realistic,' she finishes, 'you're going to prison. How you plead, and how we present any mitigating factors, might minimise the sentence, nothing more.'

But he's still not listening. He hasn't heard a damn word. Wesley has just been staring across her desk waiting for her to finish so he can deliver his own message. So she stops talking. What's the point?

Wesley's voice is soft when he speaks. His eyes project surprise and disappointment.

'Not good enough,' he says. 'I've told you how it was. The police were out of order. The pursuit was illegal and I panicked.'

Kate shakes her head.

'The pursuit may have breached Metropolitan Police rules,' she says, 'but it wasn't illegal. We won't win that argument.'

'An unmarked vehicle. No lights. No authorisation. Illegal.'

Kate is still shaking her head. 'Wesley, we're going round and round. A defendant doesn't get to define what's legal for their own benefit.'

'*Illegal.*' Wesley's stare intensifies. He just can't get through to her. 'I thought some people were after me. I can't be blamed for running.'

'The lights and siren, if they weren't deployed, would be a mitigating factor, nothing more. And the police will dispute your assertion. Your best option is a guilty plea. We can bring in the question of police tactics as a mitigating circumstance that might point more to misjudgement on your side than deliberate intention.'

Despite the cold outside, the office is stuffy. Kate needs to open the window. She needs air.

'I'm giving them possession of the goods,' Wesley says. 'They've got me on that. But they ain't gonna to bang me up just for running from them.'

'Oh, but they are.'

Wesley's voice is toneless. 'Well that's why,' he says, 'we need to kill the driving charge.'

'But the driving charge,' Kate says for the tenth time, 'can not be killed.' She sighs and sits back to put more space between them but the gesture feels weak. Hell and damn! Why does this guy scare her? The way he stares, the way he never listens. It's as if he was born without the instinct for communication. Every time Wesley appears in her office he's already run their meeting through his head and any deviation from his script is logged behind those calm, surprised, disapproving eyes. And the guy behind those eyes *hurts* people when circumstances demand. He probably has that same look when he assaults his victims, wondering why they've goaded him into it. And Wesley's driving offence has hurt someone. Badly. There's a seventy-four-year-old in intensive care as a result of him fleeing the police, and no amount of argument about police illegalities is going to impress the magistrates. Kate holds her hand up, dismayed by the tremor she feels in it.

'Wesley,' she says, 'you need to come to terms with this: a custodial sentence is highly likely. What we need to talk about is how you're going to plead.'

'Not guilty.' Wesley's surprise holds fast. So finally Kate pulls her pad across.

'Okay, we'll stay with that plea. But we won't win.'

We. The word signals to Kate that she's ceded her internal debate about taking Wesley back. She can't tell if it's momentum, the instinct to stay with a client, or simple fear of the man. She's furious with herself whichever.

'Hypothetically,' he says, 'how long would I go down for on a bust like this?'

Kate hasn't got that far but the question suggests, at least, that Wesley may be drifting microscopically towards reality. She gives it thought. Wesley is charged with multiple motoring offences consequent on his attempt to evade the police in a high speed chase, the most serious of which is the reckless driving that resulted in the injury to a pensioner by the name of John Barnes whose car was crushed by Wesley's SUV.

'We're looking at two or three years minimum,' she concludes.

Wesley's surprise shifts towards bemusement.

'The max they can hand down is six months,' he says. 'Six months suspended I could handle.'

Kate sneaks a look at her watch. Struggles to maintain a placid surface.

'The gentleman is critically ill,' she reminds Wesley. 'And you've had priors. If the verdict goes against us the magistrates will refer you to Crown Court for sentencing. Twelve months is the minimum you should expect.'

The bemusement drops from Wesley's face. His cleverness deflates. He switches back to smouldering irritation.

'That's why we need to fight this,' he says. 'There must be witnesses who saw the unmarked chasing me. We need to find them.'

Kate takes a breath. Leach is so confident that they can dig up friendly witnesses that she suspects he's already got them lined up, characters prepared to perjure themselves in his cause. That's why she'd refused to run a poster and ad. campaign three weeks ago. She won't build a defence based on perjury. When such witnesses crumbled, as they would, she'd have to stand at Wesley's shoulder and pretend that she alone was unable see the chicanery. Kate recalls, now, exactly how happy she'd been when Wesley had fired her and walked out of the door. But this road, at least, she won't travel.

'I'm sorry,' she says. 'We're not going to trawl for witnesses.'

But Wesley's eyes are burning with the force of his certainty. And she's in court with this man at 11 a.m. Monday morning.

The debacle will probably sink her whole week.

5

At one thirty Kate walks the half mile to Sharla's Kitchen, which is an eatery sufficiently distant from the office to make it her secret place, somewhere to lunch undisturbed. She's got thirty minutes until her first afternoon appointment, which leaves her, after the walk, with just ten minutes inside – realistically, less than Sharla's takes to deliver their sandwiches.

Kate enters and places her order with a new East European girl whose limited grasp of English frustrates her plea for priority. But what the hell? The sunny streets have invigorated her and vindicated her decision to come out, and if she's late back only Violet will see through her charade as she strides through the waiting room with the briefcase she's brought solely as a prop. And even Violet, fresh from her hour-long break, won't have the nerve to signal her disapproval until the afternoon backlog builds.

Kate calls her sister, Angie. She'd considered cancelling a planned shopping trip with her tomorrow in favour of a morning at the office to review Wesley Leach's file but she'll be damned if she'll ruin her weekend for the man.

In normal circumstances she'd have directed Leach to the firm's partners to let them decide whether to take him back. Unfortunately, Arthur's away, Henry is wherever he is and senior solicitor Hartley Tasker's door is, as always, barred against such threats to his well ordered affairs. But bottom line: Kate should have fended Wesley off herself. She knows it and reprimands herself yet again for the fool she is.

'I thought you'd never get back.' Angie's voice is another reprimand, for two unanswered messages.

'This damn job,' Kate says.

'I called at nine p.m. Don't tell me you were still in work.'

'I was probably in the shower.'

'You need to get out, Sis,' Angie says. 'Find a guy. You're becoming a loner.'

Which is true. Kate tries to recall how long it's been since she and her last boyfriend split and is shocked to realise that it's fifteen months. But advice from her sister, delivered from the security of her own well ordered domesticity, is something Kate has learned to ignore. And, she now recalls, she actually was out at nine p.m. last night, on her way to Liberace's.

'Loner works fine,' she says. 'Fits my schedule.'

'Your schedule will leave you high and dry. You're not getting any younger Kate.'

'Point noted,' Kate says. 'And thank you.'

She eyes the counter to see if there's any sign of her sandwich. Angie's point has been noted many times before. Kate, at thirty-two, is over the shock of slipping unexpectedly into the post youth decade when all life's gonna-be's are official late arrivals, to be considered for the first time as potential no-shows. At thirty-two the first faint worries about the future have kicked in. But Kate's focus is her job. That's where her future is happening. That's where her milestones are laid out. But the fifteen months that have slipped by since her last relationship are a worrying statistic. She hurries the conversation onwards, fixing arrangements for tomorrow.

Sharla's, despite the lateness of the hour, is not to be hurried. When her sandwich arrives Kate is well out of time. She gives herself ten minutes anyway. She'll be running late whatever time she gets back, and even if she was early, something would come up. Like a freshly dug hole on the tideline, life has a way of filling in.

~~~~~

The afternoon passes and she arrives home at a respectable seven fifteen, celebrating the fact that the weekend is hers with a glass of wine. Then as she starts her cooking she's confronted with the irritation of two blown spot lamps above her kitchen worktop. Coming after the failed bulbs in the lounge last night it feels as if the house is out to get her. She finds spares and fiddles them into place and drops the duds into the Brabantia, unsure whether this is compliant with the council's recycling policy. The bin is filling and she decides to empty it before continuing. But as she extracts the liner it splits and deposits its contents onto her kitchen floor. Kate curses and goes to grab a new liner, only to find there are none in the cupboard. She stares in disbelief. She'd swear there were several bags remaining when she last emptied the rubbish. But sight trumps memory and she's faced with a mess on her kitchen floor and no spare bag for the cleanup. With a sigh Kate roots around and unearths two cinder-thin refuse sacks from an ancient roll. If any bags are guaranteed to fail it's these but beggars can't be choosers. She clears up the mess and transports the sack gingerly outside before lining the Brabantia with the remaining one. When she's through she starts again, searching for something simple and quick, ignoring a persistent nagging from the prissy part of her brain which is pointing out that her rationale for leaving work early tonight was that she could go out for a run. But she didn't leave quite early enough and if she goes now it will be nine before she's cooled and showered and ready to eat, and she's already downed a glass of wine and... bottom line, *sod it*, she's taking the night off. She'll pick up her fitness regimen tomorrow.

But the truth is that things *are* sliding. The demands of her job have turned insidiously uphill year after year under the firm's remorseless scheduling, and Arthur's recent hints at an upcoming partnership offer have added to the temptation to let her career devour her. So tomorrow she'll take charge and go out for her exercise. Tonight is reserved for a meal that takes longer than ten minutes to eat and a drink that doesn't come from a machine.

By nine thirty she's immersed in a foaming bath, enveloped in the bathroom's warmth and the scent and flickering hues of sandalwood candles. The double glazing mutes the London night and she might be basking on a desert island. She closes her eyes and breathes out, sinks until only her face is clear, which is a better feeling by far than running along cold streets. Mind and body have differing needs. Tonight is for the mind. Kate slides her fingers across her belly to confirm the still taut definition of her muscles. Her slackening fitness regimen has not yet caused damage. She breathes, lets her fingers slide downward off her belly and find a rhythm.

Downstairs the kitchen phone rings.

Kate opens one eye. There's no way she can get to the phone and is not tempted to try but the intrusion grates across her peace. She counts the thirteen rings the service allows before the phone switches

29

to voicemail and when it does she closes her eyes again and sinks back into her cocoon.

Half an hour later she's heading for bed, relishing the prospect of nine hours' sleep, when the phone rings again. She diverts this time, a short detour being preferable to the irritation of wondering who has called. She reaches the breakfast bar and picks up, but even as she does the line cuts dead. She swears with real feeling at being caught once again by the marketing computers. The late night calls have been coming in for a month now and she roundly curses the cowboy firms who intrude at any time of day or night. She slams the handset back onto its base and heads back upstairs.

Ten minutes later she's lying in bed watching the city's light wash across the ceiling. Kate's not afraid of the dark but hates pitch black, the cloying absence of anything. She always sleeps with her curtains drawn wide. Even the faintest light has something to say. Moonlight, streetlight, passing headlights. All reminders that the world still rotates, is still there, that she is still *here*.

She closes her eyes and as the afterglow of the long soak eases her into sleep her final thought is of last night's shadowed face, her rescuer in the dark street. She'd checked his card as she slipped it into her junk drawer. His name was printed under the Wackyjack's (Specialist Curiosities and Collectibles) logo. Xavier McGeary, MA (ENS de Lyon), whatever that means. Seems you can't be over qualified to run a stall on Camden Market.

Her rescuer's face drifts across her fading consciousness just as, unexpectedly, it had drifted there in the bath, reinforcing Angie's point about her need for a guy. Well, Angie dear, whom I love dearly, and who should keep her nose out of my affairs, it's *true* that I need a guy sometimes, and it's *true* – though you'll never hear this from me, not from my dying lips – that here in this bed as I drift towards oblivion, I would happily have this particular "guy" gaze down at me as he presses his belly to mine and heats me with the fire of his eyes. Her fantasy is nonsense, entirely contrary to the unease she'd felt on the street outside Liberace's, but this isn't the street, this is her bed where *she* makes the rules and bends her fantasies to her whim and right now, Angie, this guy would do fine. The embers of the stirrings roused in her bath heat up again and her eyes flutter as her hands move across her belly, and her fantasy does indeed bend to her desire. And wouldn't she happily sacrifice an hour of her precious sleep to the delight of the guy's enfolding limbs...

Then the downstairs phone rings again. Her fantasy shatters.

She snaps awake and swears profusely in the dark but doesn't consider getting out of bed. Whoever or whatever it is she doesn't want to know. The marketing cowboys can go screw themselves. But when the ringing ceases the irritation of not knowing who called, of something unresolved, tugs at her consciousness.

'Fuck you,' she says, loudly and clearly, and that does the trick. The phone is consigned to irrelevance and Kate closes her eyes and resumes where she left off, sliding her body once again into the fire of her fantasy.

6

Kate rises late and comes downstairs to make coffee and warm a croissant. She eats at the breakfast bar, half an ear on the radio news as the day's plans coalesce.

When she's through she fetches the mail. It's all junk bar a utility bill and a handwritten red envelope. Whether the hand is human or a computer's is not clear, computers having evolved better writing than humans to force recipients to open their junk mail before binning it.

Kate opens the envelope and finds a Valentine's card, a simple arrow-pierced red heart with a penned greeting that says: "Kate. Special Love." Kate stares at the message in amazement and turns the card for a clue as to who sent it, but there's none. She checks the calendar and it is indeed February 14th, the day for such cards. But not at this address. It's not that Kate isn't Valentine's-worthy. Her occasional romances have delivered a bounty of February surprises but she's not received an anonymous card since her schooldays. She's received cards jokingly unsigned but their senders have left no doubt as to their identity. And since Kate isn't presently caught up in, running from or leaning towards romantic involvement this card sets her mind spinning to figure out who might have sent it. Her thoughts swirl inexorably into the darker territories of inappropriate suitors: work colleagues, elderly bosses, her sister's husband, the postman even. Then she bats the absurdities aside and permits herself a moment's intrigue, a daydream of a handsome admirer who's seen into her soul. But the dreaming ricochets straight back into the parade of less desirable suitors and ends, finally, in outright unease at the greeting's ambiguous words. The words are way overfamiliar, with their implication of possession. Who has the right to declare "Special Love" before he's even introduced himself?

She pours another coffee as her speculation wanders between the good, the bad and the truly bizarre. Finally she snaps out of her reverie. She's wasting time. She won't figure it out. If the sender intended to reveal even the faintest hint of his identity he's failed. He might as well have left the card unsent. She almost throws it away but a residue of intrigue moves her to prop it at the back of the breakfast bar where the red heart remains on display as she clears up.

$$\sim\sim\sim\sim\sim$$

Kate's sister looks faintly harassed as she crosses from the station. There's an air about her today that exposes every year of her seven year seniority, though Kate stops short of the term *jaded*. That would be too unkind for Angie, who prides herself in her appearance and is decked out in a fetching combination of black jeans and short quilted jacket. Kate struggles for a more suitable term. It's Angie's face and hair: a little more lined, a little less lustrous than normal, a tension across her. But no suitable term comes to mind and Kate must settle finally on the fact that Angie simply looks older, and the realisation depresses her.

But her sister sweeps into the café with her usual gusto and plants a kiss as she flops at their window table where Kate has coffees waiting. It's their habit to meet at a convenient café that will shelter whoever arrives first, which is invariably Kate. An eleven thirty meeting means eleven twenty to Kate and eleven forty to Angie. Kate's fear of courtroom transgressions have conditioned her to arrive at any appointment – her office excepted – with margin, and Angie's decade and a half reconciling teaching with rearing two children have conditioned her not to worry about such things.

Angie settles and launches into their planned itinerary for this expedition into, of all places, Brixton. But Angie's hunt is not for the exotic but for bargains. What Kate is here for is her sister's company, a day out, gossip she can never later recall.

'You're working too hard,' Angie says, breaking unexpectedly from shopping talk to seize the high ground before Kate can ask her own questions. It's as if Angie has sensed Kate's *jaded* observation and is attempting, by batting first, to deny her world-weary condition. Kate herself has slept eight hours, breakfasted leisurely, and is half way through her third coffee of the day and feels not in the least like someone who's working too hard. She's not tired, nor harassed, nor even *jaded*, and Angie's deftly cast first strike irks her for the brief moment it takes to remember that her sister means well and is always the first to tell her when she's looking tip-top. Kate assures Angie that she's fine.

But Angie persists.

'That firm doesn't appreciate you,' she says. 'What time did you get to bed last night?'

'Ten o'clock, after a long soak.'

The reply blocks Angie's attack. Kate doesn't mention, of course, that this is the first night this week that she *has* hit the sack before midnight, nor that she's been up before six every morning. 'I'm fine,' she repeats, and she means it, and Angie sees that her thrust is lost and switches to tales of overwork and stress in the world of education. But her customary war reports complement rather than interfere with their trips, and her anecdotes are a million miles from Kate's legal world which – honesty to the fore – comprises in large part the cleanup operations after the failures of Angie's education system, so Kate listens with unbegrudging attention, problems shared being, as the old adage fails to point out, problems enjoyed. And today, perhaps, the sharing of her teacher's travails brings Angie a moment's reprieve from some other shadow that Kate senses hanging over her.

The day has turned out fine. Brixton is all colour and noise. They start at the bridges and work clockwise without haste. It's the second Saturday of the month and the arches and stalls are vibrant with the Makers market, and the therapy of immersing herself in the crowd works as always for Kate. The seven years that separate the two of them meant few shared childhood pleasures and for the last decade they've been catching up. Busy though their lives are, their days out are a fixed routine.

Over lunch in a Caribbean eatery, apropos of a contribution to the day's trivia, Kate mentions her Valentine's card. The revelation can only invite mockery but Kate won't deny her sister this little opportunity. Angie duly mimes shock and intrigue and says the expected words about unknown admirers.

'You know him,' she says, forking her jerk chicken. 'I guarantee it.'

'I can think of anyone,' Kate says.

'Oh come on, there's a thousand men would send you a Valentine's card.'

'I don't know a thousand men.'

'So, fifty. You've a horde of admirers. You just never notice. You always were the oblivious beauty.'

Kate rolls her eyes the way she always has, but since her sister first made this assertion twenty years ago she's liked to imagine that there's perhaps a *mystique* about her, some sense of innocent modesty that radiates from her. She's always enjoyed her good looks without ever flaunting them and without ever depending on them. Kate's prospects at Parfitt and Quinn – case in point – hardly depend on *good looks*. But her sister is wrong on her key point. Kate is not oblivious. 'I read people for a living,' she points out. 'I'd notice if a guy was attracted to me.'

'They hide it,' Angie says. 'They might not be free to reveal themselves. Or it might not be someone close. Might be someone you've never noticed.'

Which is the least welcome possibility. And wouldn't make sense. Unrequited love might draw an anonymous Valentine's from such a person but wouldn't their message at least express their feelings of hopelessness? Those of an admirer who's "always loved you" or the regret of one who's destined "never to be with you" or even a hopeless wish that "one day..."? What's the point of a card without any declaration? But it's the simplicity of the Valentine's two-word message that is its oddity. More than an oddity: *Special Love* is damn creepy. There's a proprietorial feel about it, the abbreviated greeting only a familiar has the right to deliver – a long-term friend, a family member, a husband. This is not the greeting permitted to a stranger. So sod your *Special Love*, whoever you are, Kate thinks. Next time save the stamp.

'If you *had* a guy,' Angie is saying, 'you'd at least get dinner with the card.'

Kate snaps back. Her sister's mocking eyes are on her.

'When I get a guy,' she says, 'you'll be criticising me for my lousy choice.'

This isn't rhetoric. Angie has never been reticent with her thoughts on Kate's boyfriends, who've rarely come up to scratch. The fact that Kate is no longer *with* any of them doesn't make Angie's opinion either correct or welcome. And what does Angie know? Angie found her own true love at twenty and hasn't stuck her head above the parapet in two decades. And the scoring of a bullseye on a first attempt does not an expert make. Quite the opposite. Angie, for all her advice and opinion, has *zero* experience, having been saved from the trouble of exploring life's byways by the steady devotions of husband Ian who's steered both their lives with his insurance broker's stolid sense. And even Angie's marriage has shown the occasional rough edge. Today, for example, something is definitely bugging her. Kate wonders what storm has roared into life behind her sister's front door.

'The point is,' Angie continues, 'that you work too hard and think too little about your life.'

'I think a lot about my life!'

'Well if you *think,* Kate, you don't *act*.' Angie leans across. 'You're at serious risk of becoming an old maid, Sis, waiting for something that never turns up.'

'Well thanks, Angela, I'll note that down,' Kate says.

'Don't go cynical on me, Sis. This is serious. Look at yourself...' But then she checks her monologue and drops her attention back to her plate and for a few blessed minutes they eat in silence.

When they're through Angie returns to the primary purpose of their expedition and steers them down Atlantic Road to a boutique that's sprung up only in the last month, specialising in imported leather bags and big brand rip-offs. The shop is out of place in Brixton if Angie's information on its ludicrous price tags are true. But Angie insists that they're only window shopping, which Kate interprets to mean that, should a treasure catch her eye, an appropriate birthday present at the end of March might be appreciated, Angie not being above taking advantage of her sister's prosperous spinsterhood.

They walk through blinding sun and shadow, cross Coldharbour and leave the crowds behind, and Angie springs a proposal that when they're through Kate rides the two stops home with her for tea. Kate had planned an early return and a run in the park, but she's not seen Ian or the kids for weeks and Angie's place is on the way anyway, so refusal would be impolite. She accepts the invitation.

Then Angie goes quiet and Kate senses she's on the cusp of a new topic. They walk in silence until Angie says: 'We've a problem with Jon.'

Kate's heard this before. Her nephew has been a *problem* since he was fourteen. Unlike his older sister, whose good looks and temperament come from Angie, her nephew has inherited his father's brooding character. His sullen face has closed in over the last two years. The bright child Kate once knew has evolved into an awkward, monosyllabic ghost who flits through the house at meal times and is absent at others, busy with an outside life that has more than once brought him trouble. So Angie's report of problems is nothing new, and Kate, inexperienced in such matters, has no reassurances to offer on the fine line between youthful fecklessness and bad character, and must fall back on the standard maxim that "he'll grow out of it" without the slightest evidence to back her up. Parfitt and Quinn's waiting room is awash with those presumed, a decade earlier, to be growing out of their antisocial behaviours. So Kate's easily proffered reassurances on the subject serve simply as a mirror to Angie's own belief in her son. Angie and Ian are good parents. Jon will pull through.

They reach their destination, a shop gleaming at the end of a terrace under a new coat of paint and a signboard that promises exclusive bags and leatherwear. But Angie's mind, now she's broached the subject, needs to thrash her worries out.

'We've had a visit from the police,' she says.

Kate stops dead in the road. A cyclist diverts round them with stabs at his bell and Angie must guide Kate to the pavement.

'Do you remember Geraldine Bryson?' she asks.

The name is familiar though Kate can't quite place it.

'Geraldine's our Head of Geography,' Angie reminds her. 'The one whose house was broken into.'

Kate does now recall the story but can't imagine how it concerns Jon.

'The police wanted to question him about it,' Angie says.

Kate looks at her sister in renewed astonishment.

'They think *Jon* was involved?'

'The vandals appear to be school students, possibly from our own school.'

'Why do they think that?'

'They spray-painted those obscenities, remember? Adolescent stuff that suggested an intense dislike of Geraldine.'

Kate recalls the story. Angie's teaching colleague was away on a two day geography trip when her house was broken into and wrecked. The intruders destroyed everything and left an exhibition of spray-painted obscenities that must have been particularly distressing for a sixty-year-old spinster already fighting a losing battle to keep her career afloat. Kate recalls that Geraldine was struggling to control both her department and her pupils, suffering on both counts from the drawback of a none too affable character. School kids pick mercilessly on character weakness and Geraldine Bryson, sinking under the pressures of increasing paperchases and shrinking budgets and bottling up a consuming loneliness, had exhibited a critical vulnerability. She was the teacher the pupils loved to bait and whom few colleagues supported. Then the fateful school trip from which Geraldine returned to the nightmare of her destroyed home. Geraldine had apparently fled the building and collapsed in a neighbour's living room then spent a week in hospital. Word was that she'd never teach again. But this is the first time that Angie has mentioned that the house wreckers were from their own school, and the first time she's mentioned Jon in that context. The concept is hard to grasp.

'Why are the police interested in Jon?' Kate asks. They're outside the shop, watching the mêlée inside.

'They're talking to every pupil from age fourteen. But the officer's questions made it clear that they suspect Jonathan.'

Angie, as she speaks, truly looks older. 'I'm wondering,' she says, 'if we did the right thing letting him talk to them without a solicitor.'

Now they're in Kate's territory and she could tell Angie that it's never a good idea to talk to the police without a solicitor's advice, but also that it's not a good idea to refuse to cooperate with routine enquiries. Refusal is a great way to attract attention.

'What did they say?' she asks.

The shop doorway clears momentarily and they must either go in to inspect the overpriced offerings or abandon the bag hunt for a quiet café where Angie can get this off her chest. Their decision is mutual. They turn and walk back towards the Village arcade and find a coffee bar.

The policeman's questions, as recounted by Angie, strike Kate as little more than routine enquiries directed by whispers and hunches. He'd pressed Jon at length about his whereabouts on the night of the break-in but it was almost certainly a fishing trip, and from what Angie says no harm has been done, though Jon had only a piecemeal account of where he was, which mostly comprised hanging out with his friend Gary. Kate knows this latter name. Angie has never liked the youth whom she sees as a bad influence and who, from stories told, would be entirely credible as a house wrecker. But the constable's questioning had failed to dig up anything concrete to point to Jon, so perhaps no harm done.

But Angie doesn't touch her coffee. There's something else, something burdening her beyond the police interrogation. And when Kate states her opinion that Jon isn't capable of such a cruel act Angie cuts her off.

'I've found something,' she says.

7

Kate waits, with the sinking feeling that her nephew might have changed more than she's realised.

'Jon left his phone unlocked,' Angie says, 'so I sneaked a look to see what he and Gary have been saying to each other. And I found a photo. It was Gary at school, taken from an angle that caught Geraldine in the background. Gary's making an obscene gesture and it's clear that Geraldine's the butt of the joke.'

'Every kid's phone probably has stuff like that.'

'But I found another.'

Kate watches her sister and wonders if she's destined ever to have kids of her own. Could this be her future self? The concept of writhing in a net cast by one's offspring seems utterly alien.

'Gary messaged Jon a photo of Geraldine's house with the comment "ARMAGEDDON". It was dated the day of the break-in.'

Ah!

Now *that* communication is – to drift into legalese – *not good*. That is not something to be rationalised away.

'Did you ask Jon about it?'

Angie shakes her head. 'If he knew I'd been through his phone he'd go berserk. And what if he admitted that he was involved in the break-in? Where would that leave me? They've wrecked Geraldine's life, Kate.'

'What's Ian's opinion?'

Angie laughs mirthlessly. 'Ian was all for forcing the truth out of Jon. We had a stupendous argument about it but in the end we agreed a temporary truce to think things over. But Ian won't hold back for long. And I'm terrified that Jon was involved.'

'Perhaps it's better to confront him. Sweeping things under the carpet rarely works with youth crime.'

A bad choice of words. Kate sees it in Angie's face. But *criminality* is what this is, and not on a minor scale. Whoever wrecked Geraldine Bryson's home has directed a very vicious attack on a vulnerable person they knew would be overwhelmed. The attack had the clear element of *intent,* and the penalty for anyone found guilty will be severe. Kate has a vision of her sister making weekly trips to a young offenders' institution, of a shift in the family's standing. But as she struggles to find apposite advice Angie suddenly notices the time and pushes her untouched coffee away.

'We'd best get going,' she says. 'That is if you still want to dine at Dysfunctional City.'

Kate, to her shame, is not entirely sure that she does, but she'd be the last one to hide from her sister's problems. She shakes her head with a firmness she hopes looks genuine.

'Don't be silly,' she says. 'I'll always love calling, whatever the situation.' Though even as she says it she's pondering on whether Jon might not be home – he often isn't – and maybe not even Ian. Because the guilty truth is that the most comfortable company in which to enjoy Angie's sandwiches and cake would be that of just Angie and her daughter Claire. But she suppresses the thought and repeats her assurance, and they abandon their drinks and walk to the Tube.

~~~~~

Life rarely bends to one's wishes. At the tea table it's her niece, Claire, who's absent, and Jon who by some quirk of his social diary is present. He sits across from Kate, ignoring a story Ian is telling about the Kennington Civic Society. They're all only half listening but Jon makes his disinterest clear as he flicks through the pages of his smartphone. Kate has watched with dismay the slow metamorphosis of her nephew from a bubbly twelve-year-old to this surly teen. She's felt the change even through his always-polite exchanges with her. And the exchanges are fewer than they used to be, limited mostly to responses to her own comments. It's a long time since Jon rushed to inform her of the latest discoveries in his ever expanding world. Jon's world has long since expanded into territories that no longer require the attention of elders. He looks up now and communicates with a short despairing smile the tedium of his father's monologue. Kate keeps her smile neutral, wondering whether this boy has it in him to destroy a teacher who's crossed swords with him. She wonders if Jon, now smiling at his smartphone, has *Armageddon* inside him.

But Ian has just cast a remark in her direction and exposed her own lack of attention, and she's forced to extemporise with a vague response based on the words she did catch. She assures him that she sees plenty of that kind of thing in her line of work, whatever *that kind of thing* is. Something about misappropriation of funds. Ian's story is about financial irregularities within a neighbouring organisation – or was it his own Kennington Civic Society? – and how the perpetrator was caught through his own stupidity.

'You'd go to prison,' Ian says. 'What would they hand out, Kay?'

Kay: his name for her, dating back to the time she'd trooped around as a school student with a flower-bedecked pink rucksack emblazoned with the letter "K". Ian was already courting Angie at the time, and Kate had moved on from pink rucksacks long before he and her sister finally tied the knot but the tag has stuck, and, unlike Hartley Tasker's "Katie", is not resented.

'It depends on the sum involved and compliance with any compensation order,' she says.

'They'll go after the money, rest assured,' Ian says, and Kate agrees, though she's still not sure what sum of money they're talking about. She doesn't visualise huge sums accruing in civic society accounts.

'Seventeen thousand,' Ian reminds her.

Not so small, then.

'A custodial sentence is the starting point for that level of theft,' Kate says. 'But he might escape jail with mitigating factors and repayment of the money. They'd probably allow him to pay in instalments.'

'He's a wife and a couple of kids,' Ian says. 'So they can't take the house.'

'The house is safe,' Kate agrees. 'And if he's a professional he'll probably manage to raise the funds. I've a client of my own who's liable for costs he *can't* meet. But I'm hoping a partial reparation will keep him out of prison.'

'An embezzler?'

'Criminal damage. He wrecked his partner's flat and left repair costs he can't possibly cover. Something he didn't consider when he acted.'

The tightrope is deliberate. Kate is throwing the story in in the hope that the oblique allusion to Jon's problem might allow the subject to air without the direct confrontation Angie fears. And she senses them all pricking up their ears. Even Jon. Perhaps this might be a first stirring of the waters, might open the way for Angie and Ian to broach the subject of Jon's phone. Anything, perhaps, is better than the stagnant waters of their unspoken fears, of Angie and Ian's conscious or unconscious presumption of their son's guilt.

But the moment passes and the subject isn't broached and Kate must admit to relief, unsure where a discussion on criminal damage might have led them. Ian moves on with his story and Jon's eyes stay down on his phone and Kate goes back to wondering whether her nephew is capable of an act of malice against his teacher. Her eyes seek him a minute later and he's looking at her again with something that might be amusement. Kate casts a brief smile and wonders whether she likes her nephew as much as she once did.

They finish tea and Kate thanks Angie and they talk of another visit to Brixton to complete their unfinished expedition, and Ian offers to drive Kate to the station. She declines. It's barely a quarter of a mile and Kate will be glad of the walk. But as she goes through to collect her jacket Ian follows and repeats the offer. Her refusal is firm enough this time to deter further persuasion. Ian concedes, but stands close as she lifts down her coat.

'Did Angie mention about Jonathan?' he asks.

'Yes. Though I'm sure there's nothing behind it. I can't see Jon doing something like that.'

Ian casts a furtive glance at the dining room door, beyond which Angie is wrapping cake. He leans closer. 'I wish I could be sure,' he says, 'but I don't know what's in that boy's head any more. And I really don't like the company he's keeping.'

'Angie mentioned that,' Kate says. But she doesn't want to repeat their earlier conversation. Frankly, there's nothing she can say or do. And there's nothing Angie and Ian can say or do until they confront Jon. Angie is right to fear opening up rifts with their son, but that could hardly be worse than their corrosive uncertainty. This family, Kate thinks, is not as happy as it used to be. And perhaps it's more than just Jon. She senses that Ian pays less attention to Angie than he once did, even as he occasionally pays more attention than is strictly appropriate to Kate. His restrained flirting is, of course, nothing new and there's never been – so she's told herself – any intent behind it, but Kate has found herself wondering recently. Ian seems drawn to her, seems to like her more than, in truth, she likes him, and the truth is that she's less comfortable nowadays to be alone with him. Ian's offer of a lift was perhaps innocent but he knows that Kate is independent, fit and active and would no more desire a lift to the station than she'd hail a taxi. And now, to her surprise, Ian insists yet again that it would be no problem to drop her off, and Kate realises that he wants to talk about Jon. But that means that the one minute ride would stretch to half an hour and she really does want to get home and out for a run. Luckily Angie appears and hands over the cake and Kate can hide her non-answer in the act of opening the door. Ian stands back as Angie pecks a kiss, and Kate escapes to the street and heads towards the Tube.

8

The temperature has dropped, and a penetrating drizzle wraps Kate as she jogs to the park and starts her circuit round the cricket pitch. The path ahead is lit only intermittently and is deserted as she circles towards the distant glare of floodlights above the trees. She takes the first lap easy, though her breath nevertheless comes harsh, testament to her recent neglect. But the pain brings a sense of fighting back against a world of frustration and decay. Pain is good.

Kate's seclusion doesn't last. As she hits the main path on her second circuit she's surprised to see an approaching walker. A man, striding fast, slouched and intent, face concealed in a hood. Where on earth did he come from? He wasn't anywhere in sight on her first circuit. As they pass, Kate senses the guy's head turn fractionally then he's gone.

Her warm-up complete she pushes herself on the next lap until it hurts, alternating jogs with all-out sprints that focus her mind so that she's covered the length of the main path once again before it registers that the hooded figure is no longer there. He's vanished as suddenly as he appeared. He's either a hell of a walker or he's diverted into the trees. The latter thought brings a faint unease but Kate pushes it back. This end of Paddington is not the most gentrified, and hooded types abound on the night streets, but she's never felt threatened here.

Another circuit delivers a pain in her side and tiring legs, the cumulative effect of too many evenings at her desk, unable to beat the crush of work and the cold discouragement of winter evenings. She grits her teeth and pushes on through the dark and the now stinging rain. Then, on the far side of the cricket pitch, as she approaches the main path once again, she spots a figure under the trees. It's her hooded walker, standing watching. Without conscious thought Kate diverts onto the grass to give him a wide berth but as she moves away the sense of being watched is unnerving, and an innate caution – she won't admit to fear – brings a decision to cancel her cool-down lap. When she hits the gate she quits and leaves the park to head home, though once on the street she sneers at her foolishness. Since when were you scared to run in the park? Or was that just an excuse to cut short the exercise? And maybe it was, but the park suddenly has absolutely no appeal.

But back home even a partly completed exercise warrants the reward of ten minutes under a hot shower that stimulates her skin and washes tension away. She holds her face into the cataract, pushing at her hair until the night's cold has sloughed away.

She comes down to make dinner and spots the Valentine's card still propped on the breakfast bar. Its lurid red heart, intriguing this morning, is only mocking tonight. It's not something she needs on display. She grabs it and pushes it into the junk on the shelf, where it's not exactly discarded but is certainly no longer a part of her day.

She pulls out the chopping board and flicks a switch and is immediately reminded, by the patchy illumination of her worktop lighting, that she needs to replace the lamps. Then she stops in amazement. What she's *really* forgotten is that she replaced them last night. What on earth is going on? Has she an electrical problem? She stoops to peer up at the spots. Two blown, the same as yesterday. She tries to recall whether they're the same two and realises that at least one of them is, because it's the end one which she had to stretch to reach. And the second dud was two away, and *that* lamp is also dark again. Shit and damn! Are the electrics playing up or are the cheap unbranded spots just junk? She checks the box. Made in China. But isn't everything? She pulls out the blown lamps and pushes in replacements and they light up fine. So it's not the electrics, though if these new spots blow she'll need to get someone to check. She wonders if she's still got the receipt for the lamps. If she has, they'll go back.

Kate puts linguine on to boil and pulls shrimp from the fridge and chops garlic. The Cajun shrimp pasta she brings into her lounge thirty minutes later is a sufficient meal after Angie's sandwiches, and only marginally counterproductive to her run.

Her phone rings. It's Rache, who's out on the town investigating a new place in the West End that offers tapas and cocktails and has a great crowd – don't all London venues? – but Kate's excuse tonight is watertight. She's tired and hungry and her meal is cooling right in front of her. She promises they'll have a night soon and Rache surrenders.

As she settles onto the couch Kate recalls that she's lost the TV remote and heaves herself up to work the TV's manual controls, but just as she comes upright she spots the glint of plastic under the table nest. It's the remote. Damn! Why hadn't she spotted it the other night? It's not as if she hadn't looked, long and hard. Was she blind? But ingratitude for a problem solved is pointless. She subsides back onto the couch and retrieves the remote and channel-hops as she forks linguine. She settles on a documentary about the Hebrides, the second half of which, post wine and linguine, fades into blackness. When her eyes open it's eleven thirty.

Time to call it a day. Kate heads up to bed where she finds that she's neglected to leave the bedroom window open a crack as is her normal habit, leaving the room with a musty air. She lifts the sash now and night air chills her toes. Back at the bed, since she's noticing such things, the sheets smell like they need changing. That should be tomorrow's chore but they just don't seem fresh tonight and, Kate realises, haven't smelled fragrant since she started using a store brand conditioner when their shelves were devoid of her preferred brand a month ago. But the store's product is way inferior, and the bland fragrance that's permeated her laundry – a fragrance she now labels as *musty* – will permeate no more. She'll find her old brand tomorrow or change supermarkets.

Meantime, she'll change the sheets. She does so swiftly and re-lays the bed with linen that's been in storage for a few months and is untainted by the store's shoddy conditioner. Finally she's ready to crash.

When she slides between her clean, cool, *fragrant* sheets the effort to change them is proved worthwhile. But do other customers find the store brand conditioner unpleasant? How come it's taken until tonight for her to take exception to its cheap fragrance?

Her curtains, as always, are open, and when she kills the lamp the gentle amber reflections of the city lull her to sleep. In moments she's gone.

9

Sunday morning. The luxury of no particular place to go and no particular time to be there. Kate fills an hour with housework then goes out into a bright, chilly morning and drives to the supermarket.

She's a fast but disorganised shopper, eschewing her legal instinct for lists in favour of memory and a fixed route through the store. Speed is maximised by parking her trolley at strategic locations and foraging amongst the aisles to bring in the harvest. Today the necessities of bin liners and fabric conditioner sit dormant in her memory until triggered by her passing the shelves. The store has both the unbranded liners for her Brabantia – which despite the defect that dumped refuse all over her kitchen she again buys – and her branded conditioner which is, thankfully, back on the shelves. A single side track takes her to lighting accessories where she realises that she's unsure whether she already has replacements for the lounge lights. She has a faint notion that she does, so limits her purchase to the kitchen spots she knows are needed. Twenty-three minutes after entering the store she's in a checkout queue with only a single customer in front of her, and the new record cheers her to the extent that she exchanges pleasantries with the assistant before heading out to her car.

Back home she stores the cold stuff then goes to feed conditioner into the washing machine which is already laundering her stale bedding. In a little follow-up ceremony she pours the store brand crap down the sink and drops the container into the plastics sack. Then, as she continues unpacking, her contentment is shattered. Her list-free, efficient run through the store has delivered two screw-ups. Her quick grab for a jar of raspberry preserve was a little too careless. The brand and the label look right but she sees now that she's picked up damson, which she can barely tolerate. And a second careless pickup has landed her with a useless pack of spot lamps. To the casual glance the pack appears fine, but careful inspection shows that she's picked up the 240 volt instead of 12 volt variety her kitchen installation demands. How the *hell* did that happen? She clearly recalls searching for the 12 volt packs and comparing the prices of branded and unbranded options. What's happened, of course, is that she's fallen victim to that perennial selfish breed who prowl supermarkets and DIY stores inspecting goods and replacing them in the wrong place where, say, a pack of 240 volt spots will go unnoticed amongst the 12 volt packs. Now she's lumbered with the necessity of hanging on to the receipt and of stopping by the customer services desk next week. Shit and damn!

But whilst she's on the subject she replaces the lounge lamps – she has indeed got spares – and finishes tidying round the room, ejecting a CD from the player which has been on standby for the five days since the album played out. She searches for the CD's plastic case but can't find it, which is odd. She always leaves cases on the shelf by the hi-fi, but the shelf is empty. She spends a minute at the hopeless task of trying to spot the thing in her album rack before deciding that this is not how she intends to spend her day.

She needs to get a grip, to reverse this recent wave of forgetfulness and carelessness. She recalls the still-missing Waterman pen at her office. Even if it was stolen then it was her carelessness that permitted the crime. And the TV remote that eluded her for twenty-four hours whilst lying right next to the sofa. Now it's a CD case, an object as conspicuous as the remote but one that is never carried away from the hi-fi and should therefore *never* vanish. Perhaps Angie's right. Perhaps Kate's overburdened working life is following her home. Maybe she really should get out more.

Which is what she's about to do.

She'd considered giving Rache a call but an afternoon with her friend would extend late into the evening. And there's something that's been bugging her, anyway: the image of the ragged car-fixing guy from Liberace's has been in her mind, along with the guilt that if she thanked him at all two evenings ago it was with the briefest of words and an entirely phoney response to his invitation to look him up in the Stables. Surely the guy deserved more than that. And fact is he intrigues her. So if she's to get *out* this afternoon a trip over to Camden Market to inspect Xavier McGeary's boutique is a fun way to start. Kate changes into warm clothes and heads that way.

~~~~~

She exits the Tube into a low sun that burnishes the multicoloured brickwork of Camden High Street in a fierce winter light. The stalls are vibrant with a crowd that's shed its winter greys, lured by the illusion of spring. Kate walks swiftly up to the Lock. An exploration of the market and a coffee and croissant is the perfect antidote to the stresses of her legal world, a welcome foil against lifestyle sermonisers and defective light bulbs and splitting bin bags. She's not been here alone for years, and once she's amongst the stalls, jostled by the crowd, she's not sure if she's enjoying the freedom or is let down by it. In the past she's had Rache's commentary and mad dashes to steer her, occasionally Angie's slower explorations and longer coffee breaks. But comparison is pointless, since her mind is not *on* the goods or alluring aromas. Her random route through the market has the sole purpose of disguising the notion that she's making a beeline for Wackyjack's.

Beeline denial dictates that Kate must wander the Lock for an hour, peering at the stalls, but eventually she exits and walks under the bridge and into the Stables.

A newly recovered memory takes her up the stairs and towards the far end of the building where she confirms that McGeary was right: she *has* visited his boutique before, though it's only when she spots the garish name board and the clutter inside the door that Kate recalls what it was she purchased here. It was a scrap-metal stick sculpture, a Christmas present for nephew Jonathan two years ago. The figure was a cleverly wrought impression of a bass guitarist in full thrash whose wire braid horseshoe moustache made him a dead ringer for Mel Sánchez. Jon was fourteen and had been given a bass guitar that Christmas and he'd received the sculpture with a childlike awe a world away from today's teenage moods. With his gangly looks Jon is the antithesis of a heavy metal rocker, but he's picked up the *attitude* at least in his new sullen character. Jon hangs around with a bunch of like minds, all fancying themselves as the new Grunge generation as they shred guitar in some hopefully remote garage. They're not exactly a band, Angie says. They just hang together and make a din. Apparently the music world is safe from imminent invasion.

Kate steps into the boutique and feels the touch of electric radiants. The Stables, denied the sun, are colder than the street. She searches and spots McGeary beyond a group of Asian tourists, feet up behind his counter, reading a magazine.

The last time she was here, intent on her Christmas list, Kate had taken in little of the place and nothing of McGeary. The guy's own memory is impressive.

The boutique is floor to roof with the advertised Curiosities and Collectibles, though she can't figure which are *Curious* and which are *Collectible*, or rather, they're all Curious but probably few are Collectible. Perhaps the rack of forty-five and seventy-eight gramophone records qualifies, perhaps the shelves of old magazines, collections of fifties and sixties Marvel comics, True Detective and Parade and – Kate is living and learning today – tattered copies of Health and Efficiency from the 1930s with "full page art plates" that were undoubtedly scandalous at the time. Perhaps the Dinky toys and old dolls locked behind glass. The rest – an admixture ranging from silver-mounted otter feet and Trinidadian Limbo Drummer rum bottles to the scrap-iron sculptures that had caught her eye two years ago – are certainly Curious and presumably the proprietor would like you to *Collect* them for their somewhat eyewatering prices. The prices are what she does now recall, tags that made her think twice two years ago, but Jon's gift had simply been too perfect to pass by and so she'd taken a breath and stumped up. Kate works her way past the cabinets and racks and tables, detours round the Asian tourists and arrives at the counter where her tyre mechanic remains engrossed in a copy of True Detective that sports the trademark suspender-flashing terrified female on its cover. When McGeary looks up his face breaks into a broad smile that illuminates even his lurid reading matter in a boyish charm. 'Hey,' he says. 'The puncture lady. You came to see me.' He stands to hold out a hand. 'Zav McGeary,' he tells her.

Kate takes his hand and smiles at his turn of phrase. Does he really think she's come to Camden solely to see him? She puts him right with an assurance that she was simply passing and has called in to thank him for his assistance.

'No problemo,' McGeary says. 'Glad to help.' But he seems genuinely pleased to see her and for the first time, away from the shadowy street or forced glitz of Liberace's, she glimpses the more natural and unquestionably attractive man. He's wearing jeans and a ribbed wool sweater but his unruly hair is the same and his boyish smile is even warmer close up.

'It's Kate,' she tells him. 'And you were a life-saver.'

McGeary shrugs it away and says something about the right place and right time and Kate fills the moment by glancing at his reading material.

'You like crime?' she asks, as if the content of True Detective equates to crime in any but the most gratuitous sense. Her question, though, is only meant to provoke, and McGeary understands. He laughs.

'Only when the crime involves gratuitous violence and deviant sex,' he says. 'This mag's still published, you know. Actually there's a dozen covering the genre nowadays. But it's the vintage ones you need to read. They capture the spirit of an age. The old mags had style in the way their editors dressed the voyeuristic crap as serious reporting. Vintage publications are snapshots of their era.'

'Eras when women were attacked and murdered on a routine basis?'

'Just as today. Murder as mass entertainment.'

'The crimes are entertaining?'

'My interest's in the social anthropology. The mags dissect the evolving cultural consciousness. They beat reading research papers hands down.'

'Dissect cultural consciousness?' Kate latches onto this pompous proposition rather than challenge McGeary about whether his social studies also deliver vicarious thrills.

'Any mag. dealing with human interactions reflects the social fabric of the era,' McGeary says. He reels off a list: Life, Woman's Weekly, Harper's Bazaar, Health and Efficiency, Playboy, True Detective, Superman. All are progeny of their time.

'Time machines,' McGeary says. 'Read them and you discover what infused their readers. The editorial content, the illustrations, the adverts. The ads in particular are a treasure trove. All their gimmicks and scares and promises. You read this stuff and you're right back there in the past. Real people wrote the ads and real people read them, and you can see their naivety and hopes and neuroses, fifty years, a hundred years later. You read these magazines and you're looking at the world as it once was, the way people saw it.'

McGeary's eyes sparkle as he's drawn on his subject. Then he breaks off.

'How about a coffee?' he says.

Kate hesitates, sensing a casual visit turning into something more. But McGeary intrigues her. Their brief encounter the other night has sparked a need to know more, and so far the intrigue isn't fading. So there's no point leaving with open questions. A cup of coffee, even a cheap instant concoction in a cracked mug behind Wackyjack's counter, promises at worst an interesting interlude and at best the discovery that she might actually like this guy. So she accepts his offer. She'd passed up her planned Americano before coming in. Instant and a digestive will suffice.

But McGeary calls to a little guy in his early twenties lurking down one of the aisles. The guy has long stringy hair and a scrawny build that screams *nerd* and goes by the name of Nicholas and is apparently McGeary's assistant. McGeary sends him out with an order and when he returns with expertly brewed coffee in insulated cups and a supply of chocolate chips Kate's decision seems like a good one. Nicholas disappears with his own coffee and McGeary pats a stool behind the counter and they sit and talk amongst the clutter, and when Kate finds herself dunking her chocolate chip in unconscious imitation of McGeary a sudden warmth, which might be mistaken for contentment, flows through her. Sister Angie, with all her preaching, can eat her damn heart out. Sensible sister Angie has never dunked chocolate chip cookies with a guy this good looking and so – what's the word for someone who reads True Detective surrounded by a clutter of antique otter feet and Buddy Holly shellacs? – yes: so *cool*, in her life.

10

Wesley Leach's pre-trial review runs miraculously close to its scheduled slot and is as brief as expected, spilling Kate and her client out all too soon into the court annex for an ill-tempered leave-taking. Leach has shown up in a hand-tailored suit that has fooled neither the CPS prosecutor nor Lomax, the JP summoned at short notice to hear his plea for delay.

Leach turns, towering over Kate.

'We've work to do,' he tells her.

This is true, though not as much as he imagines since his defence will comprise only a rehash of his plea that he was in fear of his life when he fled the police and smashed into pensioner John Barnes' car. And when they lose the argument – as they will – the fear-for-life story won't count for as much as it would have if accompanying a guilty plea. Leach is treading dangerously.

And he's still refusing to connect with reality.

Even as they waited to go in he was still badgering Kate to work out a deal with the CPS that would accept a plea to dangerous driving and a reasonable chance of a non custodial sentence. Kate talked to the prosecutor as duty demanded but his response was predictable. He's not interested. Their case is solid. They'll be expecting three to five years – that's *if* the injured pensioner is still alive by the trial date. If the old guy dies they'll go after Leach for manslaughter and he'll be looking at ten. That this was an entirely predictable response did nothing to cool Leach's smouldering reaction to the CPS's non cooperation. He'd looked ready to jump out of his sheep's clothing as Kate had enacted her main business and entered a plea for a delayed trial date, which JP Lomax refused, citing the already-delayed pre-trial review consequent on the accused's whim of seeking new representation. Representation that, to Lomax's eyes, looks remarkably similar to the old representation. Lomax delivered his decision with bad grace and scheduled a slot just three weeks ahead. So Leach will stand trial in three weeks and when he's found guilty they're looking at real jail time.

'Witnesses,' he says. 'We'll prove the rozzers are lying about the lights.'

Kate shakes her head. 'We don't provide investigation services, and frankly I doubt if there are any witnesses to be found.'

In fact, Parfitt and Quinn have two consultants who carry out investigative work but Kate is not going down that road. She won't trawl for perjurious witnesses.

Leach's perplexion intensifies. He leans close. 'It's all in hand,' he says. 'I'll find my witnesses and you'll call them. I want a not guilty verdict. Is that clear?'

Kate's anger surfaces. She stares back at Leach.

'Is that a threat?'

'Do your job,' Wesley says.

'...because if you ever threaten me you'll be looking for another solicitor. Meantime,' she tells him, 'we need fifty percent of the fee in our account by the middle of the week, the remainder to be paid prior to the hearing. Can you sort that out?'

She doesn't wait for an answer. Steps round him and walks out of the building. But she feels Leach's eyes on her all the way down the steps, and her skin feels like it's crawling with insects.

~~~~~

It's lunch hour and the office is quiet. Kate goes to the kitchen to make tea and is just boiling water when she hears footsteps in the corridor and Hartley Tasker appears. As always he's brought his own mug, a pint sized tankard with the words "Street Lawyer" emblazoned around it. Hartley's story is that the mug was a gift from a nephew, though Kate assumes he bought it himself, its appellation intended as a nod to his hidden toughness, though if Hartley ever read the Grisham novel he might spot differences between himself and the fictional lawyer, the first and foremost being that under no goddamn circumstances would Hartley Tasker throw in a well paid job to go and work for a bunch of shoestring do-gooders. Hartley, of course, doesn't read and is therefore saved the irony. He acts surprised at finding Kate in the kitchen. Plants the Street Lawyer on the worktop and leans back against the fridge. His suit displays the same crisp cut as always but, it being after midday, the top button of his shirt is undone and his tie carefully loosened. Kate offers to make him tea and he accepts. She busies herself with both their drinks, searching for the minimum polite and meaningless words to fill the moment. But Hartley beats her to it. He asks about Wesley Leach.

Kate is surprised that he's been following her schedule. She shrugs and pours milk. 'We've all got our crosses,' she says. She turns and Hartley's eyes move rapidly from her legs as he nods sagely and tells her that Leach is a bad 'un. He asks how things went.

'They wouldn't budge on the trial date. Set it short, actually. Partly because Leach insists on contesting the charges. He still fantasises that he can walk away scot-free.'

'Heard the old guy's in a bad way.' Hartley's face is lined with concern.

'There's a chance he won't pull through. We could be looking at manslaughter charges before the hearing comes up,' Kate says.

Hartley nods, contemplates the consequences of criminal stupidity. 'Have you anything to contest the charges?' he asks.

'Leach wants to bring in witnesses who'll testify that the police chase vehicle was unmarked and unlit.'

'You think he'll find any?'

'Who knows?'

'If he wants to contest the charge he'd be better before a jury.'

'He doesn't have his witnesses yet. If he produces something we'll rethink.'

'That's kind of late, Katie.'

Kate picks up her cup. Wow, Hart, you think? Or is that a criticism I'm hearing? Am I to blame?

'I'm not in a position to advise on trial mode,' she says, 'until client and reality connect.'

'I see your problem,' Hartley says. 'Frankly, I'd have been tempted to show Leach the door.'

Well, Kate thinks, you already did that, Hart. Three years back when Henry's little clearout gave you the opportunity to push Leach my way. 'Yeah,' she agrees, 'sometimes I'm my own worst enemy. But client loyalty... you know?'

Hartley doesn't know. Hartley's loyalty is to Hartley. But he nods anyway as she waits for him to shift his angled legs and let her past.

'Watch that one, Katie,' he says. 'I worked with Wesley for years. Did you know he used to threaten me?'

Which is why you pushed him my way, she thinks. But she says: 'I've got it, Hart. If he misbehaves he's off our books.'

'He just might turn up his wits,' Hartley advises. 'Then you'd have a problem.'

Actually she wouldn't. Because if Leach turns up any dodgy witnesses his best course would be to elect for a Crown Court trial and Kate's problem will have ended. Arthur Parfitt is the firm's barrister. It would be Arthur who'd have the pleasure of defending Leach with a posse of ringers. But she doesn't want to see Arthur placed in that position, knowing it was she who let Leach back through the door.

Hartley has read her thoughts. 'Perhaps the firm was better off without him,' he says.

Suddenly it's clear that Hartley's come down specifically to rebuke her in his slimy roundabout way. And in rebuking her from the lofty heights of his seniority, drawing on his achievement of having sluiced Leach from his own list, Hartley is magnanimous in his lack of censure. But there's a rebuke in his every utterance and Kate can respond only with a lame agreement that yes, they'd be better off without Leach, before stepping over his legs and pushing out of the door and back to her office.

11

It's Tuesday evening and Kate has left work at an unheard-of six p.m. She's following sister Angie's advice and *getting out*. But despite the early finish and rushed shower the Tube ride has been a frustration of delays and unexplained stops, and she's half an hour late by the time she arrives at the pub off Haverstock Hill.

Zav's already at the bar. He's dressed in a mishmash. Cargo pants and waistcoat, flannel shirt, cord jacket.

'The damn Tube,' Kate says.

'Eight p.m.,' Zav says. 'That's when they switch to Siberian timetables.'

It's the eternal safe topic of London conversation, second only to the weather. The ancient labyrinthine warren beneath their feet becomes, like the weather, ever more unpredictable as its decrepit technology sparks and wheezes under the burden of three million passengers a day. But their Tube gripe is short. Sunday's coffee at Wackyjack's has eased them beyond the need for banalities, besides which, Zav has driven here and is therefore unaffected by things below ground. They continue where they left off on Sunday with the exploration of the equally labyrinthine mysteries of intersecting lives. Zav, it turns out, has dropped into the fringe retail world of Camden Market from the higher echelons of the French education system into which youthful folly and an aptitude for the language drew him as an undergraduate. Their mutual explorations haven't quite brought Kate to the stage where she feels free to ask Zav how a graduate in social anthropology at the ENS de Lyon ends up in Camden Stables but the question isn't a pressing one. For some indefinable reason the transition from Masters to stallholder doesn't seem inappropriate. Kate's own career path is less colourful but is readily embellished with the tales of the clientele who pass through her doorway, and her impressionistic sketch of the recent brawl in her office amuses Zav.

'I always imagine solicitors in these dusty rooms,' he says, 'poring over real estate codicils and composing legalese letters. I never considered the fistfighting angle.'

Kate's voice is raised against the hubbub. 'Barely a fistfight,' she says. 'Just a slap across the face. But my client went over his chair just the same.'

Zav is drinking whiskey. He swirls his glass and the amber gleams.

'I like the girl,' Zav says. 'She sounds like a firebrand.'

Kate twirls her own glass. Light sparkles in its flaws. When she looks up there's a twinkle in Zav's eyes that's more than just her storytelling. Her silk top and soft skirt, her long legs gleaming in sheer black, are working on him. He's no longer the disinterested stranger from Wackyjack's. She senses her power drawing him in. For all his boyish charm and good manners Zav would ditch his drink in an instant and follow her out of here.

'Sometimes my clients' legal affairs are the least of their issues,' she says. She's talking about Donna, the *firebrand*. 'I've represented twenty like her, all rushing towards disaster. Sometimes you can see what they might have been. This girl's sweet deep down but life has offered her a burden of hate and she's not hesitated to grab the yoke. You can see the cloud over her. And nothing I do will help. I'll try to keep her out of jail but then where will she be? Right back in the seedy clubs and hotels, or on the streets. And in ten years she'll be dead or a shattered husk. Makes you wonder what the point is.'

'The point is to help where you can.'

'But it's so little.'

'Perhaps you can steer her in the right direction.'

'I try but it's like bashing my head against a wall. These girls bear the chip on their shoulder like a jewel. They covet it, bite any hand that would snatch it away.'

'So is this one saveable?'

'I'm not optimistic.'

'A shame if she's a nice kid.'

'I didn't say she was exactly nice. I sense a sweet kid but it's buried deep. Someone's little girl who got hurt. Probably no longer fixable.'

'You mean someone who *hurt* their little girl.'

'Of course. Her family comes from social services hell.'

'Bad part of town?'

'Different town. Liverpool. A shithole estate – her description – in a place called West Derby.'

'Broken home... dysfunctional guardians...'

'Her mother's an alcoholic, her stepfather was an addict and abusive. My client spent fifteen years with them in a semi derelict house with six other kids. Her stepfather beat her mother regularly and started abusing my client when she was seven. She suffered all kinds of hell before she finally got out. Then a month after she arrived in London her stepfather was found dead from an overdose. The timing confirmed my client's view of a world that has it in for her. The overdose was going to happen sometime. Why not ten years earlier?'

'It's interesting that she's confided in you. I'd expect her to clam up for an authority figure.'

Kate catches the barman's eye and raises her glass.

'They *all* talk. They love to talk. To raise their grievances like shields against your good intentions. The whole world is against them and my client won't hear different, so she bombards me with the proof that we've all failed her. Me, the police, social services, her punters. And confiding in me doesn't mean she'll let me help.'

'No friends?'

The barman sets down her refill. Kate takes a sip.

'Imagine the kind of person who approaches runaways at Euston and King's Cross.'

'The kind they've run away from.'

'It's preordained. A day after my client arrived she was shacked up with a guy seven years older who put her straight on the street. She was fifteen. Two years later the guy ditched her for a fourteen-year-old but he's still pimping her. And my client won't break away. Sees him as some kind of protector. He takes seventy percent of what she earns and slaps her around when the mood's on him but she's never considered just walking away.'

'Could she?'

'Yes. The guy's a lone operator. She could lose him tomorrow in this town.'

'...but she'd find someone worse.'

'Exactly.'

'You say she stabbed one of her clients?'

'In the back of his car. Not exactly stabbed. She gave him a few nicks in the face and a black eye, but it's hard to walk away from a knife assault conviction without jail time. She got lucky when a patrol car disturbed their altercation before things got worse. My client's claiming self-defence but a business arrangement gone bad doesn't pull the cops' heartstrings.'

'So what's the get-out-of-jail?'

'Formally: none. Self-defence doesn't work for knife assault. Informally, my client received an incriminating text message from the punter. He'd been referred by a friend of hers who was passing her off as underage. I suspect it's a regular scam they pull. But once the guy got her in his car he realised he'd been mis-sold the goods. That's when he refused to pay up but had the idea of sampling her services for free as compensation. But sending that text was careless. It's pretty explicit about what he was expecting and when it's read out in court as part of my client's defence it's going to make the papers. So the guy's solicitor is asking him whether he'd prefer to admit his own assault to back up my client's self-defence story. That way we might reach an agreement with the CPS that my client plead guilty to something we call Section 47 which is assault causing relatively minor injury. And with the self-defence mitigation we should be looking at a fine. That's more attractive than jail time or a long community order. And the punter avoids exposure in court as a pederast. Win-win all round.'

'So you might get her off. But there'll be a next time.'

'That's the way it is.'

'A lawyer with a conscience. I'd have settled for the pretty face.'

Kate laughs off the facile compliment. She suspects she's already more than just a pretty face to this guy. She's starting to sense the power of what's growing between them, the thrilling possibly that this unruly, easy-going guy might be her next lover. It's with that thought in mind that her mouth gets ahead of her and blurts out the entirely unsubtle question about whether Zav is married.

He grins. 'Three years divorced,' he says. 'Footloose and free. How about you?'

Kate is blushing from her clumsy question but Zav shows no sign of noticing. And what matters is that his answer was the right one.

'The same,' she says. 'Footloose. How long were you married?'

'Five years. It was great whilst it lasted but then it all exploded. I still don't know what happened. Maybe I missed the footloose days.'

Which is not so good an answer. But Zav sees her disappointment and steers them back.

'I'm happy either way,' he says, 'so long as the company is right.'

And his eyes say that the present company *is* right. But there are two versions of *right,* one based purely on the physical, one that swamps common sense and dispenses with the search for the *spiritual* until the roman candle of lust has sparked out. And there's the other *right,* the one for the long term. Kate searches for any sense of the latter building, wonders if Zav's wondering the same thing. But here in this pub, right now, it's the *physical* that's ignited. The candle is flaming and the future is just a shadow beyond the fountain of sparks.

It gets late. Zav offers to drive her home but she declines, though she accepts his offer to walk her to the station. When they part she's aware that the moment could go either way, but his hand just touches her shoulder and his smile envelops her and he tells her to take care. Then he's gone.

12

Kate exits the station and crosses into Elgin Avenue. It's after midnight and the street is deserted.

Despite the dank chill she's glad she declined Zav's offer of a lift. It's good to feel the strength of her independence as she savours the thought of what might soon be. One night soon, perhaps, she won't be walking home, but she'll always be her own person. And on the brink of something extraordinary an emotion she might mistake for happiness bubbles up.

She turns into her road, whose meagre lighting has her treading carefully in the shadows, but then sixty seconds along it, half way to her house, she senses something. She stops and turns. Is there someone behind her? She sees nothing. And the only sound is the distant hiss of the Westway. But her subconscious had picked up the *sense,* more than the sound, of someone following, and the primeval filtering by which her brain resolves whispers from the background is telling her that someone is there in the shadows. Then she chides her mischievous imagination and turns to resume her walk, but the tingle is there on her neck, subsuming the cold into a more unpleasant sensation, and the unease grows steadily until she has to stop again.

And fifty metres behind her, in the shadows between the trees, she catches movement beside the glint of a car's bodywork. It's so brief that Kate can't say what it is – a man, a cat, a tumbling plastic bag? – or whether, even, the movement was of light against shadow or dark against light. It was just that one brief flicker. But what Kate's instincts are telling her is that someone has just ducked down between the parked cars. She stands her ground, challenging them to show themselves even as she admonishes herself for foolishness. Her "instinct" is nothing but mischievous imagination. She *imagined* she heard something, *imagined* the flash of something dropping between the cars. And, bottom line, she's an overworked woman dogged with problems she can't solve, and the veneer of tonight's contentment is liable to crack at the least provocation to expose her overwrought, nervous core. *Nerves* are why she's standing like a fool on this midnight street staring at something that isn't there. She needs to get home.

She turns and continues that way, refusing to be spooked further.

A minute later she's inside and has turned the key in the door just a half second before a slight tick or *clacking* sound registers. The sound comes from inside the house. Kate stops dead. What the hell was that? The house returns only silence but the sense of something amiss is back again. It's still her damn nerves, it's still nothing, but she's holding her breath, listening. Finally, she gropes for the light switch and illuminates an empty hallway. Empty because the whole house is empty. There's no one here. But the unease remains, and it takes effort to walk to the kitchen where, even as she enters, she's already identified the familiar hum of the fridge whose ticking vanes explain the sounds.

Woman, she thinks, are *you* a bag of nerves? Get a grip! You've a tough day tomorrow, and a night wrecked by idiotic imaginings isn't going to help.

Then the phone rings and Kate jumps a mile.

She grabs the handset and sees it's a withheld ID. She recalls last night's dead line. Decides that this is another marketing call. The calls are a plague and the recent shift into late night harassment is a new low. She's about to kill the call when a sudden, illogical, thought hits her that this might be Zav. That makes no sense since she's given him only her mobile number. But the thought brings the need to know. Not knowing would bug her more than a call centre operative's zombie script. So she hits pick-up.

And she's right: it's just silence at the other end, another marketing call disconnected by a computer as its quota of respondents is filled. These *damn* cowboys!

But then she realises that the line is open. The computer, or whoever, is still there. 'Hello?' she says.

There's no reply. The computer is truly inept tonight. Then just as she's thumbing for the disconnect the silence is broken.

It's a voice, an odd, warbling, barely human voice that shocks her to the core, one that's been electronically altered into an alien burble.

The voice says 'Sleep tight, Kate.'

And the line disconnects.

Kate stands with the dead phone pressed to her ear as the sinister message echoes in her head. "Sleep tight, Kate." That weird cadence, the terrifying non humanness of the words, the suddenness of the intrusion. It's like she's been shocked with a stun gun. Her limbs start shaking as she holds the handset away from her and stares into the mewling dial tone.

Then she snaps out of it. She slams the phone back into its cradle. What the *freaking* hell? Who the hell was that?

She finds no answer, and the street fear rushes back in to consume her as the two things become one with the terrifying thought...

There *was* someone out there. And he's just called her.

Kate listens, straining for sounds that are *not* the fridge. There are none, but a monstrous fear has now gripped her. Adrenaline whips her into motion. She strides across the kitchen and checks the back door. Locked. She checks the windows. The latches are antiquated but the locks are all fine. She rushes through each of the rooms checking all the windows and finishes, irrationally, at the front door which she's just locked. Then she rushes upstairs and checks the bedrooms and bathroom.

Only her bedroom window is open a crack, as always. No one could get in that way without a ladder but she's taking no chances. She closes and locks it. But even as she comes back onto the landing the thought hits her that she hadn't really *focused* in her panic. She hasn't looked carefully, calmly, double-checked that each lock is really secure, confirmed that there's no damage to the windows. So she needs to check again. She needs to know for sure that whoever just called her, whoever was out on the street, can't get into the house.

So she goes down and starts over. *Walks*, this time. She double-checks the kitchen door then inspects every window, downstairs and up, checking for any sign of damage. When she's through, when she's confirmed that the house is locked tight, she stops and waits for common sense to return and confirm that she's overreacting. The phone call was a prank, unconnected to her sense of being followed up the street. Some bastard decided to give her a scare and he's succeeded, and damn him to hell.

The extent of his success is evident in Kate's overpowering urge to repeat her patrol yet again. Did she *really* check the windows and doors adequately on her second pass? Fear urges another round, to repeat her patrol ad infinitum, OCD-like, but this time she resists. She goes through instead and pours a glass of wine to take thirty minutes in front of the TV whilst she calms down. But as she subsides onto the couch the black void of her front window catches her attention. The house is concealed by its high privet hedge but the vegetation cuts off the street light and pitch black darkness is staring at her. She rises and draws the curtains then sits down to a late night show.

But her wine glass has barely touched her lips when her overactive mind churns up the fact that in her paranoid rush round the house – in her *two* paranoid rushes – she's missed something. Two circuits of the house, up and down, every damn window and door and corner checked in case the bogeyman tries to get in and she's missed the most obvious place of all.

In the movies where does the bogeyman live?

Don't! she tells herself. Enough! The whole thing is a nonsense triggered by that stupid call. She's got work tomorrow. She needs to drowse before the TV then head for bed, forget this whole stupid hysteria. There was no one out on the street. There's no one in the house nor trying to get in. The whole thing is the workings of her jittery mind.

But where does the bogeyman hide?

Shit and damn! She *knows* where the bogeyman hides. But this isn't the movies. This is her house in Maida Vale, London, which in eight years has never thrown up a single ghost or ghoulie or bogeyman, and one malicious phone call doesn't change that.

But if she doesn't check then she'll lie awake all night, wondering.

The place she needs to check is the cellar.

Unlike the houses up on the main road with their basement flats her house has a simple, old fashioned cellar under its floorboards.

And it's the only place she's not checked. So she's going to have to go down there and make sure that the half-window is secure and that there's no one hiding down there. She plants her glass and goes to do it.

Kate rarely notices the door under the stairs, never opens it, but tonight's irrationality has endowed it with threat. She needs to open it now, go down, check that window. It will take just a minute.

She releases the latch and feels for the light switch, and the stairs are illuminated with a sinister yellow cast that's barely an improvement on the dark. Kate takes a breath and starts down, her senses now screaming that she's making the classic Hollywood mistake of descending without a torch. If the light goes out – and it *always* does – she'll be floundering in blackness. But this is a trepidation too far. Anger spurs her and she descends quickly, fear of sudden darkness be damned. She reaches the stone floor and pushes between the junk to check the half-window at the front. As she passes the hanging light bulb her shadow leaps ahead of her, startling her and inking the floor in shadow. She reaches the window and sees what she should have known, that it is tiny, barely thirty centimetres high, and that its dirt-caked woodwork is incapable of movement. It's just a solid frame, four unbroken glass panes so dirty they don't even reflect her face. She works back to the stairs and continues past them to where a coarse brick dividing wall with a narrow walk-through gives access to the rear room. Beyond the gap is blackness. *This* is why she should have brought a damn torch! But the room is empty, she recalls, except for a dresser and an ancient washing machine, and after a few seconds her eyes adjust sufficiently to let her creep over to the back wall and confirm what she also knew, that there's no window on this side and no nook or cranny that would hide an intruder. The house is secure.

Game over. Time to head back upstairs.

Then there's a touch on her face.

She snaps round with a squeal as the silky touch caresses her again, and her flailing hands become encased in a tacky, dusty, cobweb. Holy shit! *Stop this,* she tells herself. There's nothing here. No one. She curses and rushes back out and round to the stairs which she takes two at a time, capitulating finally to the childhood terror that someone's at her heels. She reaches the top and flicks off the light and slams the door then stands with her back to it in a fit of giggles that continue until she's choking. You just scared yourself silly, you stupid bitch! But she's shaking too. Stupid! she tells herself, but she must nevertheless drag her Italianate hall table from its place and tip it to jam it under the cellar door's latch because that cellar scares her tonight. But with the table in place even if the door is forced it won't open quietly, and this token defence has the desired calming effect.

She returns to the lounge and kills the TV and drains her glass then, checking the front and back doors one last time, heads upstairs. Morning will bring a more rational perspective. In the light of day the nuisance call will be just that. There'll be a hundred footsteps out in the street, and none of them a threat.

But sleep eludes her and she lies awake watching the dim flicker of light on her ceiling, still fighting the powerful sense of menace lurking. The bubbling telephone voice plays over and over, tormenting her into connecting recent events – the late night calls, the Valentine's, the unease in the park, the footsteps in the street – until she's imagining connections that can't be. But there is a connection she can't deny: these oddities have never happened before and they're all happening now.

And if they *are* connected she'd have to conclude that someone has taken a malign interest in her, has commenced a campaign of intrusion into her life, which is unthinkable.

Without that phone call the thought of someone *watching* her would not have occurred. She'd have dismissed the feeling in the street as either nothing or at worst a drunk trailing along behind her. She'd have forgotten her unease at the hooded figure in the park, dismissed the Valentine's card as a prank. But tonight's call has changed everything. Because the caller was specifically and deliberately testing her. He was ready with his voice-altering electronics, ready with his cold inappropriate message. And the call's timing, just as she got in, says that he was watching her house. In which case the assumptions that someone was following her on the street, that he was there in the park, that he's sent her a Valentine's card, aren't so far fetched. And the proprietorial air of the Valentine's greeting is creepily similar to tonight's message. "Special Love" and "Sleep tight" have an eerie resonance. But there is one difference: the Valentine's might be foolishness or a prank. The telephone message, with its mangled, altered voice, was malevolent. The telephone message dispensed with any pretence of "Special Love". It was intended to frighten her.

Kate feels as if she's on the brink of an invasion.

13

Kate rides the packed Tube, too lethargic to decide whether anger or fear is uppermost. It took last night's call to do it, but now that she's connected the recent events she wonders how she ever missed it.

She scrutinises her fellow passengers but doesn't know what she's looking for. Her tormentor's not on the train. How could he be? On the other hand... how do you double guess someone like that? He could be here, hiding behind a newspaper or a smartphone or a glassy-eyed stare. But no one catches her eye, no one seems remotely aware of her. And even stalkers have jobs to go to. Kate pictures another train racing across London on another line, a traveller whose blank stare hides a quiet satisfaction.

She strides down Upper Street and taps the front door security code and goes through to drop the mail onto Violet's desk. She's missed breakfast but can't spare the ten minutes to make a brew. The hour before the firm opens for business is too precious, and her backlog of paperwork is waiting. After which her jammed diary signals an uphill day leading almost certainly to another late night. Any thought of a second date with Zav is wishful thinking.

When Violet pops her head in at eight forty-five and catches her rubbing her eyes Kate surprises herself by admitting to a sleepless night then compounds her surprise by spilling out the details of the anonymous phone call. Even as she speaks she's dismayed that she's telling this to Violet, who's management of gossip runs on the barter principle. Kate and Violet rarely exchange chit-chat, limiting their discussions mostly to issues related to Kate's disorganised affairs. Not that Violet is unsympathetic. The telephone call shocks her. She asks if Kate has reported the incident to the police.

Kate shakes her head. 'He didn't actually threaten me,' she says.

Her words have the comforting aspects of both downplaying the incident and sharing it, as if this is some professional glitch to be talked through and not a malicious assault on her person. Violet assails her with a string of warnings, though, and annoying though they are they at least allow Kate the therapeutic repetition of the mantra that it's all probably nothing. And perhaps it is. Protected by the familiarity of her workplace yesterday's unpleasantness has dissipated like a fading nightmare. Kate draws the discussion to a close and coaxes Violet out so she can get on with worrying about the real nightmares lurking within the pages of her diary.

~~~~~

The first of these arrives at ten when Wesley Leach sits down to cast a dispiriting sheen over her day.

He tosses a manila envelope onto her desk. Kate waits for an explanation but Wesley wants her to discover the envelope's contents for herself. She clamps her lips and pulls a single sheet from it. The sheet contains three names and addresses. Wesley has found his witnesses to dispute the police version of their car chase.

'How did you find them?' she asks.

'An ad. in the *Standard*.'

'You didn't mention this the other day. When did you run it?'

'Few days back.'

'A full page?'

'Classifieds. Personal section.'

Kate's lifts an eyebrow. 'What – two or three lines?'

'Five. Standard insert.'

She looks at him. Five lines buried deep in the classifieds. What are the chances that such a scrap would raise a single public-spirited witness? She reads the addresses. Two are North London, the third Romford. So the witnesses travelled some distance to be in the right place when Wesley was fleeing the police. Witnesses who, apparently, are in the habit of searching the *Evening Standard* classifieds on the off chance they might be summoned to public service.

'You're saying these people came forward in response to the ad?'

'They did.'

'And you personally don't know them?'

Wesley's perplexity shines between the Dracaenas. 'I've never met any of them,' he says.

Kate sighs.

'Fine. I'll contact them. But if these people are summoned they'll be testifying under oath. If any part of their testimony is proved false they'll face prison sentences. It will be my duty to warn them of that.'

This deviation brings a nudge back into line.

'They're telling the truth. They can't go to jail.'

Oh, but they could. Because if Wesley's witnesses are either strangers or truthful she'll eat her damn hat. To think that she'd imagined Wesley's shoehorned appointment was routine, maybe to drop off the fifty percent fee she's requested. Now, instead of a cheque, she's lumbered with another juggling trick.

By sheer bad luck, Wesley's reckless drive through the back ways of Leyton escaped the attention of a single CCTV camera, leaving the police open to challenge on whether their unmarked vehicle was displaying lights. Just one CCTV snap could have killed Wesley's argument. If Kate brings these witnesses in the CPS will attack them with a sledgehammer, which means she's lumbered with interviewing them in a double speak charade to prepare them without provoking from them the faintest hint that they're fibbing. Kate defends clients irrespective of presumed guilt but she doesn't proffer perjurous testimony. She groans inwardly.

'How are the funds?' she asks.

Wesley smiles and hands over a cheque for the fifty percent, which, with the added cost of witness interviews, is no longer fifty percent. No matter. Wesley will settle the balance before his hearing or he'll walk into court alone.

~~~~~

Late in the morning Kate is sitting before Arthur Parfitt's antique walnut desk. Arthur rests at ease behind it, hands clasped over his stomach. His direct involvement in her work is rare, but she needs his advice. As she recounts her problem she sees her own reservations mirrored in Arthur's face. But if there's rebuke on his mind he conceals it. Perhaps, knowing Kate's record, he endows greater trust in her than she realises. But in Arthur's smile she understands that she made a bad call when she allowed Leach back in. Unfortunately, last Friday there were no partners to consult, and a decision was needed. So Arthur will have to live with Wesley, even if Kate had come here half hoping for an instruction to relinquish him to someone else. But relinquishment has not been mentioned. Leach will remain Kate's client and she must shovel the shit whichever way it falls. Tap, tap, tap. Her foot connects briefly with Arthur's desk and Kate flinches. She angles her leg away.

'Bring the witnesses in,' Arthur says. 'I'll interview them myself.'

The relief at this offer is balanced by the knowledge that in helping her out Arthur is highlighting Kate's position as a junior member of the firm. In any normal interpretation of the word Kate is far from junior. Arthur finds her indispensable. But the ladder ahead of her, he's saying, still climbs far. Kate smiles wearily. Her foot taps air. 'I'll do that,' she says.

Arthur nods and changes the subject.

'I heard you had a problem last night.'

The comment catches Kate by surprise. Has the story spread so quickly?

'Probably just a prank,' she says.

Arthur clasps and unclasps his hands. 'Perhaps. But a late night call and a disguised voice are a serious harassment.'

'If he calls again I'll be informing the police.'

'Good,' Arthur says. 'Err on the safe side.'

Kate wonders if that advice includes a backhand rebuke for her judgement on Wesley Leach. But Arthur's still relaxed and his hands lie quiescent across his belly. 'You never know who's out there,' he says.

I never did, Kate thinks. They just didn't have my phone number before.

~~~~~

Lunch is subsumed into work catch up, with the promise of a sandwich when Violet returns. The hour is broken, at least, when Zav calls. Kate pushes away from her desk and basks in the warmth of his voice even as she turns down his invitation for this evening. Any pleasure at Zav's company would be tarnished by the thought of the backlog she'd leave behind if she left work early. Zav accepts her refusal with equanimity. She pictures him reclining in his chair at Wackyjack's amongst the boutique's pervading clutter which, unlike the clutter of her office, has the charm of being intentional. When she admits that she's working through lunch, and that lunch will be, at best, a sandwich of something unhealthy on wilted lettuce, she hears his soft laugh.

'I feel so guilty,' he says. 'Nicholas brought me a sub. Prawns on fresh leaves. Dinner tonight would do you good, Kate.'

'Dinner would be a dream. But not tonight. Let's see about tomorrow.'

Though she's no surer about tomorrow. She'll give tomorrow perhaps a fifty percent chance. But they agree it as a maybe, so that today, if it must drag, can drag towards something good.

Violet, true to her word, drops off a tuna sandwich which, at two fifteen, entices her like manna from heaven. She gives herself ten and walks through to find Hartley in the kitchen, fresh from his own lunch and brewing coffee to ease him into his afternoon. He offers Kate a cup but she declines and busies herself with the kettle. She senses him waiting. It turns out that he, too, has heard about her phone call.

'That's a worrying development,' he says. 'You need to be careful, Katie.'

'I will.'

'Any chance you know the guy?'

'I've no way of telling.' She keeps it short. She doesn't want another conversation about the call, least of all with Hartley. Fool that she was for opening her mouth to Violet.

'You recall that case...' Hartley says.

Kate does recall. One of Arthur's old clients, a forty-two-year-old divorcee who was subjected to a three-year campaign of calls and vandalism. When the police failed to stop her tormentor, or even request a restraining order against the ex-boyfriend whom she suspected was behind the campaign, she'd come to Parfitt and Quinn. But restraining orders can only be applied to confirmed individuals, and all Arthur's client could do was endure the harassment and visit their offices monthly to keep the firm up to date on the guy's activities. Sadly, by the time her assailant was caught he'd already entered her house in a drunken rampage and killed her. Anonymous callers aren't taken lightly at Parfitt and Quinn.

'This isn't really similar,' Kate points out. 'This is probably just a prank.'

Hartley disagrees. 'Malicious calls are about grievances, not pranks. This could escalate.'

'Thanks for your concern, Hart.' She disposes of a tea bag. 'I'll be fine.'

'Just be vigilant,' Hartley says.

Kate promises she will and moves to pass him but Hartley stands his ground.

'It's just the one call? Nothing else?'

'Just the one,' she says. The fact that this is almost certainly untrue doesn't concern her because the affair doesn't concern Hartley. She throws him a bright smile and waits for him to move. He gets the message and stands aside but an admonition follows her: 'Don't take any chances, Katie. If he calls again bring the police in.'

Kate says she will.

~~~~~

At six thirty she's alone in her office with a mountain of paperwork for company. She attacks the mess, for once applying a rigorous discipline in her decisions about what can be assigned to the firm's paralegals such that she clears the backlog in the commendable time of one hour and ten.

By eight twenty she's home, and an almost chemical change courses through her as she closes her front door. The change is instant and powerful and renders her utterly incapable of going out for another run. Kate prides herself on her willpower but tonight greater forces prevail. She'll stay in and take a bath.

She fills the bath and lowers herself into the foam, promising herself thirty minutes, maybe forty-five, to dissipate the stress of the day. But as she closes her eyes the memory of last night's phone call sneaks back in. Harsh as her work regimen is, it's delivered the benefit today of keeping her mind off her anonymous caller. But with relaxation comes the return of her subconscious stress, even if, in her struggle to recall the electronically altered voice, she senses distance building. Maybe it *was* a one-off. Maybe the experience will recede into an irrelevant and finally forgotten mystery. She relaxes.

Then downstairs the phone rings.

Her shoulders rise reflexively from the water and her knees are folding before she stops herself.

Leave it!

She's not jumping out of her bath for the damn phone, whoever it is. She waits until the ringing stops, leaving its faint echo within the silence of the house. But when, finally, she subsides back into the foam, she remains tense.

That *sodding* phone. Almost certainly a marketing shot, but the interruption has demonstrated just how close to the surface her fears are, has shattered the fantasy that what happened last night is over. The violation of that shocking voice will be with her when she's ninety. Will she ever be able to pick up a damn phone without holding her breath? And *could* it have been him just now? She curses and closes her eyes and tries to unwind but she can't. *Bastard,* she thinks.

The phone rings again.

She tenses once more before realising that it's her mobile, lying on the bathroom worktop. She stretches for it even as the thought occurs that maybe her anonymous caller has got this number. But it's not him. The screen says "Zav".

14

'Are you at work?' Zav asks.

His voice restores tranquillity. Kate relaxes back into the water. 'Of course not,' she says. Relief draws an intimacy: 'I'm in the bath.'

'That's a pity,' he says.

'You'd prefer I was still at work?'

'I thought I'd lure you from your desk with the offer of supper. Luring you from the bath sounds trickier.'

'I'm finished with the bath,' Kate says. 'Shall I go back to the office?'

'Or I could pick you up from home...'

The offer conjures an enticing image. If Zav had called an hour ago then... what? She actually would have been at work and she'd have rushed home for a shower and she'd be turning off the tap right now. And what's the difference between getting out of a shower and getting out of a bath? Nothing more than inertia.

'Perhaps it's a little late,' she suggests. Her screen says it's eight fifty.

His laugh is self-deprecating. Supper offered out of the blue is pushy and he's playing it down. Not that Kate would call it pushy. Badly timed is what she'd say.

'Confession,' Zav says. 'I've jumped the gun. I've already something cooking.'

'Oh?' Kate slides deeper into the froth and plants her toes against the far end of the bath and stretches in a body-wide yawn.

'Crostini and piadina.'

She sighs. Sees antipasti and wine before a crackling fire. She wonders if Zav has a crackling fire. She wonders if she'd like to find out. Then pictures an untidy bachelor flat with central heating. But Zav is a style aficionado. She revises her bet: it's a spectacular place with a cosy lounge and log fire. She glances at her phone again. Eight fifty-one. She could be home by midnight... Decisions, decisions. All she has to do is exert herself and... her body tenses and her toes tangle the plug chain and it pops out and the water starts to flow.

'Are you sure it's no trouble?' she says.

Zav promises to be there in ten and cuts the line. Kate jumps from the bath and grabs the towel which is once again damp. She checks the rail. Cold, just like last week. She rotates the thermostat, puzzled that it turns in both directions. Hadn't she set it to maximum after the last failure? She sets it there now and slips on her sandals to fetch a fresh towel from the cupboard.

When she's dry she fingers through her wardrobe for something casual, but surprises herself by pulling out a body hugging black dress that is comfortable but far from casual, more suited to the West End than supper. The dress is entirely inappropriate but it's entirely sexy too, necessitating as it does the wearing of stockings.

'Tart,' she tells the figure in the mirror, but her glistening legs are elegant rather than tarty. And the dress is just right for padding around at Zav's place, and no hindrance at all for eating supper, which she hopes, as hunger kicks in, is not *too* supperish.

She goes down to grab her stuff and the kitchen phone catches her eye, reminding her of her missed call. Was it him again? Was that alien voice waiting for her? If it was, she's no time to dwell on it. She grabs a jacket and is pulling it on when the doorbell rings.

~~~~~

Zav is a man of surprises. Her foray to Wackyjack's demonstrated that. So Kate has conditioned herself to exhibit no surprise if her bohemian turns up in a Porsche. But Zav *surprises* her by walking her out to a beat-up Fiat Ducato van. She climbs onto its worn upholstery feeling a little foolish in her short dress. The dash, the floor, the door pockets are all littered with junk – if ledgers, maps and invoice pads *are* junk, though the tabloid newspaper, the broken binoculars and the empty coffee tin certainly are – but Zav seems oblivious to the mess and no more apologises for the downmarket ride than he'd have apologised for the Porsche. He fires up and they speed away through the dark streets and though his eyes are focused on the traffic he tells her: 'You look nice.' He turns briefly to lighten his words with a grin. He's just letting her know that he's noticed, as he was supposed to, but the formality doesn't lessen Kate's pleasure. She relaxes in the musty seat and says 'Thank you.'

Zav's place is another surprise. It's a three storey detached house jammed into a Victorian row on Haverstock Hill, still whole and undivided. And where Kate had anticipated the clutter of Steptoe's living room she finds a bright and cheerful place, chaotic with old, stylish furnishings. Zav has her fetch the supper fare – various breads and cheeses and fruit that are substantially more than a light bite – into a lounge heated by... dammit, a crackling fire! Or at least the next best thing. It's a stove, blazing fiercely in the old fireplace, and if stoves don't crackle they certainly blast out a cheery heat on a cold night. As she lays out the food the stove's incandescence illuminates the lounge in the *precise* cosy glow she'd imagined from her bath.

Zav is wearing woollen slacks and a striped cotton shirt with silver armbands, and his hair flames in the light as he comes in with the tray of antipasti. Kate's smile stretches.

'Lovely,' she says, restraining herself from jumping at the food like a dog. Zav gestures to the sofa and pours wine, dishes gnocchi and sun dried tomatoes then grabs his own portion and they tuck in.

'I shared lodgings with an Italian catering student in France,' he explains. 'She had to train me or live off baked beans.'

'You were an excellent student.'

'She was a great teacher.' Zav grins. 'Chef and harlot both. I'd expected the French girls to show me a thing or two but I never got to meet any.'

'Be thankful. You'd not have lured me here with frogs' legs and snails.'

'Frogs' legs aren't so bad but you need to be careful how you cook snails.'

Kate shudders in the enveloping warmth. Zav is sprawled next to her, feeding himself a finger pinch at a time from the low table. The light dances on his face. Kate laughs. 'Thank you,' she says again.

He grins at her. 'For choosing Italian girlfriend over French?'

'For inviting me. I needed this.'

'Good food and a warm hearth. My mother's formula for a happy home.'

'How many were you?'

'I've a younger sister.'

Kate pictures a tall, attractive woman with ragged hair and Zav's smile. A woman she'd like, though that's getting a little ahead. Zav is barely this side of stranger. She's glad she came though. It's not just the food and the stove's warmth or the fact that she's attracted to this man. It's the sense of security.

The realisation surprises her: she hadn't known she was *lacking* security. But yesterday's phone call has set her looking for danger everywhere in her previously safe world. And her house, with its excessive opportunity for thinking and a phone that rings late at night, is no longer the refuge it was. She opens her mouth to tell Zav about the recent odd happenings but then holds back. She's been out with Zav precisely once. And even if her instincts are drawing her towards him she's not ready to confide in him. More accurately, she's not ready to set his alarm bells ringing. So she pushes aside the strange calls and the Valentine's card, the imagined footsteps and the fact that she can spook herself inside her own house and lets Zav regale her with anecdotes of his childhood on the windswept flats of the Norfolk coast.

His father had combated the freezing winter gales that gusted soot and sparks down the chimney by installing a stove with a sealed pipe in their parlour and surrounded it with a mountain of chopped wood whose eventual depletion each year signalled the end of winter. He talks about his failed marriage and his successful business and, continuing his theme from Wackyjack's, educates Kate on the anthropological significance of past generations' trashy magazines. When he prods Kate for snippets of her own life she stays with the present, lifts the lid a little further on the pitfalls of the lower court system, the endless quest for the worthwhile amongst the hopeless. She reveals the truth about the legal charge of defending the accused, which in practice mostly comprises the protection of clients from undue harshness of sentence as they ease them, in unspoken complicity with the prosecution, towards their just and fair deserts.

'The point,' Kate says, 'is that guilt is not black and white. Circumstances are grey. Sometimes the guilty party can be as much a victim. They need help.'

She's finished eating – forced herself to stop, this being supper and not a binge – and is settled with her glass of wine, her leg folded beneath her. The leg is touching Zav's whose eyes are amused and interested and seemingly unaware of their closeness until – she doesn't know when – the knuckles of his fingers are resting on her thigh, stroking softly, minutely, back and forth along the silk of her stocking to emphasise a point. The touch, when *she* becomes aware of it, flows like electricity, a thrill amplifying by the second with the knowledge of something growing between them. And suddenly a need ignites inside her as fierce as the stove's flames. They're strangers still, but a point has been passed. Kate is reminiscing about a childhood holiday in France, but her words are a veneer on the real communication flowing between them, and impulsive images flash through her mind, obscuring her memory of the stony beach in Brittany. Her thoughts linger on an illicit anticipation of her fingers beneath Zav's shirt, his strong palms moving across her thigh. Then, almost at the moment of tipping, just as her neck turns and her muscles tense to receive his kiss, an earlier anxiety returns and the thought of a stranger waiting outside her house crashes in. The thought wrecks her mood even as Zav's hand reaches behind her neck. She acquiesces and their mouths meet but the kiss is tainted. Zav's hand is sliding softly along her thigh and she feels the heat of his body, wants it, *needs* it, but she's already pulling away but with her hand over his, pressing it against her leg so as to halt its progress without rejection. She feels a false smile invade her face.

'I'm sorry,' she says.

She can't quite find the words and cringes as a cliché pops from the vacuum. 'This is just a little sudden,' she states, but Zav's eyes show no hint of affront and she knows this is right, knows *he* is right. So the moment will happen, just not here, not tonight with her caller's malice in her head. When the moment comes she wants it to be perfect. That's what she's telling Zav in the press of her hand, in the little movements of her thumb that reassure him.

Zav squeezes playfully. 'It's okay,' he says, then lifts the hand to her cheek. 'Perhaps this weekend. I'm in Bristol until then. A trade fair, if you can believe we have shows for the junk I sell.'

She can believe it and lets his hand ease her neck forwards until their lips touch again and right now she'd believe anything this man tells her. As they kiss Kate is sure he's about to pull her to him and wonders what she'll do this time but he releases her and pecks her on the forehead and laughs. 'It's midnight,' he says. 'I'm keeping you up.'

Kate looks at her watch, astonished to see that it is indeed fifteen minutes past midnight and that the logs in the stove are white fossils on a dimming bed of coals. She stands and reaches for her jacket, appalled it's so late, even more appalled that she's terminated their evening so abruptly. She apologises again.

Zav grins and plants a hand on her shoulder and turns her towards the door.

'Let's get you home,' he says.

~~~~~

The heating is off and her house is cooling but a glow suffuses Kate as she moves about. She's still dismayed at her abrupt termination of the evening, but bottom line: no harm done. There will be other evenings. Kate even surprises herself with the need to deny that she's falling for this guy. But absence – or *abstinence* – really does makes the heart grow fonder, and a pleasure denied tonight is a pleasure to be anticipated.

Then as she heads upstairs the kitchen phone rings. She stops and her mood falters. Surely not! But you don't get marketing calls after midnight... Her first thought is to ignore the call but then she rushes back down. Not knowing would be worse. She grabs the handset and connects.

For a moment there's only the hiss of the line. Then it comes, the chilling gurgle of the electrically altered voice.

'*Nice.*'

The voice pauses. Kate's fingers grip the phone. 'I loved the cute dress,' the voice says. 'I really...' the words purr '...*loved* it.' The words bubble and ooze. 'You are *one* sexy woman, Kate. He's a lucky guy.'

'What do you want,' Kate asks.

Silence. Kate wonders if he's gone but then his reply gurgles through, fractured by the distorting electronics.

'I already have it.'

Kate cuts the line an instant before she realises that what she should have done was scream down the phone and curse this guy to hell. But it's too late. The call has disconnected. Damn and *damn!* She stands in her kitchen, watching the screen until its light extinguishes and releases her, burning with anger. She turns to look out of the kitchen window.

The bastard was watching the house! He saw Zav drop her off.

How much time is he spending out there? The answer is shocking: he must have watched for hours tonight, out in the cold, for the few seconds reward of her *cute dress*. Then another thought: he's still out there.

Panic kicks in. She starts a repeat of last night's rounds, working her way round the house, unwilling to switch on lights but fearful of the shadows, turning and twitching at every corner. When she's confirmed that everything is locked tight she looks at the table barring the cellar door. But she can't go down there tonight. The idea of descending those steps fills her with an *absolute* dread.

Dear God, who is he? What does he want? If only she'd stayed with Zav. The memory of Zav's easy-going strength, his affable nature, comes flowing back. She could call him right now. He'd turn his van right round. Impulsively she keys her phone and a moment later his voice is in her ear.

'Hi. Everything okay?'

She almost summons him. She won't need to explain. He'll turn right around and come for her.

'Kate?'

When she finds the words her voice is almost steady.

'Zav. Sorry.' There it is again. Sorry, sorry, *sorry*. For heaven's sake is there nothing else she can say? She checks herself. 'I... just thought I'd call... to thank you. That was a lovely supper.'

He laughs. *That* laugh. Safety. Security.

'I just wanted to say... I'm sorry I...' What? What the hell is she *sorry* about?

'Hey,' Zav says, 'the pleasure was all mine. Thank *you* Kate. Let's do it again, soon.'

'Of course.'

And still she's holding back, frightened of *inconveniencing* him with her fears. All she has to do is say the words. Why is that so hard?

'Well,' she says, 'thanks again, Zav. It was a lovely evening.'

'What if it was frogs and snails? Would you still be calling me?'

She laughs, though she doesn't feel like laughing. She feels sick. Yes, she'd be calling whether it was frogs and snails or caviar and crisps because there's some *bastard* outside her house watching her and making calls and she wants Zav to turn right round and rush back.

Instead she says: 'Better stick to Italian.'

'*Si signora. Decisamente.* Sleep tight.'

'You too. Goodnight.'

She cuts the line and is left high and dry in her empty house. Her feet tread heavily up the stairs.

She sets the alarm and slides beneath the duvet which she grips about her, listening. The only sound is the breath of the city. No creaking floorboards, no crunching gravel.

But she's not alone. He's out there. And the knowledge leaves her sleepless, waiting for the phone to ring.

Who is he? What does he want?

Tomorrow she'll report him to the police. The calls aren't a prank. The malice behind that altered voice, the hours he's spent watching, go way beyond that. So she'll report the calls, though she's not sure which of the other little oddities she can reveal without flagging herself as a neurotic. But this bastard won't harass her in secret.

When a faint light tints the sky she checks the time. Five thirty. The dawn brings the psychological reassurance of a new day approaching, and her subconscious finally relaxes and releases her into an hour's sleep before her alarm sounds and drags her back to cold reality.

15

Kate strides, late, through a cold wind towards the station. The single hour's sleep has left her disoriented. Sounds barely penetrate her hazy mind. She steps onto the crossing right in front of a bus and is jolted awake by a horn blast and hissing airbrakes. She jumps back but the driver waves her furiously across.

Her late start means that the station is busier than normal and she bypasses the escalators and races down the steps to the platform where she stands against the wall, searching faces. But common sense tells her he's not here. He wasn't here yesterday. At this moment he's on his way to his office or his depot, or he's stalled in his HGV on the M25 or he's just snoring in bed until it's time to *stalk* the Job Centre. The train sweeps in and it's jam packed. The passengers at the doors stand their ground, feigning blindness, but Kate is adept at commuter assault techniques and uses her briefcase to force a space. As the train accelerates she's forced to push uncomfortably close to a black girl with earbuds and blank eyes in order to leave room for a man in a cheap suit who followed her on and is breathing down her neck. Just thirty minutes delay has condemned her to this truly dispiriting start to the day. She tries to lift her spirits with memories of last night's supper with Zav but finds she can't summon the mood, can't summon the embers of the fire that flamed inside her. The drab bustle of a day commenced without sleep stymies all such attempts.

The train burrows deep under the city in a cacophony of bangs and squeals. Somehow more passengers squeeze in, pressing her forwards into the black girl who stands solid and indifferent. But as the carriage sways and rocks Kate senses that the man behind her is pressing more heavily than he need. She inches away but there's a distinct pressure on her backside as the man compensates. Kate's anger rises as last night's invasion, its violation, comes right back. The touch on her backside is now a firm pressure – dear God, is that a *hand?* – and she snaps round furiously, raking her briefcase brutally across the black girl's thigh to unleash her rage on the bastard who is *assaulting* her right here in this carriage. Her arm lifts to strike, and damned if a few feet get trodden and a few noses get pushed against the glass, because she's ready to start a damn *riot* on this train, but she finds herself looking over the head of an Asian woman whose satchel is jammed up between them. The woman starts and loses her balance and people are staggering and cursing, snapped from their zombie-like trances. Kate grabs the Asian woman to steady her and apologises then stares up at the route map in a feigned panic of a missed station to explain her convulsion. The woman pulls free with a grumble and when Kate turns to regain the handrail and extinguish the incident, to make it *never happened*, the eyes of the black girl are hostile.

'You watch what you're doing,' she says. 'You got me bleedin' leg.' She looks down, searching for laddered stockings or blood.

Kate apologises to her too and tries to smile but the mask doesn't fit and she shrinks into herself with the absurd thought that if her stalker *has* by any chance followed her onto this train then he's just been rewarded with a splendid piece of slapstick to confirm the efficacy of his campaign. He's just been rewarded with the sight of her raw *fear*.

Kate exits the station, fired by a mixture of anger and shame, and cuts onto Upper Street at a furious pace. Despite her lateness she's still first in at Parfitt and Quinn, and her morning routine kicks in to calm her: keypad; alarm; lights; post; electric fire; coat. Finally, her desk. Kate breaks with routine by brewing an instant coffee and grabbing two biscuits before returning to salvage the last few minutes of catch-up time, but she's hardly got started when Violet arrives and pokes her head round the door to ask: 'Have you had any more of those calls?'

Kate admits that she has but gives no details. 'I'm letting the police know,' she says.

All so matter-of-fact, so easily downplayed from the security of her office, though Kate knows that she *won't* find time to visit the police station today, that she wouldn't have the stomach to go through her problem for the benefit of some inattentive constable. And in the everyday surroundings of Parfitt and Quinn, with Violet's inquisitive face at her door, the distorted voice and its vile personal message start to dull, even if its miasma cloys like the flu coming on. She'll see what else happens and then talk to the police. This prankster isn't going to get away scot-free. Kate laughs inwardly. *Prankster.* That's reduced it nicely. And *scot-free!* Even better: now *she's* chasing *him.*

'I'm sorry?' she says. Violet is watching her.

'You look tired.'

Kate concedes but reports only the fact that she's not sleeping quite as she should, then smiles at Violet, willing her to leave so she can get to work. Today is hopeless. Six appointments and two court hearings and on top of it Arthur's weekly review, and she's got the energy for none of it. 'I'd better get started,' she says.

'Of course. If you need anything give me a shout.'

The offer's as unprecedented as it is futile. There's nothing Violet can do to help with either her work or her caller. When her door closes Kate takes a breath and starts on today's paperwork with the foreboding that no matter how hard she works she'll be further behind by tonight. A late finish, of course, brings the advantage of delaying her return home but that thought hardly cheers her. She must walk up her street eventually, whatever the hour. What truly dismays her though is the realisation that her street and her home are becoming places to fear.

Her appointments pass in a haze and suddenly it's gone eleven and she's the last one into Arthur's conference. The meeting passes in a blur from which she remembers little, not even her own case summaries, though she does remember the tense five minute discussion of the ethical dance necessitated by her approach to Donna Jordan's prosecution witness. The witness' solicitor is due to report back tomorrow with what Kate hopes is his client's agreement to take the route that serves both his and Donna's interests.

The meeting finally spills Kate out to return to her afternoon briefs as the others head for lunch, and she's surprised to discover that her fatigue has dropped away to leave her all but fighting fit for the afternoon's affray.

Somewhere in the middle of it though, as she argues with a client in the Highbury Corner court annex, her weariness returns without warning, and from there on it's a drudge. When she finally regains her desk at five she can barely face the thought of another three hours' clearing up, with the prospect of that walk up her deserted street when she's through.

Then she gets two calls.

The first is from Zav, in Bristol. Her day lightens immeasurably. Despite his absence, talk of the weekend lifts her spirits. They plan their activities for ten minutes and finish on promises.

The second call is from Rache, whose suggestion of a night out is a non starter, but which Kate sweetens with a counter proposal. Her schedule is light tomorrow afternoon. She could extend her lunch hour. They agree to meet then, and bar an act of God she'll take lunch away from her desk at least one day this week. Lunch with Rache and the weekend with Zav finally brings a brighter outlook and Kate goes cheerfully back to work. But at seven, when it's clear that her backlog is not diminishing, she packs up.

~~~~~

The temperature has dropped sharply. Kate's breath clouds the air as she walks from the station. The glow of her conversations with Zav and Rache has faded and thoughts of her anonymous caller have seeped back in. As she turns into the gloom of her street her nerves take a downturn and inside half a dozen steps she's tense, watching the pavement and parked cars. The cars' windscreens reflect street lights and give nothing. Someone could be sitting in any one of them, watching.

Stop! she tells herself, there's no one. Never has been. Then she shakes her head at her deceit. So you've forgotten the *cute dress?* Explain that if he wasn't watching. Get real, woman! He was out here last night and he might be here now. When Kate reaches her driveway she all but bolts for the door.

But once in the house she rebuffs her nerves. She left work for one purpose: to go for a run. And run she will, even if every cell in her body is yearning for the comfort and security of a warm bath. Damned if she'll let this bastard imprison her. As she stands looking at her door, though, the menace beyond it is real, and her determination falters. *Coward*, she rebukes herself. Stay home. Hide like a frightened schoolgirl.

But once she's cowered behind her door she'll do it again. She'll let him manipulate her until she's afraid to leave her house. That's why she needs to go back out.

She changes fast, before her courage leaks away, then pulls a three-inch paring knife from the kitchen rack. Reversed, with its blade lying along her wrist, the knife's handle sits comfortably in her palm. If anyone comes near her tonight it will be their mistake. There won't *be* anyone, of course. This guy makes calls with a disguised voice. He sends cards. He's not the face-to-face type. But if anyone does comes near...

Carrying the knife is illegal, of course, just as it has been for the hundred offenders she's represented. But so what? *So damn what?*

If he comes near her she'll kill him.

She completes a warm-up, palms the knife and goes out.

The park is empty again except for a lone dog walker and a courting couple whom she leaves well behind as her circuit cuts towards the trees. Inside the trees the path is reduced to deep shadow by the inadequate park lamps but Kate runs steadily from long familiarity. What's new is her attention to the darkness either side, the pervasive unease at the thought of someone watching, even if there's no way her stalker could be here. Even if he'd followed her from the house there's no way he could be ahead of her. But fear defies logic. Menace stirs everywhere in this brave new world.

When she breaks out onto the main path with its good lighting she feels a rush of relief.

Approaching the pavilion, she spots the distant bobbing gait of another runner on the far side of the cricket pitch, circling towards her, and a minute later they pass. He's just a momentary silhouette under the spill of the all-weather floodlights. She registers an athletic build, running shorts, sweat top, an angular face with clipped beard and hair. Senses his head turning fractionally as they meet but then she's past him and feeling foolish at the scrape of the knife against her wrist. But caution *isn't* foolishness. None of the other people out here tonight – dog walkers, lovers, runners – are getting calls or being watched. And one of them – say the lanky runner who's just passed her – could *be* her tormentor.

She completes her circuit and starts the second lap. The path is empty now. Dog walkers and lovers have dematerialised, though the runner should be coming towards her through the dark of the trees. He'll appear at any moment.

Which suddenly scares her.

But the runner doesn't appear and a minute later she's into the trees herself, scanning the shadows around and ahead of her and wondering whether he's taken another route and cursing the bastard who's put her in this state of mind.

Then half way through the trees, where the shadows are deepest, the feeble lamps go out.

In an instant she's running blind. The all-weather spotlights, where they break through the trees, dazzle her but illuminate nothing. She can't even see the ground ahead of her. She stops, disoriented. The floodlights tell her that this is not an area outage. So have the park lamps blown a fuse? Or is it possible to interfere with them?

For *her* benefit.

Deadly fear kicks in. Kate turns the knife outward and first walks then jogs then runs headlong through the dark, desperate for the break in the trees, mindless of the benches, invisible along the path, that threaten to smash into her legs. Her fear grows furiously until it's outright panic. She senses him watching, moving towards her, and terror drives her on: she must get clear, out of this hellish black. She runs, blind, guided only by half-sensed shadows, no longer doubting that he's here, that the extinguished lamps are his doing, that she'll smash headlong into him any moment. She grips the knife and *runs*.

Suddenly the trees open and she hits the main path.

She stops. Sees no one. Sets off again, towards the pavilion, still terrified that someone will step from the shadows. The park lights are dead here too, but the spilled light of the floods illuminate the path, and when she reaches the cricket pitch she angles onto the grass, seeking the safety of open ground, and accelerates, racing her shadow towards the gate.

Slowly, agonisingly, the street lights become stronger until finally she's out between the gateposts and onto the road. Her terror drops away in the light and she slows to a jog but doesn't loosen her grip on the knife. As she approaches her house she's watching every car and tree until she gains her driveway and fumbles with the key. Then she's inside and the door is slammed and she sinks to the floor in a heave of hysterical laughter. Oh, holy shit! Of all damn times those park lamps chose to blow it had to be tonight, had to be when she was right in trees. Holy shit and *damn!* That was freaky! She stays sitting, back to her front door, until she's regained the strength to pick herself up and plod through to the kitchen where she slots the knife back into its rack.

And then anger flares.

Oh you absolute *bastard*, she thinks.

Because whatever she'd told herself today, whatever reassurances she'd dug out, safe in her office, there's no hiding from the truth that she's frightened of her shadow. She's under this guy's spell.

Her smartphone rings and for a moment she's afraid to pick up. But he doesn't have her mobile number. This *isn't* him.

She touches the screen.

It's an unknown caller.

Logic evaporates.

She raises the phone to her ear and connects the call.

But it's not the altered voice. It's a woman. She's hysterical. She's telling her to come quickly.

It's Donna Jordan.

16

The interview room is over-bright and freezing, and Donna, sitting opposite Kate at the metal table, is an underdressed waif. She's withdrawn into a sullen silence staged for the uniformed constable who brought her up from the cells.

'Let's get this sorted out,' Kate says.

The navy slacks and tank top that were the first things to hand when she scrambled to dress are now sullied with her dried sweat and barely adequate for the room's arctic temperature. Donna, in a miniskirt and gauzy top, seems oblivious to the cold. Kate wonders if she's lost a jacket or was on the streets like that, a naive anachronism within the nowadays more discreet tribe of the London streetwalker.

Donna looks up. 'Tell them,' she says. 'They've no right.'

But they do. The police had every right to arrest Donna, on the grounds both of drunk and disorderly behaviour and of soliciting. Donna has come onto the streets in a bad state tonight and the catfight with a fellow worker just off Shacklewell Lane was perhaps a predictable outcome. That the police have let the other girl go with a caution suggests that Donna's behaviour was the prime catalyst, and the screaming profanities Kate heard briefly from downstairs as she arrived at the station wouldn't have impressed the arresting officers. But the police know Donna and aren't too interested in pressing solicitation charges, which is why they've agreed to drop them if Kate can take her off their hands and make sure she stays off the street tonight. The D&D will stay though.

Kate explains the situation to the girl. The best option is to agree to a penalty notice and ninety pound fine, which will avoid the need to slot a new court appointment into Donna's busy schedule. Then Donna needs someone to take her home and she needs to stay there.

But the chauffeur service won't be provided by Kate. That would be a service too far. Kate wonders how many solicitors would turn out in the middle of the night to rescue a hysterical client. But her name, apparently, was the one Donna shrieked when the police explained that she was heading for a night in the cells.

'I'll get home myself,' Donna says. Her eyes have the glaze of one not fully comprehending.

Kate shakes her head. 'The police won't release you without a chaperone. You're not going back onto the streets.'

'I'll get a taxi. I'm not going on the streets.'

'There needs to be someone with you. Is there anyone at home?'

Donna, ever keen to unload her history, has revealed little of her current personal life. Kate knows only about the guy who befriended her when she arrived in the city as a fifteen-year-old *naïf* six years ago – a predator called Wilbur Parish who became Donna's boyfriend and introduced her to the streets the same week. Parish is still Donna's pimp but the two of them are no longer an item. Maybe Donna's found someone else, and although she can't expect much from anyone who's tied themselves to this vulnerable girl the only requirement tonight is that they are *compos mentis* and available.

Donna is gazing at the table, back in her sulk. But they don't have time for sulks. The police want Donna either out of their nick or back downstairs. And Kate is dog tired and has not had a damn bite to eat since lunch.

She speaks firmly. 'Donna. We need to call someone.'

Donna remains in her trance but her shoulders come up a little and she reels off a name and number. Someone called Georgie.

'Is Georgie your boyfriend?'

'Girlfriend.'

'And she lives with you?' Kate's fingers are already tapping the number.

'Yeah. We got a place in Queen's Park...'

Kate isn't listening. She knows where Donna lives. The phone is ringing and she's praying that someone picks up. They do.

'Georgie?' Kate says. 'My name is Walker. I'm Donna's solicitor.'

'Oh God...'

'Are you Georgie?'

'Yeah. What's up?'

'She's been arrested. You need to pick her up at Stoke Newington.'

'Fuck.'

'I understand you're her partner.'

'Yeah...' Georgie's words are slow. Kate wonders if she's on something. Wonders if she'll pass muster at the counter. 'Yeah,' Georgie repeats. 'The little darlin's my partner, though that's a loose term. Mostly she's a pain.'

'Okay. When can you get here?'

'I don't know. I've got this...'

'Georgie, pay attention. You need to come for Donna now. I have to leave in fifteen minutes and if you're not here by then Donna will go back to the cells. And they won't bring her up twice.'

A sigh. Then: 'I'll come. Twenny minutes.'

'Sooner, if possible. I can't hang on for long.' This isn't exactly true but damned if Kate is *going* to hang on. She cuts the connection and smiles at Donna.

'She's on her way.'

Donna sits back. Shrugs and grimaces at the same time then drops her head.

'How long have you been with Georgie?' Kate asks. She needs to keep the girl awake.

'Coupla years.'

'Steady relationship?'

Donna thinks about it, or is maybe just staring at the table. She answers only with 'Hmm.' But then she lifts her head again and turns her chair to lift one thin leg for inspection. She traces her fingers across torn stocking. The tear, Kate assumes, is from tonight's scrap, rather than a fashion thing. Donna releases the leg, stretches it out, foot pointing, circling, then lifts it and makes imaginary motions of sliding the stocking down à la Mrs Robinson before she straightens the leg for consideration. Donna is waaaaaay under.

'Steady, I suppose,' she says. 'You tell me.'

She tilts her head and pouts, as if she's quoting a learned maxim but Kate knows that whatever strain of relationship enfolds this girl she's the baby, the one who can fall back on – who *uses* – her immaturity to protect her from life's responsibilities. Donna is simultaneously needy and cynical and will probably squander the relationship at some point. Her clouded mind, understanding only rejection and exploitation, is likely to be careless of something good. Kate wonders if Georgie is something good.

'How's the rehab?' she asks.

Donna's notionally in addiction therapy, steered there by Kate on the back of an earlier tangle, though Kate suspects that she's either quit the group or soon will. Peer support is not Donna's thing.

'Great,' Donna says.

'Remember what we said? Your lifestyle. It's...' she nearly says "dangerous" but Donna isn't receptive to warnings and the surest way to lose her is to side with the army of advisers and counsellors and do-gooders who were entirely absent all those years up in Liverpool. 'There are ways to make things better,' she says. 'Maybe you and Georgie can make it.'

Donna drops her leg to the floor and twists to the table to place her chin on her fists, cricking her neck to watch Kate. Donna's face is beautiful when the mask slips and for a second the beauty flashes through. Then the mask is back and Donna radiates a wicked grin fired in the hard realities of the street.

'Yeah. We'll make it. Thank you very much. My life is a dream...' Another switch. Donna's eyes glaze. Her head tilts. It lies on her arm. She looks sideways at Kate. 'Do you know what it's like to be fucked by your dad? Oh... sorry Kate.'

The grin mask nails Kate in its drunken, maudlin parody of humour but Kate reaches out to pat Donna's fists.

'I'm just asking,' she says. 'We need to get you home.'

'Doesn't mean I'll stay there.'

'You *must* stay there. I'll be very clear with Georgie. If the police see you on the street again tonight they'll bring you in for soliciting and that's going to be a big problem.'

'A girl's gotta make a living.'

'Not tonight.'

'You know how much I'll lose?'

'Not tonight.'

The grin slants and dissolves into something less fake. Donna chuckles and sits up. Her fists are still under Kate's fingers.

'Well... after I've paid off my pimp and bought some stuff and a couple of drinks in Gassers I'll have about twenty quidlies left.' The mask slides back. Freezes. 'Try going out on the street for twenty quid then advise me.'

But Donna draws short – perhaps only because she doesn't think of it – of asking Kate how much *she* earns per hour safe behind her desk at Parfitt and Quinn. Kate squeezes Donna's hands then pulls away.

The door opens and the custody sergeant pokes his head in to inform them that Donna's chaperone has arrived. Kate stands and eases the girl from her chair and helps her along the corridor to the counter where a tall, wide-faced woman in her mid twenties is waiting. The woman is not quite pretty but has a maternal intelligence about her, though her face is scowling as Donna lurches towards her and wraps her arm about her waist. Georgie calls her a stupid cow but slips her arm across the girl's shoulder. Her coldness is for the law. The two move to the counter and the sergeant pushes forms across and informs Georgie that Donna must not reappear tonight.

Georgie nods a cold acceptance and scribbles her name whilst Donna stands safe under her wing. Then she smiles briefly at Kate as she turns Donna for the door and although a smile has finally broken onto Donna's face too there are tears there, tracking down her cheeks.

17

Kate enters the Casa Tiziano at the bottom end of Upper Street where Rache is nibbling a bread stick, engrossed in her iPhone. She pecks her cheek and apologises for being late but Rache waves it off. When Kate sits she leans over the table towards her.

'You missed a great night, Tuesday,' she says. 'My guy knew a guy who was seriously cute. You could've hit the jackpot.'

Kate grins. She missed no jackpot on Tuesday but she lets Rache have her moment. Then Rache changes direction.

'Any more creepy encounters in the park?'

Rache is four days behind and Kate brings her up to date, describes the garbled voice of her anonymous calls, the implication that the guy is watching her. Rache looks at her, horrified.

'Jesus, Kate, go to the police.'

'As soon as I can,' Kate says.

'*Now*, Kate. You don't know what this guy will do.'

'Tomorrow,' Kate says. 'I'll see if anything else happens.'

'What if he's waiting for you tonight?'

'He won't be,' Kate says, regurgitating her theory that he's hiding behind the phone calls. 'He won't come into the open,' she says.

The words are as much for her as Rache. She still needs to believe that this is some kind of prank, the short-term fixation of a cowardly nobody, although she senses she's fooling herself. So does Rache. They bat the topic back and forth without agreement until the starters turn up and Rache gives up and switches direction again.

'You've been out with a *guy?*' she asks, picking up on a snippet within Kate's story. Kate snatches the opportunity to divert from the oppressive subject and reminds Rache about Liberace's and the guy she cold shouldered. Rache recalls him but struggles with detail until Kate's superlatives open her eyes.

'Jesus!' she says. 'You've got the hots for him.'

'I like him,' Kate says, an understatement that Rache sees right through.

'You've fallen for him,' she insists. 'You're in a damn swoon, girl.' And Rache is right. She is in a swoon.

'What does he say about your caller?'

'He doesn't know. Everything's happened so fast. I don't want to scare him off with the idea that he's dating a neurotic.'

'It's hardly neurotic to worry about some bastard harassing you. If Zav's worth anything he'll help. Tell him.'

'I will.'

'And tell the frigging *police*.'

'Eat your lunch,' Kate says. 'I've got to be back by two thirty.'

'I know you. You think you can handle this by yourself.'

But Rache is wrong. Kate is thinking no such thing. Because however she tries to fool herself, when she hears that voice, when she recalls those footsteps in the street, she's left with an overpowering sense of someone moving towards her. Something she *can't* handle sweeping remorselessly in.

~~~~~

Friday evening. Eight thirty. The house is warm with the promise of a slow unwinding, a long bath, the keen anticipation of the weekend. Zav is back tonight. She'll surprise him at Wackyjack's tomorrow.

Kate pulls a pizza from the freezer and switches on the oven then heads up for the bath. As she sinks into the water her limbs relax and her mind goes blank. But it doesn't stay that way, and she's dismayed to discover that the unwinding has only cleared the slate to readmit echoes of the week's events. There's tension even in her floating limbs, half an ear listening for the phone.

She fights back, pushes the thoughts aside, rebuffs the sense of menace as a matter to be dealt with another time. She'll tell Zav everything tomorrow. He'll protect her. And if her tormentor calls again she'll report it to the police. The decision comforts her with the sense of a way through this thing and she finally does sink into a few moments of blessed oblivion.

The heated rail is working tonight and she wraps a warm towel around her and goes to dig out fresh clothes. Pizza, a glass of rosé, an hour's TV then she'll hit the sack.

She draws the bedroom curtains closed and stoops to tidy the corner of the duvet which is rucked up. She must have missed it this morning, which is unusual. Office aside, she's a neat freak who never leaves her bedroom without patting down the pillows and duvet. She flattens the duvet now and is turning away when something else catches her eye and she's astonished to see that her pillow is rumpled. This time the sight transfixes her. Because she's now recalled that she'd patted the bed down twice this morning. The second time was after stumbling over a slipper and planting a hand on the bed to steady herself, which had necessitated pulling the duvet straight again. And when she'd done that she'd impulsively run her palms over the pillows and left them smooth.

Now that she's recalled the stumble her memory is irrefutable. There was no rucked-up duvet or hollowed pillow when she left for work.

The certainty floods her veins with a sudden, shocking cold that transfixes her, leaves her staring at the bed.

What on earth? How can her memory have deceived her like that? But it hasn't deceived her: she'd tripped on the slipper and she'd put her hand on the bed and she'd smoothed the disturbance. That's what happened.

But now...

Now the pillow is hollow from a hand or head pressing against it.

Something that's happened whilst she was out.

With a preternatural calm Kate lifts the corner of the duvet and eases it back to expose the bed sheet, then reaches out but doesn't quite touch the undulations she sees there. The sheet is not the perfect flat she'd left it this morning. Her memory is clear. She'd pulled the sheet tight as she always does, folded the edges deep under the mattress. But now it's loose. Has undulations and creases.

Kate's limbs turn to jelly. Her legs threaten to drop her to the floor. A minute passes whilst her mind struggles with the impossibility of what she's seeing.

A few creases and hollows in the bedding. Such a trivial detail. Something you'd never notice unless you were looking for them. But she *is* looking and the realisation of what it means finally detonates a bomb within her psyche.

Her bed has been disturbed.

Kate squats to look more closely. And as she does so she detects the faintest odour, the barest hint of a scent that shouldn't be there. The odour jogs her memory. Where has she smelt that recently? Then she recalls: it's the musty smell on the sheets from a week ago that she blamed on her fabric conditioner. It was this same alien smell. But *this* sheet hasn't been rinsed with the cheap conditioner.

The smell is the residue of someone lying in her bed.

Kate lifts the pillow with shaking fingers.

And confirms the unthinkable.

Her chemise has been re-folded.

Dear God.

You're crazy, she tells herself. You're dreaming.

But she's not crazy. She's not dreaming. Someone has been in here. Her sanctuary, the place of ultimate retreat and safety, her own special place in the world, has been desecrated.

And the bedroom isn't hers any more.

Her legs give way. She sinks into her chair and presses her fists to her lips and her body succumbs to a shaking fit. She doesn't move, can't *think* of moving, for five minutes, then ten.

Is she imagining this? *Is* she hallucinating?

But she's not. It's real.

And there's absolutely no doubt that it's *him*.

He's been in here to desecrate her special place, to leave her with nowhere in the world she can call her own.

Then a new fear jolts her. She cocks her head to listen. Could he be in the house?

She hears nothing but she must *see*.

In a sudden frenzy she leaps from the chair and pulls on jeans and a sweater and races through the upstairs rooms, checking behind doors, in closets, under beds. Then she rushes down to check the ground floor and even the cellar. She needs to know that he's not *anywhere*.

...And he's not. The sense strengthens with each empty place until she's finally alone in the house.

But he has been in here. He's lain in her bed.

She rushes back up and drags the duvet from the bed and pulls off its cover, strips the bedsheet and pillowcases and rushes down to the kitchen where she bundles them into a refuse sack. She unlocks the back door and drops the sack by the step to wait for morning. Then she relocks the door and rushes back to her bedroom.

She's in a frenzy of repulsion, sensing his odour, his desecration, everywhere. In a fit of disgust she cleans the bedroom, washes and dusts every corner, every piece of furniture. She vacuums the carpet, attacking it at the machine's highest setting. It takes an hour before she's satisfied that the room is cleansed.

Utterly weary, Kate digs out new bedding and remakes the bed, and finally the room is pristine and fresh.

But it's all been a wasted effort.

Because she can't sleep there. She can't even sleep in one of the spare rooms. She was fooling herself. There's no way she can be alone in this house tonight. The shaking returns with the realisation. Her eyes flood.

She calls her sister and pleads for a bed. Angie is shocked by Kate's voice but holds back questions, urges her to come straight round, and Kate fills a shoulder bag and switches off the lights and the oven, leaves the defrosting pizza to rot and steps fearfully out of her back door to face the shadows of her garage.

18

Angie opens the door and pulls Kate into a reassuring hug but as they separate all Kate can think is how harried Angie looks. Her late night face, devoid of its daytime care, is pale and almost... old. Then shame overcomes Kate and she pulls her sister back into the hug. What Angie looks is *worried*. Kate's call has given her a fright. If Kate was married Angie would assume she's running from a fight. But the single, unattached career girl does not turn up on your doorstep at eleven thirty, and Angie's imagination has been running riot.

'It's nothing,' Kate says. 'It's all a bit silly.'

But Angie knows it's not silly. Her sister isn't the silly type. She takes Kate's jacket and steers her into the lounge where Ian is rising from the sofa, the same concern on his face. Kate needs a shoulder to cry on, to spill the news of her frightening week, but three is a crowd. As Ian steps forward though, his presence, the normality of this house, is reassuring, and he suddenly emanates a comforting authority.

So: 'Someone's broken into my house,' she reports to him.

Angie and Ian both look shocked, but it's the shock of the relatively mundane, like a car accident, and Kate must start again because this isn't a car accident. This isn't a housebreaking. In fact, her house doesn't seem to have been broken into at all, which is worse. What she's running from is a house *desecration*. She rebuffs their concern with a shake of her head, not to reassure them but to tell them it's worse.

'Let's get you a drink,' Angie says.

They go to sit at the kitchen table and as Angie busies herself with cups and kettles Kate puts them right on the meaning of *break-in*. She tells them about the calls, the disguised voice, the surveillance of her house, her sense of being watched in the park and – swept along by the damn burst – a whole host of recent curiosities within her house that she has only this moment seen as a little *too* odd, things that can no longer be categorised as simple happenstance. One blown light bulb is nothing, two are coincidence, but a whole set of failures, TV remote disappearances, cold towel rails and missing bin liners following a refuse-spilling split in the one in use, all these take on a sinister air in the context of knowing that someone's been in her house. Someone who's visited whilst she's been out, who's *lain in her bed*.

Angie has stopped working. She sits down. Ian is watching in amazement. Both of them are wondering whether Kate is simply mad.

Angie, more tuned to her sister's temperament, reaches her conclusion faster. She reaches for Kate's hand.

'Dear God, Sis,' she says. 'We need to call the police.'

Kate explains that she's been on the verge of doing that, just needed to convince herself first that she was not overreacting to a few stupid calls.

'Of course it's not overreacting,' Angie says. 'Someone's invading your life.'

'Whoever it is, they know you,' Ian says. 'There's a reason he's singled you out.'

Kate shakes her head. On the drive over, and countless times in the last week, she's searched for a name, a clue, a feeling. But she's drawn a blank.

Angie shudders. 'Imagine, someone in your bed. I could never sleep there again.'

'It's appalling,' Ian says. 'But how did he get in? You sure there's no forced entry?'

'None. And the doors and windows are locked. I don't know... can you get keys? Like master keys?'

'I suppose so,' Ian says. 'Locksmiths have keys to get in most doors. But I think they keep some kind of register. You can't just duplicate them. You sure you haven't lost a spare recently?'

'Never. The only spares are one at home, the one you have, one in my office and one with my neighbour, Lottie. I'll check with her but she'd have told me if hers was missing, and if it was there's no way anyone would know it opened my door.'

'We'll get your locks changed first thing,' Ian says, assuming tactical command.

'I've a home emergency service,' Kate reports. 'I'll phone them tonight.'

Angie rises to continue with the drinks and brings Kate a mug of chocolate. Kate wraps her fingers round the mug and lets the warmth flow up her arms. She shivers violently in reaction.

'You can stay here as long as you like,' Angie says. She glances at Ian.

'Just tonight will suffice,' Kate says. 'I'll be fine once the locks are changed.'

'Really,' Ian says, 'don't rush back, Kay. You can't be too careful.' He stretches across and squeezes her wrist. His eyes are concerned. 'This guy is dangerous.'

'I'll be okay as long as he can't get into my house.'

'We'll fix that tomorrow,' Ian says. 'But he'll still be out there. Still be phoning. I think you're better with us until the police catch him.'

Kate smiles and shrugs and relaxes in the absolute security of this house. But she *can't* stay. Her own home, her own life, is too precious to her. Living in her sister's house would be as confining as prison. Even her occasional trips to distant friends, weekends sleeping in spare rooms and on couches, drain her. Tonight will be sufficient. Tomorrow she'll have new locks and new bedding and her house will be hers again.

The front door opens and a few moments later Jon comes through. He's dressed in a grungy oversized frayed shirt jacket and black pants and his hair is straggly from a night jamming in a garage with his talent-challenged friends. He's slouched himself half way to the fridge before he spots his aunt. He stops, and surprise induces conversation.

'Hiya, Aunt Kate.' He looks at the three of them for an explanation. Kate has never been a casual, late night visitor. 'Didn't know you were here.'

'Your aunt's had a break-in,' his mother tells him, staying with Kate's original euphemism.

'Oh,' Jon says. 'That's...' Kate sees him deflect away from "cool". '...*terrible*,' he declares. 'Did they, like, steal stuff?'

'No,' Kate says. 'It wasn't that kind of break-in.'

Which only puzzles.

'Somebody has been pestering your aunt,' Ian explains.

'You mean, like...' Jon's face is suddenly animated, '...somebody's *after* you?'

Kate works up a faint smile. 'Yes,' she says, 'someone's after me.'

'Wow. That sucks,' Jon says.

'Someone's been telephoning me. And watching me. They got into my house today.'

'You tell the police?'

'Not yet'

'What does he say? When he calls?'

'Jon!' Angie says. But Kate smiles.

'Stuff to intimidate me. To let me know he's been watching me.'

'But he hasn't, like, grabbed you on the street?'

'No. Not so far.'

'Does he talk dirty?'

'Jon!' Angie repeats. 'Don't be vulgar. Your aunt's shocked enough as it is.'

'I'm only asking.'

Kate smiles again. 'No,' she says, telling her first lie, because her caller's *love* of her *cute little dress* had absolutely dripped with dirt. And his *one sexy woman* compliment had almost made her heave with the sense of his filthy touch. 'Just nuisance calls,' she says. 'How's that trouble at school?'

Her entirely unsubtle switch of topic catches them all out. But sometimes the best way into a subject is to bulldoze. Since they're discussing *trouble*.

The trouble's not *at school* of course, and the police visit to talk to Jon wasn't *at school*, but Kate doesn't want to ambush Jon with any hint of inference that Geraldine Bryson's vandalised house might connect directly to him. Kate doesn't know whether Angie and Ian have confronted Jon yet about the phone photos so she's pushing out into dangerous waters. But, hard though it's becoming to sustain, Kate has a soft spot for her nephew. Beneath his couldn't-care-less attitude she suspects that he's besieged, might welcome a little neutral talk on the subject.

'It's all a crock,' Jon says. He's looking at his parents, delivering Kate the sub text.

'They find anyone yet?'

Jon shrugs. 'I didn't hear.'

'It sounded sad, that teacher getting her house wrecked.'

'Miss Bryson? Like... sod her!'

'Jon!' Angie and Ian say together.

'Sod her! She's an old cow. And why are people putting it on me?'

Kate's beginning to regret bringing the subject up. But she also hates the idea of bringing her problems here to overshadow Jon's. She needs him to know that she's aware and concerned. So she persists.

'How's your friend Gary? They giving him grief too?'

'They're giving *everyone* grief. The shit's flying everywhere about that old bat. But they can leave me out of it.'

'Jon!' Angie says. 'Stop right there! Don't ever talk about your teacher like that. Whoever wrecked her house should go to jail. They've caused untold damage to that poor woman.'

'I'm only saying. Not my problem,' Jon says. 'I could care less. At least your house didn't get wrecked, Aunt Kate. That's something.' And with that platitude he opens the fridge and pulls out a wedge of cheese then works his way round the kitchen, building a cheese and pickle sandwich and filling a glass with coke. He stops, finally, with a new thought.

'Are you staying?'

'Just for the night.'

'Cool.' He waves the sandwich and is gone.

Angie asks if Kate wants to eat. She says no. She just needs to call her emergency service then she'll go to bed. All she really wants is to be alone.

Claire's away for the weekend so Kate takes her room. Angie makes up the bed as Kate talks to her insurance service who agree to have a locksmith at her house by eight a.m.

When Angie finally heads for her own bed Kate goes to the bathroom to freshen up. Was it just two hours ago she took a bath? She feels so soiled. But the wash and brush up do the trick and she sinks onto her niece's bed with a long sigh just as her phone rings.

It's Zav

He's back in town, keen to meet tomorrow, but before he can continue Kate breaks the news. As with Angie, this is the first Zav has heard about her tormentor and he's shocked and pained by the account.

'Kate,' he says, 'I wish you'd told me.'

'That's me,' Kate says. 'Bottle things up. But I should have told you about the call on Wednesday after you dropped me off. That one shook me.'

'I'd have come right back,' Zav says. There's no rebuke, just a reassurance.

'That's why I held back. I didn't want to impose.'

'You could never impose, Kate. I hate to think of you alone after the call.'

'Sorry,' she says.

'Don't be. Shall I pick you up?'

'No. I'm fine at Angie's. I'm just getting into bed. And I'm up early. Meeting the locksmith at eight.'

'You shouldn't go there alone,' Zav says. 'I'll come along.'

'I think Ian is expecting to come with me but...'

'I'll be there. See you at eight.'

She closes her eyes. Breathes out. 'Eight,' she says.

'Sleep tight.'

His voice is gentle. If he were here now she'd sleep like a baby.

But he's not here and she doesn't sleep like a baby. Her dreams are filled with dark shadows and garbled whisperings that leave a sense of dread each of the many times she wakes.

19

Ian insists on accompanying Kate to her house despite her assurance that a friend is meeting her there. This latter mention opens up a breakfast table discussion in which it turns out, under Angie's skilful interrogation, that the friend is more than *just* a friend, leading to a hundred more questions, until Kate wishes she'd not mentioned Zav. Is she *so* close to being an old maid that the subject of a new male contact is so newsworthy? Ian persists with his offer, friend notwithstanding. He's visiting a printers in Kilburn to pick up a box of Civic Society newsletters. Maida Vale is barely out of his way and he'll take the Tube back. Kate runs out of excuses and finishes her breakfast then hugs her sister and she and Ian go out.

Zav's Ducato is parked outside her house and he appears and smothers her in a hug, a display that mortifies her after all her breakfast table downplaying. But then something clicks and the bliss of Zav's embrace washes everything else away and Kate closes her eyes and is tempted not to open them again. *Damn*, but she's tired. Then Zav grips her arms and holds her away and his face reflects his concern. Kate shakes her head and introduces Ian, and Zav grips Ian's hand like an old friend. Ian's smile is restrained. He says hi, how are you, then looks at Kate. They go in.

'I'll check the windows,' Ian says. 'Let's make sure he really didn't get in that way before we change the door locks.'

Time has all but run out for a decision on this. The doorbell rings and it's the locksmith. Kate brings the guy in and explains her predicament and the guy repeats what the call centre told her last night: that without evidence of a forced entry, lock replacement isn't covered and will be charged. Kate acknowledges the fact and when Ian reappears shaking his head the locksmith gets to work. Kate takes Ian and Zav to the kitchen where she bins her defrosted pizza and shows them the Valentine's card. They listen to her theory that it's the same guy, though the card seems small beer in the light of the other stuff.

Zav and Ian tell her it's the same guy for sure and say that this needs to be sorted. Then Ian realises that his printers are open and takes his leave. Kate thanks him and walks him through to squeeze out past the locksmith.

She takes Zav on a house tour, pointing and explaining. Zav flicks light switches and jiggles the towel rail thermostat and inspects the TV remote.

'This is weird,' he concludes. 'You're saying this guy's been breaking in regularly.'

'It freaks me out just to think about it.'

'It would freak anyone out. An Englishwoman's home and all that. It's like he was playing around in here to mess with your head and see how long you'd take to figure it out.'

'I still wouldn't have if I'd not noticed the bed. But how many times has he *been* in my bed? That's what appals me.' Disgusts her, in fact. How many nights has she slept between soiled sheets? Zav reaches to steady her hand.

'It's cool,' he says. 'His game's over. We're on to him.'

But it isn't over. Not until they find him. Not while Kate must check her bed – new locks or not – every night. She wonders if she'll ever again be able to slip under her duvet without thinking about whom she might be sharing it with.

The locksmith finishes the doors and recommends she upgrade her window locks at some point then carries his tools out. When they're alone Zav pulls her to him.

'I'm reporting it to the police today,' Kate tells him.

'Great... that's a start.'

'I've just my shopping to do, and get the place cleaned up. Then I'm going to the station. I suppose you're busy today...'

Zav glances at his watch. 'Mad busy. How about coming along? Forget the shopping. You can watch for buggers stealing from my shelves. Pay is lousy but the coffee's great.'

Kate pictures herself watching customers whilst Zav reads his Health and Efficiencys and laughs. The offer's so tempting. But she needs to get her chores done. Sunday's her usual day but she can't wait until tomorrow to deep clean the house. She says she'll try to show up later in the afternoon.

'I'll come along for the shopping at least,' Zav offers.

So they step out like any regular couple even if her compulsive checking of the neighbouring cars and gardens and windows as they drive out isn't entirely normal behaviour. Her checks reveal nothing and as she drives with Zav alongside she feels strong. Her shopping's completed fast with Zav at her shoulder, and back home he carries the bags in. His presence, the bright rooms, the heft of her new door key, bring security.

'Call me later,' Zav says.

He plants a kiss and suddenly she's clinging to him for dear life and her lips find his and press with desperation so that Zav, finally, has to ease her away. 'You sure you're okay?' he says.

'Of course. Thank you for coming.'

'Ring me.'

'Yes.'

'To be continued.'

'Yes.'

As she locks the door behind him her lips are still tingling.

'Damn,' she says.

She unpacks the shopping, keen to start on the house, to expunge all traces of her intruder and brace herself for a visit to Harrow Park. Police stations are as familiar to her as supermarkets but today will be the first time she's visited one on her own account, the first time she's discussed *soiled bed sheets* with the authorities. And the idea of throwing open her life to the vagaries of the police system repels her.

She lifts a carton of eggs from the bag and notices a yolk stain seeping through the cardboard. One of the eggs has evaded her habitual inspection at the store so she's one down and with a sticky carton as her reward.

She opens the carton to remove it and stops dead.

It's not just one broken egg. It's every egg! All twelve are crushed at the top. Every damned egg! Her heart thumps. There's no way she missed that when she lifted the top in the supermarket. Did she have a brainstorm? Did she not check the eggs at all? But her memory is clear. Zav was standing next to her and he'd grinned and made a comment about her not wanting ready-scrambled and then said: 'All good.' She can still hear his words.

But the eggs are not all good. They're all smashed. And in a moment the implication sinks in.

The carton was swapped in her shopping trolley.

She drops it into her bin and works frantically through the rest of her shopping and is entirely unsurprised to find that three tins of evaporated milk have miraculously changed to the sugar-filled condensed crap. The condensed labels are a different colour, unmistakable, and she's never made this mistake in her life. But today the wrong tins ended up in her trolley and in the rush through the checkout she hadn't noticed. But she recalls, with absolute certainty, that she picked up *evaporated* milk, just as she remembers that she picked up *unscrambled* eggs.

She recalls the other wrong items she's arrived home with in the last few weeks, the things she'd put down to carelessness. But now it's clear. It wasn't carelessness, and she wonders how she ever missed it. Her stalker has been there at the supermarket every time she's shopped, working his mischief. It would hardly be difficult, given Kate's habit of parking her trolley as she roams the aisles. She's never expected anyone to *steal* from it, after all. Nor interfere.

So it's not just the failed light bulbs and the towel rail and the TV remote, not just the calls and the surveillance and the break-in, nor his lying in her bed. This guy's been right beside her as she's shopped, watching from behind display stacks and choosing his moment.

Right there with her.

Just how crazy *is* this guy?

Kate stands with her spoiled shopping in the empty kitchen and the fear flows in again and threatens to drown her.

'Damn,' she says. 'Who the hell *are* you? What do you want?'

~~~~~

The ugly sixties edifice of Harrow Park Police Station is unfamiliar territory. It's not on Kate's legal circuit. She's never had business here so she doesn't know the uniformed sergeant behind the counter, whose name is Miller. Miller hears her out, gripping his counter with proprietary ease, but doesn't write anything down or hand her off to have her report recorded. His questions are pertinent but meaningless since he's not recording her answers, and they end with equally meaningless advice. She should take care when she's out, lock her doors and windows, fit a security chain and keep a record of any suspicious activity. Come straight back if this person approaches her directly. Their discussion is interrupted twice by calls, after each of which Miller's interest visibly wanes. When he slouches over his keyboard to open the log, finally, and record the briefest fact of her report so he can push her towards the exit Kate loses patience.

'Sergeant,' she says. Her voice is sharp enough to interrupt his typing.

'I'm reporting a serious offence. Perhaps you'd find an interview officer.'

Miller unwinds from his slouch.

'Would I now?' he says.

'Yes. Let's move this along. I'd like to have a statement on record.'

Miller raises himself to full height.

'We're a little understaffed today, ma'am. It could be an hour or two.'

'Is anyone in CID? They can fill out forms.'

As if to answer her question, a fat guy in a shabby navy suit and ridiculous red tie rolls out from the lifts at the far side of the annex. Miller calls across to him.

'Frank,' he says. 'Anyone free upstairs?'

The fat guy rotates his head in a brief shake of his jowls. Fast, dismissive. His skin is slack and the patches beneath his eyes point to either overwork or overindulgence or both. The Metropolitan's finest. 'Nada,' he growls and is gone.

'Not this morning,' Miller says. 'Would you like to wait for an officer?'

Kate would not like to wait for an officer, which would entail sitting meekly in front of Miller for an hour like a patient in a GP's surgery or, more appositely, a probationer waiting to report.

'Log the crime number,' she tells Miller. 'I'll call back.'

This will be next week when she'll find someone else to talk to. Kate is savvy enough to take the easy route. Miller pulls the keyboard across and asks for her name and address and finally her visit is logged.

'We'll call you or send someone round,' he says. 'Save you calling back.' Kate thanks him and turns to leave. No one will call her. No one will come round.

She exits the building into the racket of the flyover, penning anger and frustration behind a professional detachment. The log is open. She'll come back on Monday and kick things into gear and start to turn the tables on the bastard who's violated her house. From newly developed habit she scans the street for signs of anyone watching but the only person in sight is the fat CID guy, struggling with the lock of a beat-up Vauxhall Corsa parked on the red lines in front of the station. The car's as jaded as its owner and his struggle leaves the depressing thought that her big plan to mobilise the forces of law and order will be effected in the tatty nick inhabited by this guy. As she passes him the detective glances at her without recognition.

~~~~~

Kate parks on Primrose Hill and walks over the railway into Camden. The smashed egg thing and the uplifting reception at Harrow Park have induced a mood that would turn black in the silence of her house. Wackyjack's clutter, the tingle of its radiant heaters, its noise and bustle and Zav's laid-back presence are the only possible antidote. When she climbs the Stables stairs the chaos of the boutique greets her like an old friend. The shop is bustling and she pushes forcefully through towards the counter. Zav spots her and drops a vintage copy of Paris Match to lift the flap. She ducks through and folds herself into his hug and as she grins up at his boyish smile her cares fall away. She's safe in this bright cluttered den with Zav's arms round her. Zav sees something in her eyes though and sits her down to ask what's up. Kate grins and says *nothing's* up, she's great, and then contradicts herself with the tale of the smashed eggs and switched tins and the blasé reception at the police station. Zav calls across to a cubby where Nicholas is working a computer and gives him a coffee and croissant order, specifying something called a custard- and honey-baked rhubarb, which exotic concoction Kate knows is for her benefit, though there'll no doubt be three servings. Nicholas grins and jumps up.

'That's so freaky,' Zav comments. 'He was right there in the supermarket?'

'And he's been there lots of times.'

'I never saw anything,' Zav says.

'Me neither. But you wouldn't, unless you were looking.'

'Well, now we are. Do you think he'll try this again?'

'He might.'

'We'll be ready. I'll come along next time you shop but I'll stay out of sight. If he tries his tricks again we've got him.'

'He'll be wary,' Kate says. 'He'll know you might be with me from now on.'

'That's true. And when he finds out that you've changed the locks he'll know he's been rumbled over the break-in. He might be forced to pull back, unless pushing his luck is part of the game.'

'Let's see if he pushes it next weekend.'

'I'll be there. Maybe even the cops.'

'Assuming I can stir them into action.'

'We must. This guy could do anything.'

And there's no way to predict his next action. If someone had told Kate two weeks ago that her life was being invaded she'd have laughed. If someone had told her that someone was sleeping in her bed...

Nicholas reappears and loads the counter with coffee cups and paper bags and they gorge themselves on sugar and find happier things to talk about. Zav cleans his hands then lays out vintage magazines before Kate, true crime magazines, news and fashion from the thirties and forties, mostly American.

'Check this,' Zav says. He opens a full page advertisement that heralds "Sensational news for girls with no sex appeal". The ad. offers a rapid weight gain concoction for women blighted by the same slim figure as the specimen peering sadly from the page. The concoction's efficacy can be judged by the same woman's beatific face "just a few weeks later" as she rests her well rounded figure in the arms of a hunk, virtue of a twenty pound uptake. Scientific veracity of the transformation is delivered by a line-drawn medical doctor uncannily resembling Colonel Sanders who admonishes all women not to "let men hate the sight of you".

Kate's eyes widen.

'Times change,' Zav grins. 'Now the same people are selling you slimming pills and macrobiotic diets. But the real difference is the political correctness in modern ads. Takes all the fun out of it when the copywriters are stymied by the need to avoid the truth that men hate the sight of women who don't conform, or that menstrual cramps are a nuisance to husbands too.' He opens another page to display this assertion.

Kate is laughing for the first time in a week. Zav's social anthropology may be suspect but his magazines open a window to a world that existed only yesterday but is utterly gone, inaccessible except through the illumination of the marketing mores of its time.

'Did women fall for all this?' she says.

'The same as now. Fear and fads equal big bucks.'

They immerse themselves in more of the stuff: proud dads handing kids their first Webley rifles; spivs breathing cigarette smoke into their women's faces so "they'll follow you everywhere".

'Do advertising people live on the same planet?' Kate asks.

'They *make* the planet,' Zav says, 'then they remake it and sell you another slice.'

They break off their research from time to time to ring up sales. Zav shows Kate how to work the till and later how to spot an undecided buyer and move in for the kill. Under his tutelage she's set loose practising a new career of selling *curiosities* until, suddenly, the customers have vanished and the Stables are closing. 'Dinner on me,' Zav offers.

They eat at a trattoria off Chalk Farm, feasting on bruschetta and sourdough pizza, then walk down the High Street to a pub-cum-wine bar. Kate is underdressed in jeans and sweater but Zav's silk shirt and waistcoat go anywhere. And the evening feels better for its informality. Mingling amongst men in designer casuals, women fresh from hours-long preparation, Kate's casual attire brings a proprietary feel. It's the way you'd dress if you *owned* the place. And for a moment she owns the night. It's her night, her man by her side. She's fully alive and there's no portion of her to spare for worrying about a malign watcher out in the dark. For the moment her life is hers.

By midnight they're both a little drunk and Zav calls a taxi to take them to his place.

When he puts a match to the stove it flares ferociously and the room's instant warmth tells Kate that she won't be going home tonight. Tonight her empty house is beyond her. And the brighter the stove gets, the warmer her blood flows under Zav's alluring touch, the less is the *need* to be anywhere else. She snuggles close on the sofa and traces the hairs on the back of his arm in the flames' dancing light. His lips, when they seek hers, are all she ever wanted. She's known this man for ten days, but in that time he's flowed into her very being, transformed her world. Suddenly he's its centre. Zav's hand finds hers, finally, and eases the wine glass from her fingers and coaxes her from the sofa. His eyes are shining.

'Come with me,' he says, and leads her towards the stairs.

She follows.

20

They breakfast on warm brioche and coffee under the glow of Wackyjack's heaters. Kate is fresh from seven hours' sleep but in need of fresh clothes, and there are chores waiting at home. The house can be faced this morning, with Zav's strength coursing through her and the reassurance that he's just a phone call away. So she finishes her snack and savours one last bear hug then takes her leave and heads out into the fine, cold day.

Back home she sets about the mother of all spring cleanings, hoovering and polishing and scrubbing all trace of her intruder from the house. In her bedroom she inspects the bed sheets and though they're undisturbed is compelled to change them again, laid as they are directly against the mattress, duvet and pillows soiled by his presence. She hoovers the mattress and flips it, finds a spare duvet and pillows and re-makes the bed with fresh linen. She's just finishing when the doorbell rings.

Her front door has no security chain but the bright midday is empty of menace and she opens it to find two police constables on her step, male and female. Miraculously, they've come to interview her about her stalker.

The senior officer, a female called Cook, introduces her colleague as Sanderson and says they'd like to take a few details.

She invites them in and they sit in the lounge and listen to her story. It's the same one she gave yesterday but Sergeant Cook takes notes and asks sensible questions. She inspects the Valentine's card and asks about the park. The park, with its hooded watcher and extinguishing lamps, lacks the substance of the card and sounds ethereal before these uniformed officers. It's hard to proffer fear as evidence, and she doesn't enlighten them on the fact that she was out there with a knife in her hand.

'It was just a sense that someone was watching me,' she says. 'I'd have forgotten it if it wasn't for the calls and the break-in.'

'Probably just a walker. A power failure,' Cook says.

'It's possible. But it didn't seem that way in the light of what's happening.'

'But no one's approached you?'

'No.'

'Or threatened you in the calls?'

'The calls were threatening by nature: they were intended to scare me.'

'And you're certain he's been in the house?'

'Quite certain. He's been in my bed and he's played around with things – breaking light bulbs, hiding things, resetting thermostats.'

'Are you sure about the bed?' PC Sanderson asks.

Kate glares at him. 'Yes, I'm sure. The bed was clearly disturbed. And the smell...' this is uncomfortable. She switches her words to the policewoman: 'I could smell him.'

Sergeant Cook stays impassive. She understands precisely how that would feel but her mind is open. Apart from the phone calls there's little evidence for a stalker and nothing to prove that an intruder has been in the house or has been watching Kate. The mixed up shopping and the Valentine's card sound like something of nothing. She asks if they can inspect the doors and windows, and Kate indulges them on a tour of the house that turns up nothing.

Cook finally snaps her notebook closed.

'Thank you, ma'am. We'll get this logged. Let's see how things progress. If anything else happens let us know immediately.' She provides Kate with a direct phone number. 'Meantime we'll have a couple of patrols drive by.'

'Is it worth taking fingerprints? Could the guy be in the system?'

'We can't do that right now,' Cook says. 'But we'll log this with CID and review the situation day by day. Just lock your windows and doors and don't open the door to strangers.'

Vacuous advice. They know it and she knows it but the words are necessary, like religious platitudes dispensed over newlyweds and coffins. Kate has always locked her doors. But if someone has the key how do you stop them? And how, she wonders for the tenth time, did he *get* a key?

She shows the officers out and returns to the one action within her power, which is the completion of her purge, dusting and polishing where there's the least possibility of contamination: doorknobs, taps, ornaments, crockery, worktops, all the thousand things he might have touched or disturbed, until, if there *were* any fingerprints they're now gone. By the time she's through it's getting dark and when Zav calls she's too weary to accept his invitation. She has notes to review and an early start tomorrow and her plan for tonight must be limited to dinner and a bath. Zav is understanding. He tells her to be careful. She says she will. His voice is balm, stays with her after they disconnect.

By ten p.m. she's through: paperwork, dinner and bath. Ready for an early night. She grabs a dressing gown and completes the rounds of the house, checking locks and switching off lights, and arrives finally at her bedroom door. She leaves the room dark and pads over to gaze out of the window, wondering if he's out there tonight. Then as she turns to her bed the disgust comes back. He's lain right there under her duvet and two nights and two changes of linen have cleansed the soiling not a jot. She bends and reaches for the duvet but no matter how she tries she can't rid herself of the image of a stranger lying beneath it. She sees his head on her pillows, sees him looking at her right now...

Her fingers draw back in repulsion.

She stands for five minutes, locked in indecision. Then she turns and goes through to the back guest room. Instinct tells her that this room has remained uncontaminated. He's had no interest here. She goes in and closes the door and slides a dressing table across it then drops onto the bed.

Barricaded this way, in a place unsullied by the intruder, she relaxes and in moments she's asleep. When her kitchen phone rings thirty minutes later she doesn't hear it.

21

Donna Jordan is in a feisty mood entirely unwarranted by last week's D&D escapade. Perhaps she's emboldened by the solution to her client-assault prosecution that Kate has just presented, which is better than the girl should have hoped for. Donna has turned up dressed in what she imagines is the power fashion befitting the aristocracy of the sexual food chain, but looks, with her too-short skirt and too-slender fishnet clad thighs, a caricature of the lowest link of the chain, the streetwalker. Kate feels pity for this blind, wayward girl, trapped in the world of late night streets and seedy hotels, cold huddled groups and prowling cars. She wonders whether Donna ever hears footsteps behind her, ever changes direction from the shadows.

'Why am I always the one blamed?' Donna's asking, 'It wasn't me started that fight on Thursday, and the other bastard tried to rape me in his car. Why is it always me?'

Kate acts fast to stop this intermixing of the two affairs before they coalesce into an unmanageable soup of injustice within Donna's persecuted mind.

'One by one,' she says. 'The police witnessed the fight on Thursday. Whether you started it is beside the point. You were drunk and you assaulted the officers.'

'They friggin' assaulted *me!* They punched me down on the floor.'

'They say you were drunk,' Kate says. 'And you swung at a policeman and fell over.'

'No way! That tom bitch attacked me and the police come to *her* rescue. She should be the one bleedin' prosecuted.'

Donna's face is flushed with the incontestable veracity of her world view, which depends on neither logic nor fact. Kate glances at her watch.

'All right, Donna. Let's move on.'

Donna shakes her head and glares at the floor, and Kate can *taste* the futility of this girl's philosophy.

'The assault charge. That's a very favourable response from Mr

Porter's solicitor. It's the best you could have hoped for. I want to confirm with him today.'

'But you say they're still gonna do me for knifing 'im. It was self-defence.' Donna's furious glare is framed by the Dracaenas.

Kate holds up a hand. 'I already explained: there's no way to evade a charge of bodily harm. You were carrying an offensive weapon and you used it. And when the police arrived you were threatening to injure Mr Porter further. A GBH charge can't be contested on the grounds of self-defence. But if Mr Porter delivers an affidavit confirming that he was assaulting you, and you agree to plead guilty to a charge of actual bodily harm I think we can get the CPS to play along. We can be in and out in ten minutes.'

'And they'll friggin' fine me a fortune for defending myself.'

'If you're found guilty of grievous bodily harm you might go to prison. The very least would be a significant community order, even with your self-defence plea.'

'What if Porter doesn't tell the truth?'

'It will all be in his written statement. He doesn't want to be called as a witness any more than you want to be up on GBH. He knows the text messages he exchanged with your friend would become public knowledge and he'd be exposed as soliciting underage girls. This way you both win. He makes his statement and you plead guilty to a lesser charge and it's all over. No questions for him. A summary fine for you. Really, Donna: this is the best you can expect.'

'That bastard should be locked up. He got me in his car and then didn't want to pay.'

Kate sighs. Why can't the girl see? Why can't she just *see?*

'He didn't want to pay the *special* fee once he realised you were a little older than he'd been led to believe. He's a disgusting man who probably deserved what he got. But his interests and your interests coincide here. You both need to close this affair with minimal fuss. So... what do you say?'

Donna still wants to fight this out, to use Kate as the sounding board for her grievances, but in two weeks she'll be arguing with magistrates who, notwithstanding their contempt for the fifty-six-year-old insurance company manager who thought he was being set up with a fifteen-year-old, won't be well disposed towards Donna and her baby-faced subterfuge that enticed him in the first place, and certainly won't be impressed by her readiness to use a knife.

Donna pouts and struggles within her shadow world. This is one more battle she'll put down as a loss whatever Kate achieves for her. And the losing battles are stacking up in this girl's mind. A sex toy since she was seven, a druggie and alcoholic by seventeen, and dead, in all probability, by twenty-seven. And no one, perhaps, the worse off.

'What's a fine,' Kate says gently. 'It's better than time inside. And how about if my colleague comes to see you? She can help.'

'I don't need friggin' help.' Donna's anger is cold now. 'Everyone keeps telling me I need help. Even Georgie's like a friggin' mother hen. I wish you'd all just leave me alone. Plead me guilty if that's what you want.'

'Okay. We'll talk to the CPS and sort things out. And I'll call my friend anyway. She's a nice lady.'

Donna shakes her head and drops her gaze back to the floor to stare at God knows what vision down there in Kate's carpet. But Kate's running late. So for the moment their discussion is over. She stands and girl jumps up and walks ahead of her towards the door.

'Thanks, Kate,' Donna says. 'Thanks for nuthin'.'

But then she flashes a brief parting smile to neutralise her words, an acknowledgement of their shared understanding that the world is shit and that's just the way it is and you'd better just live with it until you're knocked out of the game. Kate shows Donna out and closes the door and goes back to reach for the intercom button. As she does so the phone rings and the light says it's an external call and she realises that she's neglected to route her line through Violet's switchboard. She almost diverts the call now but what would be the point? She was about to ping Violet anyway. Pointless to stand here waiting for her to send the call back. She punches the button and picks up on speakerphone.

The voice that flows out is female. But it's an altered, garbled travesty of a woman's voice.

'Hello Kate. You've changed the locks, my dear. Well, that's not very nice is it?'

The words freeze Kate. As much as anything her shock is at the switch to a female voice. Your tormentor is many, this voice says. Many voices, many places. We're a hoard besieging your life.

For a moment Kate can't move. It's a thunderbolt that's blasted into her office, turned her to stone and dragged her right back into her tormentor's world.

Then she snaps out of it. She picks up the phone, nulling the speaker. She won't have this voice echoing in her room.

'What do you want,' she says.

A laugh. Mangled and obscene.

'I just wanted to say hi, see how my *whore* is doing. All fresh for the new week?'

'You're a sick piece of shit,' Kate says, drawing from her creativity. 'But this isn't going to continue. The police are already looking for you.'

'Witness Mr and Mrs Plod knocking at your door yesterday. I do feel so outclassed, Kate.'

'You *are* outclassed. We're coming for you.'

'We? *Fantasy,* Kate. It's just you and me.'

'What do you want?'

'A little togetherness. A little excitement!'

'Bastard! Take your games somewhere else. You've chosen the wrong person.' Kate wishes that she too had some kind of scrambler, one that would filter the tremor out of her voice.

'I didn't *need* to choose, Kate.'

'What do you mean?'

A slow, hideous laugh comes through the line.

'Changing the locks was pointless, by the way,' it says.

'It'll keep you out, you creep.'

'No, my dear, it won't. It hasn't. I'm in the house right now enjoying your hospitality. Such a nice place, Kate. So lovely and girlish and cosy.'

He's lying. He can't beat the new locks, this freak behind a crone's voice.

'No,' she says. 'I know you're not in my house.'

'I'm lying on your bed right now.' The hideous crone voice sighs. 'Naked and relaxed. You don't mind if I take a nap? I'll be gone before you get home.'

'Go fuck yourself,' Kate says, and smashes the phone down.

If he's trying to lure her back to her house he's failed. There's no way he could have beaten the new locks, and breaking in in broad daylight would be a gamble. So it has to be a bluff.

She drops into her chair. It *has* to be bluff. But irrational doubts invade her mind and she can't rid herself of the image of him lying in her bed. She leans for the intercom but she's forgotten why she was about to call Violet, forgotten what's next on her schedule. Her mind is paralysed by the image of a stranger in her house, in her bed, *right now*.

She moves paperwork around, trying to rebuild her thoughts, clear her head, but all she can think about is him in her bed. The sickening image traps her, and ten minutes slide by as she fights the instinct to rush home, until in the end she realises that she'll have to go there. It won't take long. Forty-five minutes total if she grabs a cab. If she stays here she'll just waste the same time. What she should do, of course, is call the police. But they'd not exactly rush round to her house. It could be hours, and they'd want her there anyway. So she must either check her house now or endure torture for seven hours until she goes home in the dark of the evening.

She makes a decision, pulls on her jacket and rushes out. On Upper Street she turns towards the City and grabs the first cab she sees.

Traffic is light. They reach Maida Vale in fifteen minutes. They pull up at her driveway and Kate asks the cabby to wait and walks boldly up to her front door. But then she hesitates, fearful of what she might find inside. Better to check the building. She walks round the house. The front door's solid, undamaged, and her front windows are all intact, and her back windows and kitchen door look fine. She grabs the kitchen door handle. Locked.

She goes back round and opens the front door and waits just inside it. Hears nothing. She leaves the door open and slips off her shoes and treads silently into her lounge, alert for the slightest sound or movement. The room is empty, as is the morning room and the kitchen. All peaceful and still in the midday sun. She comes out to the stairs and stands for a full minute, struggling to hear against the suddenly noisy street. When silence eventually returns she creeps up. First port of call: her bedroom. This is where the bastard claims to be. The door is almost closed but she wonders now if it's the precise way she left it this morning. Is the gap a little wider? Doesn't she habitually leave the door open just the barest crack? She reaches and pushes the door back and her view expands slowly until she sees the bed.

It's empty.

She swings the door fully open to block the space behind it where an intruder might be waiting then takes a breath and goes in.

The room is empty. She walks to the bed and looks down on its pristine cover, its smooth pillows. Undisturbed. Then she steps across to check her wardrobe. No one springs out. And no one's under the bed. Shaking, but with a growing sense that the house is empty, Kate pads onto the landing and checks the two guest bedrooms and the bathroom. There's no sign that anything has been disturbed.

The bastard was bluffing. Unless he's in the cellar. She needs to check that one last place before she can return to the taxi. She goes down and recovers her shoes and eases the table away to open the cellar door. After she flicks on the light she listens again, illogically, for any noise in the house above and around her, not daring to risk having him come down behind her. The house stays silent. She starts down the cellar steps, hand trembling on the rail. The cellar is a profusion of hiding places but there's an empty, dead feel to it and the weak bulb is augmented today by the trickle of sunlight through the tiny half-window. She picks up a poker from an old fireplace set and walks between the junk, peering and listening. Finds only shadows and cobwebs. Silence.

She walks through to the back room and there's no one there, nowhere for an intruder to hide. She ends her search. Climbs back up the steps and switches off the light and closes the cellar door. Then she stands listening for a final minute. The house is empty. The bastard was bluffing.

She goes out, wondering, as she locks the door, if he's watching. She looks up and down the pavement but sees nothing. Her driver is gesticulating. His engine is running and his clock is still ticking but he makes money by moving and she's had him here long enough. Kate climbs back in and tells the cabby to take her back.

As they move off Kate twists for a sight of her house but it's hidden behind the hedge and in the musty rear of the cab the whole thing now seems foolish.

Foolish?

Anger overcomes Kate and she pounds a fist into the leather seat.

There's no foolishness about it. She's sitting in this damn taxi through the direct provocation of a malicious bastard who's assaulting her life, toying with her like a cat with a mouse. And she, his little *whore,* is dancing to his tune. But she's not dancing from foolishness. It's from fear. And for the first time since it began Kate dabs moisture from her eyes.

22

The afternoon drags in a tedium of lapsed concentrations. Kate's attempts to banish her tormentor fail at each break from her work, each pause in conversation. By five she's dreading going home. She's twice picked up her phone – first thinking of Angie then Zav – but stubbornness has held her back. She won't be sent scurrying like a scared rabbit.

Her desk phone is routed once again through Violet's panel but her nerves are on edge each time it rings, and when the firm shuts its doors at five and the lines revert to direct she lifts the phone off its cradle before working on for two hours. But the disconnected phone brings its own torment: he can't get through; he's frustrated; he's getting angrier; he's *waiting*. By seven her work has stalled. Kate quits and heads home.

The walk down her street is an ordeal of watching and feeling watched in a place that's become alien. He could be waiting in any shadow, behind any car. Maybe *this* car. She shivers and steps faster, anxious for her driveway but fearful that even the house will be no refuge

She lets herself in and commences her patrol, downstairs and up. The cellar beckons but there's no way she's going down there. The house is empty. He *can't* get in with the new locks. She should stop tormenting herself. She showers and starts preparing dinner, still dazed by the stress of the day and seeking comfort from the fact that her kitchen phone has recorded no missed calls and has so far remained silent, that he's not called back to gloat over this morning's little game. But comfort doesn't come. That's the genius of his game: he can scare her by doing nothing.

She's halfway through her food preparations when the doorbell rings.

She freezes, deprived for a moment of any decision-making power. Her immobility is a subconscious plea that the caller go away, or better still was never there, but when they don't go away, when the bell rings again, longer and, it seems, angrier, her trance is broken and she is goaded into furious action. She pulls the paring knife from the block and strides through, gripping it inside the front pocket of her sweat dress. She releases the door, keeping her foot behind it to thwart any attempt to barge in. Through the gap she sees a pale-faced man in his twenties wearing an oversized gabardine coat and holding up a warrant card. She stares at it in astonishment for a moment before swinging the door open for the caller to introduce himself as Detective Constable Crane. He apologises for the late hour.

The apology goes over Kate's head in the shock of discovering that they've got CID on the case, even if it's Junior Branch. She invites him in. The policeman is gangly and awkward but in the light of her lounge looks nearer thirty than twenty, though he was without doubt in uniform six months ago.

'I was just passing,' he explains.

'I see.'

Her unresponsiveness discomfits him. They stand face to face while he fishes for a smile and some words.

'We've a report about somebody following you.'

'Yes. Malicious calls, too, and he's been inside the house.'

Crane seems surprised by this last detail. Her report to the uniformed officers has not, it seems, made it through untrimmed.

'You've no idea who he is?'

Kate recalls having no idea when she reported the affair at Harrow Park and when she talked to the uniforms yesterday. Crane has either not read the notes or is easing them into the discussion. Kate doesn't need easing.

'No,' she says. 'And I've not seen him. But he's followed me to the supermarket and exchanged shopping items in my trolley.'

Which sounds a little trite, compared, say, to malicious calls and sleeping in your bed.

'What items?' Crane asks.

Kate stares at him in disbelief, then after she's found her voice says: 'He exchanged evaporated milk for condensed.'

Which puzzles Crane. 'Aren't they the same?' he says.

'No. And there are other things – jam, spot lamps, eggs. *Etcetera*.'

Steady, she tells herself.

'Eggs?'

She brings up a smile, bright and matter of fact. Her fist is still gripping the knife inside her pocket.

'He exchanged the carton in my trolley with one full of smashed eggs. It's part of his little game.'

'I see,' Crane says. 'And you're certain about this? You didn't just make a mistake?'

'I'd be less sure if he hadn't also been bombarding me with calls and hadn't broken into my house and hadn't slept in my bed.'

Crane registers the gear shift. 'Where did he break in?' he asks.

'There's been no sign of forced entry. We assume he had a key.'

'Okay to take a look?'

'Be my guest,' Kate says. 'But the two officers yesterday didn't find anything. I'm sure he had a key.'

Crane reconsiders. 'Okay. No forced entry. Did he take anything?'

'Trivial stuff to annoy me. He didn't come to burgle the house.'

'And he's slept in your bed?'

'I don't know if he *slept* there but he'd been lying in it.'

'But he's left no sign, apart from minor disturbances.'

'A messed up bed isn't a minor disturbance, Detective. It's a gross intrusion.'

Crane holds up a hand. 'Of course,' he says. 'That would be upsetting. And he's also called you, disguising his voice?'

'Some kind of scrambler.'

'Devices are easy to find,' Crane says. 'You can even get smartphone apps. When did he last call?'

'This morning. He told me he was in the house. I had to rush back from work.'

'No one here?'

As if she'd have neglected to mention that, as if she'd even *be* here if he'd been waiting for her this morning. She plants a wry smile and lets Crane figure it out. He does. He asks how many calls she's had and what the guy said, and she tells him and fetches the Valentine's card. Crane studies it and pulls out a notebook. His retrospective note taking has an odd hint of competence, suggests that Crane has digested what she's given him, is summarising it, maybe even building a picture. The same details have been taken twice already but Crane's notebook holds more promise. The detective may be inexperienced but he's interested, perhaps sufficiently to follow up.

'Who has house keys?' he asks.

Kate details her spares, all now accounted for.

'Perhaps he's had access to a locksmith's services or tools,' Crane speculates.

Kate agrees. It was this thought that drove her panic this morning. If he can get in without a key then she's got a problem. And once someone's been in your house it's hard to believe ever again that it's impregnable. Her tormentor may have taken nothing material but he's stolen something from her.

Crane asks a few more questions but it seems he actually was just passing, on his way home. He's wrapping up, keen to get going. That he's here outside his official working hours though is good, suggests commitment even if there's little that he can offer. He has Kate promise to lock all her doors and windows – cue one *more* border patrol before bed – to avoid isolated places and to call him immediately if she's threatened. She takes his card without asking whether she should call before or after using the paring knife. But Crane's concern, however fleeting, warms her to him. She asks what CID plan to do. To her surprise, Crane's response has authority, even if the substance is limited. He gives her a more specific version of the uniformed PCs' promise to have someone "drive by". A patrol car will drive past her door two or three times a night, he tells her. Anybody loitering, of course, will simply duck out of sight, but they'll know, at least, that they've no longer a free hand.

As they head to the door Kate asks if there's any way to trace the anonymous calls.

'If things escalate we'll investigate,' Crane promises. 'Your caller's probably using an unregistered mobile but we can get a feeling for his general whereabouts from tower records. If he's using a GPS smartphone we can place him accurately.'

'That's what I thought. And you don't need a warrant.'

'That's right, ma'am. Just some paperwork and approval from upstairs. If the calls persists the Guv'nor will want to think about that. In the meantime, let's see how it goes. Just take extra care.'

She thanks Crane and closes the door. Yes, Detective, I'll take care. She locks up and goes back to her kitchen and drops the knife and Crane's card into her briefcase then continues with dinner.

~~~~~

She watches a little TV then decides on an early night. But it's as if he's read her mind: she's just about to start her patrol when the kitchen phone rings. She grabs the handset and steels herself but the growl of the altered voice shocks her anyway.

'Kate. How are we tonight?'

She says nothing and a deep garbled laugh echoes down the line. They're back to a male voice.

'Did you come back home this morning?'

She can't answer. No matter how she prepares herself there's no defence against this obscene *invasion* channelling through the phone into her house, into her life. The altered voice is so devoid of humanity it's like the devil himself calling. Only when anger has built sufficiently does Kate's voice revive.

'You think I'm an idiot? Of course I didn't come home.'

Another laugh. Theatrical, phoney, scrambled into pure menace. *'Liar!'* it says. 'I watched you come rushing back in that taxi.'

'And were you watching the house an hour ago? Did you spot the Metropolitan Police detective?'

'I see everything. And I do admire your faith in the police.'

'Admire it or not, they're coming after you.'

A harsh robotic laugh.

'You think so? No: it's just you and me, Kate.'

'What do you want?' This is the third time she's asked. The question seems weaker every time and her stalker's original reply was the apposite one: *I already have it.* And he does. He has her fear, her outrage, her *life.* The bastard is revelling in the sick pleasure of taking what's not his, simply because he can. The alien voice gurgles and flows.

'Forget everyone, Kate. I'm your new friend. I'm your *buddy.* We're going to *dance,* Kate. We're going to hold each other and waltz. Shall we dance, Kate?'

'Tell me, do I know you?' She surprises herself with the sudden need to bait him, to push back. 'Because I'll bet I've seen you around and never noticed you. Isn't that right? You're invisible. A nonentity. And that's what's bugging you. Tell me I'm wrong.'

Invisible. Nonentity. Her litigator's instinct has dug up the barbs.

Words she knows will cut because his actions have the shabby destructiveness of someone the world doesn't notice. This is someone to whom the concept of being *invisible* is anathema. She knows it suddenly without a doubt. This man is a loser, a nobody, trying to change the rules.

She tells him that. 'Your game gives you away,' she says.

And the blow *does* hit home. A short, unguarded and mangled growl comes across the line before he catches himself. Then his reply drools with menace.

'I'll tell you who I am: I'm the person who owns you.' And with sudden, shocking violence the voice switches to a female shriek, an obscene laughter exploding from the handset. 'We're going to *dance*, my dear. Dance till we drop, until I *crush* you in my arms. *Be afraid*, Kate.'

Kate slams the handset onto its cradle and stands clutching the breakfast bar. Then she grabs her bag and pulls the knife out and spins round to face the black kitchen windows. The knife's tip is shaking.

'Damn you!' she yells. 'Damn you to hell!'

She shouldn't have talked to him. Shouldn't have played his game. Just check the bloody doors and windows and keep the knife close and *put the damn phone down* whenever he rings. Detective Constable Crane is on the case. He's understood the threat and he'll walk by the house (of course he will, he didn't need to spell it out) and he'll have patrol cars drive by every shift, and eventually this bastard will give himself away. So don't play his game.

She pulls herself together and commences her house patrol and when the house is secure retreats to her bedroom. She's determined to sleep in this twice changed bed tonight. No more retreating. *No more playing his game.*

But she must play his game to the extent at least of drawing her curtains and switching on the bedroom light so that she can pull back the duvet and examine every inch of the sheets for any trace. The inspection makes no sense but she must check anyway.

The bed is clean and unsoiled and when she's certain of that she switches off the light and reopens the curtains and she's just slipping under the duvet when the phone rings again downstairs. She tenses but makes no move to get up. Lets it ring out. But in the silence that follows, sleep is nowhere near. Thirty minutes later the phone rings again, faint but persistent, and her jangling nerves urge her to *answer* it and *not* answer it and it's clear he can keep her awake all night if it amuses him. She pulls the duvet round her head and blocks her ears.

Then her mobile rings beside her.

She curls away from it. It's as if he's moved from the kitchen to her bedroom. *Shit!* Please don't let him have this number. But when she unwinds herself to check it's Zav. She connects the call.

'Kate,' Zav says, 'I hope it's not too late.'

'No.' She tries to hide her breathlessness. The screen says it's thirty-five minutes past midnight. 'I'm glad you called.'

'I'm just in,' he tells her. 'Long drive. Everything okay?'

'Fine,' she says, but then she spills out the events of the day, even if she glosses over them with the positive fact of DC Crane's visit, placing her tormentor's actions safely beneath the umbrella of police business. Zav is shocked though, and despite DC Crane and his promise of police patrols he says he'll come over.

'No,' Kate says. 'Please. I'm fine now. He can't get in. If anything happens I'll ring you.'

Silence echoes on the line. Then:

'Immediately,' Zav says. 'Don't hesitate.'

She promises she won't and it's true, and Zav's closeness as she presses the phone to her ear is reassuring. He suggests they meet tomorrow night but she can't do that. Work has stacked up and she knows she'll be late in her office, the price of today's distractions. But they agree, instead, to meet later in the week. The concern in Zav's voice is unmistakable as he asks again whether she's okay and his concern stays and comforts her long after she's disconnected. His voice, his concern, finally ease her into sleep.

She wakes.

It's three a.m. and she wonders what has roused her. She searches for the echo of something that broke into her sleep. Was it a sound, a crash, glass breaking, or just a trick of her dreams? Her heart beats steadily as she lies motionless, afraid to get up and afraid to go back to sleep.

But finally she's no choice.

She finds her flip-flops and gown and, acting before terror paralyses her, goes down to check the house. She leaves the lights off, relying on her night vision. She starts with the kitchen. Lifts the phone and listens for a message waiting tone. There's none. She puts the handset back and checks the windows and continues her circuit, checking the front door and the cellar door, which she now blocks again with her Italianate table before going back up the stairs to complete the check.

Nothing. The house is dark and silent and empty.

Back in her bedroom she jams a chair under the doorknob and sinks back into her bed and slides under the duvet and finally falls into a sleep of sorts, but it's one that brings no rest by the time her alarm rouses her for the start of a new day.

23

'*Listen* to me,' Kate says.

The oration continues unchecked. Kate raises her chin and watches the winter fog beyond her window and feels the day sinking. This is the second interruption of her scheduled desk work and this time it's Jerome, whom she'd *specifically* requested to phone yesterday for a one minute chat. But when did she ever have a one minute chat with this man?

'Stop,' she says. 'Jerome!'

The edge in her voice finally breaks through.

'This is simple,' she says. 'You either come in next Monday with the ten thousand or there will be no offer to the insurance company and the sentencing hearing will go ahead without any evidence of you attempting reparations. You'll go to jail. Do you understand that?'

'They won't *give* me the money. That's what I'm telling you. They'd pay to *put* me in jail. They—'

'Jerome, you haven't talked to them. Didn't we agree that you'd explain your troubles and *see* what they say.'

'I don't know what we agreed.'

'Please, Jerome! Don't pretend you didn't understand. Do you *understand* that in three weeks time you might be in jail. Do you really fancy six months inside?'

'I hired you to defend me, not threaten me.'

'Then you'd better hire another firm. Because you've already pleaded guilty to criminal damage and if we don't make a meaningful reparation to the insurance company you'll face jail. You did enormous damage, Jerome. *Criminal* damage.'

'And that snake playing around behind my back was innocent?'

Holy mother, they're right back at the start! Kate covers the phone and groans. She isn't up to this today. Cue fantasy call: phone rings; it's Jerome; hello Kate, I've got the money; great, Jerome, see you next week; sure, and thanks for *everything* you've done for me; think nothing of it, Jerome, it's just my job; call ends.

Would that be *so* difficult?

But Kate's had enough. She isn't listening to any more of this crap.

'We're out of time,' she says. 'Go and talk to your parents. If they throw you out so be it. If they lend you the ten thousand bring the cheque in and I'll talk to the insurance company. Either way we're back in court in three weeks.'

Jerome starts up again but Kate hangs up and goes back to Wesley Leach's file. The file, at least, has been slimmed by Arthur's interviewing of his three witnesses. In the face of his incisive interrogation two wits have been consigned to the dustbin, though the third wit. is still in the game. The third still provides a viable corroboration of Leach's story that he was chased by an unmarked and unlit police vehicle, and if Arthur couldn't wear the guy down then Parfitt and Quinn can summon him in court with integrity, having no *evidence* that the man is perjuring himself. Leach is not going to be happy at losing two of his three but Kate's not here to make him happy. She's here to mount a plausible defence to the best of her abilities and within ethical bounds.

She roots in the CPS pack and pulls out the memory stick holding the police dashcam video of the chase. She's had it a week but has yet to find the stomach for a front seat view of the smash-up that put the pensioner onto the critical list. But view it she must before she steps into court. She pulls her laptop towards her.

The video opens with the police vehicle moving into position behind Leach's BMW. And Leach's reaction, accelerating instantly to eighty-five, is the first weakness in his defence. What made him so sure so quickly that the unmarked car was the "people" he claims are after him? Were his pursuers holding up a sign? The police explanation is that Leach hit the gas when they lit up the blues.

The dashcam captures it all as Leach drives his X5 like a maniac through the back streets of Leyton, commandeering both road and pavement. Kate holds her breath as Leach runs a one-way street against the flow to get across into Walthamstow. An opposing car reacts too slowly and as the vehicles converge she's thinking this is it, this is the old guy, but Leach squeezes miraculously through and opens up a gap on his pursuer. But the police vehicle has power and an expert driver and it's back up in twenty seconds as the dashcam digits flicker above eighty through narrow streets and desperate turns.

Adrenaline pumps Kate's veins as a pedestrian leaps for his life, and her mouth is forming one word, continuously and silently as she anticipates the coming disaster.

'Stupid.'

Leach's car opens another gap then jinks left and right as the brakes flare and he takes a junction at speed, cutting across the pavement and fishtailing round a flailing cyclist. The manoeuvre gives him the advantage and the BMW shrinks again ahead of the police vehicle. But suddenly Kate isn't watching. She's tapping the pause. She's freezing the action.

What the *hell* was that?

Five seconds back.

She rewinds to the junction and reruns the action and watches Wesley Leach's defence crumble. She'd barely caught it the first time but on the second pass it's unmissable. She freezes the motion at the moment the police car's blue light is reflected in a newsagent's window opposite the junction. She moves the action forward, frame by frame, and the police vehicle turns and throws a reflection of its light twice more in the glass before the window is lost to view.

Kate groans. Because she knows with absolute certainty that the CPS spotted this weeks ago, that they're planning to play the movie in court and freeze it for the magistrates to see the reflected blue light that destroys Leach's story.

Holy damn!

In a sense it's a relief. Leach's witness is redundant. His fleeing-for-his-life defence is over. The unmarked car was displaying lights just as the police claim, and dashcam footage trumps any number of perjurous witnesses.

Leach's fear-for-life plea would have bought him little, but now he's holding nothing and in forty minutes he'll be in here for a progress report and they're going to have to discuss reality. *Reality* is that his only strategy is a guilty plea and a mitigation argument that he was panicked by the police vehicle, that he maybe didn't *notice* the blue lights, didn't hear the siren. Leach's situation is now clear.

But it's about to get clearer.

With perfect timing Violet pings a call and tells her she's got Nigel Kane. Nigel is the CPS prosecutor responsible for taking Leach to court.

'Nigel.' Kate struggles to keep her voice amicable but the burden of what she's just discovered – the knowledge that Nigel has known about this all along, that he didn't think to mention the dashcam evidence to her – clips her words. For a mad moment Kate wonders if some devious malware on the memory stick has been triggered by her playing the video and has reported back to Nigel.

But Nigel isn't calling by dint of spyware. He doesn't know or ask whether she's seen the footage. He's calling about something worse.

'Bad news, Kate,' he says.

Kate's eyes close. There's only one piece of news that both of them would agree was bad.

'John Barnes died this morning,' Nigel tells her. 'We're revising the prosecution to death by dangerous driving. Evidence of Level 1. You might want to inform your client. We'll keep you in touch on the committal date.'

Kate thanks Nigel and promises to convey the information to Leach, whose hopes of a miracle have truly crashed. He'll do ten years and there's no escaping it. When she puts the phone down she buzzes Violet and tells her to send Leach in as soon as he arrives.

Horrible though the thought is, it's a weight off her shoulders. Leach is hers only for as long as it takes to schedule the committal hearing and hand him off to Crown Court.

When, twenty minutes before his appointment time, Leach's face appears in her doorway with it's eternal quizzical look, Kate doesn't bother with a smile. Leach can retain or fire Parfitt and Quinn as he pleases. His stupid actions have killed a pensioner and he'll go to jail whoever represents him.

Leach's perplexion, framed between the Dracaenas, doesn't change as she breaks the news.

~~~~~

Lunch hour is past by the time Kate clears her desk for the afternoon's business which starts in ten minutes with three back-to-back appointments. Violet has dropped off a sandwich, which must now be hoarded until she finds time for a break. Kate goes through to the kitchen to brew a coffee and maybe find a biscuit, and discovers Hartley in residence. It's just an hour since Kate phoned

Arthur with the update on Wesley Leach's predicament but the grapevine has already worked its magic.

'Your client's up for manslaughter,' Hartley says. He's fixing tea. Offers Kate one. She sticks with coffee.

'My client no longer. Leach is seeing Arthur tomorrow.'

Hartley's gaunt face lengthens. 'He still thinks he can beat this?'

'What he thinks isn't my concern. It's Arthur's. Maybe he'll push some of Leach's legwork your way.' Kate's tired and hungry and in no mood for Hartley's chit-chat. She casts the barb knowing that Hartley will recognise it for what it is. It took twenty-five minutes to get Leach out of her office this morning and his vitriol, his finger pointing, when she explained his options, have left her shaken. Her skin, it seems, is not as thick as it once was. Hartley's own skin maintains its perennial thickness. Her barb bounces off unnoticed.

'The man's a fool,' he says, referring presumably to Wesley Leach and not Arthur.

'At least he's not my fool. He's killed a man and he won't persuade any court in the land that he's not guilty.'

Hartley sips his tea. 'Coming from you that's a death sentence.'

'Simple truth.'

'If I'm ever in the dock, Katie, I'll call you.'

'Don't get in the dock. You'll find that easier.'

'Naturally. But if I'm ever in trouble you're my girl.'

Kate flicks off the kettle and brews her coffee then roots in the tin for a biscuit, fighting back a retort. She is no one's damn *girl* and if Hartley Tasker ever does end up in the dock it will be for something slimy that she'd stay well away from. So go find your *girl* elsewhere, Hart.

'How's the stalker thing?' Hartley asks.

Kate takes a breath.

'The police are on it.'

'Good. These lunatics can be dangerous. You need to keep clear of this guy, Katie.'

Which is a fatuous remark even by Hartley's standards. You don't chase stalkers, Hart, they come to you. *They* decide where and when and in what manner you meet. And it's kind of hard to *keep clear* of your own house, of your own *bed*. She glares at Hartley, furious that this is just cheap office tittle-tattle. Snippets passed around. Not that there will be any more snippets. Kate's clammed up since her outpouring to Violet last week. The unpleasant and humiliating details of her tormentor's escalating actions will never reach this office and Hartley can go fish elsewhere. But he's as oblivious to her anger as he's earnest with his advice. 'Just keep clear,' he repeats. 'You see any sign of the guy, just run a mile. Hell, I'm sure you're fitter than he.'

'Unless he's an athlete.' Kate fishes out a biscuit.

Hartley laughs too quickly and too loudly and his phoniness truly *shines.*

'Are you sure you don't know the guy?' he asks. 'Is there nothing you *sense* about him Katie?'

There isn't. He could be anyone. If he passed her in the street she'd not know. He could be an acquaintance or her client or her plumber or... anyone. She picks up her coffee and prepares to leave. *Is it you, Hart?* she's thinking. *Is stalking women a side of your slimy character we've not seen?* Then she rebukes herself. Wonders where that came from.

'Sorry, Hart,' she says. 'Things to do. But thanks for asking.'

'No prob.,' Hartley says. 'Back to the grind. Time and crime wait for no one.'

Kate smiles and leaves fast, scurries back to her office before she says something that reveals just how thin her skin has become.

24

It's ten thirty p.m. The fog has thickened on Upper Street and Kate walks to the station through a surreal haze of drifting lights and formless shadows. The station plaza is disorienting, an unfamiliar landscape that threatens to deflect her into blind, stumbling circles before the mouth of the building yawns suddenly ahead of her. As she regains the solid world she rebukes herself for being out at this hour. Zav had called at seven, and though her workload ruled out an evening off Kate had allowed the conversation to drift for thirty minutes before getting back down to it. When she'd looked up again it was ten twenty.

The haze clears as Kate rides the escalator down to the oily warmth of the deep level platforms. She finds she's the only one down there, which leaves her uneasy, but the annunciator has the next train due in only six minutes. She walks the length of the platform to kill time, only to find on her return that the due time has been revised to twelve minutes. She curses. She'll stay put beneath the damn digits for the rest of her wait. They'll not catch her again.

She hears steps in the cross corridor and waits for a fellow passenger to appear but none does. It's just someone headed for the Northern City line.

Under her scrutiny the annunciator counts down without further reversal and the train races in, braking and squealing. She rides it to Oxford Circus and changes for the Bakerloo. Her new carriage is empty. The train's direction is wrong for revellers venturing into the city, and if there's an army of workers travelling home from five hours' overtime they're taking a different line. The train accelerates and Kate plants her briefcase and checks the time.

Eleven p.m.

Shit.

Days like this, riding the late train from fourteen hours of frustration, bring questions about her choice of profession. Kate considers doctors, blessed with the certainty that they are helping –

and are appreciated by – their patients, blessed with evenings to call their own. What fool chooses the legal profession's thankless toil? And today's business had wrapped up with a truly thankless episode as a late afternoon drink-drive hearing skidded off the road. Kate had been confident of manoeuvring the court towards leniency in consideration of her client's standing as a hard-pressed and car-dependent social worker. But Tom Shipley, her perennially sympathetic magistrate, had either a migraine or a losing ticket on the horses because he wouldn't be swayed towards a discretionary waiver of the twelve month ban, leaving her client high and dry. Such things happen. You take the bad with the good. What Kate hadn't anticipated was the fury of her previously mild mannered and penitent lady as they exited the court. The woman's vitriol was shocking as she educated Kate on what the driving ban meant for her job – that she might not *have* a job – the whole speech delivered without the faintest nod to her own culpability in the affair.

The bad and the good.

Not as bad, of course, as *Twelve Months Ago*. Kate can draw faint comfort that this afternoon, odious though it was, was not in the same league. *Twelve Months Ago* stands as the yardstick for vitriol. The one she'll always remember. And it was the same thing: a drink-drive prosecution, a client rendered car-less and looking for someone to blame when his miracle failed to materialise. What was he? A company rep? Estate agent? Kate no longer recalls. What she does recall is his pulsing fury as they'd walked out of the courtroom. She'd paused for a word in the foyer but as she'd opened her mouth he'd simply continued walking as if she wasn't there. She'd called out and he'd stopped, finally, and turned to look at her as he would at an insect. He'd said nothing. Just five seconds of cold fury before he opened his fingers to let his Parfitt and Quinn paperwork and summons letter spill to the floor. Then he turned and walked out, leaving her to scrabble to recover the confidential material as an audience grinned and winked at the lawyer's come-down. He'd not said a single word but the stark message of his silence, the casting of the sheets, had more power than words could ever summon, and Kate had thought – still does think – *damn you, you bastard,* I hope the ban costs you your damn job. I hope, she thinks now, her fury fuelled by this afternoon's repeat incident, that you're in some corner pub tonight drinking your unemployment benefit away.

She snaps out of it, suddenly and angrily. What are you doing? Let the damn thing go. They're all ungrateful sods when their miracles aren't delivered, and brooding about them is not part of the service. Get a hold of yourself.

But the day has dragged her down. This afternoon's disaster, following on from the morning's doses of Jerome and Wesley Leach, has delivered an entire day-load of hostility to wash her up, abject and defeated, in this empty train.

The train pauses at Warwick Avenue, motors buzzing, then accelerates again into the blackness, and Kate feels herself drifting. If she's not careful she'll wake up in Harrow. She pulls herself together and looks round. The carriage is empty, but something catches her peripheral vision. Beyond the communicating door at the end of the coach a shadow is blocking the light.

Someone is watching.

Kate comes instantly alert, thoughts of stalkers and house invaders crashing back to displace her legal broodings. For all the job's frustrations, it's kept her mind off that problem today, but now the nightmare is back, breaking without warning at the sight of a man's silhouette standing at the end of the next carriage. Then in a jolt of fear, at the same moment she confirms that he's watching her, she knows that it's *him*.

She starts to rise, even as she's telling herself she's overreacting. How could he be on this train? Has he been watching her office all evening? The notion is ridiculous. But there he is, staring from the next carriage, and the menace in that silhouette defeats reason and floods her with a clammy terror. Then the silhouette steps forward, right to the glass, and the light from her carriage illuminates his face and it's the face of a demon, a dark, twisted mask, a grotesque snarl of blazing eyes. Eyes blazing for *her*.

Kate jumps up.

Wait! Stop!

That door is emergency only. He can't get to you unless he opens it and crosses between the carriages, and the train will be slowing any second for your station. The door's glass, though, can't repel the menace of that mask – surely it's a mask – nor dilute her terror. So she grabs her briefcase. She needs to get away and alight from the far end of the coach, well away from him, but before she's started to move the silhouette has shifted and to her disbelief the emergency door has swung open. He's stepped over the gap between the carriages and, dear *God*, he's coming! Kate flees, races up the carriage with the hideous notion that he's possessed of supernatural speed and that she'll feel his touch any second. She reaches the end and turns and he's walking slowly towards her, gripping each pole, his snarl rippling. The snarl actually *is* a mask, she sees now, but the hate shines through it.

Kate's at the emergency door with nowhere to go. And he's still moving.

She's nowhere to go but she can't stay. This can't happen! In a second he'll be reaching out...

She turns and grabs the handle and pulls the emergency door open, and without pause she's out over the couplings in the black roaring tunnel, reaching across to the next carriage. She finds the handle and wrenches it, pushes the door open and launches herself across, almost falling into the next coach. And she's through! She's given herself twenty more metres, and beyond that another carriage before she's trapped behind the driver. And even one carriage will buy time. As Kate runs she fumbles with the lock on her briefcase, scrabbles inside for the knife. But it's not there because she failed to put it back after last night's phone scare. Her fingers grab her phone but that's futile too. Even if she gets a signal there's no time. No help is going to materialise on this speeding train. She's utterly alone and the *demon* has crossed into this second carriage and is moving remorselessly behind her. She'll feel his fingers on her neck any second. Kate reaches the carriage's far end and prepares to make another jump.

Then the brakes squeal and she's pushed against the glass as the train decelerates into the bright blur of the Maida platform. Kate turns and plants her palm on the door release but it won't budge until the train's stopped. And he's moving inexorably down the carriage, still closing on her, now just ten metres away, now five, dark and vicious in a donkey jacket and cord trousers and that demon snarl. Then the train jolts and the door releases and she's out. She runs for the escalators and jogs up, muscles knotting as she leaps the oversized risers. The echo of the departing train dies behind her until the only sound is the clack-clack-clack of her feet on metal. At the top she forces the gate – no time for the ticket slot – bruising her thigh, then she's out into the fog and dashing across the zebra. She slows finally and looks back but the fog has already swallowed the station entrance and she can't see if anyone's come out behind her.

The fog cloaks her on Elgin as she strides out, looking neither left nor right, intent only on leaving the demon behind.

And that's how she thinks of him: as a demon. Yes, you bastard, maybe you *are* a demon, a sad, twisted, *terrifying* demon. In her haste Kate almost misses her turning. Only her feet, stumbling on the kerb, remind her. But the near upset steadies her. Take it easy! He's not here. He's probably halfway to Willesden by now, and the last thing she needs is a broken ankle. Kate stops and turns towards her house, alert for any sound of footsteps behind her. But the street is deserted. The fog envelops her in the quiet of the grave.

~~~~~

Kate showers and grabs her dressing gown then goes down to check the windows and doors a second time. She moves like an automaton, still gripped by periodical shaking fits as she checks latches and locks and dark rooms. Her back tingles continuously with the anticipation of a touch, of a shadow moving. All she wants is the safety of her bed. All thought of eating has gone, dropping her day's intake down to four coffees, two biscuits and a sandwich. The Scared Shitless Diet. Try it today! Watch those pounds fall off...

Her first stop tomorrow will be Harrow Park where DC Crane can tell her what *exactly* they're doing about this bastard. Tonight she'll jam the chair against her bedroom door and curl up as far from his touch as she can and tough it out. She's crossing the front room, eyeing the window as she approaches it when a shadow does indeed move outside and the doorbell rings, followed by three loud bangs.

She stands petrified.

The bell rings again. Then more knocks, rappity tap TAP, sudden and imperious. The knocks jolt her into movement and she leaves the room and walks to the door. But without a security chain she can't open it. *Why* didn't she have that chain put on? Then she hears voices. One calls out.

'Police. Ms Walker?'

She opens the door. There's three of them. Two uniformed officers and, materialising from the fog, DC Crane, his gabardine light against the shadow of the hedge. Kate stares.

'Sorry, Ma'am,' the uniformed sergeant says. 'We received a call about a disturbance. We understand you're having problems with a prowler.'

Stalker is the term. But choose your own word: stalker, intruder, prowler, *demon*. But why are they here? Crane steps up and holds his warrant card to the uniforms.

'I picked up the call,' he explains. He turns to Kate. 'Is everything okay?'

Kate shakes her head. 'No... I mean there's been no disturbance.'

The policemen look at her. Crane smiles.

'Probably a hoax,' he says. 'Are you okay?'

Kate is shivering. 'Not really,' she says.

The uniforms perk up but Crane sends them on their way. Kate invites him in. Crane looks tired. Too much overtime. They stand in her hallway and she tells him about the Tube demon.

'And you think it's him?'

'Who else would pull that kind of trick? He must have been watching my office. And I assume it's he who's just reported the disturbance.'

Crane concurs. But there's nothing he can do tonight. He promises to review the situation tomorrow and try to put someone on the case. The words bring a faint hope. Kate pictures a detective, P.I.-like, walking the streets, hunting down her assailant. Fantasy, of course, but if Crane or one of his colleagues starts actively *looking* for her tormentor then that would be progress. And after tonight she needs to know that *someone* is looking because she's damned scared.

Crane dispenses advice about not going out alone and not taking late trains – got *that one,* Detective – and staying alert for anything out of the ordinary, advice she's already given herself. Then he asks again whether she's okay and she says she'll be fine and he leaves.

Kate locks the door and restarts her patrol, checking slowly and diligently, and when she's finished, fifteen minutes later, she falls wearily onto her bed where she's already drifting off when the distant annoyance of a car alarm intrudes. She comes fully awake. The problem with car alarms is you don't know whose they are, and the morons who habitually trigger theirs by leaving car windows or doors open are always the last to imagine that their vehicle is the cause of the disturbance. But the alarm sounds worryingly like hers. Could the guy have got into her garage? The horn continues intermittently and she lies awake, wondering each time the alarm shuts off whether it's over. But it isn't. The alarm starts up again every time and in the end the suspicion that it's *her* car is too great. She scrambles to pull on jeans and a sweater and goes down. On her way through the kitchen she retrieves her trusty paring knife before unlocking the door. Outside, the fog is as thick as ever and now it's two degrees below zero. Kate grips the knife and crosses to the garage door from behind which the alarm is quite clearly sounding. When she opens the door the noise bursts about her. She flicks on the light and presses the remote to silence the alarm. Beyond the Mazda she can see that the up-and-over door is partly raised. Someone has been in. She checks the car and finds the driver's door open and its window down but no obvious damage. Whoever came in here didn't come to steal or vandalise, just to scare her and bring her out in the dead of night. Despite her knife, fear slides back in and Kate stands rigid under the garage light, transfixed by the thought that he's nearby, terrified of going back out into the garden. But in the end what choice does she have? She can't stay here, cowering against her car. She finally moves, pulls the up-and-over closed and jams a rusty claw hammer into its mechanism so that it can no longer be opened from the outside. Then she switches off the light and peers into the fog and summons the courage to step out.

She finds it and crosses to the house. Goes in and locks the kitchen door. But even as she does so the tingling on her neck increases with a sense of something malign right here in her kitchen. Whether it's imagination she can't tell, but every sense screams that the *demon* is nearby. Kate stands with her back to the door, trembling. But there's nothing in the kitchen and eventually she forces herself to move and tiptoe yet again through the house with the knife at the ready. She walks the rooms and checks the shadows, her nerves taut at each opened door and cupboard. She stops frequently to listen but there's nothing. He *hasn't* come into the house.

But it doesn't *feel* that way. She opens another door, lets the shadows flow out...

She completes her patrol and no one has jumped out, and the ebb of tension admits fury. She curses her tormentor. This has gone way beyond a game. The guy has dedicated his whole night to tormenting her. From her office to the Tube to her house. Pulling on masks and jemmying her car door and...

The phone rings.

In a fury she races down and snatches it from its cradle and waits for him to speak but he doesn't. She grips the phone, unable either to speak herself or to break the connection.

Then she hears it. Stertorous breathing and a groan that sounds like the ecstasy of sexual passion, a groan without electronic distortion, a clear, rising, uncontrolled passion that ends in her name.

'Kate...'

Kate hurls the handset across the kitchen and rips the wires from the wall mount in a spray of fine, coloured entrails and the phone is dead. Nevertheless, she walk across and stamps on the handset. It cracks and shatters.

She stamps again. And again.

25

Two days have opened up distance. Tonight it's hard to recapture that obscene voice in the dark of her kitchen. Even the memory of foggy streets and demon masks, desperate leaps in roaring tunnels, is more like a dream, cannot drag her down as she pulls Zav closer. She's sandwiched between the heat from his stove and the warmth of his skin, caressed by the sheepskin rug and still aroused by the trickle of his lust inside her. She inspects his eyes, sees amongst the tiny reflected flames a shadow that must be her. Kate closes her eyes and drifts.

'Staying?' Zav asks.

She opens them again, shakes her head.

'Better not. It'll be too much of a rush tomorrow.'

'Start late. Scandalise them.'

She smiles. 'I've finished twice this week at a sensible hour. That's scandal enough. And the work's piled up.'

'Work shouldn't be your priority at the moment.'

Her smile widens. 'Is that impartial advice?'

'Not in the least. There are perks for the adviser when you're lured away from the office.' He traces the tips of his fingers across her breast. She shivers. Zav has every interest in freeing up her evenings. And his unexpected call at five thirty today aligned perfectly with her decision to avoid late night streets. He was calling from outside her building, parked in the red zone, and she'd barely registered the annoyance at his presumption before she was clearing her desk and grabbing her jacket. After all the recent unpleasantness she deserved a night off.

They'd dined at a bistro in Covent Garden then spent the rest of the evening on Zav's sheepskin.

'I don't just mean tonight,' Zav says. '*Stay* here. You'll be safe.'

But she's not ready for that. In a week or a month, perhaps, she'll give up her freedom for what this man promises. She runs her palm along his thigh then touches her fingertips to the deep bush of his chest, feels his breath on her cheek. A week or a month. Or maybe only a few days. But not tonight. She won't come to Zav as a fugitive. She's already exposed her weakness by unloading her fears onto him as they ate at the bistro. His eyes were wide at her stunt in the Tube tunnel, her smashed phone, the fear of the shadows in her house. He'd said it then: 'Stay with me.' And there'd been fear in his eyes. She'd reached across the table for his hand.

His hand cups her face now, then slides away and his fingers go back to teasing her breast. A week or a month or a few days. How easy it would be to surrender even tonight. But she won't. Tonight Kate must reclaim her own house or it will be forever foreign territory.

'The guy's not rational,' Zav says. 'We don't know what he'll do next.'

'I'll not take chances until the police find him,' Kate says.

'I wouldn't place too much faith in the police. They'll not put effort into this until...'

The thought falls unspoken. Kate thinks of the young detective in his gabardine coat. He'll try, she knows, but catching a maniac who's waging a guerrilla war might be beyond him. And how much time has he been authorised to spend looking into her complaint? Not much, she guesses. She won't be a priority until, as Zav almost said...

But that's another time, another place. She reaches round Zav and coaxes him atop her where he brings absolute safety, stills her fears. And in the strength of her hug, as she opens herself to him, she feels something like love.

~~~~~

It's one thirty a.m. when she climbs from the Ducato. Zav waits until she's in the door then drives off.

She readies things for a rapid exit tomorrow then showers. The hot cataract envelops her like armour, suffuses her with a sense of strength enhanced by the consideration of her shattered kitchen phone, her symbolic fight back. The phone won't ring tonight.

She pulls on a chemise and slips into bed for five hours' sleep, and is beginning to drowse when her smartphone rings on the bedside table. She picks it up and sees an unknown caller. In an instant she's wide awake. Surely not! He doesn't have this number! She's tempted to take no chance, to ignore the call. If it's important the caller will leave a message. But she's never ignored her mobile in her life and the fear of hearing his voice is insufficient to suppress habit. Against her instincts she connects the call.

And it's him.

The woman's voice again, the garbled crone.

'Slut,' it says. 'Whore.'

He's more to say but Kate kills the line and hits Zav's key and when he picks up she blurts out her terror. He asks if her doors are locked and tells her to stay put. He's coming round. After the call disconnects Kate stares at the screen and wonders whether she's been too hasty. So much for strength. This is the real her, indecisive, turning on a whim, blown this way and that at the pleasure of her tormentor. This is what she wanted to avoid. She's safe in the house. Should have ignored the call. Instead, she's becoming a habitual damsel in distress, endlessly crying wolf. Even if the wolf is real, even if he's out there, she doesn't want to be that helpless person.

Damn!

She almost calls Zav again but that would be even worse. The damsel who can't make up her mind. With a groan she throws her head back onto the pillow, all the joy of the evening gone.

Fifteen minutes later a vehicle stops outside and her phone rings again.

'Everything okay?' Zav asks.

She hesitates. 'I'm sorry, Zav. He just scared me.'

'No problem.'

'I'll let you in.' She starts to rise.

'No need. Unless you want me to stay. I'll just walk round. Check there's no one about.'

Kate rises and walks to the window and looks down onto the street but sees only her high hedge and gleaming car tops, frost on the roofs. Her phone rings again.

'All clear,' Zav says. 'I've checked up and down the street and in your garden. There's no one out here. I don't think he's around.'

She walks back to the window and sees him looking up from her drive and she's sorrier than ever that she's brought him back out into the freezing night. She asks if he'd like a drink but he tells her to go back to bed.

'Damn,' Kate says. 'I'm truly sorry, Zav.'

'Don't be,' Zav says. 'Call me anytime. This guy's going to regret his stupid game.'

She thinks she can discern a hardness in his lamp-lit face and, in a nonsense of contrariness, is saddened that it's capable of such expression. Zav has been, until now, wholly soft, her cuddly toy.

Zav's still speaking.

'You want me to stay?'

She does but she can't. She tells him she'll be fine now but something in her voice catches him. He gestures to her door and strides towards it and she almost runs down to let him in.

He stands away from her, careful not to freeze her with his chilled jacket as she locks up. Then he takes her hand and leads her up the stairs and she sits with the duvet round her as he pulls off his clothes. When he joins her his body is warm and his arms are a fortress.

There's nothing to say. She closes her eyes and permits herself the briefest smug thought of her stalker. Is he out there, freezing his butt off in his mad fixation? She hopes so. She hopes he's seen Zav, hopes he waits all night in the black street for him to reappear. She hopes he freezes solid.

Then her thoughts snag on something that's lurked in her subconscious since that call two nights ago. Did she hear, through the pall of its obscenity, something in that undisguised voice as it cried her name, something deeper inside her tormentor? Something beyond the cold of his previous contacts? Does this bastard have some kind of warped feelings for her? Is he burning with rage down there? The thought chills her but she pushes it away and lets Zav's chest and arms enfold her world and falls into a sleep deep as death.

26

It's Saturday morning and Kate has woken refreshed. Even without Zav's presence – he's away at a Brussels collectibles fair – her body deferred to Friday night and released her into deep slumber, undisturbed by three calls that lit up her silenced phone in the early hours.

A surprise call from DC Crane yesterday afternoon confirmed that the police are still on the case even if their actions are limited to detours down her street by night shift patrol cars and a couple of late night walks round her neighbourhood by Crane himself. On the negative side Crane reported that his boss is not yet inclined to raise a request for phone data that would allow them to track her anonymous calls.

Kate completes her housework and heads out to meet Angie for a day's shopping therapy. The bright morning enhances her feeling of strength, the sense that she can beat her stalker or at least fend him off until he gives himself away. She's maintaining her safety routine, checking the house, avoiding late night streets and empty trains, but she's going to live her life. Fresh from two nights sleep she can tough this out. She'll prevail.

~~~~~

It's Angie who looks weary when they meet. Kate senses Jon's troubles hanging over her. Kate's own problem, though, is the first topic on Angie's lips and Kate spends half an hour both reassuring her sister and fleshing out details of Zav, whose confirmed status as official boyfriend brings a demand that they all meet. Kate deflects Angie's attempt to organise an immediate dinner with the fact of Zav's absence at his trade fair, the latter being made to sound like a regular thing such that diaries will need consulting before any such meeting can be dropped on her in future.

The Oxford Street crush is hard work and they divert into the side streets where Kate asks about Jon. Angie's response confirms that this is what's bothering her. Kate's love for Angie, who's pushed her son's problems aside in her concern about her stalker, is as warm as ever, and her ear, now, is gladly lent to her sister's fears.

They cut down to Grosvenor Square and sit beneath the Roosevelt Memorial, warmed by the sun even as their breath clouds.

'They wanted to talk to us,' Angie says.

'The police?'

'The school. Although they implied that the police are still looking at Jon.'

An old guy arrives with a bag of bread and conjures a storm of pigeons so that Angie's words can hardly be heard.

'What did they say?' Kate asks.

'The school are making their own enquiries. Keith, our head, wanted us to know that Geraldine had a problem with Jon.' Angie smiles. 'You'd think I'd know such things.'

It's Kate's understanding that Geraldine Bryson had a problem with most pupils. From Angie's descriptions it's clear that the woman was an anachronism, her teaching style lacking the natural gift of connection, a woman with a declining career stranded among her disorderly pupils by the insidious ebb of school discipline. Disliked sufficiently to induce the house wrecking. But Jonathan, for all his teenage sullenness, and despite that photo on his phone, is not malicious or vindictive. Friend Gary, of whom Kate knows nothing bar Angie's disapproval, *is* perhaps malicious and vindictive. And it was he who'd sent the "Armageddon" message from outside Geraldine's house. So it's just possible – it's what Kate has been assuming – that he is the culprit and that Jon is linked to the affair only by association. But now here's Angie talking about a problem between Geraldine and Jon. Here's Angie changing the picture.

'Apparently Jon allowed Gary to crib from his coursework,' Angie tells her. 'The two turned in essays that matched word-for-word in parts. Keith has no doubt which way the copying went – you've only to look at Jon and Gary's respective grades – but apparently Geraldine marked both essays down equally. So Jon's A-grade work was given a D. Maybe he deserved it but Geraldine might at least have talked it through with them. She knows how hard Jon works.'

'Have you spoken to Jon about it?'

'At length. But it's difficult to make headway. He started by denying that Gary had cribbed from him which put him in a corner. He knows the essays prove otherwise so his denial only locked him into a defensive shell.'

'What does the headmaster say?'

'He let us know that the police have talked to Gary again. Implied he's their prime suspect. But he thinks they'll talk to Jon again. He wanted to know if we suspected anything. Wondered whether Jon might be willing to own up to any part in it.'

The pigeons take flight suddenly in a thunder of wings. Kate glares at the old guy and wishes he'd take his damn breadcrumbs elsewhere.

'Ian was angry at the insinuation,' Angie says. 'He was adamant that Jon wasn't involved but I was shocked that Keith sees Jon as a potential culprit. That's without even knowing about those phone pictures. That "Armageddon" text scares me, Kate.'

'What does Jon say about that?'

Clouds have darkened the sky in the space of five minutes and freezing rain suddenly pricks their faces. They both look upwards and stand, head for shelter.

They find a café that's filling fast and grab a table by a radiator. Angie slumps down and toys with the menu.

'We talked to him last night,' she says. She shakes her head. 'We should have done it sooner. But I was afraid of a fight between Ian and Jon.'

'How did it go?'

'We had the fight. Jon tried to go ballistic at us for sneaking a look at his phone but Ian wasn't in the mood. I thought they were going to come to blows. Ian threatened to take the phone away if Jon couldn't explain what we'd found but Jon just dug in. Claimed it was nothing. Wouldn't talk about it.'

'Do you think he might have been involved in wrecking the house?'

'I don't know.' Her voice is a whisper. The uncertainty is sitting heavily on Angie. She starts to scan the menu then breaks off and looks up.

'What could they do?' she asks.

What could they do, she means, if her son *is* found to have destroyed Geraldine Bryson's house and life. The question distracts

Kate's thoughts for a moment back to her own problem. At least, up to now, her stalker hasn't wrecked her house with a sledgehammer, but the image of smashed rooms is suddenly frighteningly real, and in the vision she's trapped in the building as her madman rampages. Jesus, woman, she says, get a hold of yourself. She forces herself back to the subject. Angie is waiting for reassurance that if worst comes to worst it won't be so bad. But it will be bad. Kids are sent away for that kind of offence. Kate shakes her head.

'I'm sure it won't come to that,' she says. 'Perhaps Gary *is* involved but the phone doesn't implicate Jon. You know how kids are. They send each other all kinds of stuff.'

'But if they come back to talk to Jon?'

Kate knows what Angie's asking.

'You're not obliged to mention the photos or text,' she says. 'Those would never be more than circumstantial evidence and it's up to the police to talk to Jon and find what they will. If they've reason to think there's evidence on the phone they'll get a warrant. They won't need your help.'

'Jon has probably deleted the picture,' Angie says, a statement of hope more than fact.

'All the more reason to say nothing.'

What Kate doesn't tell Angie is that if the police arrive with a warrant then they'll recover any incriminating photos and text, deleted or not, nor that they might already have such evidence from Gary's phone.

'We've forbidden him to see Gary,' Angie says. 'And Ian wants him home by seven every night until this thing is over.'

'Will he comply?'

'I doubt it. He'll see Gary for sure. We can only hope that that does some good. If Gary's feeling the pressure it may scare Jon enough to make him talk to us.'

'This is all speculation, of course,' Kate says. 'Gary may not be involved in the attack. Jon neither. We may be misreading the whole thing.'

But her sister's face, as she orders lunch, says she believes otherwise.

27

Kate declines Angie's invitation to tea. She has an appointment. They part at the station and head for their separate lines, but once Angie's out of sight Kate backtracks and descended to the Central for a Mile End train.

The knife had given her the idea. She'd sensed its power even if reason said that her lack of skills would probably render it useless if she was attacked. But the idea of arming herself had taken root. She'd resisted the foolhardy idea of placing herself on the wrong side of the law until the accumulating fear and anger of the week conspired to invent the nonsensical maxim: "Better the iniquitous survivor than the virtuous corpse." Convincing herself of the truth of this aphorism she'd called in a favour from Eddie Hazel. Eddie was a petty criminal whose son she'd rescued from a scrape two years ago and who'd told her, after she secured the boy's freedom and rehabilitation, to call him any time he could return the favour. Kate's not a big fan of illegal favours and she'd have forgotten Eddie entirely if she hadn't bumped into him six months ago in Holborn. They'd barely slowed in passing. Just a nod and smile and three words from Eddie: 'Call me! Anytime!'

So now she'd called, and asked Eddie about personal protection devices.

'A shooter? I can get you a lovely piece.'

'Not a gun. Just basic protection. A bit like those dye sprays.'

Meaning *not* like those dye sprays. *Not* like the UK's only legal weapon which, as its name suggests, will mark a guy with an indelible dye just before he kills you. Kate was talking about the other kind of spray. The kind that was as legal as a paring knife but perhaps more effective.

'You want a pepper,' Eddie advised. 'Special, like. Something with stopping power.'

Exactly. Something that would well and truly *stop* someone. A spray. Special, like.

'Leave it with me, darlin',' he'd promised. Then this morning he'd called her back.

Kate exits Mile End Station and finds a brick shoebox pub a hundred metres up the road. Eddie is waiting at a corner table. He opens a padded envelope to show her a surprisingly small canister with Chinese hieroglyphics printed over a skull watermark.

'This is not your regular stuff,' Eddie cautions her. 'Don't go tryin' it out.'

Kate thanks him and asks how his son is getting on, and they make small talk for five minutes before she grabs the packet and leaves. Pepper sprays are easy enough to get hold of, imported illegally from the USA and the Far East. But Eddie's spray, with it's unreadable hieroglyphics and death's head warning, isn't targeted at the delicate end of the market.

The can's size suggests a limited load but she's guessing that a single brief blast will leave her assailant with serious medical issues. If she uses the spray she'll have questions to answer, but if she uses it it will probably have saved her life. Her tormentor comes near her now at his peril.

It's seven p.m. and dark by the time she's back at Maida Vale, walking towards her house. She watches hedgerows and parked cars, wondering if Crane or his people are out here. But she sees nothing until she reaches her drive and discovers a figure standing at her door. She hesitates. Then the light catches his face. It's Ian.

'I was wondering where you were,' he says.

'Is everything okay?' she asks.

'Fine. Just passing. Angie asked me to check you'd got home.'

She puts the key into the lock and invites Ian in. When she closes the door they stand for an uncomfortable moment before she offers him a drink. Ian declines.

'Can't stay. Angie says this guy's getting worse.'

'Yes. More overt.'

'Have the police picked up any clues?'

'None that I know of. But they've assigned shifts to watch the house.'

Kate can't think where that lie came from. Why does she need to mislead Ian into believing she's got protection?

Ian nods and purses his lips. 'They need to stay there twenty-four hours,' he says. 'This guy is dangerous.'

And so, Kate thinks, is Eddie's spray. The can will stay close to her from now on even inside the house. If her assailant makes a move he's blinded. 'I'm sorry to hear about Jon,' she says.

Ian grimaces.

'I don't know what's happening with him. Before that imbecile Gary came along he was fine.'

'I warned Angie that Jon could be in trouble if he was involved in the incident. You should be prepared for that.'

'I am. I just don't think *Jon* is. But he wasn't involved directly, Kay, whatever happened. It's just not him. Jon wouldn't destroy someone's house. He wouldn't spray that vile stuff on the walls. It fits his friend Gary to a tee but not Jon. Did you know that Gary's father served time?'

Kate didn't, and the information doesn't dilute her suspicion that Gary is indeed the guilty party, her solicitor's training and total unfamiliarity with the youth holding back her judgement not a jot.

'Do you think Jon would listen if you talked to him?' Ian asks. 'He knows you deal with stuff like this. He needs to understand the position he's in – the risk that he could be sent away.'

'Certainty,' Kate corrects him. 'If Jon was found guilty of wrecking that house he'd receive a custodial sentence. Please God it won't come to that.'

'Please God. But I'm worried what will happen if the stuff on his phone comes out.'

'Without direct evidence the photos and text would mean little in court. At the worst they might suggest that he was on the periphery, encouraging Gary, but they don't implicate him directly in the crime.'

Ian looks at her.

'That little punk Gary knows what happened. And he dragged Jon into the mess somehow. If they interview them again I'm worried they might try to play them off one against the other.'

'As long as Jon sticks to his story, and there's no proof he was in Geraldine's house, he'll be fine.'

'I think it would really help if you could speak to him, Kay.'

There's no obvious way to refuse Ian's request, though Kate has been thinking fast since he made it. The last thing she wants is to be dragged into the affair but fact is that no reasonable grounds for refusal come to mind.

'We'll set something up this week,' she says. 'And thanks for calling, Ian. Appreciated.'

Though all she wants is for him to leave. All she wants is to lock her doors and grab something to eat and settle down with her new best friend, Skull Can.

'No problem,' he says. 'Thanks for helping with Jon. Angie and I have hit a dead end.'

He moves towards the door but as she turns to open it he plants a palm on her back.

'Really, Kay,' he says, 'keep yourself safe.'

'Of course,' she agrees.

And when I can't, Skully comes out.

But Ian is waiting, watching her, and he seems to be leaning imperceptibly in, and Kate realises suddenly that he's looking for a reciprocal sign, the subtle body language that would invite him closer. He's ready to pull her towards him. The thought hits like a shock wave and repulses her so profoundly that she steps backwards into the wall and has to hide her reaction with a hefty tug at the door.

'The world's just crazy,' she says. 'I don't know how any of us can keep safe.'

She uses the door as a shield and Ian registers the rebuff and steps quickly past to eradicate the moment. Then he's gone.

Kate locks the door behind him, stunned. What the hell was that? What was going through Ian's mind? Has she *ever* broadcast wrong signals, let him imagine that there could be anything between them, that she'd ever harbour inappropriate feelings towards him? There's always been an undercurrent, of course, and Kate has always sensed that Ian's play-flirting is never wholly play. But what just happened has stunned her.

Or did she just imagine it?

Did she read too much into their brief physical contact, sense body language that wasn't there?

She replays the contact, his words, but the moment is fading, and she can no longer say what was real and what was imagination.

Still shocked and perplexed she commences her patrol, doors and windows, upstairs and down, then takes a bath and eats. By the time she's in bed, lying in the dark with the pepper spray beside her, waiting for her phone to light up, waiting for the dead kitchen phone to ring, the incident with Ian has faded against her real problem. But no one calls. Out in the garage the car alarm stays silent.

She senses him out there, though, watching and planning, her fantasy police surveillance notwithstanding. And she lies for an hour before fatigue drops her into a troubled sleep beneath the watchful gaze of Skully, standing sentry on her bedside table.

28

Delight and disappointment. Give and take. Gain and loss. Kate is looking at the living embodiment of caprice sitting expectantly on the far side of her Dracaenas. Jerome Welland has just handed her the cash for their prospective insurance company settlement. But, of course, there's a catch.

Two catches, in fact.

First: Jerome's envelope contains cash, not a cheque, and that's going to be a problem.

Second: the cash counts out at six thousand. Ten was what they'd agreed as the minimum meaningful settlement offer. Ten was the figure she'd waved before the London Century rep. to take back to his recoveries department. The company may or may not be disposed to go after Jerome in civil court but six thousand won't be enough to decide the matter.

Six thousand, though, is too big a gesture for her simply to dismiss out of hand. Give and take. With Jerome there's always a catch. And *cash* for heaven's sake. Kate listens to the traffic on Upper Street and breathes in deeply.

'Lady, you don't know the crawling and pleading I had to do to get even that. I told you. They hate my guts.'

'Then how come they gave you anything?'

'It's a buy off. To get me the hell out of their hair. They don't want to see my face again. Take the cash, Jerome. Disappear, Jerome. See you in twenty years. They didn't even invite me for dinner. I should never have gone.'

'You had no choice. This wasn't a social visit. It was either find the money or go to jail.'

Jerome turns to look out of the window. His attention is evaporating. 'I'd rather be in jail,' he says.

'This may not be enough,' Kate says. 'Ten thousand was already on the low side. I don't think it's enough to squeeze an affidavit from London Century for your sentencing hearing.'

'They can take it or leave it. What am I supposed to do?' Jerome quits gazing at the rooftops and starts his damn squirming and bouncing again. Take it or leave it. Let someone else clear up the mess. The philosophy of someone who doesn't realise just how close he is to a world that will decide to *leave it* and drop him into the grinder. His offence is minor by the standards of the wider criminal world but if Jerome goes to jail then his narcissistic self-destructiveness will ensure he's in for a very bad experience.

'Just another four thousand, Jerome. Can you not explain to them that that's the minimum?'

'I did explain.' He goes back to watching the rooftops. 'It was like getting blood from a stone.'

'Could you ask just once more?'

'No. Not doable.' He drags his attention back. 'That's the most they'll go. They're quite happy if I go to jail.'

Happy to see their son in jail but they'd given him six thousand anyway. It makes no sense.

'Why is it cash?'

'It's what they had to hand. If they'd had two thousand that's what I'd have got. Bitches.'

'Your parents had six thousand lying round the house?'

Jerome's eyes glitter through the Dracaenas. He shrugs. Squirms and bounces.

'They probably have a million quid in their accounts,' he says. 'But they had six thousand to hand so they just shoved that in my face and pushed me out. I think it's enough. Those insurance bitches will settle.'

Kate pushes the money back into the envelope. Jerome's expertise she can do without. Confidence in miracles is something he shares with many of her clients. They see simple solutions everywhere, though the world's not sufficiently simple, apparently, that they can keep out of trouble. So Kate will talk to London Century. She's obliged to do that. But favourable words from them at Jerome's sentencing hearing are unlikely. The most she might salvage is to offer Jerome's modest payment as evidence to the magistrates of his remorse and his desire to pay his dues. That might still sway the hearing towards a lenient outcome. Whether the insurance company chase Jerome afterwards is up to them. Not her problem.

Her problem is the cash. Has Jerome really visited his parents or is Kate about to deposit monies of dubious provenance into Parfitt and Quinn's escrow?

She stands and thanks Jerome and escorts him back out.

Jerome jigs alongside her towards the waiting room. 'The crazy bitch,' he says, 'she around today?'

He's bobbing and dancing like he's badass, ready for another round with Donna, but Donna's not due in today and for a moment Kate regrets it. Wouldn't she just love to watch Jerome's bravado evaporate if the feisty Liverpudlian appeared? The mood Kate's in right now, she'd just love that.

~~~~~

It's a beautiful winter's day and Kate's new determination to take control of her working life has her pushing paperwork aside at one thirty to head out for the ten minute walk to Sharla's Kitchen.

Upper Street is bustling with traffic and workers on lunch break. She walks fast into a dazzling sun and makes the deli in nine minutes but is dismayed to find the place still busy, every table taken. She stands undecided in the doorway but then one of the window tables catches her eye and she stares in astonishment.

Hartley Tasker is sitting there with a coke and sandwich.

Before she can turn away he looks up and catches her eye and his face lights with a gaunt delight. He beckons her across and it's too late to hide, so Kate plants a smile and walks over, her stunned mind trying to fathom how Hartley has found this place. The furthest he ever walks is to the deli fifty metres from the office. But now he's here, and her secret eatery is no longer secret.

She reaches his table and half sits, maintaining her sideways stance to let him know she's not staying.

'Katie,' he says. 'Surprise.'

Surprise, hell! Hartley isn't here by chance. Hartley would no more walk half a mile to his lunch than stand in a fish and chip queue. Kate can only construe that the bastard has discovered her lunch haunt and has started coming here, waiting for the day she'd drop in. Is that what you've done, Hart? Have you found me out? Is this a lunch date?

'Amazing,' she says. 'Is this your regular place?' Going along with the pretence. Kate usually eats here two or three times a week and Hartley has never once shown up.

But he says: 'I come in from time to time.'

'Me too,' Kate smiles, continuing the pretence. 'Mostly...' and the lie flows as smoothly as syrup, 'just for takeaways.'

'Hey,' Hartley invites her, 'eat in for once. There's no rush.'

His smile is innocent but he's sensing that his game's about to be ruined, that his trips down here, the twenty minutes of foot slog each time, will have all been for nothing if Kate runs away.

Kate appraises her position. It's a fifteen minute wait whether she stands at the counter for a takeaway or eats in. Better just stay seated and make the best of it. With luck Hartley will be through and headed back to the office before her food arrives, though even as she turns the thought over she suspects it's a false hope. 'Sure,' she says, 'I'll eat in.'

A waitress appears. It's her East European girl, businesslike, eyes on her pad. Kate orders a baguette and coffee and pulls off her coat and Hartley returns to his pulled pork sandwich, shredding the meat with his teeth and devouring it like a wood chipper.

'How's your stalker thing?' he says. 'The guy still bothering you?'

'He's still around. Making calls. The police are looking for him.'

Hartley stops for a moment.

'They getting anywhere?'

'Maybe. They've not updated me.'

'But you've not seen him? He's not approached you?'

Well, I've seen a freak in a demon mask, Kate thinks, but he didn't get near me since I leapt between train carriages in a Tube tunnel. But I'm not talking about any of this, Hart. My stalker's antics aren't for my work colleagues' entertainment, least of all yours. So:

'Just the calls,' she says. 'The police are tracking them.' She shrugs. Something of nothing.

But talking of *stalkers*, Hart, how dare you follow me here, how *dare* you hijack my lunchtime retreat? It takes effort to hold her smile but Hartley is oblivious. He slurps his coke and devours his sandwich.

'Sorry to ask,' he says. 'I guess everyone's pestering you. But we don't want anything to happen to you.'

'Nothing will happen, Hart.'

Hartley puts down his sandwich and snaps one of his cards down onto the table, finds a pen and circles a number.

'This gets me anytime,' he says. 'You're in Maida Vale, right? I'm Golders Green. Ten minutes. If anything happens call that number. Anything.'

Kate takes the card and thanks him. She's not, of course, going to call the number, fuck you very much. But why did you follow me here, Hart? Are *you* stalking me?

'Wesley Leach's committal this morning,' Hartley informs her. He's back to his sandwich. 'Apparently he's sticking with Arthur.'

'Good luck to Arthur.'

'You can say that again,' Hartley concurs. 'We can all do without clients like that.' Condescending. As if we can do *without* them but a legal powerhouse like Hartley Tasker would nevertheless stand up to the breach if called upon. As if Kate – though no one could blame her – has simply found Wesley Leach too much to handle. Hartley takes another bite and chews furiously and gives Kate his opinion on Leach's chances, and Kate glances towards the counter, barely resisting looking at her watch. How long has it been? Three minutes, maybe four. At least another ten before her sandwich arrives. But where the hell's her coffee? She needs something to distract her from listening to Hartley, observing him eat.

Hartley drones on, oblivious, and Kate nods and smiles at the right places until her coffee does arrive. But her hope that Hartley will disappear after he's eaten is dashed. When he finishes his sandwich and she mentions that she'll be here a while, a covert invitation for him to feel free to walk, he smiles and says he'll hang around. He needs the damned break.

Kate smiles thinly. 'Don't we all,' she says.

Her sandwich, when it arrives, is tasteless.

29

Arthur is phlegmatic over Jerome Welland's cash deposit. He listens to Kate with the same calm temperament that sways juries in Crown Court. As a mentor Arthur can't be faulted.

It's another fine day outside. The sun mottles Arthur's face and illuminates his faint smile.

'So what do we do?' he asks. Arthur rarely dispenses solutions. He prefers to coax the right ones from his protégés.

'It's not our job to refuse the cash,' she says. 'But I don't like it. So I'll have to check it out.' Spoken as a plan of action, not a question. But it is a question. If it was truly a plan wouldn't she be in her office *implementing* it?

Arthur nods and asks what enquiries she'll make. Parfitt and Quinn's business routinely involves research ranging from phone-arounds to hiring private investigators, time and cost varying accordingly. But Kate's *plan* comprises only the first step which is to check the telephone directory and locate Jerome's parents.

'They live in Lambeth,' she says. 'If there aren't too many Wellands in that area I'll find them.'

'Will they talk to you?'

'I think I can squeeze them about whether they've funded Jerome's legal affairs.'

'And if they haven't?'

'I'll have to think about it,' Kate says, though she's already thought about it and doesn't have an answer. Does a solicitor handle client money of uncertain origin? Many would, and do. But it's not an issue that's come up at Parfitt and Quinn. So her vision is limited on this issue. For once, Arthur needs to assist with more direct tutelage.

But all he says is: 'Fine. Let's do it.' His smile holds steady.

~~~~~

Kate checks the phone directory in her lunch hour and finds that

Lambeth has dozens of Wellands and her plan for a quick ring-around over a sandwich isn't practical. She'll have to put one of the paralegals onto the job.

Damn Jerome and his tricks! He'll be billed every penny of this extra work, payable before his hearing. And it will *not* be taken from the six thousand recompense pot. Jerome either finds the extra or they *will* take the fee from the pot but return the balance to him and the insurance company negotiation will be dead. Jerome will go into his hearing absent any meaningful mitigating factor. And he can find another firm if London Century pursue him with a civil suit.

Then Kate recalls that Jerome's father is a jeweller. A "fat pig bling broker" to use Jerome's term, though she assumes the man poses as a normal jeweller. But when she searches the businesses in Lambeth she comes up blank. With nothing to lose she widens her geographical area and gets a hit. There's a Steads Jewellers operating across the river in Fulham that has a Peter Welland in its list of directors. Kate calls the shop and is handed to Peter. She introduces herself and explains that she's acting for Jerome and the man's reaction is the surprise: he's unaware, apparently, of his son's legal problems. Kate persists, dancing around the topic in a way that avoids breach of client confidentiality. The dancing mostly comprises ignoring Peter Welland's questions.

'These are just peripheral enquiries, Mr Welland.'

'Peripheral to what? Is Jerome in trouble?'

'I'm not permitted to discuss particulars. Has Jerome not talked to you?'

'Jerome never talks to us.'

'Not recently?'

'Not in the last five years.' Peter Welland pushes out an exasperated sigh. 'We never hear from him.'

Asked and answered. If Jerome hasn't talked to his parents in five years then it's highly unlikely that they've just loaned him six thousand pounds.

'What kind of trouble is Jerome in?' Peter Welland persists. 'Do we need to help?'

'I'm sorry, I can't say. This was just a peripheral consideration.'

'Just tell us. What do we need to do?'

But the call is over. Asked and answered. Kate apologises and finds a few polite words and rings off.

So...

As she'd expected.

Jerome's six K didn't come from his parents. Which means she must now take this back to Arthur, inform him that the firm is indeed likely to be holding dodgy money in escrow. But she elects for the easiest route, the coward's way out. She writes a short note and runs up to drop it onto Arthur's desk whilst he's away at lunch. The note says that she's continuing to investigate, whatever that means.

~~~~~

The week progresses over the next two days by fits and starts.

Progress of the *start* type is that earlier today, Thursday morning, Kate had received Arthur's approval to call in the firm's investigator, Mike Price, to check the provenance of Jerome Welland's six thousand pounds. Normal procedure would simply be to call Jerome back in to explain, but the result would likely be an angry tirade and a story that could be neither believed nor immediately dismissed, leaving them in a no-man's-land of further checks and accruing billable hours. The simplest route is Mike Price. For a fixed fee Mike will get a sense of whether Jerome has legitimate access to that kind of cash. Such money would certainly not be the product of honest toil but if it's not actually illegal then they're in the clear. If the cash appears dirty then Jerome's account will be debited all fees and they'll return the balance for Jerome to take elsewhere.

The *fits* side of the week's affairs is a statistical rise in the chance meetings with Hartley Tasker in the firm's kitchen. Kate hasn't forgiven Hartley for invading her lunchtime retreat at Sharla's Kitchen, and though the encounters with him in Parfitt and Quinn's kitchen may be only marginally above the two-per-week norm they nevertheless stand out – at four and counting, this week – as a significant deviation. And, incredibly, Monday's lunchtime *rendezvous* has instilled in Hart the nonsensical notion that there is common ground between them, that there might be some sharing of confidences. When they meet he's always ready with queries and comments on the subjects of Kate's problematic work cases and her even more problematic home life, Hartley presuming that when Kate needs a shoulder to cry on it might be his. Kate visits the kitchen at most twice a day but Hartley seems to have some kind of sixth sense that steers him there just minutes ahead of her visits, until it finally dawns on Kate that her *stalker* (devil's mask variety) has germinated a *stalker* (kitchen variety) desperate to hear about it. Hartley is actually nosier than Violet, who, at least, has given her space this week.

Continuing with the *fits* side of the ledger, her stalker's activities seem to have levelled out at an average of five calls per night to her silenced smartphone, and although the calls go unanswered his assault is no less effective for their having become routine.

And the chaos can't patch over the fact that she hasn't seen Zav for five nights. He returned from Brussels Tuesday and phoned with the news of a bug picked up in an airport lounge, an ailment he was loath to pass on to her, so they've agreed to defer their next meeting until tomorrow or the weekend, leaving a monster hole in her uncharacteristically long evenings. She's filled the hole with indulgent dinners and hot soaks and mindless TV, from which routine even Rache's invitation to a night out yesterday failed to deflect her.

Perhaps the dark winter streets are to blame for her stay-at-home yearning. Kate no longer sees the streets as safe, even with her pepper spray. And though Crane has phoned twice since the weekend to ask questions and repeat advice, inform her that they are still keeping an eye on the house, his assurances don't comfort.

So Kate must wait and endure and keep the pepper spray handy. And perhaps that will be enough. Perhaps it won't.

30

It's Thursday evening and Kate is feeling good.

What she's just done was risky but it's given the finger to her would-be jailer and taken back the dark streets and the park. She's gone out like she's always done and run her five miles and he hasn't come near her, which was fortunate for him because she was just itching to find out just how good a protector Skully is. But no one had approached. No one was watching. And she's regained a part of her life. She's feeling good.

Her bathroom is roasting and she's floating beneath the thick foam that tops her bath. Her legs are stretched way out and feel not the slightest twinge from the punishment they've just received. Kate rests her head and lets her body rise under the foam. She's *floating*, drifting down a magical river to a tropical sea.

She breathes out. Her body sinks. She breathes in, it rises but doesn't break the surface and she could lie here forever if she didn't have dinner to make. She closes her eyes and pictures Zav, his smile, his body pressing atop hers. In fantasies a bath is as large as you wish and there's ample room for two within the foaming cocoon.

Kate's breathing softens and she's on the verge of dozing, a blissful reward for her grit tonight. She awards herself another twenty minutes before she makes dinner.

Then a distant sound encroaches. It's like the thump of a car door. Then, after a while, a second thump.

A faint unease stirs inside her at the odd notion that the sound came from inside the house.

But bumps and bangs often sound like they're coming from inside and it says something about the state of her nerves that such fanciful nonsense now has her on edge. Relax, she tells herself. Take a night off from scaring yourself.

Then she hears the thud of a door being closed. Not exactly slammed but pushed firmly enough to register through the floor. She opens one eye and then the other and watches the tiles beyond her feet. One of her toes is peeping through the foam. She presses it against the sharp metal of the chain and strains her ears. The thud was definitely a house door, and it sounded distinctly like it was from downstairs. Her neighbours are habitually quiet as the grave, just occasional faint voices and feet on the stairs. She's never once heard their doors bang.

So which door just closed?

Kate floats silently, listening, but there's no repetition to calibrate her hearing and confirm the door as her neighbours'. The silence is broken only by the faint rasp of her toe on the chain and the drip of the tap. Contentment starts to re-surface, buoyed by her reasoning that she's heard nothing of significance.

But she can't entirely lose the tension. The silence now isn't wholly easy. She can't rid herself of the sense of something wrong. This is crazy, she tells herself. *What* is wrong? This is all in her mind. She's simply geared up for torment. Thanks to her stalker she's thriving on nonsense and gratuitous scares. She's an expert at frightening herself.

The silence extends and finally the tension does ebb to allow peace back in. That's it. Scare over. Time to pull the plug and make dinner, if she can coax her limbs into motion. But just as she's willing her legs to move she hears footsteps. And this time she's not imagining it: she's just heard the soft tread of feet on her stairs.

Dear God...

Her limbs lock rigid. The concept's an absurdity. There's no one on the stairs. She checked the doors and windows right after she came in, and she left the keys in the locks to ensure that they couldn't be unlocked from the outside. So there *can't* be anyone in the house. Her overwrought mind is distorting sounds into things they're not.

But the sound was *so* like someone coming up from downstairs.

So like it.

Kate looks at the bathroom door. It has a lock but she's not secured it. If someone was out there there'd be nothing between them but a turn of the knob. With that thought she watches the door, mesmerised by the anticipation of it swinging open. She looks for her phone and realises she's left it down in the kitchen. Oh you stupid bitch! What's the good of a phone you can't reach? And how effective is pepper spray when it's lying in a bag on the coffee table? It's taken true brilliance to get herself trapped, naked and defenceless, behind a door that needs just one little push...

She's barely breathing now in her effort to catch any further sound. The drip of the bath tap, when the next drop falls, is like crashing metal. She waits, muscles taut, heart racing, for two minutes. For three.

Then a floorboard creaks right outside the door.

And this is no trick of acoustics, no fabrication of her overwrought mind. There actually is someone on the other side of the door.

Kate stares at the doorknob, knowing that it's about to turn, that she's about to see the demon mask.

She knows with absolute certainty and absolute terror that he's there, staring through the wood, savouring her presence, smelling her fear.

Then the doorknob does indeed start to turn, ever so slowly.

Urine jets on Kate's thigh, tickling her through the cooling bath water. She should have jumped from the bath and locked the door when she first heard him but now it's too late. She needs to find a weapon, do *anything* but lie here helpless, waiting for the door to open on that demon snarl, do anything but lie helpless as he strides across. But her limbs simply won't function. She *is* helpless, able only to wait. Her heart beats the slow pulse of a funeral drum.

The doorknob stops rotating. Now the push. She watches transfixed.

But for the moment the door doesn't move.

Thirty seconds. A minute. He's waiting on the far side, savouring the moment, choosing his time.

Kate's world has contracted to that doorknob. Her heart beats another minute, then five, and still the door stays closed as the tap drips and her mind toys once again with the crazy thought that this is all hallucination. And still nothing happens. *Could* it be imagination? Is she going nuts? Is she seeing and hearing things?

Ten minutes have passed and the bath water's cooling and Kate senses suddenly that she's alone, that whoever was outside the door is gone, if there was anyone in the first place. Perhaps she really is going crazy, a thought that frightens her almost as much as the demon mask.

Then, below in her lounge, her hi-fi blasts out at a full booming volume that vibrates the floor and shakes the building. It's a track from one of her old albums, and the shuddering familiarity of the music assaults her, a rape-like obscenity that tears at her innermost self. It's the CD she'd left in her player pending rediscovery of its plastic case, an old Muse album that she'd played way too high on phones after a Friday night with Rache. But the music now is like the summons of some monstrous doppelganger roaming her house, mocking who she is, flaying her life.

The pounding music confirms that she's not going nuts. But this is worse. He's down there in her lounge and he wants her to know it.

She needs to jump from the bath and lock the door and don her discarded running gear to cover her nakedness. She needs to block her ears against the awful booming music, the malice that thumps through the fabric of her house. She should open a window and scream for help. But she can't. She's caught in her paralysis waiting for him to come back up.

She won't hear his footsteps this time. The first she'll know is when the door opens.

The album track ends and she listens, tries to sense whether he's there. Hears nothing. Then the next track kicks in and the house is pounding once again with the racket.

The resumed onslaught paralyses her while the album plays out its tracks. She's unable to function, barely able to *breathe*. The single movement she can summon is to push a tear from her cheek. Coward! she tells herself. Do something! Fight this bastard! But her body has given up. All she can do is imagine Zav, will him to turn up, unannounced, to ring her door bell. He's saved her before. He'll do it again. Or Detective Constable Crane and his posse of police vehicles. They're out there somewhere right now. If they pass the house they must hear the music. Surely an official fist will pound the door any moment. Crane's voice will call through the letterbox. She waits for *someone* to save her because she can't, absolutely *can not*, save herself.

But time passes and the music crashes on and the bathroom door stays closed. Perhaps this is his game. To keep the door between them and leave her own mind to torment her, to cow her before he steps in for the finale? The music plays and plays and the bath water is stone cold and then suddenly the last of the album tracks has faded into a stunning silence, leaving Kate shivering and weeping in her freezing bath.

173

It's the dripping tap that rouses her, finally. Without conscious decision she launches herself from the water and rushes across to lock the door then pulls on her sweat-cold tracksuit and sandals and stands dripping and shivering, clutching a pair of nail scissors as her token defence.

Silence.

Is he gone?

When she can't stand the tension any longer Kate slides back the lock and eases the door open. The landing is deserted. She tiptoes out and walks the upper floor, switching on lights. The rooms are all empty. She creeps down the stairs and checks each dark room, reaching with unbearable tension to flick the light switches, expecting a hand to shoot out and grab her wrist any moment. But no one grabs her. The house is empty. The only sign of disturbance is the array of LEDs that say her hi-fi is alive. She checks the front door. It's locked and secure. She checks the kitchen door and finds that the handle rotates. She opens it a crack then slams it shut and turns the key, baffled. She'd locked the door. She's certain of it.

But all her patrols, all her locking of doors have been for nothing. She can't stop this maniac.

Kate fumbles with her phone and calls her sister.

~~~~~

'But how?' Angie asks. She's dressed in a robe, fresh from her bed. Ian is sitting beside her, still in his day clothes. Jon, who came in right behind Kate, is slouching against a worktop eating chocolate mousse.

'I don't know,' Kate says.

'You must have missed the kitchen door.'

Her sister's face is concerned and Kate hasn't the heart, or the energy, for anger. Her house patrols miss *nothing*. The checking of doors and windows is not a routine. It's an obsession.

'Ange.' Ian touches his wife's hand. 'Kay double checks everything.' He looks at Kate.

'I checked them last night and this morning,' she confirms. 'And right after I got back from my run.'

'Might he have got in,' Ian says, 'while you were out for the run? There was no key in the front door then. Perhaps he was hiding in

174

the house when you went up for the bath.'

Was he there whilst she did her patrol? Had she locked them both in? Kate shudders.

'Wow,' Jon says. He digs at his chocolate. This is too cool. His aunt turning up a second time with this weirdo after her. Weird. 'All that patrolling round the house,' he says. 'It's like, OCD or something. He's got you checking and checking...' he licks chocolate from the spoon, 'until you start to make mistakes. You turn the key the wrong way and you've just unlocked the back door.'

'Jon!' Angie snaps, 'I'm sure your aunt knows what she's doing.' A neat reversal from her own comment ten seconds ago.

'I'm just saying,' Jon insists. 'If you're doing all these endless checks you're gonna screw up.'

Kate forces a faint smile. 'You're right,' she says. 'The way I rush round double-checking everything is a recipe for disaster. But it's just hard to believe I *unlocked* that door tonight.'

'The main thing is that this maniac got into your house again,' Ian says. 'And this time with you right there. This is escalating, Kay.'

'So you're staying here,' Angie finishes, 'until they catch him.'

'Thanks, Angie,' Kate says. 'I appreciate it. But I don't know when or if they'll catch him.'

'However long it takes,' Angie says, 'safety comes first. You can use the spare room.'

Her sister has a sofa bed in the tiny spare bedroom. Strictly emergency only. But the discomfort of the spare room is the least of Kate's tribulations. There is a bed, of course, that's far more comfortable and certainly available. Zav would have come running, bug or not, but her instinct tonight had brought her to someone who's always been there, someone she trusts absolutely.

Not that she doesn't trust Zav, but she's still reluctant to let desperation push her into his arms. Zav deserves more than that. *She* deserves more than that.

Or is it, deep down, that she *doesn't* entirely trust him? The hateful thought chills her.

'Stay as long as you need,' Ian agrees.

'You should, like, get a knife,' Jon says.

Angie's eyes are hard, furious. 'If you've nothing sensible to say,' she tells her son, 'go to bed.'

175

'I'm just saying. Aunt Kate needs protection.' He's scraping the tub, licking the chocolate.

'Knives are dangerous,' Angie says. 'And stupid.'

Dangerous and stupid: picture Kate, a few nights ago in the park, ready to slash anyone who came near. Picture Kate, now packing something even more dangerous and stupid.

'You've gotta protect yourself is what I'm saying,' Jon says. 'Like, those Taser things. They give you a quarter of a million volts. You zap a guy with one of those and he's down.'

'Thanks, Jonathan,' Kate says. 'I'll think about it.'

Meantime I'll stick to the pepper spray that's right here in my bag. The non regular type. The one with Chinese hieroglyphics. How about *Mr Skully* for cool, Jon?

Trouble is, this guy terrifies her whatever protection she carries.

'Did you phone the police?' Ian asks.

'Tomorrow. I just wanted to get here tonight.'

'Good decision,' Ian says. 'Safety first. But don't forget tomorrow. Maybe the cops will step up their investigation.'

'I'm going to insist on it,' Kate concurs. 'This guy's just a step away from confronting me directly.'

'Cool,' Jon says. 'You've a right to protection.'

Kate smiles again at her nephew, so certain of his rights, certain that *rights* are the same as *solutions*. But if rights were protection we'd all be safe and Kate would be out of a job.

'Tomorrow,' she says. 'Right now I just need some sleep.' It's barely after midnight but her need is not related to fatigue. Kate just wants to be alone, to lie in a safe, dark room with the door closed. Because she's about to cry, and in a few moments she'll be beyond holding it back. She won't be driven from her home, she says. She won't have her life hijacked. But that's what's happened and this bastard might be in her house right now. Maybe he'll sleep in her bed tonight. She's not using it.

So, stupid weak bitch that she is, she's about to weep, and she doesn't want Ian or Jon or even Angie to see how far this guy has brought her down.

176

31

'I won't be forced out of my house.'

It's Friday night. They're in a cab, heading to Zav's. They've been going round this all night.

'He's got the advantage at the moment,' Zav says. 'It might be better just to disappear for a while.'

'He'd just bide his time. This is just a hobby for him. Waiting would be part of the game.'

They've spent an evening at The Playhouse and eaten a late supper dominated by a conversation that's turned endlessly on what her tormentor is up to. Zav is ever patient. He's talked her through the situation as calmly as he elucidated on the Priestly play. He's urged caution. Stay away from this guy. Stay with *him*. She'll be safe there. And she would, of course. Or with Angie, or with Rache, whom she's not seen for ten days. But Kate won't be evicted from her own house – though since this madman can walk in and camp outside her bathroom door any time he pleases it's not exactly clear that the house *is* hers any more. But hiding isn't her way.

'The police should be watching the house,' Zav says.

She's nestled against him in the overheated cab, gazing at the lights dancing beyond the driver's silhouette.

'Apparently it's a resource issue.' Kate is quoting Crane. She'd caught him at Harrow Park this morning and they'd had ten minutes in a cubby where he'd listened earnestly but left her with the feeling that this is beyond or above him. His only proposal was to chat to his boss – his *guv'nor* – to see if they could free up some hours. Personal protection is not easy to fund unless a person has been attacked or received specific and credible threats. Kate wonders what constitutes a specific and credible threat compared, say, to being chased between Tube carriages or having a stranger camp out in your house. Her ten minutes with Crane ended with apologies and a rush back to the foyer. She'd smiled and accepted his reassurances at the front desk but had already decided on her own plan of attack. The *plan* is to return unannounced to Harrow Park on Monday morning and commence a blitzkrieg. Kate is about to become a bugbear for both Crane *and* his guv'nor. Because they are not, absolutely *not*, going to investigate her case as a murder enquiry.

Zav agrees. 'Make them sweat. If you want me to hassle them just say the word.'

'They wouldn't talk to you.'

'I've got ways,' Zav says.

She can't see his face but knows he's smiling.

'I hate to be such a drag,' she says.

His arm tightens round her. 'You're not a drag. And I've an ulterior motive for keeping you close.'

'I'm well aware of your motives.'

'What are you doing Sunday?' he says.

'Sunday?' The switch throws her.

'I've a pallet coming in and Nicholas is off. If you're still alive by then it would be good to have extra hands at the boutique.'

She elbows him. Maybe a little hard. If he feels pain he makes no sign.

'Is that your only interest in me?'

'Of course not. There are side perks.'

She elbows him again.

'Let me put it another way,' Zav says. He eases her gently and takes her face in his hands and then there's nothing gentle about his mouth as he finds hers.

~~~~~

The gentleness comes back later, in his bed, in the crush of his slow limbs, in the glide of his lips across her skin and in his passion. And his body is the ultimate bastion against the hostility of the cold streets. It's been too long since Kate had a lover, someone whose life braided hers with purpose and strength. And now Zav, stranger, rescuer and one-night delight, *is* that purpose. He enfolds her soul as he wraps her body, and it's as if she's known this unruly, twinkle-eyed, scandal-magazine-addicted proprietor of gimcracks forever. As he pushes into her body he flows into her soul through the doorway of her awakened, astonishing, uncontrollable desire. And then he calls her name and grips her shoulders, pulls down hard, and her own pleasure bursts unstoppably even as a sudden, dreadful, untimely memory of another voice calling her name, of the malice that flowed through her phone line, echoes alongside Zav's. Even as she cries out she's pushing Zav away and the moment is sullied by fear and disgust. Then she catches herself, pulls him back before he's registered her panic, and grips him desperately, eyes closed tight against the memory of the perverted phone ecstasy, its garbled obscenities. She holds Zav ferociously in utter despair that her tormentor has reached even here. Being safe is not the same as being whole. Even *here* he's taken part of her.

She lies awake afterwards as Zav sleeps with his arm across her, fighting a new fear that's creeping insidiously in, a new, chilling notion assaulting her.

Her assailant's voice, calling her name in his perverted passion, is repeating endlessly, and the harder she tries to push it away the clearer it gets. It's an obscene mockery of Zav's passion as he'd breathed her name and pushed his face into her neck as he finished, but with growing horror she realises that the voices are almost indistinguishable. But all voices in moments of passion sound the same, and it is a pointless self torture, to compare Zav's voice with her tormentor's. But the obscene, hateful thought grips her and gains strength. Two voices, the one she's come to love and the one she hates, merge and germinate and finally the horrible thought holds her prisoner: her stalker could be anyone.

Anyone.

And two weeks ago she didn't know Zav.

Stupid! she tells herself. You stupid, masochistic bitch, intent on tearing apart the most wonderful thing that has ever happened to you. Zav is *not* a stranger. Has surely never been. Perhaps he's been waiting for her forever. And if she's met a kinder, more gentle man in her life she doesn't remember it. So how for shame can she invite her malicious tormentor in to sully this man, to shred their shared contentment?

Kate's eyes are damp. She lies in the dark, raging at this soiling of her mind. To doubt Zav is monstrous. But she does doubt. It's a ludicrous and baseless doubt but there it is and it torments her like tiny shards of glass. The idea has taken over. It lies across her consciousness the way Zav's arm lies across her stomach until she feels herself shrinking away from his touch. The arm pins her down and she must press herself into the bed to lessen the contact, escape the weight. All she wants to do is hold Zav. And all she wants to do is escape from him.

The tears roll down her cheeks. How can you ruin this, she thinks? The man beside you is the best you'll ever meet. Follow your instincts. Turn to him.

But she can't. She *just can't*.

Her stalker could be *anyone*, and Kate is pinned beneath that arm, petrified and disgusted and hating herself for not fighting. After an agonising hour Zav stirs and frees her and she rolls away to open a space between them . Then lies terrified.

Follow your instincts. Turn back to him!

But she can't. And when dawn's light creeps through the window she's still lying rigid and cold at the very edge of his bed. At six o'clock she slips from under the duvet and gathers her clothes.

32

Hell is a wet winter's dawn with nowhere to go and poison in your mind. Kate can't return home and she can't face rousing Angie. She flees through a fine drizzle and seeks refuge in the Northern Line. She takes the train down to Angel. The carriage is empty but she doesn't fear stalkers or demons. The train is devoid of threat.

If only it *wasn't*. If only the communication door would swing open for that demonic snarl to announce that her stalker is *here* and not asleep in the bed she's just left. But the glass reveals only the rocking metal of the next carriage.

It's not her stalker she should fear, it's *herself*, the destructive impulse within her that relishes the bad, is afraid to embrace the good. It's her own foolishness. What will Zav think when he wakes alone? She checks her phone. No calls. He's still asleep.

She exits into the ill-lit streets of Islington and walks the quarter of a mile to Sharla's Kitchen. The café is almost empty. Kate takes a window table and orders coffee.

She'll ring Zav at eight once her nerves have steadied. She'll have seen sense by then. Zav is not her stalker. Zav is the sweet, caring guy she's starting to love and could never be anything else. But paranoia is stronger than logic. Paranoia has just paralysed her for five damned hours lying beside him, unable to disentangle Zav's innocent passion from the obscenity of her stalker's phone ecstasy.

The sky continues to lighten. Traffic and people animate the street. Caffeine drives away the fug of her lost sleep and common sense begins to surface. Of course Zav is not her stalker. It's to her absolute shame that she can think such a thing. But her fears sit obstinately within her subconscious and when Kate searches for evidence to bolster her certainty nothing substantive appears. Zav really is, when she lets truth speak, a stranger. They've spent at most a few hours together and she's no way of knowing where he is, what he does, when they're apart. But the argument swings back. So what? There's not a person in the world she *could* alibi for each occasion her assailant has phoned or donned his mask or broken into her house. And the very last person she should suspect is Zav. Trust your instincts, she tells herself. Don't play this game. Fear and despair are what this monster wants.

Her phone rings at quarter to eight. It's Zav, and she's caught out, not ready with her story.

'You should have woken me,' Zav says.

'You were out of it. I wish I could have stayed longer.'

'Me too. I dreamt you'd be there when I awoke.'

Kate laughs. 'I will be. One day.'

'This feels very good to me, Kate.'

'And to me.'

'So what was the rush?'

'Busy day,' Kate says, which would be true if only her mind could dredge up the chores she'd earmarked. 'And I'm at Angie's tonight.' She throws this in as if it's an arrangement already made, before Zav can invite her to stay with him again and force a refusal that would break her heart. But the drop in his affable voice, his disappointment, breaks it anyway.

'You sure you should be on your own today?'

'Gotta catch up. I'll be fine.'

'How about tomorrow?'

'I'll be there.'

'Pick you up?'

'I'll drive.'

'Okay. Bring a sweater. Wackyjack's is an ice box till the heaters get going.'

'Well, I'm sure we know how to solve that.'

The ersatz flirting fails to deliver any feelgood factor and when they end the call Kate is alone once more with her coffee, still unable to face her empty house, afraid to find that her stalker has been in again and afraid to find that he's *not* been in. She orders an omelette and sits for an hour with the breakfast crowd and at the end of the hour she's still lost, still can't go home. She hogs the table for the duration of another two coffees before making a decision and calling Rache. Rache is busy with Saturday trade but agrees to come out at lunch time and finally Kate's day has a purpose.

~~~~~

Rache's bright-eyed cheer is a palliative, though it's extinguished by Kate's update on her tormentor, which excludes only her nonsensical suspicions about Zav. Rache's interrogation on the latter topic draws from Kate a picture unsullied by destructive paranoia but leaves her stranded in the wash of Rache's undisguised delight at the burgeoning romance. She's relieved when they switch back to the darker subject.

'I've an idea,' Rache says. They're in a window above Oxford Street, finishing lunch, and Rache must soon rush back to work. 'I've a friend has a pad in Bermondsey. She's working in the USA for three months. I'll call her. She'll let you crash there. The bastard won't know where you are.'

Despite her determination not to be forced from her home, last night's onslaught of insidious suspicion, piled on top of the bathroom scare, makes the concept of heroic resistance less of a virtue. And with the idea of seeking refuge with Zav now blocked – a fact that might overwhelm her if she thinks about it too long – the offer of a respite in Bermondsey sounds like a godsend.

A respite. To think and plan.

'I'll talk to her,' Rache promises. 'Don't worry, girl, we'll keep you safe.' She stands and plants a kiss

And Rache, of course, will do everything in her power to keep Kate from harm. In a world dissolving into corrosive uncertainty her best friend and her sister are her two rocks. But Kate is realistic. While her tormentor is out there, watching and planning, unseen, she's not sure she *can* be protected.

~~~~~

Reluctant to arrive early at Angie's, Kate wanders the West End like a lost soul, and by five p.m. her bones are weary. The Tube to Kennington takes forever.

Angie welcomes her and keeps the interrogation about last night as short and subtle as circumstances allow. The whole family bar Jonathan is at the dinner table, though it's not an entirely happy circle. Ian is keen for an update too but beneath his concern, and despite his assurances two nights ago, Kate senses that her presence in the house is a burden. Her sister's family has a cloud of its own, and she's still to make good on her offer to talk to Jonathan.

That opportunity comes at midnight as she watches a late movie, unwilling to retire to the sofa bed until her eyes are leaden. The front door opens and Jonathan's face appears in the lounge doorway. He's ruffled and sweaty. He's a little drunk.

'Hi, Aunt Kate.'

The greeting isn't a conversation opener. Jonathan disappears before she can respond. She kills the movie and follows him through to the kitchen.

'Good night?' she asks. Jonathan pulls a carton of milk and a slice of apple pie from the fridge. 'So so,' he says. In deference to her presence he searches for a glass.

'In town?'

'Brixton.' He takes a bite from the pie and talks while he eats. 'Just jamming. We've a store room over a shop.'

'You playing any gigs yet?' Kate asks.

Jonathan chews. 'Working up,' he says. 'We'll probably do the pub circuit next year.'

It's mid February. "Next year" seems a long way off. Perhaps it's a metaphor.

'Are you in for the night?' Kate asks, glad she's not a parent, glad Jon's answer isn't critical to her either way. Jon swallows the last of the pie and downs more milk and emits something like a "yeah" through his working jaw.

Kate pours herself a glass of water and leans against the sink.

'Are they still hassling you over that teacher thing?' she says.

Jon shrugs. 'Not much.'

'Good.' She watches her nephew. 'They find who did it? Someone from the school?'

'Dunno.'

'Your mum says no one liked her.'

Another shrug. 'She's not exactly popular. She's this, like, character defect. She just hates everyone.'

'Even her students?'

'Everyone.' Jonathan plants the glass on the draining board. 'Mum's all pious and shit because she works with her but she never liked Dyno either.'

'Dyno?'

'Miss Bryson. Dyno. As in Dinosaur. Big and obsolete. None of the teachers like her. I heard Mum call her "anal" once.' He chuckles. 'Now they're all, like, she's a freakin' saint.'

'I guess what happened wasn't nice, even if she wasn't popular.'

'Yeah. It was kinda extreme. They shoulda, like, just locked her in there or something. That would have been enough.'

'Who should?'

'Whoever it was. Maybe her neighbours.'

'Was she the teacher who marked you down?'

Jonathan wants to leave. He's not comfortable with this conversation but he can't see how to escape it. 'She marked everyone down,' he says.

'But your Geography's good. I heard you did a great dissertation.'

Jonathan shrugs nonchalantly. If he holds a grudge he isn't showing it.

'She marks everyone down,' he repeats.

Kate crosses to the table and pulls a chair out and pats it and now Jonathan's *really* wishing he'd gone straight to his room. Embarrassment tautens his face but he comes over and drops heavily into the chair. They used to be friends, the two of them. He used to race to sit in her lap.

'Jon,' she says, 'your mum's worried about those texts, about that photo of your friend Gary.'

Jonathan's embarrassment shifts to hostility. He rolls his eyes and shakes his head.

'Was Gary involved in what happened to Miss Bryson?'

But Jonathan just stares at her, and Kate realises that she's pushed a little too fast. They're not friends any longer. Just relatives who meet occasionally. This youth with beer on his breath is a stranger to her.

'They shouldn't have been in my phone,' Jonathan says, finally. 'That's private stuff.'

'I guess they were just worried.'

'It's *private* stuff. You should tell them that, Aunt Kate. And there's nothing there now: I've wiped the card.'

'*Was* there something there?'

'There's nothing there.'

'If someone asks your mum and dad what they saw...'

'They saw nothing.' He stands and crosses to yank at the fridge door. Pulls out a tub of chocolate mousse and roots for a spoon.

'But you can see why they're worried,' Kate says.

Jon walks back over but doesn't sit.

'They don't know anything!' he says. 'It's like, I'm guilty automatically.'

'Is Gary guilty? Did he drag you in?'

'No one dragged me in. I'm not in anything.'

'But the police are still looking?' she asks. Meaning: have the police come to speak to *you* again? Perhaps that's the tension she felt at the dinner table tonight. But Jonathan repeats that he knows nothing. He says no one's talked to him, and Kate wonders if perhaps the police are really *not* interested in her nephew despite the school's insinuation. But there's more in Jon's demeanour than simple irritation. He's nervous. She's seen that defensiveness in a hundred clients.

'You should get that knife,' Jonathan says.

Kate snaps back.

'For protection,' he says. 'If he's breaking into your house he might come after you.'

Kate smiles.

'It won't come to that. I'm keeping out of his way.'

'You still need protection.'

'I suppose so. But we're not allowed to carry knives.'

Any more than you're allowed to carry pepper spray with Chinese hieroglyphics. She could pull the can out of her bag right now and that would be really "cool" to Jonathan.

'You shouldn't underestimate him, is what I mean,' Jon's saying.

Kate smiles again. 'Thank you, Jon,'

Jonathan smiles back then turns to take his mousse upstairs. His smile lingers in her vision.

~~~~~

Angie feeds Kate a huge breakfast before she sets off for Camden. The day is bright and the night's sleep has lifted the cloak of fatigue and fear and when she reaches the Stables Zav's cheer and industry mock her fears. When she'd called in at home to shower and change and pick up her car even the house held no sense of threat, no sign that anyone had been in. Maybe she really had left the kitchen door unlocked on Thursday night. Maybe he can't get in now. In the buzz of Wackyjack's her fears evaporate and hope returns as Zav's smile enfolds her once more.

The boutique is manic. The pallet must be brought up and unloaded in the back and customers must be watched and advised and cajoled, and sales must be rung through. In the few quiet moments, Kate and Zav stand close, each signalling their desire, and Kate's fears have faded to an abstract shadow. Her stalker could be anyone in the whole damn world *except* this man. The day flies and at the end of it the takings are an eye-opener. Zav is working a gold mine.

At five they close up and when Zav offers food in lieu of wages Kate follows his Ducato up to Haverstock Hill.

Dinner is a homemade lasagne that bloats her mercilessly as self control is subjugated by Zav's culinary skills. He clearly spent as much time a decade ago in the kitchen with his Italian girlfriend as in the sack. When she comments on this Zav grins. 'I learn fast,' he says.

'In the kitchen or in bed?'

'Both.'

'So who was the tutor in bed?'

The dishes are cleared and they're on the sofa with a nightcap and the night has closed in to this warm, sensual moment. But as Zav's mouth finds hers she's utterly dismayed to sense a returning shadow. For barely a second she lets the fear in and that's all it takes. She tenses under Zav's slow touch. She wants him. She's aching with desire for him. But she can't imagine lying beside him tonight, wondering who he really is. She wants him but it must be good. Must *only* be good. Gently, firmly, she lifts his hand away.

'Better go,' she says. 'Angie's expecting me.'

'Phone her. Stay over.'

'Better not. She's worrying herself to death about me. I don't want her lying awake.'

Zav strokes her cheek. His eyes dance with hers.

'Of course,' he says. 'We're all worried.' But his eyes are asking her why she's fleeing him, going back out into the night when safety is here. His eyes have the faintest hurt and they shame Kate. She touches his cheek but wonders whose cheek she's touching.

~~~~~

She lets the engine warm and calls Angie to apologise and announce that she's had second thoughts: she'll go home. Angie protests but Kate promises to be careful, to check her doors and windows, and to phone if anything's amiss. The truth is that the thought of sitting late at Angie's waiting for the moment she can head for the sofa bed is more than she can face. She'll risk her own house this one last time. And tomorrow, if Rache makes good, she'll cart her stuff to Bermondsey.

She leaves her car on the street to avoid the shadows of her garage and opens her front door. The house is quiet.

She switches on lights and, pepper spray in hand, completes her patrol, checking windows and doors and hiding places. Then she manoeuvres a hallway dresser against the front door and de-plumbs the dishwasher to drag it over and block her back door. The cellar door is still jammed by her hall table. If anyone has materialised down there they'll have to fight their way out.

The tension eases with each reinforcement of her castle but the anger at her flight from Zav has grown to a cold fury.

She'll talk to Crane tomorrow. She'll *demand* they go after this bastard. This is a crime in progress and it's their job to investigate. She isn't living this non-life. She won't lose Zav.

She hits her bed at midnight, resisting the urge to make a final patrol, dismissing the notion that the hall dresser and the dishwasher are not heavy enough, that somehow her tormentor will, like a will-o'-the-wisp, pass by all defences and materialise right here in this bedroom. She lies awake for an hour, fighting conflicting impulses, before fatigue wins out and drops her into a fitful sleep.

33

Kate wakes at seven, facing a morning schedule squeezed by the need to call in at Harrow Park Police Station.

The prospect of forcing the police to move into gear puts things on a businesslike footing that helps control her fear. And tomorrow's move to Rache's Bermondsey hideaway will get her clear of this bastard's clutches, perhaps bring a more objective view of her situation.

Clear of his clutches is, of course, a joke. She could live the rest of her life in Bermondsey, covering her trail home from work each day, frightened of every shadow, suspecting everyone, even poor Zav. Precisely how *clear* of this maniac's clutches is that?

As she gathers the mail from behind her door she spots a white envelope with a handwritten address reminiscent of the Valentine's card and her mood drops.

She goes through and opens it.

There's a single sheet inside, a message in blue ink.

> *Kate,*
> *Enjoyed our time Thursday.*
> *Again soon, when you're not out whoring.*
> *Love the album!*
> *Always close.*
> *XXX*

In an instant the *businesslike footing* of her situation evaporates, and Kate realises she's about to weep. But she resists. Refuses to break down. He won't reduce her to a blubbering weakling. You knew he wasn't going away, you silly bitch. Dear God, he was in your house four nights ago. What's a letter in comparison?

What the letter *is* is a material reminder, something she can touch, something that solidifies their foul relationship and draws his presence right here into her kitchen. *Always close.* Kate stymies the tears and jams the letter back into its envelope and drops it into her bag, and the businesslike approach returns. The letter will be Exhibit A for this morning's chat with Crane, hard evidence of her tormentor's actions. And from now on Kate is a forwarding service. Letters and cards all go straight to Harrow Park. Write to the police, you bastard!

When she walks into the police station the original sergeant, Miller, is guarding the counter, bright eyed with Monday morning bonhomie. He recognises her but can't quite recall why she was here previously, which gives him the rationale to interrogate her from scratch. But Kate hasn't the time or patience. She tells Miller she's got an appointment with Crane, a straight lie. Miller glares suspiciously but picks up the phone and Crane, thank God, appears and invites her towards the lift. As the lift doors open the fat detective from her earlier visit comes bowling out with a consort and almost flattens them. His shoulder catches Crane and knocks him aside with barely a hand raised in apology as he blasts on out. Crane grins at Kate and shakes his head but she's not in the mood. The Met should either put their coppers on diets or teach them manners. The fat guy is obviously a hotshot Baloo in this nick, which explains why he's been exempted the self-improvement courses, but if he ever barges into Kate he'll know about it.

They traverse the office to the same cubby as before where Crane apologises that he's only got a few minutes and asks what's happened. Kate hands over the letter, which is the only new thing since Friday apart from the corrosive assault of her own intellect. But she's about to flee her home and this criminal will have beaten her unless the police get their fingers out. She conveys to Crane, via her brusque demand for an update, that the rules have changed. She's going to be a regular here. Crane's easiest route will now be to work with her and actually *chase* this guy. Crane hears her out then goes to bring over an older guy whom he introduces as DI Andy Heldt. Heldt gives her a brief handshake and sits to read the letter.

'Wasn't there another letter? Some calls?'

'A card,' she corrects him. 'And a few calls.'

Heldt puts the letter down. 'So, you believe this person is stalking you?'

Kate looks at him. Then glances at Crane but he's watching Heldt.

She takes a breath.

'The problem's a little more serious than that,' she says. 'DC Crane has the details.'

'Quite,' says Heldt. 'DC Crane has briefed me fully. I asked him to keep an eye on things.' He smiles at Kate.

'Of course you did,' Kate says, wondering how the hostility in her voice is helping. But the condescension in Heldt's manner is clear. This is not a priority for Crane's guv'nor.

'Have we picked up anything?' Heldt asks Crane.

'Nothing, sir. We've had a few cars drive past Ms Walker's house and I've put in a few hours but we've not spotted anyone. We could pull some turns. I could manage a couple of lates with Alan. And Theresa's back in tomorrow.'

Heldt flaps his hand and cuts Crane off. He looks at the letter again.

'It's always the same story,' he says. 'Never the resources.' He looks at Kate. 'Complaints about stalkers are very common. But it's easier to act if the suspect is known.'

'That doesn't mean,' Kate says, 'that where he's not known you do nothing.'

'Not at all. We prosecuted twenty cases here last year. But I hope you understand the pressures. In this instance, apart from the letter and nuisance calls there have been no specific threats or approaches, no assaults.'

Holy fucking *mother*, Kate thinks. *Nuisance* calls are the things marketing cowboys make. 'He's broken into my house,' she tells Heldt. 'He's slept in my bed. He's stood outside my bathroom door whilst I was trapped naked inside. Is that the kind of *nuisance* you're talking about?'

Heldt stays impassive. Anger doesn't impress. *Easy*, Kate tells herself.

'There's no damage to the house?' Heldt says. 'No evidence of a break in?'

'He appears to have some locksmith's capabilities.'

'Or a key?'

'I've had the locks changed. He's still got in.'

'But he's not left any evidence?'

'He's moved things about, exchanged light bulbs for duds, left my bed soiled. And he's entertained himself with my hi-fi while I was in the bath. You mean that kind of evidence? Or are you asking whether I'm imagining it all?'

'I'm considering all possibilities,' Heldt says. 'But I'm puzzled that he's left no tangible evidence other than what you yourself can observe.'

Kate says nothing, afraid of what might come out, while her mind adjusts to the new situation. She's come here to prod the police, to get them to focus and tell her what they plan to do. But DI Heldt has her on the defence. He's not even convinced this is real.

'What evidence would you like?' Kate asks. 'A body?'

Heldt's calm expression doesn't change.

'Have you considered whether it's someone you know?' he says.

'It's not.'

'...because nine times out of ten a victim at least recognises their stalker. Seven out of ten they know his name.'

'Well I'm the *one* out of ten, Inspector. I don't know who the hell this person is but he's dangerous. How many stalkers break into houses? How many chase their victims between carriages on the Tube?' She takes a breath. 'I need you take this seriously, Inspector,' she says. She's waiting for Crane to back her up, to expand on his earlier proposals for stepping up the surveillance and tracking the phone calls, but DI Heldt has turned him to stone. He's standing back, silent. Heldt is the guy she must convince.

But Heldt looks at his watch and stands to leave.

'We'll review your case,' he says. 'We don't take *any* stalker lightly, Ms Walker. But this guy's not accosted you directly and he's left no material evidence bar this letter and card. And it's a puzzle how he'd get in and out of your house so freely. So let's just see how it goes. If anything else happens bring it straight in, and if you do think of a name bring that in too. If you feel threatened then perhaps a move to alternative accommodation would be in order.'

'I'm already doing that. I'll be in hiding until you can catch this bastard.'

'Good. That's best.'

'No,' Kate says. 'It's not good. It's not best. There's a very real threat against me and the response from this nick is inadequate.'

'Please,' Heldt says. He lifts a placating – a patronising – palm. 'Be assured we're taking this very seriously.'

Kate glares at him and sees a bureaucratic fool juggling resource against workload and imagining that that's what defines a policeman's job. Despite his platitudes Heldt hasn't shown the least awareness that she's brought him a crime in progress, one that's set to end badly. Heldt takes her tight-lipped silence as concurrence. 'DC Crane will be in touch,' he says. 'He'll let you know what we're doing. We do have some options as soon as we free up a few hours.'

Heldt turns to Crane. 'Keep Ms Walker in the picture,' he says. 'Thank you for coming in,' he tells Kate.

He walks away. Crane hesitates, embarrassed, bereft of reassurances. He's just the junior guy. Kate is tempted to take it out on the young policeman but holds back. There's no point antagonising Crane. When she speaks to him next she'll wheedle the name of his Superintendent from him. Maybe *he'll* have the experience and clout to prod Heldt, or to steer round him. Because she knows Heldt isn't going to prevent the approaching disaster.

~~~~~

By ten thirty the morning has sunk further.

Kate is standing in the annex of Highbury Corner Magistrates' Court willing the schedule to slip so that Donna Jordan might still get here. She should have reported half an hour ago but hasn't shown. Her hearing is a little down the list – sixth on the morning's schedule – but the first four have raced through in little more than five minutes apiece as Kate made repeated calls to the wayward girl. After all her efforts to get Donna her deal this is her thanks. Yvonne Hughes, the CPS prosecutor, has acquiesced in the face of victim Charles Porter's affidavit admitting attempted assault (attempted *rape*), and has taken the pragmatic route of allowing Donna to plead guilty to ABH where she'll argue fear for life and will proffer her ongoing attendance in addiction therapy as evidence of a new straight and narrow. They should be home and dry in terms of a non-custodial sentence, and within reasonable expectation, even, of a summary fine, for what is by no stretch of the imagination a minor offence. But if Donna doesn't show up in the next few minutes any mood of exculpation will evaporate. The court will issue an arrest warrant.

Kate tries again. Donna's phone is still off. She kills the line and curses. Damn you, you stupid girl. And Damn Heldt and damn Crane. When Kate is through killing herself with unappreciated efforts to keep miscreants out of jail, when she's through salvaging other people's wrecks, she must rush off and hide from her *own* miscreant who has come precisely *this* close to a direct assault on her, *this* close to unleashing who knows what urges, and Kate could be lucky, very lucky, to escape with only the damage suffered by Donna Jordan's victim. Kate pictures another day, another court annex, a public defence solicitor waiting for his client to be escorted up for a committal hearing. The schedule will still be running late and the clerk will still be juggling the list and the magistrates will still have an eye on their morning break as Kate's stalker is walked into court to plead guilty to murder.

Damn you, damn you *all,* Kate thinks.

The next hearing stretches out, takes them to near eleven a.m., but it's not enough, finally, to magic up Donna. The doors open and the usher nods and as Kate and Yvonne Hughes walk in together the despair on Yvonne's face is perhaps genuine. There are three magistrates in attendance and Kate absolutely *knew* that one of them would be Dennis Brigdon, that she'd have to address an adjournment plea to the one member of this court whose ignorance of law is matched only by his gratification by its power. Brigdon is the last person to look favourably on no-shows, the first to remember such disrespect when the hearing does continue. Kate needs only an adjournment over lunch so she can drag the stupid girl in, but if Yvonne's not available this afternoon – and so far she's stayed tight-lipped – or if Brigdon is so minded, Kate's request will trigger only the issue of a warrant for Donna's arrest and committal, and an assured hardening of the Court's disposition.

Kate pulls herself together and smiles briefly at Yvonne, an exchange of "tell me about its" that is not reciprocated. Then she faces the bench and looks squarely at JP Brigdon as she draws from a reserve of humility and patience that's all but depleted to give the court the bad news.

~~~~~

Donna shares an address with her girlfriend Georgie over in Queen's Park, north of the canal. The new-century redevelopments to the south have barely touched this side of the water and the cab drops Kate alongside a heap of uncollected refuse sacks in a run-down street of struggling family businesses and boarded up shops. Kate asks the cabby to wait. If Donna's here she'll bring her straight out and keep hold of her until the rescheduled hearing. 'Five minutes,' the cabby says, though he'll probably not give her even that.

The address is a flat above a dry cleaners in a terrace overlooking the canal. Kate climbs the stairs and is astonished at the turn of the first landing to see the fat detective from Harrow Park rolling down towards her in his crumpled suit. His over-bright yellow tie hangs disembodied in the dim light.

The detective is surprised too. He stops on the landing, blocking her way, and his face folds into a bulldog's frown of recognition. So he *was* awake when he shouldered Crane aside this morning. And he's wondering why she's here. Then in a moment of stunned apprehension Kate realises that their meeting is no coincidence.

The detective jabs a thumb over his shoulder.

'You going up to 3-b?'

Kate's blood chills. 'Yes,' she says.

'Donna Jordan?'

Her blood has all but stopped. She looks at the detective in the gloom of the stairs.

'What's your connection?' he asks.

'I'm her solicitor.'

The detective cocks his head and raises his bushy eyebrows.

'House calls? That's a nice service. Do you bill for travel?'

'I don't discuss client billing.'

'I suppose not. What's the reason for this visit?'

Kate should tell him that *that's* none of his business either but a cold fear tells her it is. She shrugs, law officer to law officer.

'My client's late for a court hearing. I've three magistrates and a CPS lawyer waiting for her.'

The detective's eyebrows rise further. 'Have you now?' he says.

Something in his tone, in the way he's watching her, deepens Kate's fear. She feels an absolute dread.

The detective's face relaxes. Cracks into a smile.

'What's Ms Jordan charged with?' he says.

But Kate isn't going to discuss that. If the fat detective has business with her he can spit it out. She asks her own question but he ignores it. Instead he says: 'Tell your magistrates not to hurry their lunch.'

Kate's blood turns to ice. Finally the detective sees something in her face and his own face changes.

'I'm sorry,' he tells her. 'Ms Jordan's dead.'

The words leave Kate's ears ringing. The detective speaks again but his words are mush. Dear God! Donna! Feisty, foolish, bittersweet Donna! Kate had allowed her ten years of burning and fading before she met the wrong person or the wrong drug or simply the wrong dose of everything that life was throwing at her. But not here. Not today. Kate's not ready to believe that Donna's already gone. Pain clamps her chest.

'How?' she whispers.

'She was attacked in the early hours. Beaten about the head. Multiple stab wounds. They took her to St Mary's but they couldn't revive her.'

'Where did it happen?'

The detective angles his head. 'Just over the bridge.'

Kate's eyes close. When she opens them the stairwell is darker. 'Was it a client?' she asks.

'We don't know,' the cop says. 'What was her hearing about?'

'She's been charged with assaulting a client.'

'What kind of assault?'

'She used a knife.'

'That how she usually handled business?'

'The man was trying to rape her. He'd hired her believing she was underage and got violent when he was disabused.'

'I see. I'd like to stop by and get some details. Of him and of any other of Ms Jordan's legal adversaries.'

He hands her a card. Detective Inspector Frank Feather, Harrow Park CID. Kate fishes out a card of her own. Her hand is shaking. She looks up the stairs. 'Is Georgina there?'

'She is.'

Feather repeats that he'll need to talk to her then pushes past her and on down the stairs and Kate stands frozen, not sure which way to go. Going up seems pointless but sneaking away would be shabby.

Georgie deserves at least a word. She takes a breath and climbs the rest of the flight.

Georgie opens the door and her plain, motherly face is so collapsed in misery she doesn't recognise Kate. Senses only another official presence, maybe one of Feather's colleagues. Kate reminds her who she is and tells Georgie how sorry she is. Georgie blinks and invites Kate into a dingy lounge then subsides onto her sofa and weeps. The pain cuts through Kate.

'If there's anything I can do...' she says. Georgie's head is down. She's weeping into her hands and saying 'Jesus!' over and over. Detective Feather has just exploded a bomb in here. His visit has blown apart everything that matters to this woman. Kate pictures Angie, Rache, Zav similarly broken and weeping over *her*. She shakes the image away and tells Georgie again that she's sorry. But she doesn't know this woman, doesn't know what to say. Her presence here is an intrusion. She lays a card on the sofa beside her. 'In case there's anything,' she says, feeling instantly cheap, as if she's touting for business. She finds a pen and squats and writes on the reverse of the card: "Call anytime. Kate". She leaves the card and goes out.

Her legs barely get her back down the stairs.

Her cab, predictably, is gone so Kate walks up the ramp to the bridge and crosses the canal. The path brings her into a quiet street of nineties redevelopment, brick and concrete apartments and clean pavements. A hundred metres down she sees a cluster of police vehicles and walks towards a taped-off side road. The side road is bounded on one side by a small park and on the other by a Catholic church, Our Lady Of The Holy Souls. The church is a modern brick building with a heavy stone arch over its street doorway. On the steps below the arch white-suited figures are inspecting Donna's final stop in this world. Feather and a female detective are there, head-to-head. Feather is gesticulating, pushing with his hands towards the doors, acting out movements. There are just a dozen onlookers. The crime scene is old. Interest has faded. There's nothing to see but a bright empty street, and any sense of what happened by those doors last night is gone.

Feather's gesticulations throw out questions but the day has no answers. And when they find the answers Donna will still be gone, as if she never existed. All that's left are Georgie's tears.

34

Kate stands at her window watching Upper Street as she calls Highbury Corner reception. No point wasting their time this afternoon.

A shower has passed, leaving traffic spray, bobbing umbrellas and blinding roof slates. The call is unanswered. The justice system is on lunch hour.

She tries Yvonne Hughes, the prosecutor. Yvonne picks up and listens to Kate's news then thanks her and says she's sorry, and perhaps even means it. Arthur was sorry too, when she told him fifteen minutes ago. Kate's not quite sure whom Arthur's sorrow was directed towards. Donna isn't her *daughter*, for Chrissakes. But something in her face had drawn Arthur to suggest that she take the afternoon off, which Kate declined. Of course Kate cared about Donna. She tried to help her. But she knew it was futile. She knew what the end would be. Things have just run their course. A little early but there was never anything Kate could do.

She wonders how it happened. A client Donna picked up over in Kensal Town? Or just a random thing, the bad guy she was always destined to meet? Was Donna just in the wrong place at the wrong time? Kate smiles at the irony. Unavailable in court to face prosecution for assault on one violent man due to a priority appointment at the morgue virtue of another.

Beaten, the detective had said; multiple stab wounds. What were Donna's final moments? Fear, or fiery anger? Was she drunk? Off her mind on drugs? Perhaps not: Donna had assured Kate she'd be bright and early this morning for her court appearance. A skirmish which in the end turned out to be not so important. Take the afternoon off, Arthur said. Go home. Violet will reschedule your diary. Perhaps Kate would have taken his advice if she'd had a home to go to. She cuts the line. Turns from the window and walks back to her desk.

In the event, her diary is rescheduled anyway because at three fifteen Violet buzzes the news that DI Feather is here. He comes through and almost fills the room with his rumpled suit and luminescent tie. He shakes her hand briefly and drags a chair to a central position before her desk where he sits and eases the Dracaenas further apart to improve his view.

'Is this convenient?' Feather says. His eyes bore into her.

'It's fine, Inspector.'

'Good. Now with your client being dead I assume we're not going to dance around confidentiality issues. If there's anything you know that can help catch her killer then disclosure will be in your client's interests, wouldn't you agree?'

'Within limits.' Kate has already discussed this with Arthur. In principle the lurid details within Donna's files, her history and present activities assembled in defence of her drink and drugs charges and two earlier assaults, should remain confidential to protect her family. But the confidentiality rule protects first the client, and any extension to protect family and associates is subject to discretion. Which permits Kate to decide whether the grotesque family sketched within Donna's case notes are worthy of protection. The only person who might realistically be hurt by disclosure of Donna's affairs is her partner Georgie, and there are things she'll hold back for this woman's sake, things unlikely to be relevant to DI Feather's investigation.

The details related to Donna's assaulted client Charles Porter were covered by the agreement to keep the affair under wraps in return for Porter's truthfulness and cooperation at Donna's hearing. But since the hearing will no longer go ahead Kate has leeway with what she gives Feather, and she decides that the man's details are justifiable fodder. If Porter gets dragged in, so be it. The solution to Donna's killing, though, won't be found in the girl's legal files, an opinion she gives Feather.

'Doubtless,' he says. 'If we hadn't chanced to meet, Ms Walker, it would have been a while before we got round to digging after this stuff. But the assaulted client interests me.'

'Call me Kate,' she says.

Feather humours her. 'Kate,' he says. 'Tell me about that case.'

Kate lists the facts of Donna's ruse about her age that snared Porter, of Porter's realisation that he'd been had and his refusal to pay for services demanded, of Donna's use of the knife when he assaulted her. She tells the story straight, dispenses with the nuances she'd rehearsed for this morning's trial, the implication that Donna was an innocent victim forced to defend herself. The facts can speak for themselves. Let Feather make what he will of the affair. Kate doesn't believe that Porter tracked Donna down and killed her and guesses that Feather doesn't believe it either. He's just covering possibilities.

'Does Porter have any convictions?'

'None. Though he's probably assaulted girls before. He just got unlucky this time.'

Feather shifts and his chair creaks.

'What other trouble has Donna been in?' he asks.

Kate smiles. 'The list is endless. She's had troubles since she was a kid. We've represented her four times. Four and a half, in fact: I bailed her out of a night in the cells a couple of weeks ago. That one's not on our books.'

'How come?'

'Not worth the paperwork. Just an hour or so one evening.'

'Pro bono? Admirable.'

'We're not all sharks.'

Feather watches her through the Dracaenas. His eyes have a fierce light. Then he sits back and crosses his arms over his tie. The jacket strains and the chair creaks ominously.

'Did Donna tell you about her habits? People she knew? Places?'

'Nothing from her immediate past. I didn't even know she had a partner until I went to bail her.'

'Georgina.'

'Yes.'

'Are they close?'

'It looked that way. Georgina was furious at Donna for ending up in custody but it was clear that her instinct was to protect her.'

'And you've no knowledge of other contacts? Work or personal?'

'I'm her solicitor, Inspector. Not a confidante.'

'But she talked to you.'

'Her drug and alcohol problems were part of her troubles. We invariably touched on those things. I persuaded her into addiction treatment. But she was always selective with what she gave me. I don't know who her friends are or the places she hung out.'

'You mentioned the guy Parish. Her pimp.'

'He picked her up when she first arrived from Liverpool. She was his girlfriend for a while but it's just business between them now. She pays him off for some kind of protection.'

'She ever hint that Parish slapped her around?'

'Barest details. Parish would get heavy handed from time to time. He's the archetypal pimp. It's amazing how these girls always home in on the type.'

Feather returns a smile but isn't inclined to discuss street girl psychology. 'The fight in here,' he says. 'What was that about?'

The question catches Kate out. How in hell does Feather know about Donna's scrap with Jerome? The detective waits, enjoying his moment.

'You work fast,' Kate says.

A faint movement of Feather's shoulders, a tightening of his crossed arms.

'Just something we picked up,' he says. He releases one of his arms and circles a podgy finger. 'Chit-chat,' he says.

Chit-chat be damned! Who the hell is telling tales out there? Was Violet so desperate to poke her nose in that she let the detective draw her into gossip? She'll burn the bitch's pants if that's the case. Feather picks up on Kate's irritation.

'I chatted to a colleague of yours,' he explains. 'He gave me a few impressions. I understand Donna was well known in the firm.'

A colleague.

There's only one colleague who'd shoot his mouth off to a visiting policeman. Hartley. Just the guy for a smart detective to corner. Mr Ethical Piety would never divulge an iota of confidential client information but a set-to in Kate's office would be just the tittle tattle to exchange with a copper here on murder business. Hartley must have spotted Feather checking in and couldn't resist offering assistance.

'Donna's temperament got the upper hand, one time,' Kate admits. 'She had an altercation with another client. It was a flash in the pan. There's no connection with your investigation.'

'Did she know this client?'

'No. They met right here.'

201

'What was the fight about?'

'Nothing. A clash of temperaments.'

'A male client?'

'Yes.'

'He start it?'

'He was as much to blame as she was. But Donna finished it. She knocked him out of his chair.'

'This chair?' Feather looks down.

'That chair, Inspector. But we sorted it out and that was the end of it.'

'Was the guy threatening Donna?'

'No. It was just an exchange of words. The client can be a little annoying, even to me. He managed to rub Donna up the wrong way.'

'Did he retaliate? After she knocked him from the chair?'

'No. He was stunned. Donna can – could – be quite scary.'

'What's his name?'

'Jerome Welland.'

'What was he here for?'

'I can't discuss that, Inspector.'

Feather smiles. 'Is your assessment of Mr Welland's character, his behaviour, part of your confidential information?'

'No. I can talk about that. Mr Welland has a certain adversarial attitude. He doesn't have a high opinion of people. He directed that opinion towards Donna and met his match.'

Feather rises suddenly and crosses to the window to stare out at the street, hands jabbed into his trouser pockets.

'So Welland didn't fight back. Not a strong guy.'

'Not a strong character. Persecution complexes aren't associated with strength. Mr Welland tends to shrink from uncomfortable issues.'

'Did he get angry later?'

'Perhaps,' Kate says. 'He's inclined to brood.'

Feather walks back and peers down from above the plants.

'I'd appreciate the contact details for Mr Welland and Mr Porter,' he says.

'Fine. I suppose you've got to eliminate all possibilities.'

'Exactly,' Feather says.

'As long as you get the killer. Donna didn't have a great future but no one had the right to take it away.'

'My feelings too,' says Feather, and Kate sees that he means it. He wants to catch whoever left Donna bleeding on those church steps, whoever they are, whatever she was. Her death actually matters to the fat detective. Kate ups her opinion of him. He may be an ill-mannered slob but he cares, and that's something they both share.

Feather reaches out and moves the Dracaena pots back where he found them whilst she writes out Jerome's and Charles Porter's contact details. Then he tells her he'd like a full list of Donna's previous tangles – offences, verdicts, adversaries. Everything that's permitted by confidentiality considerations. At her earliest convenience. Then he snatches Jerome's and Porter's details and is gone.

~~~~~

Kate muddles her way through two client appointments and then hits a late afternoon lull. She takes Donna's case folder from her briefcase and consigns it to the cabinet where it might hide indefinitely in denial of it's subject's new-found indifference to the workings of the law.

At four thirty Rache calls with news that her friend has okayed the Bermondsey apartment. She offers to meet Kate and help pick stuff up from her house. Better than Kate going there alone. Who knows, this guy could be waiting for her. They agree to meet at a café on Elgin Avenue and Kate thanks her friend profusely. 'You're a life saver,' she says.

'Just doing my job,' Rache says. 'You sound down, Kate. Don't let this guy get to you.'

Kate *is* down, but her stalker has faded today behind the vista of the police tape by the church doorway. People like Donna are watching over their shoulders their whole life, evading predators everywhere. For them it's the natural order. In the end, though, even street-savvy Donna couldn't protect herself.

Kate has barely ended the call when Zav rings, asking what they're doing tonight. Kate reacts with a story about an arrangement with Rache and deflects further discussion by proposing a meal out tomorrow. She doesn't mention the Bermondsey move, which feels truly bad. But if she's to have peace of mind the hideaway must be a secret from everyone except Rache, though how long she'll be able to keep up the pretence that she's still living at her house she can't say. But no one must know about Bermondsey. Innocent and guilty alike. That's the point of the move. She can't even tell Angie, because if Angie knows then how many others will know? Or is she thinking of someone specific? Dear God, is she hiding from *Ian?* Or from her *nephew?* And how long can she keep her secret from Zav when all she wants to do is run to him? That thought brings a new fear: that when this is over, when she's through deceiving Zav, treating him as a suspect, there might be nothing left between them.

She's packing to leave when Violet connects another call. It's Mike Price the firm's P.I.

'Got something,' he says, and Kate's heart sinks. This is about Jerome Welland's six thousand cash presently locked in Violet's safe for transfer to the firm's escrow account. What she needed to hear was that Mike had *nothing*, no reason to eschew the cash. But it's not to be. Kate takes a breath.

'Not good?'

'Not good.' Price's voice is gravel. Kate used to think he was putting it on for the job but his sandpapered vocal chords are as natural as his frown.

Mike describes what he's found and *not good* really doesn't cover it.

To him it's just detail. A job done.

To Kate it's a bombshell in a day already foundering. She shrinks in her chair.

'Are you still there?' Mike asks.

She's not sure.

35

The day has worn her out utterly. Kate quits work at five forty-five desiring only a hot meal and a bath but facing the prospect, instead, of a hasty packing and a drive across town, the setting down of her bags in an empty apartment.

Violet is still at her desk and looks ready with questions but Kate delivers a curt "Goodnight" and steps smartly past and out onto the street. The freezing air outside is a palliative, invigorating her as she walks swiftly to the Tube, distracting her from the grit that's worked into the cogwheels of her life.

She rides the packed train, watching faces withdrawn behind thoughts of tea and telly, credit limits and deceptions and desires. She catches her own reflection in the glass but that face is unreadable.

At Maida Vale she exits the station and walks up Elgin to the café where she'll meet Rache. She peers in through the window but Rache is not there. She's fifteen minutes early and Rache will probably be fifteen minutes late. Kate hesitates for a moment then turns towards home. She'll take the risk, one last time. By the time Rache arrives at the café she'll be packed and ready to go. She'll drive round and pick her up.

Her street is alive but dark. Cars chug past with clouding exhausts. Workers trudge homewards. At her driveway Kate suppresses yet again the sense of someone watching. Was Donna afraid as she walked towards that church? Was her own stalker following? The thought is fleeting, layered on the backdrop of Kate's fears as she roots for her key.

She lets herself in and reaches for the light switch, then as she turns to close the door a figure steps from behind it.

The shock is a searing thunderbolt that stuns her utterly, stops her dead with a scream rising in her throat. She barely has time to register the face, to give the malicious campaign, the myriad rancorous misdeeds, finally, an identity – and see that it could never have been anyone else – before he steps back and points something and there's a bang and wired darts hit her chest and extinguish her scream in the agonising crackle of fifty thousand volts. Her nerves shatter. Her legs fold.

She sits on the floor and is barely aware, a few moments later, of being turned, of the door closing. Her vision has shattered into black and violet shards that whirl and dance to the cacophony of her ringing ears. She barely senses her wrists being secured and a gag being pushed between her lips, a cloth wrapped tightly to secure it. As her ankles are tied she's locked in black and violet turmoil.

He's got her.

And she hadn't even thought about the pepper spray.

PART 2

The sand should talk

36

DI Frank Feather backs the Corsa in between two bollards, splitting a refuse sack under his rear tyre. He climbs out and walks across the pavement, and his jacket flaps in a sudden freezing gust. There's a faint light in the back of the dry cleaners but the shop is closed. The residential door alongside is shut but when he presses the bell the security latch clicks. He goes in.

He hears feet descending the stairs and waits in the vestibule as a guy swings round the landing and skips down the last flight. He's a big ugly bastard with fighter's paws but light on his feet. He reaches the ground and steps aside, rocking his head to invite Feather past, and Feather reaches for the banisters and heaves himself up the steps. When he looks back down the guy is still there, watching him. Their eyes lock for a moment then Feather continues up.

Georgina Trent looks no better than earlier. She's a tall, plain woman who'd opened her door this morning with her chin up ready for trouble but now she's a hollow husk. Her face and hair are a mess, her eyes are glittering pools. She's not surprised to see Feather again, seems incapable of any emotion bar misery. If she's any friends she's not bothered to call them.

'Sorry to impose again,' Feather says. 'But I guess there's no good time for this.'

He walks into a tiny lounge choked by an oversized leather suite and bamboo-and-glass table set. A gas radiant fire hisses under a mantel jammed with figurines and photo frames. Georgina closes the door but doesn't invite him to sit.

'Was that guy just in here?' Feather says. He tilts his head towards the door.

'Darren. A friend of Donna's.' Georgina's voice is slow, a little slurred.

Darren. Feather tags the name onto the mnemonic he's already attached to the guy on the stairs, which is "Meatloaf".

'They close?'

Georgina purses her lips but her eyes seek the floor. Her voice is soft.

'He's nothing. A nobody.'

'Why was he here?'

She thinks. Lifts her eyes.

'Questions about Donna.'

'What kind of friend is he?'

'A nobody,' she repeats. 'He thought he had a thing with her. *As if.*'

'As in boyfriend?'

'Donna doesn't have a boyfriend. She's through with men.'

Through with everything, in fact. Georgina will adjust the terminology in her own good time.

'Does he call here often?'

'No. I don't allow it. He's trouble Donna doesn't need. She's told him to go to hell but the message never gets through.'

'What did he want just now?'

'He wanted to know what happened, what the police told me. I said the police have told me fuck all.'

Feather is looking round. He lifts a figurine from the mantel. An elegant woman holding a parasol, glazed china, colours washed out, tacky as a bar of Brighton rock. He puts the figure back. The photo frame next to it has a snap of a couple in Edwardian dress. Could be Georgina's great grandparents. More likely just the junk picture that came with the frame.

'What's Darren's full name?' he says. 'What's he do?'

'Stokes. He's on the doors. A porter at Billingsgate when the clubs close.'

'How long has he known Donna?'

'A year or two. Donna's round all the clubs. You pick up shit like that.'

'And he thought Donna had something for him?'

'In his dreams. Donna wouldn't touch a gorilla like him.' Drink amplifies Georgina's anger.

'Did it bother him that she didn't reciprocate?'

'Who knows? He's too stupid to recognise a brush off.' Georgina's words are slow. Her mind is working to put things together.

'He seemed calm just now.'

'You can't tell what Darren's thinking.'

Feather picks up another figurine.

'Have you called anyone?' he says, but Georgina is back watching the carpet. Feather plants the figurine and squeezes between the furnishings to a CD rack, pulls out a few cases. Hip hop, indie, one-album garage punk, market stall rip-offs. 'What music does she dig?' he says.

'She listened to mine.'

'This *all* yours?' Feather indicates the wider room.

'Yeah. Donna travels light.'

'How long have you been together?'

'Three years.'

'And you were getting along? Things were okay?'

'Yes. I'm the only family Donna's ever had.'

'She got her stuff here?'

'Some.'

She escorts Feather down the short hallway. There's an open door onto a dark bedroom. 'You mind?' he asks. He flicks on the light. Georgina stands back, too lethargic to object. It's the bedroom they share, cluttered like the lounge. Tidy but overpowered by a massive four poster that's a mess of drapes and tassels. How they got the thing in is anybody's guess. The remaining floor space is taken by two free standing wardrobes, a dressing table and an armchair. There's barely room for Feather's girth. He opens a wardrobe and sees a rail hung with skimpy dresses and short skirts, expensive jackets. Donna's. It's all neatly hung but there's stuff on the floor too: jeans and tops, underwear, toiletry stuff, piled in a heap beside a small travel case that's open and empty. Feather closes the door and eases himself past it to the second wardrobe which houses larger sizes, more expensive cuts. Georgina's. He looks at the dresser which is covered by a forest of cosmetics that could be either woman's. Stuff Georgina and Donna couldn't use in ten years. Maybe gifts from satisfied customers, though Feather doesn't see Donna's customers as the giving type. He guesses that Georgina's in the same game, a notch up. Georgina will have patrons, a few sugar daddies, though they'd have to be men of particular taste, given Georgina's plain looks and her disposition towards the opposite sex. Maybe she has a speciality that draws her clientele.

Georgina may have an act for her customers but there's a distinct matronly air about her that perhaps drew the dead girl in. Feather nods his head to invite Georgina ahead of him back to the lounge. Her cheeks are glistening. The dam is ready to burst. He treads behind her, taking the short walk that had been most familiar to Donna, a million miles from the streets of North London and the freezing steps of Our Lady Of The Holy Souls.

Feather continues into the kitchen. It's a tiny place with a waste bin jammed by takeout cartons, a stained electric hob, dirty cups and plates dumped in the sink. The kitchen is on the verge of becoming a tip.

Feather takes off his jacket and hangs it, then lifts plates and cups from the sink into a bowl and runs the water. Georgina watches.

'What time did Donna go out last night?' he says.

'Sometime before ten.'

'She meeting anyone in particular?'

'She was going up King's Cross.'

The same story as this morning.

'She always pick her clients up there? No prearrangements?'

'She's usually there or Finsbury. Hackney sometimes. She's got three or four clubs. There's always punters in.'

Feather works a sponge, scrubbing the crockery, stacking the wire rack. 'We're covering the clubs,' he tells Georgina. 'Talking to the girls. We'll see if anyone knows who picked Donna up last night. Did her clients ever drop her back here?'

'No. Usually where they pick her up.'

'Why was she walking round Kensal last night?'

'She was probably in Gassers.'

'What's that?'

'A club on Ladbroke Grove.'

'She go there often?'

'Two or three nights a week, if she's not busy.'

'Then she walks back? Past Our Lady's?'

'Yes.'

'So a taxi or customer might have dropped her off at the club and she walked home from there?'

'Probably.'

Week-old solidified grease resists Feather's sponge. The water's not hot enough and the cheap washing up liquid barely touches it.

Feather grabs a scouring pad.

'What do you know about Wilbur Parish,' he says.

'A piece of shit.'

'How come she knew him?' He glances sideways at Georgina. She's staring at him but her eyes are glazed.

'He got his claws into her when she arrived in London. They had a thing going but he put her on the streets anyway. She was fifteen.'

'How long were they together?'

'Two years. Then Parish found a younger girl and threw Donna out. But he still "manages" her.'

'Still pimps her out?'

A coughed laugh. 'He doesn't even do that. She works independently. Wilbur just takes his cut. He doesn't know what she's doing or how much she's really earning but as long as she hands him enough he leaves her alone.'

'Why didn't she ditch him?'

'He said he'd find her. Hurt her.'

'I heard Donna had legal problems.'

'She's up for assault on a guy who tried to rape her.'

'A client?'

'Yes. Wanted to sample the goods without paying the bill but he met his match. You need to talk to him. He's a violent man.'

'We'll talk to them all. Did Donna mention a problem at her solicitor's? A bust up with a fellow client?'

'Yeah. A creep called Jerome. The little shit got what he deserved.'

'Do you know him? Did Donna?'

'No. He was just some jerk with the same solicitor who thought he was tough. Saw Donna as a pushover.'

'Donna was no pushover,' Feather says.

'No. Donna fights.'

Most of the time.

Feather stacks the last plate and wipes the draining board. The kitchen looks half decent again.

'Have you got anyone?' he asks. 'It might be better if you're not alone tonight.'

Georgina shakes her head and stares at the rack of dishes as if they've miraculously cleaned themselves.

'It's going to sink in,' Feather says.

'What do you care?' Georgina says. 'Do any of us matter?'

Feather finds a roll of paper towels and dries his hands. Reaches for his jacket.

'Darren Stokes,' he says. 'Donna's admirer. You got an address?'

37

It's twenty four hours since they found Donna Jordan on the church steps and DCI Peter Clough senses time ticking like the meter in a dodgy cab. The case needs resolution. Get the perp and get the people off the job before the team grows like a rampant amoeba. It's not that streetwalkers don't count. Donna Jordan deserves justice the same as anyone, but this unglamorous, scrappy killing can't be allowed to drain resource. The killing's not a gang hit nor a serial killer. There's no wider consideration, no threat to the public. Donna's body is the messy outcome of a chance encounter, a lone and one-time killer who was as unprepared as she and who will be incapable of hiding. He's out there right now looking over his shoulder and they need to get him while he's running scared. Deserving they may be, but streetwalkers are many and imperilled and DCI Peter Clough is one and resource-strapped.

He crosses before a collage of crime scene photos and rests his backside on the desk, waiting for Feather to finish a call. The detective gives him the eye as he grunts parting words and disconnects.

Clough's about to speak when Mary Charlton arrives and hovers, lanky and leggy. Feather raises an eyebrow.

'We've got a car,' Mary says.

'Time?' Feather is already up and moving towards the board.

'Ten fifty. Seven Sisters. Donna talked to the driver for five minutes then got in.'

'Get it checked. But we need something later. Ten fifty's too early.'

'Yes, sir.'

'Anything from Lawrie?' Feather asks.

'Not yet.'

Lawrie Mercer is back out canvassing for wits. Last night's turns netted only three snippets of Donna's movements. They've confirmed that she was in a club up Finsbury Park at ten, which ties in with Georgina Trent's timing, though not her location, and was in some kind of argument with another girl a little after that. Then she picked up a punter on the street and disappeared. That would be the ten fifty pick up Mary's just given them. But if there was another pick up before two a.m. they need to get it. They need to bridge the gap between Seven Sisters and the church steps. Lawrie's people will need to go into the clubs and bars tonight.

'Send Lawrie home after lunch,' Feather says. 'We'll run a late turn.'

He looks at Clough for endorsement. Clough says nothing. If they need a turn they need a turn. Waiting for CCTV scans to give them another pick up isn't going to be enough. Clough has joined Feather at the board. He plants a hand on the fat man's shoulder.

'Names?'

Feather fingers the names, some with photos.

'Donna's partner, Georgina Trent. Out of it at the moment but I'll be talking to her again. Wilbur Parish, the character who was pimping her out. Possible candidate if Donna was playing games with him. Darren Stokes. I bumped into him at Donna's flat. Some kind of acquaintance but I don't know if he's friend or foe. And a few long shots from Donna's legal affairs. This one's a client she assaulted, for which attack she was presently standing trial. Word is the guy wants to keep things quiet but sometimes grudge is stronger than sense. We'll talk to them all today but we need another pick up. I'm still liking a punter for it.'

'If we get the pick up we'll scale down the late turn,' Clough says. 'We'd have her covered until the early hours.'

'She might have called in for a drink or bite in between. Spoken to somebody. Made arrangements for later.'

'If she stayed in Finsbury Park that would limit the places. Maybe a few DCs can do the rounds.'

'Let's wait for the CCTV,' Feather says.

~~~~~

The waiting room is less congested than last time he was in. Parfitt and Quinn's receptionist has perhaps been cancelling appointments.

'Might she be ill?' Feather asks.

'I can't think why she wouldn't call or answer her phone. I'm having to cancel everything.'

'Who stands in when Ms Walker's not here?'

'No one. We cover for holidays but otherwise Kate's always here. She doesn't need stand-ins.'

'You have her address?'

'I'm not sure we can give that out.'

'This is police business. I'm sure you can.'

'Well... it's in the phone book anyway.' The receptionist taps the computer and scribbles an address. 'Ask her to give us a ring,' she says.

'Is there anyone else who could talk to me about Donna Jordan?'

'Only Arthur and he's in court.'

'Fine. If Ms Walker appears, ask her to call me.'

Violet smiles up at him and now there's a purpose behind her smile.

'Donna Jordan...?' she says.

Feather smiles back. 'Still dead,' he says.

He walks out and almost bumps into the guy he spoke to last time. Feather has a technique of filing names and faces using mnemonics. He's hung the present guy on a peg labelled "Undertaker". Real name, Hartley Tasker. Tasker's suit, unlike an undertaker's, is bespoke and crisp, but the rest fits. Tasker is barely an inch shorter than Feather but travels seven stones lighter, much of it donated from the face. And the dusty grey of Tasker's sunken eyes is just about right for the burial scene. In past times the guy would have sported a comb-over but Tasker has followed fashion and buzz cut his skull like an advert for the hereafter.

'Detective,' Tasker says.

'Sir.' Feather continues doorwards.

'Any progress?'

Feather stops.

'Katie's client,' Tasker says.

'No,' Feather says. 'Nothing yet.'

The guy acts businesslike but he's after tittle-tattle the same as the receptionist. He's casting for a bite. So maybe he'll dispense a little bait Feather's way.

'I heard the girl was up for a knife incident,' Feather says.

Hartley Tasker's mouth slants. 'That would be confidential, I'm afraid, Detective. But it's no secret that Donna had enemies.'

Bait withheld. Feather stays with the snippet Tasker threw yesterday. 'The fight here – was that one of her enemies?'

Tasker's mouth straightens and puckers simultaneously. The eyes shine like diamonds. 'I understand the two of them met only here,' he says. 'But who knows what animosity was kindled. You don't meet the most rational people in this business.'

'Mine neither.' Feather's watching him.

'Donna's killer was probably a stranger,' Tasker tells him. 'But Katie can tell you about the client who had the set-to.'

'A guy called Jerome,' Feather says.

'Right.' Tasker nods his skull. The badger eyes glitter surprise. 'Bit of a ding-dong. I actually heard it from my office.'

'I forget – what did Ms Walker tell me about Jerome's prosecution?'

But Tasker is not so easily drawn.

'I'm sorry, Inspector,' he says again. 'Client confidentiality. Haven't you spoken to Katie?'

'She's not in.'

Tasker's eyes glow. His skull nods.

'Well, I'm sure you'll catch up with her,' he says.

'Yes,' Feather concurs. 'I will.'

He leaves.

~~~~~

Feather drives back towards Harrow Park. Kate Walker's address is just up the road and what he wants to know will be in her head, not in Donna Jordan's case file. It's perhaps worth a quick detour to see if he can catch her. He spins the wheel and the Corsa creaks and turns and coasts north through midday traffic on the Edgware Road. Kate Walker's house is barely a minute away, a white pebble dashed semi behind ten-foot hedges on a tree-lined street in Maida Vale. If she's sick she'll not appreciate his calling but Feather lives to be unappreciated. He lives to bully out facts and hunt down the likes of Donna's killer.

As he parks he spots a couple standing at Ms Walker's front door. He climbs out and they turn to look at him.

'She in?' Feather asks.

The guy answers. He's big with unruly hair. 'Are you a work

colleague?' he says.

'Police.'

The couple's faces switch to concern.

'What's happened?' the girl says. The girl is a stunner. She triggers Feather's mnemonics and picks up the tag "Ruth", a girl he once knew. The guy is "Worzel".

'Just a routine business call,' Feather says.

'What's happened? Why are you here?' Worzel says.

'Routine,' Feather repeats. 'And Ms Walker's not at work, which you clearly know.'

They say nothing.

'Any reason you're here?' Feather says.

'Why do you think? She's missing,' Ruth says. Her anxiety contrasts with the guy's calm. The two seem more like individuals than a couple.

'Well,' Feather says, 'I'm sure she'll turn up.'

Ruth stares in amazement. 'That's your response?' she says. 'When are you people going to take this seriously?'

'I don't follow, ma'am.'

'Are you looking for her or not?'

Worzel touches the girl's arm. 'He doesn't know,' he says. He turns to Feather. 'Kate's missing. There's been a guy stalking her.'

Feather cocks his head.

'You people were supposed to be investigating this bastard,' Ruth says. 'And now that she's missing you're *still* doing nothing.'

A light goes on in Feather's head. 'I see,' he says. So Kate Walker wasn't at Harrow Park on legal business.

'The guy's dangerous,' Ruth says. 'He's been *in* here, he's followed Kate around, and now he's probably taken her. And what are you doing?'

Feather doesn't know what they're doing.

The guy touches her arm again. 'This officer's not involved, Rache,' he says.

'Fuck "not involved". He's the police.'

Feather smiles. Yeah, he's the police. But he's not here about some stalker or a missing person report. 'I'm sorry I can't help,' he says. 'Go in and talk to your contact. Ms Walker's probably fine.'

'She's not,' Worzel says, but Feather doesn't care what he thinks.

He needs to shift.

'Kate was moving out,' Ruth-Rache says. 'To hide from this guy. But she didn't make it. She's disappeared.'

Feather sees the fear in their eyes and he wonders. But this isn't his business. 'Who's your contact,' he says.

'An officer called Crane,' Worzel says.

'Know him,' Feather says. 'Good guy. Go and talk to him.'

He nods at them and takes off. As he unlocks the car the guy is watching him.

~~~~~

Feather backtracks towards Marylebone Road and pulls in at the nick. Leaves the car on the yellow zone outside the doors.

DC Crane is at his desk, pushing paper. Feather walks across and hovers.

'You got a missing woman, name of Walker?'

'Yes, sir.' Crane quits his paperwork and sits back stiffly. Feather's not in his chain of command but he's intimidating nevertheless. Crane's smart enough to recognise a true copper, and junior enough to be wary. Feather plants his backside.

'What's the story?'

'Report of a stalker. Phone calls, letters, someone following her around. Indications that he'd been in her house. And Ms Walker's missing since last night.'

'Is she credible?'

'Yes. I think someone's been harassing her. And she's not contactable today.'

'What's Andy say?'

'He's concerned. We're talking to people who know her. If there's no sign by the end of the day we'll pull a team together. How did you hear about this, sir?'

'She's Donna Jordan's brief,' Feather says. 'She's my murder victim's lawyer.'

Crane's eyes widen. The whole department knows about the body on the church steps. 'Small world,' he says. 'I'll inform DI Heldt.'

'Good idea,' Feather says. He heads back out.

38

Feather parks on double yellows behind Joey Obasanjo's job car. Obasanjo is waiting on the pavement, checking the fascia of a fast food takeaway that promises everything from fish and chips to kebabs and spring rolls, all conjured up within premises the size of a sardine can.

'Upstairs,' Obasanjo says. They go into the shop.

Lunchtime customers are queuing inside in the stink of burnt oil and curry. Fryers bubble and spit. The display glass is steamed.

Obasanjo calls to an Asian girl working a fryer. She shakes her head.

'No here.'

'Where is he?'

'No here.'

A wiry black guy in a chef's apron appears with a tray of fish. He sees trouble and plants the tray. 'Whatcher want?' he says.

'Wilbur Parish back there?'

'He don't work in here, mate. He owns the place.'

'He upstairs?'

'Sometime.'

Feather lifts the flap and walks through. The black guy yells and comes after him but Obasanjo blocks his way, holds up his card.

'You can't go in,' the guy says. 'These is private premises. Where's your warrant.'

Feather heads up the narrow stairs behind the takeaway. The first floor is storage and junk. He continues up. By the time he's reached the second floor he's breathing hard. Obasanjo catches up and they stand outside a door with no name or number. Feather knuckles it and it opens and a white teenage girl peers out.

'Wilbur Parish in?' Feather says.

She tells him no, contradicting herself by turning to peer back into the flat for approval. She's maybe seventeen years old, maybe not, but her gaunt face and stringy hair say she's on the edge. Feather pushes the door open. The girl steps back and he's past her and into a seedy lounge overlooking the street. The room's littered with ashtrays and takeaway cartons and in the middle of it on a striped sofa is a short black guy with a Mohawk fade hairdo and goatee. He jumps up and grabs a baseball bat lying at his feet but Obasanjo steps up smartish and his fist connects with the guy's face sending him sprawling back onto the sofa. The bat goes flying. 'The *fuck?*' the guy's yelling. 'Fuckkas! Geddouta here!'

Donna Jordan's pimp is a mean looking bastard, though it's hard to get a clear picture since his face is a mess, for which Obasanjo's fist can claim only part of the credit. Parish has taken a beating recently. His eyes are puffy and his cheeks have cuts and a sheen of heavy bruising. His nose is bleeding – which *is* Obasanjo – and the girl's screaming behind them, flailing her way through. Feather grips her wrist and holds her clear. Obasanjo stands over Parish.

'Stay there, Wilbur,' Obasanjo says. 'Nice and quiet.'

Parish stays seated but he isn't quiet. Neither is the girl. Feather steers her out of the room and closes the door and stands with his back to it. Her fist pounds the wood.

'The *fuck* you doin'?' Parish says. 'What you at?' He's staunching the blood with the sleeve of his hoodie, flicking dazed looks between the two of them. Obasanjo flashes his brief. The ID doesn't change Parish's dialogue. He asks them what the damn *fuck* man. He tells them *gedd*outa here. They wait till the protests die off and the pounding on the door quits. Then Feather comes over and sits on a chair arm.

'You look like a bus hit you,' he says.

'Fuckka.'

'What happened?'

'Fuckka!'

'I heard first time. Who's been smacking you?'

'Nonna your business. The hell you doin' bustin' in here? Where's your fuckin' warrant?'

'We don't need a warrant. We've just come for a chat.'

'No fuckin' way. Fuckin' chat. You come in here brutalising me you got a complaint coming, coppa.' Parish is dabbing his nose, making it worse.

'You pick up a baseball bat on me again,' Obasanjo says, 'and you'll

222

have something to complain about.'

Feather sighs. 'What happened to you?' he repeats.

Parish shuts up.

'Lost his tongue,' Obasanjo says. 'Or are you in shock, Wilbur, from hearing what happened to your prize tart?'

'Fuck you,' Parish says. 'Bitch got what was comin'.'

'She get it from you?'

'Gedd*outa* here.'

'She and you have a falling out?'

'I'm callin' my lawyer.'

'Did the two of you have an argument?' Feather says.

Parish laughs through his blocked nose. 'She don't never argue with me. Bitch knows better.'

'So what happened?' Feather says.

'What *happen*'? Bitch got herself offed is what happen. Met her match. Got cheeky one time too often. An' I give a *shit!* Bitch can rot in hell.'

'You've just lost income, Wilbur. You must give a shit, a good businessman like yourself.'

Parish lifts a lip. 'I ain't got no income from that bitch. You talking out your ass.'

'Not what we hear,' Feather says. 'We hear you were pimping her out. In a lazy kind of way. You dispensed with the actual pimping and just banked the cash.'

'I ain't no involvement with that bitch. You're crazy.'

'No Wilbur. We know you're lying.'

'You got nuthin' to prove nuthin'. Geddouta here.'

'You had a thing with Donna, we heard.'

'History.'

'So you *were* together?'

'History, man. Old an' forgot.'

'So you no longer work Donna?'

'Nah.'

'We've people who say otherwise.'

'Well fuck them people an' their grannies.'

'When's the last time you saw her?'

'How should I know?'

'Last year? Last week? Sunday night?'

'Fuck should I know?'

'You need to know, Wilbur,' Feather says. He leans forward. 'Because we've people who put you with Donna last week. And given your relationship with her – I mean as a parasitic louse – you're top of our suspects list for her death.'

'You're fuckin' *crazy,* man. Why I gone murder bitch if I'm pimpin' her? You ain't talkin' no sense.'

'So which is it?' Obasanjo says. 'Were you pimping her or did you kill her?'

'What? Go fuck yourself. I'm puttin' a complaint in.'

Obasanjo steps forward. Gets right over Parish.

'This is a murder investigation,' he says, 'and we need answers. So you can talk here or come down to the nick.'

'You got nuthin' on me. You can't take me in.'

'Where were you on Sunday night?' Feather asks.

'Howd' I know? Roun' about. Doin' stuff.'

'I need details,' Feather says. 'Times and places. And I need a little more clarity on your relationship with Donna. If you don't give me those you're coming to the station.'

'You ain't nothin' on me! Get the fuck out.'

Feather's still leaning. 'Wilbur, listen: you look good for Donna's killer. I'm tempted to put you through the wringer until we know one way or the other.'

'Then I'm callin' my lawyer. Geddouta here.'

'Tell us about Donna. What you and she were up to.'

'I don't know the bitch no more. This is just shit.'

'Word is she was holding back,' Obasanjo says. 'Thinking she shouldn't pay her dues. People are pointing the finger.'

'I ain't saying nothin'.'

'Where were you Sunday night?' Feather says. 'Did she and you have a fall out?'

'I'm callin' me lawyer. Arrest me or geddoutahere.'

'Did you have a fight with Donna? Is that what happened to your face? Let me guess. She hit you. Messed you up before you could get out of reach. And you ran away and got mad, being humiliated by the scrawny bitch you were pimping. So when you got brave again you went back with a knife.'

'Fuck you. This is shit.'

'Where were you Sunday night?'

'Mindin' my own business. I was with friends.'

'Did you meet Donna that night?'

'I din' see the bitch. She was prob'ly out workin'. You think I'm gon' be out on the streets middla winter?'

'I don't know. Maybe you needed to catch up with her. Maybe to collect arrears she owed.'

'Bullshit! You ain' got nuthin'.'

'How much did she owe? Was the bitch holding back on her payments?'

'You crazy. If bitch owed me money I'd make her pay. No one holds back with me.'

'But someone's messed with you, Wilbur. Her or someone else. Who gave you the face?'

'I ain't bin near the bitch. I got people to vouch. Bitch got what was comin', is all.'

Feather looks up at Obasanjo. 'You believe him?' he says.

'No,' Obasanjo says. 'Not a single fucking word. I think he and Donna had issues.'

'Me too,' Feather says. He sighs. Leans across, close in to Parish's messed up face. 'Give us their names,' he says, 'the ones who can vouch for you. And don't go anywhere.'

~~~~~

Obasanjo suggests lunch but the stink of Parish's takeaway has turned Feather's stomach. He tells Obasanjo he'll meet him back at the nick and Obasanjo heads off. Feather sinks into his car and calls his desk number. Mary picks up and brings him up to date. Lawrie has talked to the owner of the vehicle that picked Donna up at ten fifty Sunday night. The guy claims he dropped Donna back off at Gassers, the club Georgina mentioned, around eleven forty-five. They need to confirm the story but it sounds credible. The guy wouldn't know the club unless he'd dropped Donna there. So the next step is to find out who saw Donna in the place. Maybe she left to pick up another customer or maybe she stayed put until she was wasted. Mary is about to head over with Lawrie and talk to anyone who's in the club right now. Ian Platt and June Smith are trawling

CCTVs for any sight of Donna in the area after midnight. They may get lucky and spot another vehicle. And they'll go back into Gassers tonight to catch the late crowd. Feather tells Mary to keep him posted and drives down to the City where he parks in the utility entrance of an office block above a delicatessen off Aldersgate. The foyer plate directs him to the third floor where a receptionist makes a call and brings out a squat guy in an off-the-peg suit and a grey pall on his face. Feather shows his card and asks if there's somewhere quiet, and the guy leads him to a small meeting room. The guy's name is Porter. He's the client Donna knifed after he got irate over the scam about her age. There are two livid scars on his cheek and the faint sheen of a fading black eye. Feather wonders what story Porter worked up to cover the marks. Porter sits but Feather waits, standing over him to let the implications of his presence sink in. Porter had thought his tussle with Donna Jordan was over with his signature on the statement exonerating the girl and consigning her prosecution to an uncontested and un-newsworthy magistrates' hearing from which his name would never become public. But now here's a detective showing up at his workplace and the nightmare is back.

'I hear you're the main witness in Ms Jordan's prosecution,' Feather says. He nods towards the marks on Porter's face. Sits.

Porter's shirt is staining beneath his jacket. He's already trawling for the story he needs for his work colleagues when they go out of here.

'The prosecutor agreed to my statement,' Porter says. 'The charge against the lady was reduced.'

'That's what I heard. You admitted that she was just defending herself.' Feather sits back and clasps his hands behind his head. 'It kind of let her off the hook, though, didn't it?'

'We agreed to let it all go. The girl believed she was provoked.'

'And is that true?'

'It's what we agreed.' Porter's tongue dry-clicks in his mouth. He's rigid with the fear of where this is going.

'A girl slashes your face and escapes with a slapped wrist. I wouldn't be happy with that.'

'I made my statement. I've nothing more to say.'

'Did you ever see the girl again?'

'No.'

'Do you still drive round Hackney?'

226

'No!'

'You've not been back there?'

'It was only that one time. A mistake.'

'A mistake? That's a nice word for soliciting for underage girls.'

Porter flinches. This was supposed to be over. And there was absolutely no mention of underage in his statement. His eyes glint and his odour floats across the table. He licks his lips and reaches for a lie.

'I don't know what you mean,' he says.

Feather's smile conveys to Porter that they both recognise the lie. But he wants Porter on the defensive. 'We've got it on record,' he says. 'We've got the texts you sent her.'

Porter's mouth clicks twice more and he swallows. What in hell is this cop after? They'd agreed. They'd given the girl's solicitor what she needed. The CPS accepted it. So why are they coming after him? Porter feels his world start to crumble right here in this room, in the citadel he's inhabited for thirty years. The partition walls are paper thin. Anyone could be listening. Any of his work colleagues, until now unaware how their Adjustments Manager spends his evenings. 'I don't know what you mean,' he repeats, quietly, afraid of the thin walls. He shrinks before Feather, a rabbit in the headlights.

'Must have been a good story you told them...' Feather inclines his head to the office beyond the walls. His own voice isn't quiet.

Porter swallows again. 'This will ruin me,' he says.

'Let's talk about the assault. She cut you up and got away with it,' Feather says. His voice is not quiet at all.

Porter's voice is small, psychological compensation. 'We had an agreement. I admitted culpability and we let the whole thing go.'

'The CPS let things go, not you.'

'We agreed this wouldn't go any further.'

Feather pins him in his stare.

'What did you tell them here?' he asks.

'A car accident.'

Feather nods. Purses his lips. 'So you kept your dirty habit under wraps. Got away with it. But Ms Jordan still got away with knifing you.'

'This will ruin me,' Porter says. 'It was a single mistake.' He's still not switched track. His noisome fear flows across the table but it's the fear of who might hear, of work colleagues and neighbours, of acquaintances and whatever church group he belongs to.

'She got away with brutalising you in your own car,' Feather says. 'Don't you think she should pay for that?'

'I don't want her to pay for anything,' Porter says. 'I think I should call my solicitor.'

'You've seen her again, haven't you?'

'No.'

'Did you harbour a grudge?'

'What?'

'Did you kill her?'

Porter stares back without comprehension.

39

Feather is snarled for forty-five minutes on the Euston Road so it's four p.m. by the time he gets back to the incident room where Mary Charlton walks him across to the board. Donna Jordan's final night is coming together. They've confirmed her at Gassers until two a.m. and she's there in company. A thread leads from the timeline down to a pinned note in Feather's own scribble. The note says "Darren Stokes. Friend? Fixation? Brush-off?"

Joey Obasanjo joins them. 'That's the guy you bumped into at her place?' he says.

'Yeah. What's the story?'

'He works the door at Gassers,' Mary tells him. 'He was off Sunday but the proprietor says he was in the club with Donna for a couple of hours. They both left around two a.m. The guy can't say if they were together.'

Feather eyes the timeline. Cancel the punter who'd dropped Donna off at eleven forty-five and bring on Meatloaf, aka Darren Stokes, who's now the last guy seen with her. They're together until two a.m. By three Donna's dead on the steps of Our Lady's. Did she leave with Stokes or was there time to squeeze in another punter? A quickie from a chance meeting in the club or out on the street? But the gap is narrow and closing. If Stokes has no alibi they'll sweat him. If he's in the clear they're left with one blank hour and Feather will bring pimp Wilbur Parish in while they close it.

There's another note, another name in Feather's handwriting at the bottom left of the board. Jerome Welland, linked to Donna through that confrontation at their solicitor's. Welland's name is alongside Porter's and both are tacked beyond the left extreme of the timeline in an area marked "History". Feather grabs a pen and crosses out Porter's name. Writes "desperate for quiet" beside it. That leaves Welland. He's a long shot but they'll check him anyway.

'Go back in,' he tells Mary. 'After midnight. Let's see if any of Gassers' regulars recall seeing Donna, whom she left with.'

'I'll take Lawrie,' Mary says.

Feather turns and finds Clough at his shoulder.

'Nearly there,' Clough says. 'It's one of these.'

'Let's see what we pull in,' Feather says. 'Who've we got?'

'Two plus four,' Clough says. 'Your two in the club. And we can get four out in Kensal Town. Pubs and clubs. Talk to late night regulars. See if Donna was spotted after two a.m. You okay for the streets, Joey?'

Obasanjo nods. 'I'll net some volunteers,' he says.

'Six pairs of feet. Three hours each.'

'We need more,' Feather says. 'We need every sighting and speculation, any rumours. If Stokes comes up clear we'll need to know which way to go.' His face is patient but Clough shakes his head.

'This is Kensal Town,' he says. 'There's nothing there. Four will cover it, Frank.' He's pulling on his jacket, ready for the off. 'We'll bring in extra tomorrow if we must. Better if we don't need to.' He pats Feather on the back and heads for the door.

The incident room is emptying. The late night crew are heading for a few hours R&R, a bite to eat. Feather nods to Mary and Obasanjo. 'Keep me informed,' he says.

He goes out to grab a black tea at the machine. He hasn't eaten or drunk since seven this morning, which given his poundage is no bad thing, but dehydration is making him light-headed. The machine spits out a concoction whose aroma assaults the nose before it gets near the lips. Feather holds it away to take a breath then sips. The tea tastes of powdered liquorice. When he opens his eyes DC Crane is beside him, jabbing the machine's buttons. The machine grinds and screeches.

'What's happening?' Feather asks.

'She's definitely missing. The Guv'nor's concerned.'

'Who's on it?' Just a copper's curiosity. None of his affair.

'Right now it's just me and a couple of others, sir. DI Heldt is reviewing the situation. He'll pull the in troops tomorrow if she's not turned up.'

Feather sips again.

'You checked known associates?' he says.

'I've talked to the friends, sister, work colleagues. She's nowhere to be found. And the disappearance is unprecedented. She's never dropped out of sight before.'

'The friends kosher?'

'Seem to be. Her girlfriend's worried sick. She'd arranged a hiding place across town to get her away from the stalker. Ms Walker didn't show up for the move. The boyfriend's playing hell too but we need to look at him. She hadn't known him long.'

'The stalking thing is real?'

'DI Heldt thinks so. Agrees she may have been abducted by the guy.' They turn to head back to CID and Feather is musing on the oddity of his murder victim's solicitor disappearing. Entirely unrelated, of course, but odd. Feather's met Kate twice and she's stuck in his mind. It would be good if she turned up safe.

Feather walks with Crane to Heldt's office and stands in the doorway, sipping tea. Heldt's fluorescents are playing up, flashing and snapping and throwing light pulses off the black windows. Heldt looks up and beckons him in and Feather plants his backside against his desk. Crane hovers.

'Progress?' Heldt says. He's talking about the murder enquiry.

'Some,' Feather says. 'We've narrowed down her movements, got a guy with her near the end. We're close.'

'Funny thing, our missing solicitor,' Heldt says. 'I heard you were talking to her only yesterday.'

'Yeah,' Feather says. 'Funny.'

'Neil's been banging on about this stalker for a fortnight but we can't chase up every report or we'd never get home.'

'Tell me about it,' Feather says.

Heldt sighs. Leans back in his chair and looks at Crane. 'We've no alternative but to assume this nutter's taken her,' he says. 'I'm talking to the Guv'nor first thing. We need bods. It's going to squeeze your homicide, Frank.'

'Worst case they'll transfer some people. You'll have no problem with priority.'

'I suppose she mentioned nothing when you spoke to her?'

'Nothing. It was just Donna Jordan business. She was a little jumpy but I assumed that was the news about her client.'

'We've had this thing two weeks,' Heldt says. He picks up a file folder, hefts it as if weighing consequences.

'No one in the picture?'

Crane leans back against the visitors' table. The fluorescents strobe his pale face and give Feather a headache.

'We've half a dozen males in regular contact,' Crane says. 'Boyfriend, work colleagues, brother-in-law, nephew. None of them jump out. I'm working up the wider circle – clients, passing contacts, people who work in the same building, regulars where she eats, neighbours, postman.'

'She may still show,' Heldt says, 'otherwise we'll need feet on the ground. Plenty of them. It's been twenty-four hours.'

He looks at Feather and Feather clamps his lips. If someone's taken her the odds are not good.

'Her firm cooperating?' he asks. Kate's own caution when he came asking about Donna Jordan seems a little ironic in hindsight.

'They've given us some names,' Crane says. 'Not their clients so no confidentiality issue. Ms Walker has fought a few battles over the years. We've half a dozen people who might hold a grudge.'

'There's one of her clients, too,' Heldt says. 'Had some issues with Ms Walker's representation. Got into a fight with another client right in her office.'

'Jerome Welland,' Feather says.

They look at him.

'The client he was fighting with was my murder victim. But it's a big leap from troublesome client to stalker.'

'That's what I figure,' Heldt says. 'If it's work related it's either a colleague or an adversary she's beaten in court.'

'It's not the fight that's the oddity with Welland,' Crane says. 'I talked to a guy who does investigation work for the firm. The firm are about to ditch Welland over some dodgy funds he's paid into their account. Apparently Ms Walker had exposed the irregularity.'

'I don't see it,' Feather says. 'If someone's been stalking her, planning the abduction, it's something long standing.'

'We've a request for her phone data on Clough's desk,' Heldt says. 'We'll run that tomorrow. See who her anonymous caller is, or at least where he was calling from. And we'll get the CCTV coverage. Neil's built the timeline of the stalker's contacts. There must be a sight of him somewhere.'

Feather tosses the empty cup and folds his arms.

'Time,' he says.

'Time,' Heldt agrees.

'You've got a little, perhaps. Not much.'

'Yeah,' Heldt says. 'If this was a spur of the moment thing she'd be dead already. But assuming it's her stalker, assuming it was planned, he wouldn't finish it right away. We've a little time.'

'Hope it was planned,' Feather says.

40

The electric fire roasts her when she's close but leaves her freezing whenever she vacates the zone of its radiant heat. She lies on a camp bed in front of it, turning continuously to balance the heat. She's been down here for twenty-four hours, and fear is growing with the remorselessness of a dripping tap. She's over the initial shock of being dragged from her world as if it had never existed. She's even over the disbelief at *who,* the face behind the mask, though she can't stop telling herself that she should have known, should have opened her eyes. But wasn't it easier to imagine a stranger, to file a report and berate the police for doing nothing than to look closely herself?

She should have seen him, sensed the face behind the mask. But it's her *not seeing* that's been burning inside *him* all this time, has slowly poisoned him.

When someone's so close shouldn't you sense it? Shouldn't you *know?* Couldn't she have stopped this?

Don't! she tells herself. Don't play his game with its perverted logic in which *she's* responsible for bringing them to this foul cellar, the logic in which this is not *his* doing, not *his* plan.

It's his self-absolution that really frightens her, together with her cold, clawing fear that none of this was planned. He hadn't intended to bring them here, did not have this destination in his mind. And he can see no way out.

Kate's face is burning. She turns and presents her back to the fire, and as she does so there's a tug at her ankle as metal slithers across the matting, and that's another thing she can barely comprehend: that she is chained to the wall.

The chain tests her sanity more than anything. She can barely reconcile what was real yesterday with what is real now. Yesterday she was just another Londoner muddling through life. Today she's chained to the wall of a goddamned cellar. Reality now is a horror movie cliché. But the tempered steel links snaking from their anchor are all too real. She'd spent an hour this morning attacking the cement in which the chain is fixed using a blunt chisel she'd found amongst the cellar's junk, but she'd barely left a scratch. The movies are right. The cliché works.

After her bout with the chain she'd spent another hour hammering at the wooden joists over her head, hoping someone would hear, but no one did. She's heard no voices or movements upstairs except for his. If there are properties adjoining this building they're vacant. All Kate can hear is the occasional low rumble of traffic. Another movie cliché verified: in cellars, no one can hear you scream...

It's been twenty-four hours. Rache and Angie would have reported her missing last night but there won't be a full blown search yet. The police will still be making enquiries, feeling their way towards the conclusion that she really has been abducted. By tomorrow, though, she'll be news headlines. A full scale operation will be underway. But will the police connect the dots where even she failed? And how long will it take?

Because she may not have long. *He's* trapped just as much as she is. She sees it in his anger. He prepared for this a long time ago – the chain wasn't cemented in overnight – but it was all fantasy, something that might or might not ever happen. Then she returned to her house at the wrong moment and caught him and he'd no choice but to act. But with a major police search about to start her presence down here can only be a liability. And neither of them knows how to resolve that. That's what really scares her.

At eight this morning he'd brought her a sandwich and a bottle of water but they'd hardly talked. The old adage says get to know your captor, make a connection, force him to see the real person so that you might influence his ultimate decision on your fate. But his eyes had been angry and evasive and Kate fears that he has seen their destination and doesn't *want* to connect. It's as if he knows where they're going. So it's been a long day of shivering and baking in front of the fire, of hacking away at her chain and hammering at the joists and trying not to imagine how short their time might be.

And if he hadn't planned this he's nevertheless been *preparing*. Not just the camp bed and shackle but everything in this cellar, the whole creepy collection displayed around her. She's trapped in a mad museum that is a distorted shadow of her life, a crazy collection of artefacts that relate to her. Things she recognises and things that are inexplicable.

Her camp bed sits within a perimeter of old furniture whose surfaces display the collection by the mean light of a caged lamp hanging from the joists. And the whitewashed walls behind the furniture are displays too, a collage of photographs in which she is the subject, some new and some very old. And the old ones shock her with their testament to just how long he's been watching. All those years, hiding with his camera. How could she not have known?

The furniture is a former tenant's leavings. There's a bureau and a teak-veneer gramophone, a folding dining table and a treadle table, a bookcase and a bedroom dresser, an old upright piano. Kate can't stop wondering how they ever got the piano down here, as if that's of the least consequence.

But it's what covers the furniture that's frightening. At first sight it's just so much bric-a-brac but when she'd started to take it in she'd realised it was far from that. These are no obsolete household appliances, no paint tins or mouldering magazines, no ancient tennis racquets or board games or wine bottles. The furniture's surfaces, instead, display the carefully arranged icons of a shrine.

Atop the gramophone is a pattern of carefully spaced and perplexing objects: a tiny bottle of Coco eau de parfum, a pencil lying atop a faded notebook, a black hair band, a tattered pocket dictionary, a white sock, a shiny, silver, obsolete Sony Walkman, a lipstick. There's a plain white envelope and a small transparent polythene bag holding what might be a tuft of hair. There are a dozen folded and flattened confectionery wrappers. And at the back of the cabinet, against the wall is, on the left, a pyramid of six Coke cans and on the right a line of four Sprite cans, all open and empty.

Some of the things tug at Kate's memory as if they might have a significance, but no meaning has come yet for a stack of soft drink cans.

There *is* meaning to be found on the folded dining table, where the mementos of her recent torment are laid out: a collection of light bulbs and spots, without doubt taken from her house as the non-working substitutes were left; several inconsequential household items that she now recalls missing; and cans of supermarket produce removed from her trolley as the mischievous replacements were substituted. There are two keys, one each for her front and back doors, obsolete since she changed her locks. But how did he get those copies? And how did he get back into the house after the locks were changed?

Behind her, on the ancient treadle table, a demon mask stares at her to rekindle the terror of that Tube ride, the leap between the carriages. And beside it the bookcase whose shelves are lined with photo frames displaying selected pictures of her recent life. She's out running in her summer gear beneath trees heavy with foliage and blossom. She's striding down the street in a business suit, clutching her briefcase. She's sitting in the park with a book. She remembers that particular day: early September, a sense that summer would last forever in her warm and safe world, devoid of any sense that she was being watched. In another photo she's walking through the park scattering golden leaves and in another she's running under its winter lamps, determination – but not yet fear – on her face. A later, recent, photo first catches the fear, a portrait of her mid avenue, running from something, eyes darting. Her senses had not misled her out there.

On the wall beside the bookcase, more photos: in one the lighted windows of her house, in another her barely visible silhouette against the faint gleam of her wardrobe's courtesy light through her uncurtained bedroom window. Thank God she's always kept the room dark. The thought brings a bitter smile: would it matter, given the present circumstances, if he'd snapped her *butt naked?*

Adjacent to the cellar's door are the part-open drawers of a chipped pine dresser displaying folded items of underwear and a blouse, a pair of pyjama bottoms, all stolen from her bedroom and laundry basket. She recalls puzzling over the blouse and pyjamas a few weeks ago but hadn't noticed the missing pants. But he's lain in her bed. Why shouldn't he steal her knickers?

Completing the circle is the old upright piano, its lid raised to expose a row of uneven and missing keys. A music rack hangs down over them and supported in the rack is a plain sheet of paper on which are glued the scraps of two torn tickets, concert admissions from a decade and a half ago, as mystifying as anything in the room.

But what's on top of the piano is not mystifying. It's disgusting.

It's a leather-bound photo album with a button clasp. The album was fanned out to stand in pride of place atop the piano and Kate had stretched her ankle chain and taken it down out of curiosity. Inside the album are pornographic images of a naked woman in every licentious pose and state of abandon. And the woman is her. At least it's her face blended onto the bodies with exquisite PhotoShop skills. Kate senses a work of love, hundreds of hours spent searching out body images to match his photos of her face, each selected for perspective, light and shadow and skin tone, so that where he's blended face and bodies you can't tell the difference. One of his photos had caught her in an innocent yawn that he's mutated into a woman in naked abandon, at the height of her pleasure. It's pure porn and it's her and it's so real it makes her skin crawl. Kate pictured his arousal as he pored over his album and had thrown the thing back atop the piano in horror. It's clear that the recent instances are not, in his mind, the first times he's slept in her bed.

This is his lair, his hobby room, where he's given reign to his twisted mind, where he's planned his fun, written his Valentine's cards and ventured forth with the demon mask, where he's returned with the snippets of her life. It's the war room of a mad campaign directed against what she'd thought was hers. He hadn't planned to take her yesterday but he's been anticipating it for a long time. And so here she is, trapped at the centre of his mad fixation. This foul cellar now bounds her life, and despite all her crazed work at the chain, despite all her hammering and shouting, she can't see any way out.

41

It's eight fifty p.m. Feather coaxes the Corsa onto the Edgware Road and points homewards. The radio reports zero degrees and there's a drizzle coming down. He circles Hyde Park Corner and steers towards Fulham. Late shoppers are scurrying for taxis outside Harrods, pinched and cold. No bargains in sight. Feather thinks about the streets, those going out into the night. Down by the river he pulls into a residents' spot outside his building and goes in to climb the stairs, two floors, thirty-eight steps. By the time he reaches his door he's wheezing.

He showers but resists the temptation to crash out, rummages in his kitchen and puts two chicken breasts under the grill, chops a bed of salad and adds a scatter of oven fries then sits at the window looking at his sliver of river and eats. When he's through he's just as hungry but energy is coming back. He washes up and checks his phone. A message from Suzanne. He'll call her tomorrow. He thinks about Donna Jordan, discarded on those church steps. He thinks about Donna's history and how he'd like to catch the train up to Liverpool and take a look at the people who sent her here. There's a place called West Derby, a blighted street in the outer wastelands of the city, where it started, where the first blows were thrown that put Donna down on those church steps with her bruised face and rucked up skirt and her shoeless foot trapping a windblown scrap from last week's *Standard*.

Feather goes back to the window and watches the black river. The building is silent around him bar the murmur of a TV and the hiss of his gas fire. But what's the point of quiet when there's no one to share it with? Where's the purpose in lying awake in bed? It's ten thirty p.m. and rain sprays the window and wrecks his view, and Feather grabs his coat and heads back out.

~~~~~

He drives up past Brompton Cemetery, aiming for Kensal Town. Mary and Lawrie will be in Gassers in an hour, chasing wits who were there in the early hours of Monday, but Feather will go in first, get a head start.

The lights catch him at the Old Brompton Road and he sits sixty seconds on red, heater blasting and wipers smearing the screen. When the lights change he spins the wheel and diverts. He passes the Exhibition Centre and rounds the ESB into a narrow maze of shoebox houses. At the far end is a cul de sac of brick and timber units thrown up by a shoddy builder from third rate blueprints. He checks numbers and coasts up to a garage door fronting one of the houses and climbs out into a biting wind and pin-sharp rain. He looks round and shakes his head the way he always does when he comes to places like this. The place will look even worse in the light.

He squeezes behind the garage and presses a bell. Paint flakes off where Feather's knuckles catch the wood.

After thirty seconds the door opens and a mottled mid thirties face peers from a smog of cannabis. Feather pulls out his brief and asks if Jerome Welland is home. The man curls his lip.

'Christ, the fuzz.'

It's icy behind the garage and the rain is soaking Feather's neck. He palms the door open and goes in. He doesn't need to ask about Welland again because the first door he tries opens into a squalid lounge where a scrotty fuzz-haired youth is jumping up from a couch and jabbing a spliff into an ashtray where a cop wouldn't notice.

'Hey,' the youth says. 'What the fuck?'

'Jerome Welland?'

'What the fuck?'

Feather turns and tells the older guy to scarper and shuts the door on him.

'How's tricks?' he says.

'What the fuck?' Dope is entirely wasted on Jerome. He's dancing like he's on crank. Jumpy, Kate Walker said. She'd got that right. 'The fuck...? You can't come in here. Where's y'warrant?'

'Just a few questions,' Feather says. 'Routine enquiries.'

'Questions, fuck. Where's y'warrant?'

The door opens again behind Feather and the guy comes in to watch. Feather turns and plants his palm on the guy's chest and pushes him back out.

'If I see your face again,' he says, 'I'll improve it.'

He closes the door and Jerome is dancing like a string puppet. His eyes dart every way.

'Did you hear about Donna Jordan?' Feather says.

'Who?'

'You know who. You had a bust up with her in your solicitor's office.'

'That stupid bitch? I don't know her.'

'You were scrapping with her but you don't know her?'

'I never met her before. You here for that stupid bitch? What's she said?'

'What was the fight about?'

'Fuck should *I* know? The bitch was crazy. And you just assaulted Lionel. I'm a witness!'

'So you don't know Donna?'

Jerome's eyes finally meet Feather's, wide with fake virtue. 'Fuck no! She's just a crazy bitch. Mental. She attacked me in my own lawyer's office. I nearly whopped her right there, thrashed some manners into her. If my damn lawyer hadn't been there she'd have got a lesson.'

'What was the fight about?'

'Told you. Don't know. Miss Mental just come on all attitude. She was *lookin'* for a fight. Good luck with the magistrates, bitch. You can claw *their* eyes out.'

'I heard she smacked you around,' Feather says.

'*Fuck,* no! She surprised me, got the advantage. Came clawing at me, but if her lawyer hadn't been there I'd have put her teeth down her throat. All these bitches figure the world's gotta be politically correct. Think they can create havoc and walk away because a guy doesn't smack a lady. Fuck, *no,* bitch! I'll smack you into the back end of tomorrow, you claw me like that again.'

'So you didn't know her before the solicitor's?'

'No!'

'And you don't hold a grudge?'

'What?'

'For slapping you about like a pussy. That had to be a little humiliating.'

'*Fuck* you talking about? That uppity bitch was playing with fire. She just got lucky her lawyer was there.'

'But she didn't stay lucky.'

'How should I know? As if I give a shit. I hope she got hit by a bus.'

'Did you see her again after that time?'

'No. And she'd better hope I don't.'

Feather watches Jerome twitching and dancing, positioning himself between Feather and the ashtray, between Feather and the rest of the room. Jerome's nervous as hell, because none of the stuff in the room is legit. Who brings home phones and Xboxes and tablets and leaves them stacked in their boxes? Seems Jerome and Lionel have a little supply chain going. No wonder they're squealing about warrants. Feather strolls over and picks up a boxed smartphone. Hefts it.

'Samsungs just don't compete,' he says. 'Got one of these myself. Must be great to have ten of them.'

'The fuck! The fuck's your warrant? *Fuck!*'

'Is this how you funded your lawyer's account?' Not that Feather cares. He doesn't give a shit about stolen goods or dodgy escrows. He's just baiting the guy. It's wet and freezing outside and at one time he'd have been home with Sally, laughing at one of the old films. Perhaps not on an *exact* night like this, with Donna Jordan lying cold in the morgue. His job always had first call, but Sally understood. So maybe on a night like this he'd be out, prowling the streets, visiting shitty holes like this and talking to turds like Welland, who hasn't murdered anyone because he's too cowardly ever to face anyone down, and murder is as face-to-face as it gets. So Feather's not interested in Jerome. He's squeezing him simply because he doesn't like him.

'Where did you get six K in such a hurry?' he says. He plants the phone and crosses to the fireplace. The mantel's crammed with figurines and ornaments, ivory figures and diamante clocks. The mantel's flusher than an old lady's dream and the expensive glitz is as out of place here as the sixty inch screen propped behind the sofa. This is a den of thieves – fences, rather, Jerome not being the face-to-face type – and Kate Walker's suspicions about the escrow funding are spot on. Her investigator didn't have to dig hard.

Jerome didn't kill Donna Jordan but Feather asks anyway.

'Where were you, Sunday night?' he says.

Jerome's eyes are on the mantel, fearful of any further probing. He's not fearful about Donna Jordan, because he's not the one. If Jerome has no alibi then one of the team will follow up but it will be time wasted.

'A party,' Jerome says. 'The fuck's it to you?'

'I need the address. People who were there.' Feather pulls out a notebook.

'The fuck...'

Feather walks over and gets in Jerome's face. Jerome shrinks back.

'The bitch who knocked you about,' Feather says. 'Someone killed her. She got what was coming, and she got it from someone like you. So I need an address and names or I'm taking you in.'

Jerome catches up. His eyes leave the mantel. His eyes widen.

'Bitch is dead? Some fucker offed her? Man, that's karma.' His face stretches into pure euphoria. The fat pig's not here about drugs or knock-offs! Jerome twitches and jigs but now it's from pleasure. '*Karma*,' he says.

'Address,' Feather says. 'Names.'

~~~~~

It's eleven thirty. The rain has quit but the breeze has strengthened and the chill factor bites as Feather walks up to the club entrance.

The guy is right there on the door. Meatloaf, aka Darren Stokes. The one Feather met at Donna's yesterday. Stokes is an inch taller than Feather and unlike Feather's his physique is toned, but the main asset he brings to his job is his mean, ugly face. It's one that has deterred a hundred fights, though the rumbles he *has* been caught in have left scars. Feather flashes his brief. Wonders if Mary and Lawrie are already inside. If they are, Stokes doesn't mention it. He grumbles and calls behind him.

'Bring Bluey out.'

Bluey comes out to take over and Stokes walks ahead of Feather into a tiny cloakroom.

'Whatchya got?' he says. His face is grim.

'What've I got? I've got a murder enquiry.'

243

'Anno. Who done it?'

'I heard you were friends with Donna.'

'She was my girl.'

'Your *girl?*'

'I'll kill the fucker who done it.'

'Take it easy.'

'I'm gonna kill the fucker. The law ain't gonna protect him.'

Feather holds up a finger. 'Darren,' he says, 'stop.' He waits until he has Stokes' eye. 'If you're going to talk about killing people don't do it in front of me.'

'She was my girl. I'll say what I want.'

'Long as that's all you do. But not to me. Don't tell me about your murder plans.'

'Yeah.' A rumbling laugh rolls out then cuts dead. 'Well you just find the fucker.' Stokes pulls out a fag and lights up as if it's normal in here, which it might be. No one in Gassers is going to tell him otherwise. He takes a drag and Feather steps back.

'She was your girlfriend?' he says.

'Yeah.'

'That's not what I heard. Word is you were being a nuisance.'

'You 'eard wrong. We was good.'

'Donna had no time for you but you wouldn't listen.'

'We was good. Who's telling you this shit?'

'What was she? Seven stone? Something a breeze would blow away. You could have put her in your pocket and you'd not have noticed. That's a funny match.'

Darren's fag flares and fades.

'Fuck what you think,' he says. 'We was good, the two of us. I loved her.'

'But did she love you?'

'Yeah, she loved me. Who's been spreading this shit? I never caused no nuisance. We was a pair. Donna was moving in with me.'

'So why's everyone saying she wasn't interested?'

'Who's sayin' it? That cunt Trent? You bin talking to the dyke?'

'Donna was a dyke too, is what I heard.'

'Bollocks. Donna likes men. Real men, know what I mean?'

'You saying she didn't like girls? So what was that relationship with Georgina Trent?'

'Relationship, shit. Donna was hacked off. Georgie was always complaining, controlling her. Donna and me been steppin' out for a while.'

'So you say. I heard different. I heard you were following her around, wouldn't take no for an answer.'

'You heard bollocks. Donna and me was an item. If she'd been with me this bastard wouldn't have got her.'

'Which bastard? Someone you know?'

'If I did he'd be dead. And she'd never have been out there if it was up to me.'

'Not out roaming the streets? You'd have kept her under control? '

'She wouldn'ta had to work. I told her.'

'So who wanted to kill her?'

'The fuck I know? You're the copper.'

'But you were with her on Sunday night?'

Stokes throws the fag down and grinds it. Locks Feather's stare with furious eyes.

'Yeah. We was here. Talkin.'

'Did you leave with her?'

'No. She wen' out first. I'd business with the crew.'

'So you didn't walk her home?'

'I was in here.'

'Can anyone confirm that?'

'Bluey will tell you. The lads. I was with them. Donna went off on her tod.'

'Home? Or back on the streets?'

'She said home. I dunno.'

'Some boyfriend.' Feather smiles and jabs his hands into his pockets. 'You let your girl go wandering about at two in the morning?'

Stokes' eyes spark and his fists tighten. Feather looks at them then looks at Stokes. His own fists are ready inside his coat. Stokes' eyes stay locked on him but then his arms relax.

'I offered,' he says. 'She didn't want me to. She knows the streets better than anyone.'

'You think?' Feather says.

'Fuck you,' Stokes says.

'Did you follow her out? Had she told you not to?'

'Fuck you.'

'Been in a scrap?' Feather switches subjects and nods at Stokes' knuckles. They're calloused from years of fighting but something recent has aggravated them.

'Bit of bother the other night.'

'Here on the door?'

'Whatever.'

'Because Donna's killer knocked her about and I'm wondering how your knuckles got scraped.'

Stokes laughs, another deep rumble.

'You think my knuckles are grazed 'cos I hit her? I could have smashed her to pieces and it wouldn't show on me.'

'So who did you hit?'

Stokes grabs another fag and turns away to light it and Feather's just thinking that they're on their way to the nick when he speaks.

'I give that fucker Parish a slap,' he says.

'Wilbur Parish, Donna's pimp?'

'Yeah.'

'Why'd you do that?'

'So he'd know to stop messing with her.'

He turns back. Blows smoke. Their stares lock. No one's going to mess with Donna Jordan any more, of course.

Feather recalls Parish's puffy eyes, the bruising on his face. 'When?' he says.

'Sunday night. The fucker got wind that Donna was shackin' up with me an' told her he'd break her arms if she ever tried to do a runner. So I paid him a visit an' delivered his retirement package.'

'You beat him up?'

'Fucker had it coming.'

'Was this in the early hours?'

Stokes shakes his head. 'I done him before I come to meet Donna. When she came in here I told her she was free. Off the fucker's books.'

'But she was still working the streets?'

'She wouldn't listen. If it was me she'd be out of it. We was talking about it Sunday night. She said it was her life. Her decision.'

'A decision you didn't like?'

'I didn't kill her,' Stokes says.

'So you say.'

'Fuck you.'

'You say Donna was moving in with you?'

'We'd been plannin' it. And Sunday night she was ready. Said she was tired of working for Parish, living under that dyke's thumb.'

Feather pinches his nose. When he opens his eyes Darren Stokes is dragging at his cigarette and still talking about getting the fucker. Georgina had painted Stokes as an ape with a fixation, too stupid to recognise a brush off, a guy who handles life's problems with his fists. Donna would have found that out, sooner or later. You never know what Darren's thinking, Georgina said, and maybe she was right. Maybe Stokes is lying or maybe he's telling the truth or maybe he *thinks* he's telling the truth, but he's still the last person seen with Donna that night.

'Fetch your mates,' Feather says. 'The ones who can alibi you.'

~~~~~

Feather wakes after four hours' sleep and rustles up breakfast and two cups of black tea then goes out and fires up the Corsa. He leaves it running while he climbs out to scrape the windscreen. By the time he's finished the car's no warmer inside. The car's like a hearse. Feather grips the freezing wheel and finds the gear.

Six thirty. Headlight dazzle in the black cold. Traffic growing as he swings round Bayswater and turns up Ladbroke Grove, drives into Kensal Town. He crosses the railway and turns just before the canal, down towards Our Lady Of The Holy Souls. There's nothing there now bar a remnant of police tape littering the steps. Feather parks and steps out. The sky is lightening but the doorway's deep in shadow and the steps are desolate, an icy sheen that could suck the life out of anyone. Was Donna alone as she got here? Did a car creep from behind? Did she find a late punter? A five minute quickie? But the church is on the route between Gassers and home and it's more likely that Donna was just passing on her way to her bed. She was cutting onto Kensal Road to cross the canal. What was the chance of meeting someone here in this backwater? Unless they were expecting her, had come to meet her. Perhaps, after it was over, that person continued over the canal. Feather walks up the road and cuts between the buildings to climb the ramp to the bridge and leans on the railings over the centre of the canal. The water's a freezing black, dotted with icy reflections of lit windows along the terrace that backs onto it. Feather peers down into the infinite black.

After a while he continues across the bridge and descends to Harrow Road. He walks a hundred yards and arrives at their doorway. He stands and looks up for thirty seconds then sighs, turns and retraces his steps. Back on the bridge he keys his phone. He wakes up Phil Ashley who greets him with profanities and Feather says yeah, yeah, tell it to the Sleep Police, I need your people here at eight. Fuck no, Ashley says, no can do, I can't get them into the water before ten, I've gotta break into John's day off and Roger comes in from Slough. I need them in the water by eight, Feather insists, as soon as the light's good. Nine, Ashley says, earliest. Soon, Phil, Feather says, as soon as you can, though there's not really a rush. He kills the line and turns to stare the other way, past the apartments and condos to the bend of the water.

A taxi horn blasts on Harrow Road for no reason at all.

42

It's one thirty in the afternoon when they bring it up. The water's less than a metre and a half deep but there's a god-awful mess of junk down there. Ashley's team have covered twenty yards either side of the bridge and landed everything to clear a sight of the bottom. The tow path's littered with detritus. It used to be worse, Ashley said. Before the renovations you'd find TVs and bicycles, all kinds of stuff down there. More trolleys than at Sainsbury's. Feather and Obasanjo have been pacing the bridge for three hours, trying to keep warm and thanking God they're not in the water, which is exactly one degree above freezing. Then the divers' heads break the surface. They wade in and heave themselves onto the path and Ashley waves something. Feather and Obasanjo descend the ramp and Ashley holds out an offering.

'This it?'

It's a four inch kitchen knife with traces of what look like rust on the blade. Yeah, Feather says, that's it. Thank Christ, Ashley says.

Obasanjo touches his toe to a wheel-less child buggy beached amongst the crap. 'What happens to this lot?' he says.

'As if I give a shit,' Ashley says.

'Council job,' Feather says. 'Bag the knife.'

The vehicles are parked in the stub road. Mary Charlton has takeaway coffees there. She looks at the knife.

'Both ends were used,' Feather says. 'Donna took blows from the handle, clenched in a fist, but it probably didn't quieten her. Her attacker got madder and switched to the business end.'

The coffee's lousy but it's hot. 'Take it in,' he tells Obasanjo. 'Prints and blood.'

There's a gash bag in the back of Mary's unmarked. He leans in and deposits his empty cup. Heat envelopes him. He slams the door and opens the front one and slides in.

'Take us round,' he tells Mary. She climbs in.

~~~~~

The flat is the same mess but at least the sink's still clear. A sole takeaway carton on the draining board is testament to Georgina's culinary efforts of the last twenty-four hours. Feather reaches beyond the rack where the dried plates are still stacked and pulls a knife block towards him. There are five knives in the block and an empty slot where a four inch blade belongs. Feather tilts the rack.

'It wasn't in the washing up,' he says.

Georgina's hair is tidier but her eyes are desolate pools. Her arms are crossed. She hugs herself.

'It's around here somewhere,' she says. She puzzles it over, trying to work it out. Mary Charlton watches from over her shoulder. Feather pulls out a knife from the adjacent slot. Its handle is slightly longer but it's a match for the one retrieved from the canal.

'Donna was leaving you,' Feather says.

Georgina's confusion deepens. 'What?' she says.

'You told me she wasn't interested in Darren Stokes. But she was.'

'No.'

'Donna hadn't given him the brush-off. She was about to move in with him.

'No,' Georgina repeats. 'That's not true.'

'Stokes says different.'

'He's lying. Donna wouldn't go near him.'

'And Wilbur Parish's story corroborates.'

'That animal? Why would you believe anything he says?'

Feather smiles. 'Parish told me plenty of lies but when I spoke to him this morning he came clean. Stokes had given him a beating to let him know that Donna was off his books. She was moving in with him.'

'Liars. I'm all Donna has.'

Feather drops the knife back into the block. 'I think you were,' he says. 'All she had. But Donna didn't see very clearly. Abused girls have limited vision. They're blind to what's good for them. That's why the two of you could never have lasted. She'd have walked away in the end.'

'She loved me. I was her protector.'

'Yeah. You just couldn't protect her from herself.'

250

Georgina is shaking her head but Feather's still smiling. He's smiling for Donna, wondering what he'd have done if his own girl had ended up on the streets.

'Donna's biggest enemy wasn't Parish. It wouldn't even have been Stokes when that affair went bad. It would always have been herself. You could see how it was but you couldn't do anything about it.'

'I'd never hurt Donna.' Georgina is shaking.

Feather takes Georgina's arm and eases her past Mary. He walks her through to the bedroom and opens the wardrobe and they look at the heap of clothes beside the empty travel case.

'She should have packed more discreetly,' he says, 'but that wasn't her style. She'd announced that she was leaving. Packing right in front of you was her grand gesture.' He sighs and closes the wardrobe. 'And she'd arranged with Stokes to pick her up yesterday.'

'No!' Georgina's eyes gleam. 'It was bluff. She wanted to hurt me. But I was everything she had.'

'You were here alone on Sunday evening,' Feather says. 'Maybe having a drink or two. Alone and scared that you were about to lose her. The thought was unbearable. So you came in here and emptied the case, tipped her stuff out as if that could hold her back. Then you went looking for her. You were torturing yourself with the thought that she was in the club with Stokes. You were so terrified of that that you had to go out and confront her. Anything was better than waiting here alone.'

'She hated him. She hated all men. She needed me.'

'You were so scared,' Feather says, 'that you took the knife. It was just an instinct, a defence against the terror. If you'd not met Donna on her way back here, if you'd not had the knife in your hand, it would never have happened.'

'I loved her,' Georgina whispers. 'But she was in such a state. We met at the church and the drink had made her evil. She laughed at me. Told me she hated me. *Hated* me. But she never could have.'

Georgina sinks onto the bed and falls sideways to rest her head on a pillow. Tears flow across her plain face. 'She didn't hate me. But she said some terrible things. I just started hitting her and then she *spat* at me and said we were through. It was only the handle. I didn't mean to hurt her.'

Mary Charlton comes into the bedroom and stands back to let

Feather squeeze out. Then she crosses to take Georgina's arm. Feather waits in the lounge and looks at the mess.

43

The second day has lasted an eternity. Once she'd wracked her mind for ideas that didn't come, spent another futile hour attacking the chain and hammering at the joists, Kate had been left with the truth that there is no way out. There's no way she's leaving the cellar without his consent. She's powerless to evade whatever is coming. She'd fought to resist that terrible truth all day, searched and searched for solutions, but in the end the hours and the silence and the *nothingness* have delivered her to this shivering and stunned despair.

On the wall over the folding table is an electrical box. Kate had experimented with the switches last night and found one that extinguished the cellar light, leaving only the soothing glow of the fire's radiant coils. But at six this morning when she'd roused herself to put the light back on, the instant suffocating press of the cellar walls had battered her anew and her frayed nerves had finally betrayed her. When he came down at eight with her food she was a pleading, weepy cur. But her pleas and tears elicited from him only a frightening mix of contempt and fear. He hadn't planned this. He's stuck with the situation and he's afraid. He'd put down her food and fled.

The day has lasted an eternity.

When she hasn't been lying stupefied on the camp bed Kate has prowled the territory permitted by the chain, checking the artefacts around her again without further enlightenment. And at every move the chain has tugged at her ankle and slithered across the matting to test her sanity. Each new sight of the white flaking walls as she turned and turned has made it harder to reconcile what was real *then* with what is real *now*. This afternoon she'd gone to work again with the chisel, levering at the chain's anchor flange until the blade snapped. Then she'd resumed hammering against the joists, screaming until her throat hurt. But the cellar returned only silence. Where the hell is this place? Is there no one next door? *Is* there a next door?

She'd forced herself to focus and *think,* but as the afternoon had worn on without a single useful idea the fear had seeped back in. She'd considered the electrical box. She can control the house's supply from here but what would that gain? If she put the cellar in darkness he'd just bring a flashlight. If he left the house above with lights blazing she could perhaps signal by flashing them on and off, but would he leave lights on? And would anyone – *could* anyone – see the windows? She could lure him down here by shutting off the electricity but he'd be ready for her, and her chain prohibits access to the space behind the door, so there's no hiding there with a weapon.

Ideas had failed and the hours had ticked by in numbing silence. By the end of the afternoon she'd retreated into a listless trance, moving only when the heat from the fire forced her first one way then the other, pushing the camp bed back, moving it forward, achieving nothing.

~~~~~

It's seven p.m. The day has finally passed and in the world outside she's in the news. There's an Incident Room in a police station where men and women are working urgently. They're talking to everyone she knows and many she doesn't, all who've had contact with her. She wonders when they'll talk to *him,* how good are his acting skills.

He's been moving about upstairs for an hour and finally he comes down. She's not eaten the whole day but dinner is another unappetising supermarket sandwich and a banana. She'll cram them down her throat once he's gone, a miserable feast to keep her strength up, keep her alive. But the meanness of the meal, his lack of effort, tells Kate that he doesn't see food as a significant factor in their situation. He nevertheless stays to talk to her and that's what counts. She fights to stay calm and identify the cracks in his armour, to pull him back from wherever he's leading them. Her abduction has changed him too, has locked him as much as her into this surreal world that split off from normality two days ago. His mad fixation, his actions in stalking her, his preparation of this cellar, have placed him all along, of course, much nearer to that world, but we're all allowed a little of the dark side, we're permitted our fantasies. Fantasies can go on forever. This new world can't.

'It's not too late,' Kate says.

He's standing at an angle to the fire, taking its heat as he gazes at his collection. She watches, still unable to fathom him. The way he's standing, rocking on his soles, suggests thought or trance, and his facing away from her is a psychological palliative. He's keeping his problem out of sight.

'It will destroy you too,' she says.

He surprises her then. His shoulders shake and he emits a low chuckle as he scrutinises his museum – The Museum of Kate's Life (Parts Unverified). His head lifts to the patchwork of photos on the wall and he scrutinises them, left to right, as if for the first time.

'Listen to me,' Kate says. 'This isn't you.'

Now, finally, he turns to her.

'This is *all* me,' he says. 'I'm nothing else.'

'We need to stop it,' she says. 'To find a way out.'

'There is no way out.'

'Of course there is. There's no harm done yet.'

He forces another laugh, phoney, shot through with anger and fear. Maybe a little hate.

'That's so *you*, Kate. Just what I'd expect you to say.'

Kate's reply is over harsh. 'But what the fuck did I ever do to you...?' Then she checks herself. Careful. 'If this is my fault...' she says.

Of course it's her fault. That's the mantra directing every iota of his anger. If they're to understand each other, if they're to progress, her penitence must be the first step. But penitence for what?

'The harm was done a long time ago,' he says. 'We can't go back.'

'But how? I was never aware of doing anything.'

His smile loses interest. He's drifting.

'Why didn't you talk to me?'

He returns. 'I tried to.'

'I never noticed.'

He smiles. A forced, frightened, *powerful* smile.

'That's true. You never noticed. You never saw me.'

'You must stop this. It's not you.'

But his smile falls away.

'It's all me, Kate. It's what you made me.'

44

It's ten p.m. and the Donna Jordan incident room is a silent tableau of vacated desks and dead screens. Up on the board the final threads of the girl's life are mapped out in a mosaic of notes and photos. They'll be cleared out tomorrow and then she'll be gone. Feather flicks off the lights and walks out. He's beat.

Down the corridor C4 is bright and busy with the missing lawyer incident. Feather stops by the door and jabs his hands into his pockets. He watches the team, twenty police and civilians, taking calls, sifting data. Heldt's got another thirty on the street. They need to blitz this. Feather has what he calls his Two-Seventy-Two Rule: get to an abducted woman or kid inside two hours and you'll get them alive; beyond seventy-two you'll bring them back cold. It's ten p.m. on the second night of the search. They're forty eight hours in and sliding towards a bad result. If they haven't found Kate Walker by this time tomorrow they'll have lost her.

Six of Feather's own people are in the room, pulled across from Donna Jordan. Mary's here. And Lawrie. They both look whacked. They were in Gassers until three this morning, back on shift at eight. Feather needs to catch Heldt and make sure the Donna Jordan crew are thrown out at eleven or they'll be good for nothing. He spots DC Crane, scribbling in a pad and working a keyboard. He walks across and eases into a seat by his desk.

Crane looks up and angles his head towards a card folder lying on the desk. His original notes. 'We should have stopped him,' he says. 'There was enough.'

'There's never enough,' Feather says, wondering why he's in here and concluding that it's the directionless aftermath of the Donna Jordan case. Whilst you're working a murder you have focus. You fool yourself that you're doing something for the victim. Feather's had homicides that have taken twelve hours to clear and he's had cases that have stretched years, and every day is driven by the belief that you're moving towards a destination. But when the cases close, when the perpetrators are caught and are found to be no different to all the other perpetrators, to have motives no different – it's always greed or power or hurt, nothing else – when the files close you're back where you started: the victims are still dead and nothing has helped them. The dead *can't* be helped. So you switch off the lights and hope that the emptiness is gone by the time you reach home. But Feather's home lost its power to heal when Sally died. So he's dog tired but he's still here, wanting to know – *needing* to know – that the lawyer is okay but thinking that she's probably not.

He pulls Crane's folder across and lifts the flap. Everything's now in the system, everything Crane had and everything that's coming in, and the card folder is redundant but he opens it anyway, and the first item he sees is the media photo, the only new thing in there. Feather slides it out and stares at it and truly hopes the lawyer's okay because God help him she's the spitting image of Sally. A decade younger than Sally was, but the picture would fool him if he didn't know different. Maybe Kate's nose, in the angle of the picture, is straighter, but from the front you'd never notice. To tired eyes the missing lawyer is indistinguishable from his wife and Feather is dog tired and deadly afraid.

He sighs and pulls out the rest of Crane's old notes.

They *should* have stopped this guy, of course. There are always people being stalked and harassed, but once an assailant is breaking into the house, once he's confronting his victim on the Underground, trapping her in her *bath*, it's time to act. Heldt should have been watching Kate and her house six days ago. The guy was there for the taking. They'd have picked him up within forty eight hours and there wouldn't be thirty people on the streets tonight searching haystacks.

He reads the notes and sees the picture Crane was building. Things are always clear after the event but Heldt should have caught this.

'Anything on the calls?' he says.

'They're an unregistered PAYG. We've requested the data so we'll get the call locations at least.'

'Anything from the TV appeal?'

'Still coming in, sir, but nothing positive. She's not been seen since she left work on Monday night. The door-to-door's not given us anything. We're checking CCTV but if the guy chose his route his vehicle won't be on anything near by.'

'Family? Friends? Work?'

'We've talked to them but they've nothing that helps. Her closest family is her sister's. That gives us a brother-in-law and a nephew who are both a little jumpy but claim to know nothing. And there's a pushy boyfriend – he came on heavy when he reported her missing. Pointing the finger, throwing blame.'

'Long standing relationship?'

'Two weeks. And we've screwed up. He's been in here five times in the last forty-eight hours yelling in our faces and we've still not sat him down to check *him* out.'

Feather looks at Crane, astonished. This isn't good. What the hell's Heldt playing at?

'We took a statement when he reported her missing but that's it. DCI Clough did his nut when he found out we'd not sweated him.'

'I bet he did,' Feather says.

'We'll have him in tomorrow morning. I don't get the sense that he's playing games but we should have cleared him first thing.'

'Yes,' Feather agrees. 'What else? Neighbours? Locals? Services?'

'Still working through them. There's a guy lived six doors down from her who'd been seen talking to her but he's moved away. We've not located him yet. She has a regular milkman but he only sees her once a month for collections. We've three postmen who cover the street. Early morning workers. I don't see them hanging out for hours late at night, watching her.'

'Clients?'

Crane's paperwork has a bare list of Kate's recent clients, which is all the detail her firm would release. Another sheet lists the results of a dig through the last two years of court proceedings in which Kate was involved. The team are digging out detail on all this right now. It's unlikely that a former plaintiff or defendant has snatched her but stalkers crawl from the strangest corners. Feather scans the list and spots two names from his murder enquiry. Donna Jordan is there, but the morgue's her alibi. And Jerome Welland is there, but he's not an abductor any more than he's a killer. Overleaf, under the heading "Opponents" is a shorter list: plaintiffs, victims and defendants Kate has acted against. The firm has been freer with information here, confidentiality not being an issue. Kate, it seems, has knocked a few people about in the courts and amongst them he spots another name from his murder enquiry: Charles Porter, Donna Jordan's assaultee, on whom Kate was apparently turning up the heat. Crane's notes tag Porter as unlikely for the abduction for the same reason Feather dismissed him in Donna's murder enquiry: the guy is looking for quiet, not for trouble. You don't admit culpability in a court case to avoid publicity then rush out and start a war with the opposing solicitor. Feather scans the rest of the list but sees nothing.

'You say the family males are jumpy?'

'They're frightened about what's happened, but there's something else.'

'Unrelated?'

Crane shakes his head. 'I don't know. Just a feeling. They were all there when I called in – parents and two kids – but it was like they were pulling together for show. And the boy had an attitude like he resented me intruding over his aunt. I just got a feeling.'

Feather shrugs. All families have problems. He shuffles the rest of Crane's sheets, a mixture of computer printouts and hand written notes detailing the facts of the stalking. The affair is nascent by stalking timescales. Harassment campaigns can stretch five years, ten even, but Crane's notes have this starting only a couple of months ago, though as Feather reads the detail he senses a longer campaign. The guy was watching Kate before he started his tricks and maybe the tricks went unnoticed for a while. This started at least six months ago. The guy moved into the overt phase when the urge to be noticed got the upper hand. It's a standard pattern, though most stalkers stop short of face-to-face confrontation. But when the victim is taken things rarely turn out well. He reads the details again. The house break-ins, the intrusion whilst Kate was in the bath, the devil's mask. These are extreme.

He fishes a pad from his jacket pocket.

'Give me the sister's address. And these two. I'll take a look.'

Crane brings the info up. He doesn't ask why Feather's poking his nose into something that doesn't concern him. He doesn't quote procedure. The big guy's way above his rank and no one tells Frank Feather what to do. Even his guv'nor watches his toes.

And some extra footwork would do no harm. Crane takes Feather's pad and writes addresses.

45

Feather drives east along the river in early morning traffic and crosses at Vauxhall. He eases the Corsa into a narrow tree-lined street of four storey Victorians and parks up. Climbs the steps to one of the doors.

The brother-in-law, Ian, opens it in a suit and tie. He eyes Feather's brief, wondering why it's not Crane and what the early morning visit implies. Feather reassures him, and Ian calls ahead to save his wife the shock. Angela Harris is wandering her kitchen in a dressing gown. Her hair's a mess and there are bags under her eyes. She's older than Kate and sadder, which might be her permanent look if they don't get her sister back. Her hands are unsteady. Feather nods to a teenage girl spooning cereal and declines an offer of coffee but shakes off his coat. The kitchen's a furnace. He pulls out a chair and sits, a psychological gambit to get them focused. Angela sinks into a chair opposite. Ian checks his watch but stays put.

'How many people have you got looking?' Ian asks.

'Around forty,' Feather says. 'More civilian staff will be on from nine.' He doesn't mention that he's not part of it, is circling the periphery fresh from investigating the frozen corpse of a woman who was one of Kate's clients. 'The guy has left traces somewhere,' he says. 'They'll get us to him.'

'But how quickly?' Ian says. He plants a hand on his wife's shoulder. The girl pushes her bowl away and stands.

'Not in time,' she says. She's been crying.

'Claire!'

'Why didn't you stop him?' The teenager comes to stand beside Feather. 'Why didn't you listen to her?'

Feather has no answer.

'If you'd just taken Kate seriously,' Angela concurs, 'she'd be safe. What did this guy have to do to make you act?'

They all know the answer. He's done it.

'It's perhaps not much consolation,' Feather says, 'but we're doing our utmost now. We're committed to getting her back.'

'We appreciate that,' Ian says. His hand squeezes his wife's shoulder. 'But you took way too long to act. We need to know that you're not holding back any effort now.'

'Believe me,' Feather says, 'we're not holding back.' He's not come here to stand in the dock. He's here to understand this family. 'We're still trying to get a picture of your sister's life,' he says.

'Is it relevant?' Ian asks.

'It's central. Her abductor is someone she knows. Maybe only peripherally, but she knows him.'

'Have you a profile? Anything to steer you?'

'Just a generic picture,' Feather says. 'Stalkers and abductors fall into a narrow band but they can be good at hiding. We look at the victim's environment for flags.'

'She's been gone two days,' Ian points out.

'Yeah,' Feather says. 'And your cooperation is appreciated. We may get the best idea about who this is from the people who know Kate best.'

'You have our full cooperation,' Ian tells him.

'That's good. That's why I'm here.'

'But we told DC Crane everything we know. The boyfriend Zav is the biggest unknown. Kay has become involved with him very recently. We've not even met him.'

'*You've* met him,' Angela says.

'In passing. Hard to get his measure.'

'He the big guy with messy hair?'

'That's him.'

Worzel. The guy outside Kate's house two days ago.

'Any particular reason you mention him?' Feather says.

'He just appeared at a funny moment. We get the impression Kay rushed in.'

'The stalking started before he met her,' Angela says.

'That would still fit,' Ian replies. 'Guy harasses Kay from a distance then moves closer.'

'We've talked to him,' Feather says. 'We'll probably talk to him again. I'm here to see if you've any more thoughts.'

'Kay has her own circle,' Ian says. 'She can be a dark horse.'

'Don't!' Angela says. 'Kate's completely open. Having her privacy doesn't make her a dark horse.'

'I'm only saying that she leads an interesting life. She's thirty-two. A professional. But she's still footloose. Does her own thing.'

'Unlike us,' Angela says.

'Any particular thing? Anything that concerns you?'

Ian shrugs. 'She likes to be out, socialising, meeting people. Nothing wrong with that, of course.'

'Exactly,' Angela says. 'So forget dark horses. If we want dark horses we don't have far to look.'

Ian casts a wry smile at Feather. When Feather doesn't return it Ian takes his leave.

'Excuse me,' he says. 'I've things to wrap up at the office then they'll have to fend for themselves for a day or two. You coming, Claire?'

The girl is still beside Feather. She shakes her head. 'I'm meeting Nikki. I'm not going in.'

Ian nods at Feather. 'If I think of anything,' he says, 'I'll let you know.'

'Do,' Feather says. 'But one moment while we're all here. Put me right: none of you have seen Kate since early Sunday?'

Ian stops. 'That's right.' He looks at his wife. 'She stayed with us on Saturday night. Friday and Sunday night she was elsewhere. Her fears seemed to be up and down.'

'She stayed with Zav, Friday night,' Angela says. 'And she was at her own house on Sunday.'

'When did she last talk to you?'

'Monday afternoon,' Angela says. 'She phoned to let me know she was okay, wouldn't be staying here that night.'

'She could have stayed as long as she wanted,' Ian says. 'I just wish she'd done that.'

'So none of you saw her after Sunday morning?' Feather says. 'Do you all recall what you were doing, Monday night?' He's watching Ian, who's stopped in the doorway.

'I was working late,' he says. 'I got home at ten. Angie and Claire were here.'

'With your son?'

'Without our son. He was out that evening.'

'He came in an hour after you,' Angie says. 'Just before eleven when the police called. Does it matter, Inspector?'

262

'He's checking our alibis,' Ian explains. 'But don't waste time too close to home, Inspector.'

'Close to home is rarely a waste of time,' Feather says. 'Thank you for your time, Mr Harris. Just a few more minutes with your wife then I'll leave you in peace.'

Ian and Claire go their separate ways but then there's a commotion by the front door as someone comes in. Feather hears heated words and a scruffy youth appears. He stops when he sees Feather, then pulls himself together and heads for the fridge.

'Jonathan,' Angela says. She's more to say but she's holding back.

'Gotta rush,' the boy says. 'Gonna be late.'

'You're *entitled* to be late,' his mother says. 'We're in a horrible nightmare, in case you hadn't noticed.'

Jonathan roots in the fridge and comes out with a slice of leftover pizza and a can of Coke. He snaps the tab. 'Doesn't matter where I am,' he says. 'I can't help Aunt Kate. I hope she's okay but I gotta go to school.'

'In that state? Where've you been all night?'

'Already told you. I crashed at Gary's.' He closes the fridge and looks down at his mother. 'Interrogation over? May I go?'

'Get a shower,' Angela says, 'at least.'

'I'm on it,' Jonathan says. He checks Feather out again.

'Good morning,' Feather says. 'Heavy night?'

'Kinda.'

Feather smiles. 'We're just bringing your mother up to date. Still no news, but we're looking.'

'Cool. That's good. We can't imagine who's got her.'

'No ideas at all?'

Jonathan shakes his head. 'As if we'd know anything. Aren't there, like, suspects yet? There's gotta be some weirdos you're on to.'

'Do you know any? Anyone who'd be interested in your aunt?'

Jonathan aligns the sagging pizza with his mouth. He waits, like he's about to answer, then pushes the pizza in and chews and shakes his head. Feather waits. Jonathan swallows the mess and says something that sounds like: 'Could be anyone.'

'We're still wondering why anyone would stalk your aunt. Why they'd take her. That's our main puzzle.'

'There's a million weirdos would do it,' Jonathan says. 'She's like a...

MILF or whatever.'

'Jonathan!'

'I'm just saying. There's people out there. They notice.'

'What do they notice?'

'I don't know. Like...'

'That she's good looking? That your aunt's attractive? So people would notice?'

'Yeah. I guess.'

Feather works up a wry grin. 'I sure never had a sexy aunt like that,' he says.

'Yeah. She keeps in shape.'

'I met her. Very good shape.'

'So – there's guys would like a piece, is what I'm saying.'

'Jonathan!'

'You figure that's the reason?' Feather says.

'Some guy wanted to come on to her,' Jonathan says. 'Liked how she looked and dresses. Makes sense.'

Angela is tight lipped. 'Go get ready for school, Jonathan,' she says.

Jonathan looks like he's going to say more but then takes another bite from the pizza and heads out. Feather watches for a moment. Turns back to Angela.

'He often stay out at night?' he says.

Angela pulls a carton towards her and pours milk into her coffee.

'Just occasionally at his friend's,' she says. 'But we're going to put our foot down. If it hadn't been for what's happened we'd have made him come back last night.'

'I guess all kids stay over.'

'When their parents allow it. But Jonathan's going to be spending more time here.'

'You worried what he gets up to?'

'When he's hanging out with the wrong people.'

'There a girl involved?'

'I wish,' Angela says. 'We're worried about the crowd he does hang with. They're getting him into trouble.'

'This Gary he mentioned. He a close friend?'

'Unfortunately. And a bad influence. We've had some problems recently.'

'Alcohol? Drugs?'

'Jonathan's got mixed up with something at school. The police have talked to him.'

She lifts her coffee but doesn't drink. Gazes into the distance.

'Mixed up in what?' Feather says.

'We don't believe it. We know our son.'

'What happened?'

She tells him. Describes her son's gradual slide, the bad company, his friend Gary, a teacher's house wrecked. Angela Harris is in denial but she fears she's losing her son. Feather thinks of his own son Karl. He's thirty-one, a doctor who buys him gym memberships and dispenses advice. But Angela's story mirrors his relationship with Karl a decade and a half back. For a while Feather couldn't tell which way the boy would go, still can't say what pushed him in the right direction. Maybe it was nothing. Maybe it's all inside. You just go in your own natural direction even if you bounce around a little first. It wasn't easy, after Sally died. He and Karl fought all the time. But deep down Feather always had faith. And Karl never wrecked a teacher's house, demolished a life. Maybe Jonathan Harris didn't either but he's keeping bad company and he's entrenched behind a wall of bad attitude and his mother thinks she's losing him.

And maybe she is.

Feather wonders what Jonathan Harris is capable of.

46

C4 is packed for Heldt's briefing. Feather gatecrashes and leans against a desk beside Peter Clough. Clough gives him a world weary look. He's just pulled in another ten uniforms and seven civilians plus the remnants of Feather's Donna Jordan team to boost the search. Mary Charlton catches Feather's eye. Her face is grim and she looks tired but she'll pull her weight. Feather's here to see DC Crane but he doesn't spot him. He listens for a while to nothing much new then shrugs at Clough and walks out. He heads to his desk to start on the Donna Jordan report for the preliminary CPS conference.

Ten minutes later there's feet and voices outside. The briefing is over. The team has dispersed to hit the streets and computer screens. They've got maybe one last day to get to Kate. Probabilities. The Two-Seventy-Two. The chances are already down to fifty-fifty. By tonight no one will be expecting a good result.

Feather works his report up fast, leaving blanks for consulting the log, placeholders for precise times, the autopsy summary, the print and DNA from the knife. The words come fast in cold formalese. Feather pictures Georgina Trent, shivering in her cell. She wanted to protect Donna but you don't protect people by killing them. Feather jiggles the mouse and brings up Donna's proforma, and her old family address is there on the screen, and what Feather would really like to do is ditch the damn report and drive over to Euston and take the train to Liverpool. He looks up and Crane is standing there.

'I talked to Kate's family,' Feather tells him, but he's little to give. Just an undercurrent that may be nothing more than the stress of the situation, plus the boy's troubles. If it was his case he'd sweat the boy and husband but for now nothing jumps out with them. He asks if Crane has had Kate Walker's boyfriend in yet.

'I'm just in from chasing my tail after him,' Crane says. 'He's not answering his phone and he's nowhere in sight.'

Feather sits back. Gives Crane a look that says he's lucky he's not working for him.

Crane's look concurs. Like he said: a screw up. Feather shakes his head. 'Want me to drive round?'

Crane shrugs. They're out of time. They need all the bods they can get. 'Better than sitting at a desk, sir,' he says.

'Better by far,' Feather agrees.

~~~~~

Feather drives to Camden. He shouldn't be doing this. He should be fleshing out the Donna Jordan report ready for the CPS meeting which is precisely fifty minutes away. But he can have a quick look for McGeary and still get back. Boyfriends that pop up from nowhere in the middle of a stalking campaign are worth talking to. Worzel interests him, even if it's not his case, even if he shouldn't be anywhere near it. Clough and Heldt have it covered. But Feather can't put Kate's face out of his mind. He can't put the Two-Seventy-Two Rule out of his mind. If they don't find her today then it's over.

Bar the McGeary oversight Heldt's doing all the right things. They're on the streets, canvassing. They're taking calls, checking CCTVs, sifting dozens of names for background. But right now they've got nothing. The net's still being cast wide when they should be moving in for the kill. They know that Kate was taken from near her home but where did he grab her? On the street? In her drive? Inside the house? How did he get her away? Worzel's a big guy. He could have overpowered Kate without any problem and he has a van. And if Clough wants him back in maybe Feather can snag him. Save them precious time.

McGeary's business is open and there's an undernourished hippie behind the counter who doesn't know where McGeary is. The hippie's nervous at holding the fort alone and the only information he has is that McGeary was set to meet a wholesaler down Stamford Bridge today and maybe he's gone straight there, though why the hell he didn't tell him he can't imagine. Feather leaves him to it and drives to McGeary's house but the guy's not there either. He heads back from the wasted trip and he's already fifteen minutes late for the CPS conference so he makes a call and cries off. Drives straight past the nick and fights traffic down to Chelsea. McGeary's wholesaler is an unlikely bet but what's another thirty minutes? Feather eases the

Corsa round the stadium and turns into North End Road and gets snarled between delivery trucks and oncoming traffic on the narrow street. His blood pressure starts to ratchet like he's on his damn stairs. Then a guy crosses in front of him and he comes alert. It's Jerome Welland, large as life and twice as jumpy. The guy was never a serious candidate for Donna's killing but he's one of the names on Crane's talk-to list, and even if he's no more a contender for abduction than murder Feather can nevertheless save Heldt's people an hour.

Jerome's moving with a nervous urgency and he's hauling a rucksack. He skips along the pavement and disappears into a corner pub. Feather turns and leaves the Corsa on yellows and follows him in.

The pub's dark and there's maybe ten people in, drinking early lunch. Jerome has crossed to a table on the far side of the room and is sitting with a black guy. The rucksack has disappeared. The black guy is sporting short dreads and has a pint of mild in front of him and Feather's mnemonics tag him Natty from the cover of one of Sally's old vinyls. Jerome's just jumping up to order himself a shot when Feather's paw lands on his shoulder. Natty's already spotted the danger. His eyes flash but he's sharp. He picks up his mild and sips like any regular punter. Jerome doesn't know what regular is. He curses and twitches like a rabbit but the weight of Feather's hand is unremitting as he eases himself into a spare chair and smiles across the table.

'Introduce us,' he says to Jerome.

'The fuck I will. What you doing following me?'

Natty doesn't need introductions. He's got a nose for the filth, but Feather pulls out his brief anyway and holds it up, so they're clear. The guy looks at Jerome. The look says that they're going to talk about this.

'The fuck you doing?' Jerome is saying. 'This is harassment. This is the second time. You've nothin' on me.'

Feather says: 'Nothing? Is that what I'll find if I look in that rucksack?'

The black guy's face is stone. Jerome licks his lips and brings up his next line, which is as stupid as it's predictable. He says: 'What rucksack?'

'You telling me there's no rucksack under the table?' Feather says.

'The fuck you talking about?'

'So. If I were to reach under right now, if I were to pull a bag out, it wouldn't be yours?'

'I've nothin' under there.' Jerome is talking to Natty. 'You anything under there, Ray?' He's talking to Natty-Ray and trying to be smart but it's about the stupidest question he could have asked because they all know that if neither of them owns the bag then it's Feather's. No warrant required. Feather guesses that the bag's full of knock-offs or maybe dope, but what's in the bag doesn't interest him.

'I thought the murder was solved,' Jerome says. 'It was that freakin' dyke. Why you still harassin' people?'

'Your alibi didn't hold up,' Feather says. Not that he's checked. Just a reasonable supposition.

'What the fuck's my alibi matter? The case is closed.' He's still talking to Natty, making eyes.

'You wasted police time,' Feather says. 'So I've orders to bring you in. And the rucksack can come too.'

'I ain't *got* no rucksack,' Jerome repeats. 'This is bullshit.'

'Then you don't mind if I take it.'

Feather is looking at Natty. The guy takes another sip of his mild, playing it cool but his eyes are smouldering. If he's not handled the rucksack and left prints, if he's not already paid for what's in there, he may be okay.

'Either that or talk to me,' Feather says, turning to Jerome. 'I need another alibi. Different day.'

'Fuck you do!'

'Did you hear the news yesterday?'

Welland thinks. Makes the connection. His lip curls. 'Yeah, I heard. My brief. She disappeared. What's it to do with me?'

'We need to eliminate candidates.'

'Eliminate me? Fuck, man, she's a useless bitch. Why am I goin' to kidnap her?'

'You didn't kidnap her, Jerome. I know it the same way I knew you didn't kill Donna Jordan. Because little turds like you don't ever face up to people. Am I right?' He's looking at the black guy for an opinion but Natty's sitting quiet.

'Fuck you, man,' Jerome says. 'Get outta here. This is harassment.'

'Orders are orders,' Feather says. 'I've gotta check out where you were on Monday night or take you in. If you've an alibi then we're done for the moment, though since we both know you're a lying little shit we'll be checking out your story double quick.'

'The fuck you are. I've got my rights. I don't have to give you no alibi.'

Feather sighs. 'Then I'll take that bag and you and I will go up to the nick and you can read me your rights up there. Is your pal coming along?'

The black guy's eyes are on Feather. The eyes say he's going nowhere. Feather can handle the guy but he's not interested. He's not interested in Jerome's rucksack. He just wants to tick the damn box and save Heldt's people some footwork. 'Your choice,' he says. 'Here or at the station.'

Jerome swears again for effect but his act is lost on his pal. Natty's eyes hold him like a leopard watching prey and Jerome sees how it is and talks.

'I was with some people,' he says. 'All night. I didn't kidnap the bitch.'

'Who were you with?'

'Fuck you.'

Feather breathes out and reaches under the table and grabs the rucksack. 'Okay,' he says. 'Let's go.'

'Stop,' Natty says. He's still looking at Jerome. His eyes are steel. 'The fuck you messing with, Jerome? Tell the man.'

Feather waits.

'Shit,' Jerome says. But he tells Feather. He gives Feather his alibi for Monday night and Feather's eyes widen. His face stays straight but his eyes open. He asks Jerome for detail and Jerome squirms like he's in fibreglass pants and talks about rights and the law but he gives all the details, and Feather had known the little runt was no stalker or abductor but now it turns out that he's something else. He releases the rucksack and pushes his chair back and tells Jerome that if he has to come back there'll be trouble.

Jerome looks at Natty-Ray and believes it.

47

Feather sits in the Corsa watching a beat-up Volkswagen Golf on a school car park. It's lunch hour, and the kids are in and out with takeaways and drinks but so far there's no sign of the one who owns the Golf. But Feather will give it another fifteen before heading back to the nick. He's still calculating the odds on Kate Walker. It's swings and roundabouts. If the guy's got her close by then he's had her for too long and the clock may have run out. If he's taken her on a trip then they might have a few days' breathing space, but the outcome is even more assured.

Time.

The sand's flowing fast and there's nothing he can do except wear out shoe leather in a futile chase. And sitting here at this damned school is more futile than anything. This is totally unrelated. But he'll give it another fifteen before heading back to take another look in Crane's file.

And he's thinking of McGeary.

McGeary's wholesaler hadn't seen him today and now Feather's interested in the guy because he's AWOL at the wrong moment. Feather thinks back two days, sifts impressions from their brief meeting.

Worzel. Big. Strong. Boyish face that attracts the girls. Hair a mess. Good Worzel or Bad Worzel? McGeary impressed Kate, anyhow, and she seemed the sensible type. Feather thinks of all the sensible women who've hitched up with the wrong guy and ended up behind police tape.

He comes alert.

An acne scarred youth in sagging trousers and hooded sweater is opening the Volkswagen. He gets in and music starts thumping. Feather steps out of the Corsa and goes across and opens the passenger door. He bends and rolls himself into the seat and the pressure pulses from the grunge assault his ears. The kid's eyes are wide beside him and he's yelling something that Feather can't hear.

Feather stabs the console and shuts off the din then holds up his brief and twirls a finger, and the kid kills the ignition.

'Gary Stewart?' Feather says.

The kid's staring at him. There's a parochial toughness to him but he's never had a cop bust into his car. He's not that kind of tough.

'What?' he says.

Feather stashes the warrant. Watches the boy's face and knows his hunch is right.

The kid looks away. Looks back. 'Shit!' he says.

Feather grins. 'Shit,' he agrees.

'What do you want?' the kid says.

'You know what.' Feather drops the smile. Stares the boy out then turns to watch the kids drifting back into school.

'Fuck is this?' the kid is saying, but he knows.

Feather takes a slow breath. He shouldn't be here. He needs to get back. If this was Sally missing he'd be bulldozing the city. He could have left this until tomorrow. Better still, till never. This kid isn't his business any more than Kate Walker is.

'I was talking to Jerome,' he says.

'Who?'

'Don't play games,' Feather says.

'Jerome who? You're crazy, man.'

'Don't play games,' Feather repeats. 'Tell me you don't know Jerome once more and I'll knock your head through the window.'

'You're crazy! What've I done?'

'You know what.'

'This is bullshit. I wasn't involved.'

Feather gives Gary Stewart the eye. The little bastard knows, all right.

'Jerome says it was your idea,' he says.

'No friggin' *way!*'

'Jerome says you were the instigator.'

'No way! That *fucking* prick. No way!'

'He says you talked him into it.'

'No fucking way!'

'He told us everything.'

In fact, Jerome has told Feather nothing apart from the fact that this kid, Gary Stewart, Jonathan Harris' friend, is his latest number.

272

Jerome had had no choice but to spill that little secret because Gary is his alibi for Monday night. Jerome clammed up after spilling the name but Feather has connected the dots.

'Jerome's in the nick,' Feather says, 'reviewing his statement. He puts you at the centre of it. It was *your* idea to wreck her house. Geraldine Bryson's not *his* damn teacher. He's no beef with her.'

'Oh man, that's so not true! He was the one had the gripe. I was only bitching how the cow needed a lesson. She's been totally on my back since forever. I'm gonna fail my GCSEs because of her.'

'That's not how Jerome tells it. What does he care about your damn teacher?'

'Because this was *his* school. She was *his* teacher. And Dyno got him thrown out. Jerome hates her guts. When I told him how she was on *my* case he was, like, let's teach the bitch a lesson.'

'Demolishing her house? That's a lesson?'

'The guy's totally crazy. He wrecked his ex's flat. Like, totally destroyed it. He said Miss Bryson could do with the same treatment and I said okay, if that's what you want to do. I was thinking maybe just go in and break a few things.'

'You practically demolished the house.'

'The *dude*. He's plain crazy. We trashed a few things and I was, like, okay, that's *that* bitch sorted, but Jerome found some hammers and stuff and said let's wreck the place.'

'And you helped him. Do you know you've destroyed her life?'

'I couldn't stop him. The guy's crazy. Fuck, I was shitting myself. When I saw what he was doing I got the fuck out.'

Feather's heart bleeds. It truly does. They should do PTSD therapy for vandals and muggers and rapists. The forgotten victims. This kid's got his heart bleeding so much he'd like to knock his head through the screen. No wonder Angela Harris was worried about her kid hanging with this one. Feather leans across and lets his anger show.

'What about your pal Jonathan? Did he lead you on too?'

'No, man. Jon wasn't there.'

'No? You saying he doesn't hate that teacher just as much as you? You saying he doesn't have pictures taken outside her house?'

'Straight, man, he wasn't there. He hates that old bitch like the rest of us but he wasn't there. I just got a problem and asked him for

273

help.'

'What problem?'

'I'd been taking pix but when Jerome started totally demolishing the house I was, like, freaking, like, *whoa,* I'm out of here. But I'd put my phone down in there. I didn't realise till I got home.'

'And you didn't have the guts to go back in and fetch it. You got Jonathan to go in for you.'

'I told him what happened and he said okay, I'll get the phone. Only when he came out of the house he was, like, what've you *done,* man? You're in trouble.'

'He got that right. You *are* in trouble. You and your lover boy.'

'He's not a lover boy. We just hang.'

'You telling me you're not a fag?'

'Fuck! What is that? We just fool around a little. The guy's got some kind of fixation on me. It's no crime.'

'Until you go into people's houses.'

'Shit!'

'Do Jonathan and you "fool around" too? Is it like that between the two of you?'

'Fuck, no! Jon likes girls. We just hang. Play thrash.'

'So do you like girls? Or just the boys?'

'Fuck. I don't know.'

'Do you hang at Jonathan's house?'

'Time to time. It's cool.'

'You hear about his aunt?'

'Yeah. She got kidnapped.'

'You ever see her?'

'A coupla times.'

'But you don't like girls. So you wouldn't say she attracted you, for instance?'

'The fuck you saying? She's, like, middle-aged.'

'Not so old, Gary. Boys your age are always drooling after the MILFs.'

'Not me. Shit, no! What are you sayin'? Fuck! Are you going to arrest me? Otherwise you shouldn't be in my car.'

Feather reaches across and eases the key from the ignition.

'Yeah, Gary. I'm arresting you. Over the teacher attack. We're going to take a ride to Kennington. They'll take care of you.'

'I don't have to say nothing. What I told you here means shit.'

Feather nods. 'That's right. So now I'm going to tell you your rights and take you to Kennington, and the first thing you should do there is call your parents. They'll get you a solicitor.'

By the time Gary's solicitor arrives, they'll have raided Jerome Welland's flat. They'll have identified the loot from Geraldine Bryson's house and Welland will be cosying up to his own solicitor, who won't be Kate Walker.

They get out of the car and Feather arrests Gary and says the words, and that's when Jonathan Harris appears. He jumps a mile when he sees the two of them.

'Wait,' Feather tells Jonathan. He takes Gary to the Corsa and sits him in the back then returns to Jon whose face is a treat. He knows Gary's copped. He's thinking about what's coming his way.

'He told me everything,' Feather says. 'If his story's straight you obstructed a police investigation.'

Jonathan's eyes flicker but that's all. If he's scared he's covering it well. He stares at the horizon, almost amused.

'Go home,' Feather says. 'Tell your parents. There may be charges.'

Not Feather's problem, of course. Once he's dropped Stewart off he's not involved in the thing. Not with Kate Walker, either, but he'd like them to get her back. Jonathan looks across at the Corsa. He shrugs.

'I hope you've read him his rights,' he says.

'Worry about us reading you yours tomorrow,' Feather says. 'Go home. Tell your parents.'

'Sure,' Jonathan says. 'They'll understand.'

'I'm surprised you're so keen on school, with what's happening,' Feather says.

Jon shrugs again. 'Life goes on,' he says.

'But you've gotta be worrying about your aunt. You must be scared for her.'

'I am.'

'Must be hard to concentrate in class.'

'Sitting at home isn't going to help.'

'You don't think so? It won't help you to take a day off?'

Jon cocks his head. Smiles.

'I don't need help,' he says. 'Shit happens.'

'Losing your aunt is some bad shit.'

'Yeah. Very bad.'

'You never know who's got her. Or what he'll do.'

'He's a smart guy. We know that much.'

'Smart how?'

'Doing all that stuff. Driving her nuts. Snatching her from under the cops' noses.'

'The guy impresses you? That what you're saying?'

'He's smart, is what I'm saying.'

'Basically, a cool guy?'

'Just saying. I don't have to admire him.'

'But you admire your aunt.'

'She's cool.'

'Attractive, didn't you say this morning? You agree she's cute?'

'Not for a police detective who's looking to bust someone for taking her.'

'But she *is* attractive. That's what you said. Someone a guy might fixate on.'

'I guess. Guys would go for her.'

'Including you? Would you go for her?'

'She's my freakin' aunt, Detective. What do you think?'

'I heard you weren't home on Monday night. And you weren't with your pal over there.'

'Right.'

'So – you have an alibi?'

'Alibi for what?'

'For not being fixated on your aunt. For not thinking things you shouldn't. For not doing something to her.'

'Man, you're sick.'

'So were you fixated on her? Were you stalking your aunt?'

'Fuck no. As if I'd tell you. Can I go please?'

'Sure,' Feather says. 'But tell your parents. And stay home tonight. We'll be calling round.'

'You're crazy,' Jonathan says. 'You've got crazy ideas, you know?'

Feather knows.

But it's crazy ideas that are often the right ones.

48

Dark comes early and the conference room windows return black and yellow reflections in which Feather's bulk shifts beside CPS prosecutor Paula Stone as he lays out the evidence. They've got motive and opportunity and they've got Georgina Trent's statement. By the middle of next week the knife forensics will complete the package. Paula's taking Georgina into court tomorrow – Feather's AWOL having screwed any chance of getting her there today – and the machinery will fire up to complete the final spin of the threshing wheels that have turned for twenty-one years to spit the body of Donna Jordan cold and grey onto the steps of Our Lady's.

They finish and dispense with chit-chat. Paula has places to be and Feather isn't in the mood. He goes back through to drop the paperwork onto his desk then drifts towards C4. Crane's not there so he collars Joey Obasanjo who reports that the team are still interviewing everyone who's had contact with Kate and are working through the fallout of a TV appeal that went out last night. The abduction location is confirmed. CCTVs caught Kate exiting Maida Vale station then retracing her steps from her abandoned café meet three minutes later. She crossed towards home and disappeared. She was snatched at or near her house. The records for Kate's anonymous caller are also in: the phone's never been used except to make those calls, and most were connected via a mast a quarter of a mile from Kate's house, suggesting that the guy was close by, maybe right outside. The phone was switched off between calls, denying them further location data, and the information has the feel of trial evidence rather than something that might get Kate back.

Feather walks back and spots Clough in Heldt's office. He joins them. Clough's eyebrows lift at the realisation that Feather's still here but what the hell else should he be doing? 'Going home,' Clough says. 'Getting some sleep. You look like shit.'

'I *feel* like shit,' Feather says. 'It's how I always feel. When are you getting that damn light fixed, Andy? The thing gives me a headache.'

Andy Heldt looks up at his strobing fluorescent as if he's stopped noticing. He gestures towards Clough.

'Tell Peter. It's been reported six months. We never catch sight nor sound of Works Services up here.'

Clough twists his neck to scrutinise the faulty light. 'The bastards don't listen to me,' he says. 'Just nick one from downstairs.'

'I'm not paid to climb ladders,' Heldt says.

'Then get someone else to do it.' Clough couldn't care less. It's not his damn light.

'I want to look at her house,' Feather says.

'We already did,' Heldt says. His sparking fluorescent has him mesmerised. 'We're running prints.'

'We need to know what he was thinking,' Feather says. 'What did he see in there? How did he get in? Are we looking at a magician or was she careless with her keys?'

'He got in after she changed the locks,' Heldt muses. 'It wasn't carelessness.'

'Maybe a locksmith,' Feather says. 'Maybe he was in there Monday night and got caught out. She was home earlier than usual.' He jabs his hands into his pockets and leans against Heldt's desk. 'From harassment to abduction. That's a big switch. I'm wondering if it was unplanned.'

'Go home,' Clough says. 'Take the night off, Frank. If she's anywhere to be found we'll find her.'

Feather smiles. Shakes his head. 'You're out of time, Peter,' he says.

He pushes himself off the desk and heads out.

~~~~~

'Go!' Feather says.

Crane steps out of the still moving Corsa and jogs across the road to where the van is pulling out. He slaps the stubby bonnet and holds up his card and the engine dies. Feather manoeuvres into a space and walks back and Xavier McGeary is just climbing out of the Ducato as he reaches them. The three of them form a triangle outside Kate Walker's house. Their breath clouds the air.

Feather smiles at McGeary. 'How are we this evening?' he says.

McGeary glares.

278

'Funny, seeing you here again,' Feather says.

'I'm looking for her,' McGeary replies.

'Well, that's a fine thing.' Feather's smile shines under the amber light.

McGeary hunches his shoulders. 'You people are getting nowhere. Am I right?'

Feather turns to check the house. 'So you think maybe she's home?' he says. 'Is that why you're here?'

McGeary shakes his head. 'I've been watching in case the guy comes back.'

'Her abductor? Why would he do that?'

'No reason,' McGeary says. 'I'm grasping at straws, same as you.'

'Why's your phone off,' Crane says.

McGeary breathes deeply. 'The battery's dead,' he says. 'And I've been chasing all over town. No chance to recharge.'

'Chasing anywhere in particular?'

'Places Kate goes. Where people know her.'

'And you've not seen her?' Feather says.

McGeary looks at him. The three of them face off on the freezing pavement. 'Shit,' McGeary says. 'You think I took her?'

'Did you?'

'Give me a break!'

'So where've you been?'

'Everywhere.'

'And you think you'll find her where we can't?'

'I doubt if I could do worse.'

'Give us some places,' Feather says.

'I've been here three times. I've called at her office and two cafés she uses. I've walked every inch of the park where she runs. And I've talked to her friend and called at her sister's.'

'And what do they say?'

McGeary's eyes are flat. 'What do you think? And, no, I didn't spot her body in the park, since you ask. I might have saved your people a job but I didn't see any of them in there.'

'She's not *in* the park,' Feather tells him.

'Well, fuck you for that insight. So what are you doing to find her, Inspector?'

Feather pulls out his phone and calls Angela Harris and she

confirms that McGeary was indeed at her house just two hours ago, asking questions. She tells him that McGeary's off the rails. Feather looks at Worzel and thinks she may be right. The guy may indeed be off the rails. But there are different ways of being off them.

'Call the friend,' Feather tells Crane. The DC finds the number and talks to Rachel, the one who reported Kate missing, and she confirms that McGeary has called her three times, presumably from pay phones. Crane disconnects. 'She's out searching too,' he reports.

Feather bunches his fists inside his pockets. Their breaths cloud. A car races by and illuminates them. When it's gone they're just amber and shadows.

'So you've not seen Kate since Monday?' Feather says.

'Jesus,' McGeary says. 'How have I seen her? I don't know where the hell she is. I'm scared to death.'

McGeary looks like he might indeed be scared to death. And he could be off the rails. He's certainly not rational, rushing round the city after a lottery win.

'Why did you come here?' Feather repeats. 'There's no way her abductor would return. And if he did he'd spot you and your van. You'd never see him.'

McGeary looks at the sky. 'What am I supposed to do?' he says. 'Jesus. If anything happens to her...'

'It's *already* happened,' Feather says. 'Okay, Xavier, so you've been searching around. Any bright ideas?'

McGeary drops his gaze. He's no bright ideas.

'If we look in your van,' Feather says, 'will we find anything?'

McGeary holds up the keys and they stand at the rear doors to watch Crane open the vehicle. If there's anything out of place they'll tow it in. But all that's in there is some junk in a mostly empty space. They step back onto the pavement.

'Where were you, Monday night?' Feather asks. They need to sit McGeary down and interview him as they should have done two days ago but this is the bottom line: has he an alibi or not?

'We had a traders' association meeting,' McGeary says. 'I went in at six and was there until Rachel phoned to say that Kate was missing.'

Feather looks at him and sees no obvious sign of bluff. If Worzel's trade cronies can vouch for him he's in the clear. Feather tells Crane to make the calls and Crane gets names and numbers from McGeary.

Feather watches the street, the cars and buildings, the tiny front gardens. Kate's stalker spent time here. Hours, days, weeks, soaking up her life. Someone must have seen something. He leaves Crane to his calls and walks in to take a look at Kate Walker's house. He's fishing just as much as McGeary but places will talk sometimes, walls whisper. He lets himself in the front door and switches on the lights. The door's solid, undamaged, the lock brand new. He goes through and checks the back door. The same. Crane's notes say that Kate checked the windows and doors ten times a day and never noticed anything. And the guy got in even after the lock change. He's either a locksmith or a magician or he had access to her new keys. Only her sister had a copy of the new ones. Kate kept another in her kitchen drawer and one in her desk at work. So if the abductor is not a locksmith or phantom then either sister Angela got careless or someone had access to Kate's bag or office desk.

Feather goes upstairs and flicks on her bedroom light. Illuminates a stylish room, decked out with the kind of stuff Sally collected – porcelain figures, chintz nightshades, cosmetics. There's a romcom paperback on the bedside table, a bookmark halfway through, and the bed's made up from when Kate left for work Monday morning. The room is spotless apart from the print dust. A woman's safe place. Must have been hell finding that someone had been borrowing her bed while she was out. And the other stuff, the messing with her household things, all evidence that he was playing with her. The guy is weird above and beyond his fixation. But the key question is why did he take her?

His game – the slow poisoning of her life – was a long term hobby. It would get hot if and when the police took Kate's complaint seriously but her tormentor would adapt. The game would change its shape but the thrill of controlling her life would remain. Kate's tormentor had time on his side. Why switch the play?

One answer: he got caught, Monday.

Feather goes back down. Crane and McGeary have come into the house.

'I talked to two association people,' Crane holds up his list. 'They confirm Mr McGeary's story.'

McGeary holds Feather in his cold stare which Feather ignores. He turns and walks ahead of them into the kitchen and lifts the ripped out phone. Blows carbon dust from his fingers. They'll finish the print match this evening but Feather's not holding his breath. Unless the guy has a record there'll be nothing to match. But the guy left *something,* all that time in this house and all that time in the street, watching. So why is there nothing coming back from the door-to-door?

Feather walks back to the hallway and stops at the tipped table jamming the cellar door.

'What's down there?' he asks.

Crane shrugs. McGeary shakes his head.

They ease the table away and open the door. Feather feels for the light switch and goes down, watching the steps. Crane and McGeary follow. McGeary they could do without, but Feather just can't be bothered to kick the bastard out. The cellar's dank air chills him, and Feather feels like he's moving away from Kate Walker as he pokes around under her house.

The room is cold and dingy, cluttered with junk inherited from a previous owner. Feather works his way to a tiny opaque half-window at the front, decades sealed. He inspects the furniture and the boxes around him without much interest. There's nothing to point him towards Kate. He lights up his LED torch and pushes through a gap in the dividing brickwork and comes into a rear area. The area is mostly bare but there's an ancient dresser against the left wall, purchased perhaps in the forties when the previous-but-two occupants moved in, a soldier home from the War, washed up with his bride and their twelve month old child in the inner suburbs and stretching their seven quid a week to its limit. They'd picked the bare essentials, left most of the house empty for a decade. And this faded blue dresser was maybe their one concession, her pride, though it's a cheap, stapled construction. Feather runs his finger over its surface and ploughs up dust. Then he spots something and calls Crane over and plays his beam across the dresser. The dust is disturbed round its edges where fingers have gripped it, and the floor is a mess of scrapings and smearings where it's been swung out from the wall.

Crane and McGeary step forward and pull it round and out, and Feather aims the torch into a three foot access hole in the brickwork. The space beyond is as black as soot, reflecting nothing. Feather feels a draft, sniffs the air.

'That's how he got in,' he says.

McGeary looks at the hole. 'What is it?'

'The old coal cellar. Coal was delivered down a hatch outside. You filled the scuttles from this hole.'

They go back up and out into the garden where Feather walks to a metal hatch set inside a brick surround under the back wall. A line of garden tubs cover the hatch, but if they move the tubs the hatch will lift.

'She probably didn't even know it opened,' Feather says. 'But the guy just pulled off the tubs and worked it loose, maybe smashed a rusted bolt. Then he slid down the coal chute and pushed that dresser out and he was in her cellar. All he had to do was to slide the dresser back against the wall and work the door open upstairs. Once he'd replaced the tubs over the hatch no one would know he'd been in.'

'Shit,' Crane says. 'All her checks. Changing the locks.'

'For nothing,' Feather says. 'The guy had this way in. He's familiar with these old properties.'

With this mundane explanation something of the stalker's mystique drops away.

Crane curses. Feather thinks.

49

This is bad. He should have been here at six p.m. with food and fresh water. He should have taken out the filthy bucket she's been squatting over. His morning and evening routines have been dependable, the only responsibilities he's acknowledged, demonstrating at least a token concern for her welfare. If that concern has waned, if her welfare is no longer of significance, then that's bad. Very bad. So where the hell is he?

Kate sits shivering with her knees drawn up on the camp bed. The day has been another torment of endurance, fighting the overpowering oppression of the cellar walls, their denial of any world beyond.

Staying calm, thinking, has taken all she has. But her search for a way out has again been fruitless. And the cellar's mad contents are as much a mystery as they were three days ago. When calm finally deserted her this afternoon her shouting and hammering went, as always, entirely unnoticed. And just as she's found no way out of here she's found no way through to him. When he's been down here he's not stayed to explain why he's done this. And tonight, finally, he's not come at all. What seemed inconceivable three days ago, even in the first shock of finding herself in this foul place, can no longer be denied: she may actually die here.

Kate is scared as hell.

She checks her watch. It's after nine. Far too late. She can hear occasional thumps and creaks from upstairs but something has changed. He's abandoned his routine. And now she's dreading his appearance.

But eventually he comes. His feet sound on the steps and the cellar door opens.

~~~~~

'Just tell me,' she says, 'why you're doing this.'

He's brought nothing. The need to feed her has slipped his mind. She wants to remind him, to demand food and water and the removal of her soil bucket but this is more important. His reason for taking her, the blame he's put on her, is a gulf that blocks communication. 'Tell me,' she says.

But his response is unnerving. He stands watching her as if the answer's too deep to elucidate – or as if he has no answer. He seems shaken, confused, and his stare scares the hell out of her. The stare says he doesn't know the reason. Doesn't know what happens next. But just as she's about to repeat her question he speaks.

'This wasn't the plan.'

Of course. That's perfectly clear. The camp bed and shackle were down here by chance. A person never knows when they might abduct someone, after all. And all the weird shit displayed down here, that wasn't planned either. But she knows what he means. She knows that taking her on Monday was unplanned. But the question is why any of it has happened.

He turns to inspect the exhibits of his warped museum, and his face, side on, alternates between the familiar one and the one she once knew. He didn't have the trimmed beard back then. He didn't have the clipper cut. He didn't have the muscle-bound physique under his shirt. The figure before her is barely reconcilable with the scrawny youth of her memory. No wonder she hadn't recognised him. Even his name hadn't helped. Back then she'd known only his nickname. *Gimp*. And more recently – until he'd brought her here – he'd not given the slightest indication that she meant anything to him.

The photos on the wall behind the fire – she's counted ninety-three – have unnerved her more than anything, more even than the piano porn album. Unlike the photos on the wall behind her, which are recent, these ninety-three are old. Breathtakingly old. In the ninety-three she sees a carefree schoolgirl tripping in and out of her house, alone and with friends, going places, returning. She sees herself at her high school, laughing with those friends. Three of the photos have caught her with her arm round the waist of a boy who was her short-lived romance in the first year of sixth form. Another group captures her walking alone, a reflective smile on her face. Ninety-three photos. A collage of her life fifteen years ago, obscenely out of place in this cellar. And the implications of the photos are terrifying: she's looking at a madman's hobby. She's lived her life for nearly two decades unaware that it was being documented frame by frame. It's like discovering that your parents are the crown prince and princess of Monaco, that your whole life's been a sham.

She waits, but he's content to inspect his wall, the Ghosts of Kate Past.

'What wasn't the plan?' she says. She knows but she must ask.

'This,' he says. 'You caught me at your house.'

'I see. And it was just luck that you happened to have a stun gun on you.'

Stop, she tells herself. Antagonising him isn't going to help. But anger has the upper hand.

'If I hadn't caught you out how long would it have been before you took me anyway? Before you brought me *here*?'

Kate bends and grabs the chain and hurls it at him but it snaps short, held by her ankle, and crashes onto the matting.

'I don't know,' he says. 'I'd have brought you when it was ready. This. Your room.'

'My room? This fucking place?' Kate blinks back tears. *'My* room?'

He turns to her. His smile is cold, and it's frightened. 'Yes, *your* room, Kate. It's dedicated to you.'

In the flat whites of his eyes, Kate sees that she shouldn't be baiting him. She's chained to the wall and he's in charge of the runaway train that is this *unplanned* abduction and they are racing towards a wreck.

'It's not too late,' she says. 'We can forget this happened. If you just stop following me, leave me alone.'

He shakes his head. 'Of course it's too late. It's been too late for a long time.'

'I don't understand,' Kate says. 'This...,' she gestures, 'has crossed a line. We both know that. But let's stop here. I'll say I don't know who took me. We'll let the whole thing go.'

'I don't want you to let it go,' he says. 'And that's the point: you *don't* know me.'

'Please. This will get you into a lot of trouble.'

He shakes his head. His eyes are powerful and afraid. 'Don't patronise me,' he says.

'You know the police will find us. It's just a matter of time.'

Another shake of his head. But he's scared. The police *will* find him. Which makes her a liability.

'Tell me what you want,' she says.

'I want you to understand.'

'But I *don't* understand. I've done nothing to you. We don't even know each other.'

His anger comes suddenly in a contemptuous laugh.

'You're wrong, Kate. I *do* know you. But you've hit the nail on the head. *You* don't know *me,* because you've never seen me.'

'Of course I've seen you.'

The anger hardens.

'No,' he repeats. 'You haven't.'

Kate stifles her own anger. She's seething that this bastard has given himself the right to complain about her, to make any demand of her as if this was any regular situation and not a criminal act that will see him spend his future life in prison. And what was there to *see* of him back then? They weren't friends, they didn't hang together, they weren't even in the same class fifteen years ago. Sure, Kate recalls him now but her memories are so hazy as to be meaningless. So hazy that she'd not recognised him when he reappeared twelve months ago.

'How long were you watching me?' she asks.

She's looking at the ninety-three photographs, peering into the past at the carefree schoolgirl. 'You must have spent hours taking those,' she says.

'Hundreds.'

'For what? If you'd just spoken to me...'

He looks down, and the caged lamp makes black pits of his eyes.

'I lived in a different universe,' he says. 'How could we talk?'

'That's not true. Just because we weren't close friends...'

He barks a laugh and shakes his head as emphatically as if he was shaking off a blow. 'We weren't any kind of friends,' he says. 'You weren't aware that I existed.'

'Of course I was aware.'

'In the abstract way you knew pygmies existed in the rainforest. That grains of sand exist in the desert.'

'You should have talked to me. We might have got on.'

But he's still shaking his head, flicking a hand to stop her.

287

'The *pygmy* should talk to you,' he says. 'The *sand* should talk to you.'
'You had your friends. I had mine. Can't you see?'
'I didn't exist. That's what I see.'
'We were just never thrown together.'
'And I loved you.'

~~~~~

'You ask how many hours I watched you?'

He's pulled a canvas garden chair from behind the bookcase and set it beside the fire, out of its direct heat. He's sitting, straight-backed, his feet planted on the matting in a proprietorial pose. He's king of this place. But he's stayed to talk. That's what matters.

But he's uneasy. Something is bugging him. Their eyes meet and the reality of her situation amplifies her fear. They're chatting away like normal people but she's chained to the wall.

'I bought a digital camera,' he says. 'It became my hobby.'

Along with housebreaking and phone calls and kidnapping. A man needs hobbies. Gets him out.

'Each photo...' he tilts his head towards the ninety-three, 'represents about ten hours' watching. I'd wait all day, all evening, sometimes and get nothing.'

'That was crazy,' Kate says. 'Whatever you wanted, that was unnecessary. What normal person spends hours hiding with a camera?'

This brings a smile. 'Actually, you've a point. I could have stood out in the open and you'd still not have seen me. I was there every day, right in front of you. We even exchanged odd words at school. One time I caught your eye and you smiled,' he says, 'and I built this whole fantasy that the two of us had an understanding, that you'd secretly acknowledged me from within the ranks of your moronic friends. What a fool.'

'Why didn't you *talk* to me?'

'Bust into your circle? I'd have been a carbuncle.'

'No.'

'If you'd given even the slightest *real* sign maybe I would have talked to you. But deep down I knew my fantasies were just that. I repulsed you so you made me invisible.'

'No one repulsed me. Not you, nor anyone. And all young girls are fools. They miss all kinds of opportunities. They never see what's in front of them.'

His smile snaps away.

'You think I'm so shallow? You want to patronise me? To tell me it was all schoolgirl naivety? You loved your world, Kate. You basked in your ring of admirers, you played for the good-looking guys. Remember Marty Martins? The *looks* you gave him. We all thought you were about to fuck him right there in the classroom. Marty's a carpet salesman now. That's where your hunk landed. But you had your world and you put up the shutters against anyone who didn't fit. You never imagined there was a guy out there who loved you. So don't insult me, Kate. The love's gone, so we need to stay on good terms.'

'You should have talked to me,' she insists. 'If I wasn't interested I'd have told you so. But we didn't have to be enemies.' She says it and it's true, though she can imagine no universe where she *would* have been interested in Gimp. She'd never known how he got his nickname, had never used it herself, but nicknames have a way of sticking, of reducing their owners, of seeming *right*.

He stands and turns back to the photos, touches the scraps of her life, and Kate shivers violently. They need to stay on good terms. She'll not disagree with him there. Because this maniac – yes, I see you *now* all right! – has got both of them into a situation. He'll go to jail for fifteen years even if he lets her go and there's no hiding from that. And *Christ*, where are the police? What are they doing?

But what *can* they do? What is there that will point them towards him?

He picks up the plastic bag with the tuft of hair from the display. Lifts it to the light. Inspects it, distracting himself from his anger.

'This is yours,' he says. 'I'd sit behind you on the bus when I could. Most of the time you had a crowd round you but one time I got the opportunity. Your hair was hanging over the seat behind you and I used a knife to cut some off. Scissors would have been better but the knife was all I had. You never noticed, anyway.

'And this.' He walks across and retrieves the photo album from the piano and hands it to her. She takes it but can hardly bear to open it. She turns the pages only to placate him.

'I guess I *was* crazy,' he tells her. 'It's the kind of thing I was driven to.'

Kate thinks of her last school years, the friends and places, parties and romances, she oblivious to a boy alone in his room, working at this obscene album. She closes the album. Her hands are trembling.

He turns away and walks round the cellar touching and moving things, picking them up. 'All this stuff,' he says, 'is you.'

He picks a Coke can from the top of its pyramid. 'I collected your throwaways. I used to kiss the lip of the can where your mouth had been, to taste your saliva. When there was no more taste I'd collect another.'

He lifts the notebook and pencil, the hair band, the pocket dictionary, the Walkman. 'All yours,' he says. 'The Walkman was a risk. I thought you'd miss it.'

She had missed it, but not sufficiently to be certain where and when it had disappeared because she already owned a new gadget that made the Walkman obsolete. She'd been carrying an iPod round in her bag since her seventeenth Christmas and the Walkman had probably lain discarded in her school desk for months before he took it. She'd never been sure if the player had been taken or was just misplaced somewhere, and eventually she just forgot all about it.

So all this junk is hers. Old stuff and recent stuff, scavenged from her life and hoarded in this cellar. Even the confectionery wrappers are hers, discarded obliviously. How could she ever have imagined him following and retrieving? How could she ever have imagined that one of her fellow students was off his damn rocker? And time has turned his fixation into something very dangerous.

'What do you plan to do?' she asks again.

He quits his patrol but says nothing.

'How long have you been planning this?'

He shakes his head. 'I didn't plan it.'

'Of course you did. You prepared this place.'

'It was just somewhere to keep the memorabilia.'

'This chain is not memorabilia.'

'That was just a mad rage,' he says, 'after we met again last year. It brought it all back. It's why I've been toying with you. I had a fantasy of bringing you here one day, but not now.'

'But now you've done it. So what are you going to do?'

He smiles. It doesn't touch his eyes.

'I don't know,' he says.

50

Feather drops Crane off at Harrow Park. Crane asks Feather where he's headed and Feather says maybe home. Crane climbs out and disappears into the building and Feather watches him, engine idling. There'll be nothing new in the Incident Room. They're out of time. They aren't going to save her.

He drives out and drifts with the late traffic down the Edgware Road, a vague idea of home in his head and Crane's folder under his seat. In the end, hunger decides. Feather hasn't eaten all day. He diverts west at Marble Arch and drives towards Notting Hill Gate. He swings the Corsa into Pembridge and parks on a taxi area beyond the roundabout to walk back to Terry Timms' café. The windows cast an orange glow onto the street and there's a handful of late night diners in. Feather grabs the corner table by the counter and hangs his coat. Settles on the padded bench. The table's his regular, furthest from the door, warm air vents right under the seat. There's something called Jumbo Lump Crab Cake up on the specials board. Terry likes to impress. He runs a greasy spoon and thinks he's Ramsay, though in truth he turns out nice plates.

Hilary spots him and comes over to ask what he's having and Feather decides on the crab cake, which saves going through the charade of pretend-reading the menu before ordering his usual all day breakfast. The crab cake comes with a salad garnish, and Feather orders chips and wholemeal bread to bulk it up and gets Hilary to bring tea across. He asks her how she is and she says she's fine and how's *he* doing and Feather lifts Crane's folder and says he's doing just great when they're not working him to death.

Hilary says she knows how it is and brings a stainless teapot over and tells him that the crumble's good tonight, and Feather adds it to his order. Hilary's looking at the folder. 'You should take it easy, Frank,' she says. Feather smiles at her. 'I am taking it easy,' he says. 'This is me, taking it easy.'

'Nine thirty at night and you're lugging paperwork around, miles from home? That's not taking it easy.'

Feather smiles. 'Home's a little quiet,' he says. 'This is just some homework. Keeps me from getting bored.'

'You've always got homework, Frank. You're always solving murders at midnight.' Hilary shakes her head and walks back to the counter to put a slice of crumble into the oven. She'll bring it out later, crunchy as cornflakes. Feather pours his tea.

He pulls the sheets from the folder. Fifteen pages summarising the enquiry. Names, contact details, shorthand bio's and interview notes. Feather counts fifty names. Family, neighbours, friends, work colleagues, clients, adversaries, café waitresses, regulars at a couple of bars and gym members. Most with summary notes from the team's interviews and most unaware that Kate was being stalked. None of them saw her after she left work on Monday evening. Feather sips his tea and runs his biro through names. By page fifteen he's left with only three that interest him.

One guy's a sex offender on the losing side of a civil prosecution in which Kate participated. His name is Norman Hill. Fifty-eight years old. Two convictions for indecent assault. Suspected of multiple offences. A young single mother was terrorised and later raped by Hill but was failed by the criminal prosecution system. Apparently she was an acquaintance of Kate's which is why Kate had assisted one of her firm's civil lawyers pro bono to file a suit. They won the suit and the guy was hit with a hundred thou' damages plus costs and an additional penalty for an outburst against the plaintiff and her lawyers in court. Hill lives in Willesden, two miles from Kate. The team talked to him yesterday. His lone lifestyle has left him without an alibi for Monday night but he let two detectives look round his house and held up for two hours in interview. Feather has him as unlikely but not ruled out. Ideally someone would be watching the guy until this is over, but Clough's resources only stretch so far.

Subject number two is a guy called Marcus Wain. One of Kate's clients. Confidentiality rules permitted her firm to deliver only the bare fact of their representation but the team has fleshed things out from court records. The guy is thirty-three, an estate agent, convicted of a drink-driving offence a year ago. Kate had acted for him at a hearing that saw a fifteen hundred pound fine and twelve month ban handed down. It's possible that Wain has a grudge against his solicitor for failing him, but it's stretching things a long way. Feather wouldn't be interested but for the fact that they've not yet caught up with him, and that his involvement with Kate fits the timescale.

The crab cakes arrive and Hilary stands patiently while they go through the usual rigmarole of making space on the table. Feather shuffles the paperwork and gets it stacked on the bench seat beside him, drops the folder on top and they're sorted. Hilary plants the food and Feather piles the chips onto the salad and grabs a slice of bread, all one handed. His other hand is pulling sheets back onto the table. The crab cakes are hot and tasty and cooked up for a tenth the fee Ramsay would charge and Feather waves his fork to Terry who's appeared behind the counter looking for accolades. They should do Bake Off here. Terry would walk away with the prize. But a waved fork must suffice. Such is life.

The third name's another hard-to-locate. This one has caught Heldt's eye. A shorthand note says there's a DS and three DCs out searching. The guy's name is Victor Alexander, and he has lodged six houses down from Kate's for the last two years. Thirty-something. Unknown origin. His landlady put him on the street recently when rent arrears hit three months. He'd moved in without references or evidence of a job, and all the landlady knew, beside the fact that Alexander was in arrears, was that he spent hours watching videos in his room and that he'd taken an interest in Kate. The landlady had spotted him more than once leaning over the gate to speak to her as she'd passed. There was something unwholesome about the guy, the landlady said. She was well rid of him. But she has no forwarding address and Heldt's people are struggling to trace him. Feather doesn't see Kate's abductor as an itinerant but you never know. They need to catch hold of him.

Chances are they'll have talked to these last two names by tomorrow and added other ten names to the list from the blitz of information and rumour the TV appeal has brought in, but it will be too late. It's been seventy-four hours since Kate Walker disappeared and Feather suspects that it's over. She'd seemed like a good woman, and too many bad things happen to good people. In his mind Sally is watching him the way she used to when he blundered out of the house late at night on some equally futile chase.

Feather pushes his plate away and Hilary comes over with his pudding. He smiles up at her. Shakes his head. He shouldn't be eating this shit late at night. Nor starving himself all day. Feather knows it. He knows a lot of things. Most have never helped him.

The café is filling with youths in heavy coats, in for a burger or Coke. At that age you eat what you want, when you want. You're invulnerable. And you're out late because you want to be out late. Feather sighs. Terry Timms' is cosy and the streets are desolate and it's tempting to sit here until they close but he's restless. Maybe he'll go home, watch a TV show, get a night's sleep. Maybe not. He catches Hilary's eye and smiles as he reaches for his coat.

~~~~~

The Corsa's a hearse. Feather turns the heater high but it blasts cold. He kills the fan and drives slowly east.

Marcus Wain. Name number two on his of-interest list. Kate Walker's former client. Not at work today, not home, not answering his phone. Maybe a house call will catch him now. Wain lives up by Caledonian Park, a thirty minute round trip at this time of night. Feather drives up through Barnsbury watching street names. Kate's abductor isn't likely to be a former client but if he can catch Wain he can save the team an hour tomorrow. If nothing else the detour will delay his arrival at his own empty apartment. The hollowness of the Donna Jordan case is still with him, the understanding that nothing he's done has helped her. Maybe he can't do much for Kate Walker but if he eases the team's work, if it kills thirty minutes of a long night, he'll have achieved something.

He parks on a corner outside a three storey end-of-terrace house. The terrace is a remnant in an area ravaged by uninspired sixties development. There are three bell pushes by the door. The upstairs properties are for sale and the boarded-over windows suggest they've been empty a while. Wain's is the ground floor flat.

Feather sees a faint light in the door glass. He presses the button and hears a bell deep inside. The building has a deserted feel but the light suggests otherwise. Maybe Wain is home, maybe not. Maybe he doesn't answer the door at night. Feather pokes the bell again and raps on the door and finally gets a response.

The door opens and a man wearing a faded red tee shirt and jeans is there. His arms have the smooth curves of a gym jock, a guy who likes mirrors, and Feather's mnemonics tag him as Gyminy Cricket. Gyminy's a step up from Feather which puts them eye to eye. Feather flashes his brief and the guy confirms he's Marcus Wain.

'Mind if I come in?'

'What's happened?' Wain doesn't move. They stand on the step.

'We've a missing woman. We're talking to people who know her.'

Wain's face stays blank. 'Is she someone I know?' he says.

'Maybe only in passing. Did you see the TV thing?'

Wain shakes his head.

'You have a solicitor named Kate Walker?'

Wain seems uncertain. Takes his time before pulling up the name like it's old, forgotten.

'She represented me once. I don't know her personally.'

Feather rubs his hands and kicks the step. 'Can we talk inside?' he says. The cold doesn't bother him but he doesn't want Gyminy comfortable. He doesn't want him safe behind his door. He doesn't want him a step up. The guy hesitates but Feather moves and closes the space so it's either step back or go nose to nose. Wain steps back and they're in the vestibule.

'So you didn't see the TV piece?' Feather says. The vestibule and hall are communal. Stairs run up to the right, and to the left a hallway goes back to where Wain's apartment door is open and throwing out light.

'I don't watch TV.' Wain folds his arms. His muscles flex. 'Has something happened to her?'

'She's been missing since Monday.'

Wain purses his lips.

'Have you seen her recently?'

Wain shakes his head. 'Not since the court case a year ago.'

'...because we're talking to everyone who's been in contact with her.'

'I hope she's not hurt.'

'Your case was a driving offence?'

'Yes.'

'And you didn't know Ms Walker before that?'

'No.'

'And you've not seen her since?'

Wain's face is neutral but it's a hostile kind of neutral. His conviction has left him without wheels for the last twelve months. The system and its officials are no friends of his.

'Not after the court hearing,' he says.

'How was she? As a lawyer?'

He shrugs. 'She did her job.' He's holding his ground in the vestibule, unconcerned about discussing his legal affairs out here, not about to invite Feather back to his apartment. Feather glances at the stairs. Empty for sure up top.

'Would you recognise her still?'

'I'm not sure.'

'Nice looking woman. Stands out.'

'Maybe. Possibly.'

'Attractive.'

'I don't know.'

'You didn't notice?'

'Attractive,' Wain recalls now. It's been a year but it would take more than a year for Feather to forget Kate's face.

'And you've definitely not seen her since? Even in passing?'

Wain frowns like he's searching the twelve months. His fingers tense and un-tense round his biceps. He's nervous. His big, bland face is tense too. Razored hair disguises encroaching baldness. He releases his left biceps and strokes his buzz, massages the back of his neck. His mouth purses, turns down. 'Definitely not,' he says finally. 'I can't help you. But I hope she's okay.'

'You think she might not be?'

'If she's been kidnapped you never know what might happen.'

'Yeah. So we're just asking everyone who's been in contact,' Feather says. 'Just to rule them out. Checking alibis. That sort of thing.'

Wain smiles. 'I've got an alibi, don't worry.'

'Good.' Feather smiles. Takes out his notepad. 'If it's no bother...'

Wain waits. Feather looks up.

'The alibi.'

Wain hesitates. 'Monday, you say? Any time in particular?'

'Evening. But all day, too.'

'I was out in the evening. At work in the day. I travel round but it will be in the book.'

'You got the book?'

'It's at the office. I can let you know tomorrow.'

'Can I catch you at work?'

'Sure. Any time after nine.'

'Good. So what about the evening?'

'You want to know now?'

'Unless you keep *that* in a book.'

'No. Sure.' Wain laughs. 'I was out with a couple of friends,' he says. 'We were in the Duke, off Caledonian Road.'

'Would you happen to have those friends' names and addresses?'

'Not the addresses. I'll have to call them tomorrow.'

'Numbers?'

'They're in my phone. I left it at work.'

'I got the impression you weren't in work. We couldn't contact you.'

'You were trying to contact me? Sorry. I was off. Only called in first thing to drop off some keys.'

'No one seemed to know where you were.'

Wain shrugs. 'Doesn't surprise me. But I'd booked the day off.'

'Okay,' Feather says. 'Just your friends' names for the time being. We'll pick up the other details tomorrow.'

Wain reels off two names and also throws in the Duke's landlord, a guy called George who'll confirm that he spent Monday evening there.

'To be clear, what time were you in?'

'From just before seven until ten or eleven. George will confirm it.'

'That's good,' Feather says. 'That would cover our window. Any chance I could take a quick look in your flat?' He shrugs. 'Just box-ticking.'

'It's kind of late, Inspector. What about tomorrow?'

'Won't take a sec.'

'Sure, but... you know. The place is a bit of a mess. I'm just about to hit the sack. This really isn't a good time.'

Feather smiles. 'Five minutes, max.'

'Legally, must I let you in?'

'Legally – no. This is just on a voluntary basis.'

'Well then, Inspector, tomorrow. I'd prefer that. If you come here I'll have the addresses and numbers for you too.'

Feather looks at Wain.

Gyminy Cricket.

Every inch of the man is tense. He might have Kate back there or he might have some porn up on his TV or he might have illegal substances lying about, though Feather detects no whiff. He might this and he might that, and Feather's just pushed him way up the suspects list. He smiles.

'Thanks for the names,' he says. 'I'll call by tomorrow morning.'

'Nine thirty. I'll call back here from work.'

'I'll see you then. Have a good night.'

Feather turns and walks out onto the street. When he unlocks the Corsa he turns and sees that the light is gone behind the closed front door.

51

'Please,' Kate says. 'Just think about this.'

He's come back down but despite her protests of hunger and thirst has brought nothing. And there's a new hardness to his face.

'It's too late,' he tells her.

Keep talking, she tells herself, find a way through. She reaches for an old memory, an ancient connection, something that has been in her mind for three days.

'You called on me one time,' she recollects.

It's a hazy memory of a face she can barely reconcile with the one before her. The memory is of a clean, bland face. But there was something else about it. *That's it:* an attitude. What was it? Defeatist? Judgmental? The details are coalescing, little by little: his particular way of walking, that self-conscious gait, arms down at his side.

He says nothing as Kate continues to coax out the detail. It was her seventeenth birthday and she'd been out with Simon Cadet, supposedly at Pizza Hut but actually at his place. His parents were out and they'd spent two slow hours in his bed where she'd received – to use Simon's endearingly crude term – her *birthday fuck,* and she'd arrived home, still dazed and tingling, on Simon's arm, only for her planned *Pizza Hut* nonchalance to evaporate at her mother's announcement that she had a visitor. She'd followed her mother through, trying to fathom the cryptic announcement but wholly unprepared for the sight of the figure rising from the sofa.

Gimp!

What on earth was this boy – who'd never been more than a passing shadow, the awkward boy with a funny gait, just another face around the school – doing in her house?

She and Simon had stopped dead. It was like finding Santa Claus in the room.

Kate wonders now how the memory had ever faded: the shock of Gimp waiting in her lounge on her arrival back from... *Pizza Hut.* She, facing him, still tingling and damp, with her perplexion switching to an utter, cringing, apprehension that he'd come with a birthday gift, that he was here with some kind of dreadful, inappropriate expectation. The moment drifted towards catastrophe. This poor *nobody* caught in an utter *faux pas* in her living room, with her mother behind her and the heartless bastard Simon grinning merrily beside her. The moment had blossomed towards a pinnacle of teenage embarrassment, to be cringed over ever after. But then... disaster averted. Gimp explained and the tension evaporated. And even if Gimp's embarrassment at being the focus of this group was palpable and his explanation a little odd it was, at least, mundane. He'd come with a request for help, which Kate had been unable to supply, and when she'd informed him of such he'd shrugged and said no problem. Then he'd thanked her mother and left.

'You needed tickets,' Kate recalls, and suddenly sees a connection. She looks at the piano. The torn shreds of ticket reassembled on the music rack are what that visit was about.

'You thought I could get hold of last minute tickets for you,' she says. 'But I couldn't. It was something of nothing.'

But clearly it *wasn't* nothing. Something had happened that day that she'd not understood. But how could the simple request be misunderstood? He needed tickets for a Muse concert. The band was a favourite of hers. She'd been to two of their gigs in the last twelve months, and now Gimp needed last minute tickets for the Brixton Academy. So he'd come to ask if she knew any way to get them without going to the touts. But she'd had no such knowledge, no special contacts. So she'd apologised and he'd said no problem, worth a try, and she'd walked him to the door and he'd disappeared with barely another word. She'd forgotten the incident within days and it is inexplicable that it could be of significance in the confines of this cellar, but the reassembled tickets on the piano say otherwise.

He walks across and lifts the sheet holding the tickets.

'That's not what happened,' he says.

He proffers the sheet and Kate takes it. When she's finished inspecting the tickets, no wiser, he's looking down at her.

'I can still see your face,' he says, 'when you walked in with Simon. The look on your *mother's* face. If I could have died and gone to hell I would have.'

She looks again at the tickets, looks at him. And his cold dead stare scares her to death. Something terrible happened that day and she never saw it. When she understands what it was perhaps she'll know why she's here. But she's afraid to understand.

'I loved you,' he says.

A cold draught flicks the wall photos and touches Kate's cheek. *He loved her.* What the hell does that mean? So he had a schoolboy crush. Is all this for a crush? She starts to rebuke him then stops. It's his script. Play along, she tells herself.

'If you'd just given me an idea how you felt...' she says.

'Then what?'

'I don't know. We'd have sorted it out. But this... is all this because of how you felt back then? It can't be. This isn't right.'

'I decide what's right,' he says.

'No! You don't.'

'I can. I have.'

'Tell me what happened.'

'This...' he gestures at the old photos, the artefacts atop the gramophone, 'was a little crazy, I admit. I was collecting this stuff and I knew it was crazy. But then I looked at it one day and realised that the crazy thing was my hiding how I felt, and I realised I couldn't do it any longer. I had to talk to you. I had to let you know I existed.'

'That's why you came to my house?'

'Yes. And I walked into a disaster.'

'What disaster? It was just a favour. You thought I could get tickets for you and your girlfriend.'

He laughs and retrieves the torn tickets from her.

'I already had the tickets,' he says. 'These. I didn't have a girlfriend.'

Kate waits.

'Muse. The band of the moment. And their number one fan was you. I'd spent three months' savings on the tickets but I'd prepared a story that I'd been given them and was looking for someone who liked the band. Just a casual thing. If you said you couldn't make it, meaning you didn't want to go with *me,* I'd say I was offering you *both* tickets. I wasn't interested myself. That was the way out, to save us both the embarrassment of you refusing me a date.'

'You bought the tickets for *us?*'

He ejects a sad laugh.

'I shredded them outside your house but then I couldn't bring myself to throw them away.'

He inspects the reassembled shreds. Smiles.

'I hadn't done my homework,' he says. 'Do you recall that you'd broken up with that turd Paddy Martin? I thought it was my opportunity. Bought the tickets on impulse and worked myself up all week to talk to you, but I couldn't. Until on the Saturday I just gritted my teeth and marched up to your house before I could chicken out. But I never imagined you might already be shacked up with someone else. And I sure as *hell* didn't know it was your birthday. I just walked right into a trap.

'I didn't know if you'd be in that day. It was just hit and miss. Subconsciously I probably hoped you were out so that I wouldn't have to go through with it. And you were. But your mother said you'd be back shortly and invited me in, and I was so hyped up that I never saw the trap until it snapped shut. Suddenly I was sitting on your sofa listening to your mother explaining how you were all going out for your birthday meal later and I could have died when I heard it. It was your *frigging birthday!* So there was no way that my turning up on that day could look casual. Your mother didn't know who the hell I was but she assumed I was there with some kind of birthday greeting.'

'Embarrassment is what growing up's about,' Kate says. 'What's wrong with giving a girl a birthday present?'

For a moment he can't find the words. His eyes close. Agony shakes him. Then when his eyes open again they're blazing. 'What was *wrong?* A birthday present from a dork who's never even spoken to you? From someone you didn't even know, had probably never noticed? Or didn't like? How uncool was that?'

Very uncool, Kate thinks. And so like the bland-faced boy with the awkward walk. So like Gimp.

'So there I am, a fly in the spider's web, waiting for you to show up and wondering how I could still make the tickets look casual. But I couldn't. I was trapped in your lounge like some idiotic suitor.'

His voice has risen. He's been living this humiliation for a decade and a half.

'So I'm sat there, sweating like a damn pig with your mum hovering and asking all these questions because she'd never seen me before and all I'm wondering is how this could possibly get any worse, and then it does. Because when you finally come in... *Holy Christ!* it's only that prick Simon Cadet on your arm and you could see a mile off that the two of you were fresh out of the sack. Your own mother could see it! And there I was, ready to jump up and ask if you'd like to come see a concert with me sometime when you're not busy fucking Simon who was standing right there grinning his fat head off. Do you know what we called him? Simon Sez. Because he never stopped talking about all the girls he was laying, how he was this real big stud, and we all just had to make like we admired him. Believe me, I just wanted to be dead when the two of you walked in that door.'

'Shit,' Kate says.

'Yeah. Shit City. Final curtain and applause. Bow out and die.'

'But all this?' Kate gestures around them, at the hideous crime in the making. It still doesn't make sense. The tormenting, the abduction. Kidnapping a thirty-two-year-old professional who hasn't thought about that boy in fifteen years can't come from teenage humiliation. If it did the whole world would be in flames. There has to be something else.

'Your story about wanting *me* to get *you* tickets,' she says. 'That was quick on your feet.'

'We can be creative in dire straits,' he says. 'I switched the story in the nick of time but I didn't know if any of you bought it or just pretended. But the charade suited us all. It let me walk out through the door and out of your life to go die somewhere.'

He's right: the story had seemed odd but in the absence of any other explanation they'd accepted it as the truth, mundane and forgettable. Forgotten by all except the angry, humiliated tormentor standing over her in this cold cellar, stooping now to check her chain.

And the way he pulls the chain, the ferocious tug, shows the depth of his anger, that he's nurtured his humiliation over the years into a burning need to hurt her. His next words chill her. He gestures at the museum-cellar.

'This is what you made me,' he says.

~~~~~

He's prowling the cellar, fingering his memory shard collection, torn between staying and leaving. Kate breaks the silence and asks for a drink but she gets no response. His movements are urgent, nervous. He darts to each place, spends long minutes scrutinising the mementos and photos of her life. When his gaze catches her occasionally he turns away fast. Then finally he speaks, his back to her as he inspects his photo wall.

'It must be good to have it all,' he says.

The comment is barely worthy of a reply but she needs to keep talking, to invest in a show of sociability that says they're in this together, because he's her only way out of this cellar. He's not a stranger predator, a serial killer in mid spree. He's just a weak man who's let his grievances fester and steer his life into this blind alley from which he sees no way back. But there has to be a way back. She must lead him there.

'That's unfair,' she says. 'I've worked hard for what I have.'

'You didn't have to work at being attractive,' he says, 'at being the centre of everything. At being bright. Success was guaranteed.'

'Nothing is guaranteed.'

'Guaranteed! You apply yourself and the golden gates open.'

But his words aren't about her. They're about him. Every gate opened to her is an opportunity denied to him. This is the blame psychology of the loser. And *loser* is what you are, Kate thinks, silently and cruelly.

'So what happened to you?' she asks, even though that's a dangerous question. Because *what happened* can't be good. *What happened* featured no golden gates. *What happened* is why they're here. But it's a subject she must breach. Because until they've got through *what happened* they can't move on to *what will happen*.

His answer surprises her.

'I did okay,' he says.

Sure you did! Doing okay explains the gigantic chip.

'I was in trading,' he says. 'Then banking. And property. Made a few bucks.'

The résumé's as brief as it's wide. And it's clear that he didn't do well in trading or banking or property. It's hard to extrapolate from a cellar but Kate doesn't picture a palace upstairs. For all his *trading* and *banking* and *property* the "few bucks" he made actually *sound* like a few bucks, as opposed to *plenty* of bucks. Kate almost laughs. This lousy cellar, the police hunt in full swing up above, they're both the marks of a guy who's done okay!

'You stopped watching me,' Kate says. She's referring to the fifteen year gap between the school photos and the recent campaign.

He continues scrutinising the old photos. His words strain for a casual tone.

'I got over you,' he says. 'I had a life. You think I'd circle forever like a moth round a flame?'

Kate hadn't *thought* anything. She hadn't known he existed until three days ago, the egotistical prick. And their very presence in this cellar gives his words an irrational slant. But she needs to play along.

'I suppose the thing weakened,' she says. She can't bring herself to say "love" and dare not substitute any more trivial emotion to stir his sense of grievance. He's no such inhibition though.

'I loved you even after that disaster,' he says. 'Even after we left school. You went to Durham. I travelled up twice to see you. I didn't have a clue where your digs where so I just hung round the campus for two days each time. Didn't spot you once. Two rail tickets and six nights sleeping rough and not a single sight. The trips were the lows of my life. I just wanted to end it all as I huddled in my sleeping bag in bus shelters and pictured you out partying, or in the sack with a new *Simon Sez*. I bet you never imagined in a million years that while you were being fucked in your student bed someone was out there in a stinking bus shelter thinking of you?'

He's right. No one in their right mind would imagine such a thing. And no one in their right mind would voluntarily *be* in a bus shelter. She pictures an open metal shell on the outskirts of the city, this pathetic person curled against the cold as *she* snuggled with her arms round the greatest boyfriend she ever had, and *FUCK YOU,* you piece of shit, for imagining that anything I did, whomever I loved, is anything to do with you. I hope those bus shelters were freezing and noisome with the stink of piss and puke and I hope the rain sprayed across you all night. Yes, she'd enjoyed life and love and never imagined other universes. But that's the way it should be. One pathetic loser wrapped in a dirty sleeping bag doesn't change that.

But the images of those long bus shelter nights, of the smelly student riding the train back south, are testament to the full weight of this guy's neurosis. This guy was beyond normal even then, and the thought scares her to death. She needs to reason with him. Even if that means risking offending him with the *trivial*.

'It was infatuation,' she says, 'not love.'

'You've no idea what it was.'

He turns suddenly from the wall. His tee shirt is stretched across gym-honed muscles that project the impression of an undersized head, and if she ever did know this person she doesn't know him now. He says he had his life but did he? Has he moved on? Or have his *love* and his *doing okay* festered and mutated? Because it's clear that this person hates her.

But then he says, casually, surprisingly: 'I got over it. Really.'

She looks at him in disbelief.

'The trips to Durham were eye-openers. On those long train journeys back I saw what a fool I was. And I finally decided not to waste my life.'

Kate says nothing.

'Do you know what happened to Simon Sez?' he says.

Of course she knows. She doesn't forget the boy she slept with on her seventeenth birthday. She'd cried her eyes out a decade ago when she heard, pictured Simon lying in the squalor of a squat, dead from a drug overdose at twenty two, and *fuck you*, you bastard, Simon was with me barely a year but he gave me more than you could in a lifetime. So the betrayal of her next words is hard, but she needs to connect with this bastard if she's ever to get out of here, so: 'Yeah,' she says. 'Drugs or something.' As if it was nothing. She hates herself for the words but she has to find common ground.

But his own words are puzzling. *Over her* is hard to reconcile with the stalking campaign, his calls and cards, his intrusion into her life, with this dingy cellar and the chain round her ankle. She *still* doesn't understand.

'Why have you been stalking me?' she asks.

He smiles his cold, scared smile and bends to retrieve the photo album from beside the camp bed. He turns its pages. Kate shivers as his eyes absorb the obscene images. For a moment he's distracted with his salacious inspection. If she leapt up from the camp bed she'd take him by surprise but his bulk is intimidating and she's no weapon. And her lack of a weapon is foolishness. When he leaves this time she'll find something, arm herself ready for another chance. It may be the last she gets.

'I've been *over* you a long time, Kate,' he says. He's still studying the album.

'So why did you start stalking me?'

He snaps the album closed. 'Because it began again,' he says, 'when we met last year. Not the schoolboy love. That could never rise from the dead. But things were just the same in every other way: I was right there and you didn't see me.'

'Of course I saw you. You were my client.'

'You didn't *recognise* me. Didn't remember me. I was nothing to you. Just another drink-drive court case, a fee earned. Sure I was your client, and you went through all the motions, but when your defence failed you just moved on to the next business and forgot me. And you hadn't recognised me, still hadn't seen me. Fifteen years on and it was happening again. You walked away with no idea what that conviction, what losing my driving licence, did to me. So I decided that you *would* notice. You'd notice when your perfect world was turned upside down.'

He drops the album onto the bed and his smile is angry and frightened and powerful.

'And it was a great game. I realised I could toy with you for years. And when I tired of it I'd bring you here and make sure you understood.' He smiles. 'Do you know: even if I didn't plan on us being here so soon I'm glad we are.'

'We need to stop this,' Kate says. 'Before it goes too far.'

'No,' he says. He lifts the tee shirt and reveals the pitted metal of an old automatic pistol tucked into his waistband.

'We need to finish it,' he says. And his hands are shaking now.

Oh dear God! Oh shit! Not here. Not right now. Why didn't you find yourself a weapon you stupid bitch? You had all day. You've had *three* fucking days.

'Please,' she says. He pulls the gun free and his hands are shaking but his eyes are steady.

'I wanted you to see me,' he tells her.

'Please,' she says.

But she's talking to a burning void.

'And now you have,' he says.

52

Feather drives slowly down Caledonian Road. Neon dances on the windscreen. Sterile shop windows illuminate empty pavements. He turns at Copenhagen and nearly runs down three girls out bingeing in light jackets and short skirts. They totter out against the lights and though he stamps on the brake they collide. The Corsa is stationary when they hit but motion is relative. The bodywork thumps and a girl falls sideways onto the wing. Another spins clear, holding a bottle high. The last one goes down in front of the car.

There's screaming and shouting.

The first girl slaps the bonnet. Feather kills the engine and climbs out.

'Crazy old git!' the bottle girl says. 'You've killed her.' She's staring at her friend on the ground. 'Allie! Talk to me.'

'What happened?' Allie says. She's staring up at the night.

'Fucker ran over you.'

'What happened?' she repeats.

'Ohmygod I think she's hurt.'

'Stupid old git. You shouldn't be on the roads.'

'Allie!'

Allie is sitting in the road. A Captain Morgan is rolling towards the gutter. Her friend squats beside her. The other lifts herself off the wing and comes to meet Feather.

'Silly bastard. Why don't you look where you're going?'

'Help her up,' Feather says.

'You coulda killed us.'

'Where are you girls going?'

'Nonna your business, you cheeky old fart.'

'Enrico's,' the sitting girl says. 'What happened?'

Feather stands over them. 'Help her up,' he says. The bottle girl gets her friend up and they stand in a hug, one palm each on the Corsa's bonnet like they're on the deck of a rolling ship.

'Give us yer name,' the other says. She's grabbing at Feather's arm.

He lets her take it and walks her to the far pavement. Traffic's stopped. Headlights blind them. 'Stay there,' he says but she follows him back out.

'The fuck you tell me what to do! You nearly killed us. I'm reporting you.'

'Get his number, Sarah!'

'I already got it.' The bottle girl's released her run-over friend and is holding her iPhone up.

Feather puts his hand on her back and she curses and points her phone at him and says Hey! Hey! but he moves her across in front of the waiting headlights and her friends follow. People have gathered. They've stopped to watch the show. They're clapping and cheering.

The girls huddle together and give Feather lip. He looks at them. They're fifteen, maybe sixteen years old, Donna Jordan's age when she arrived at Euston. 'Go home,' he says. 'It's freezing.'

'Fuck you.'

'And kiss your licence goodbye, grandpa. You nearly killed us.'

'Get his number, Sarah.'

'Go home,' Feather says, 'before you get hurt.'

But they won't. The city's their playground and they've no concept of danger. The bright lights have yet to cut them and leave them bleeding. They know nothing of walking the streets for the price of their next fix, nor of cold, broken bodies on church steps.

Feather crosses back to the Corsa, waving at the headlights. The girls are yelling behind him, calling for the cops, but by the time he's rolled the Corsa twenty yards and parked it in front of the pub they've just vacated the girls have drifted off towards the next place that will let them in with dirt on their hands and tears in their stockings. He goes into the pub and pushes through a noisy crowd, half of them clones of the Teen Princesses. He asks at the bar for George and a rotund guy in his sixties walks over and asks how he can help. He's all smile and propriety. His territory. Feather reaches and pulls out his brief and George drops the smile because he's not checked his clientele's ages tonight. But Feather's not after teen bingers.

'You got a regular, name of Marcus Wain?' he asks.

'I've lots of regulars. I don't memorise names, pal.'

Feather describes Wain. George looks sour but nods his head.

'Yeah,' he says, 'there's a guy like that comes in.'

'How about Monday night?'

'Don't remember.'

'Three nights back? You don't remember?'

George holds his hands wide and waggles his head in pantomime ridicule. 'I don't remember who was in *last* night,' he says. 'We get busy.'

'And you don't know Wain well enough that you'd recall seeing him?'

'That's right.'

'Any idea *when* was he last in?'

'Not a bloody clue. Coulda been Monday, coulda been a montha Sundays. Really, officer, we're a busy place.'

Feather snaps his warrant back and works his way back out. Alibi neither confirmed nor disproven. Very smart, Gyminy. Have you got Kate Walker, Gyminy Cricket?

He fires up the Corsa and continues to King's Cross and turns towards Paddington.

There are three people in the incident room. Crane, Obasanjo and Mary.

Obasanjo looks up first. 'You got no home?' he says.

'Sir,' Feather says. 'You got no home, sir.'

'Sir,' Obasanjo says. 'We thought you'd knocked off, *sir*.'

'I was never on.' Feather lowers himself into the chair by Crane's desk. 'Marcus Wain,' he says.

Crane's ears prick up. Mary comes across to sit sideways on the desk. 'Bring him up,' Feather says.

Crane scrolls his computer.

'I had a chat,' Feather reports. 'He worries me.'

Obasanjo joins them and they cluster round Crane's desk in the empty room.

'Something about him,' Feather says. 'He's got the temperament and he's nervous and he was too quick with his alibis. He was sure he was covered before he even knew the time window.'

'His alibi hold up?'

'He gave me a pub landlord who may or may not have seen him Monday, plus two of his cronies. But no contact details until tomorrow. So right now it doesn't hold up.'

'He'll know we'll follow up on the names.'

'But not till tomorrow,' Feather says. 'Maybe that's all he needs. You've got him as an estate agent. Which firm?'

Crane swivels the screen. The background notes give the firm's name. Feather raises his eyebrows. 'Well that's interesting,' he says. 'They've got a property for sale across from her house.'

'I'll talk to them,' Obasanjo says.

The firm's number is an office hours commercial number. It's going to take some digging via the registered holding company. Obasanjo heads to his phone, leaving them reading the notes on Crane's screen. There's not much, just the bare bones of Wain's life. He's thirty-three. Single. No criminal record. Brought up and educated in Kingston. Ordinary degree in Marketing and Management at UEL. Worked three years at a city stockbrokers before moving to Lloyd's Bank. Spent five years there before moving on again, to the estate agents. Feather wonders. He calls Angela Harris. It's ten-thirty but Kate's sister is wide awake and scared as hell. Feather reassures her and asks if she knows Wain. She doesn't. Another question: where did Kate go to school? Angela tells him that Kate went to Rowledge High in Kingston, which is another interesting fact because the school's name is up on Crane's screen. It's Wain's old school. And Wain is just a year older than Kate so what's the chance the two didn't know each other? What's the chance he wouldn't recall her after he's hired her as his lawyer? Feather kills the line and stares at the blank windows.

'It could be him,' he says.

'There's nothing that precludes him,' Mary agrees. 'And he doesn't sound like someone who's career gives him a purpose in life. His job progression isn't upwards.'

'Maybe the stockbroker job was his shot at the big time,' Feather says. 'Lousy qualifications don't bar you from that game. But he was out after three years and into the banking job. A step down. And selling houses is another rung lower. Wain's not wealthy and he's got some bad habits, ones that lose you your driving licence. A once-high-flyer on a downward track. Someone who might find alternative ways to get his kicks.'

'But why target an old schoolmate?' Crane says.

'Beats me,' Feather says. 'But why did he lie about not knowing her? Do we have any names from his old jobs?'

Crane works the internet and pulls up the stockbroking firm and Lloyds Bank. The stockbrokers have two names on their bio page. The bank lists three contacts at Wain's old branch.

Mary goes to make calls. Gets mostly unanswered numbers. The single conversation she has is short and frustrating. Obasanjo's at her shoulder when she returns.

'I reached the Lloyds branch manager,' Mary reports. 'He won't discuss staff without a notice. We'll get one started.'

'Wain's boss at the estate agents is Wendy Grey,' Obasanjo says. 'Address in St John's Wood.'

Feather taps his finger on the two other bank contacts and Crane searches the telephone directory. The printer spits a list and he brings it over. The names are not common. The first has only a single entry. Crane calls and confirms it's the bank worker but he's a recent recruit and doesn't recognise Marcus Wain's name. The second name has four entries. Obasanjo and Crane call the numbers and eliminate three. The last one isn't answering and she's probably the one. A woman called Andrea Oglethorpe, Small Businesses Manager at Wain's old branch. Feather stands and gestures to Mary

'Keep digging,' he tells the others. He and Mary go out.

~~~~~

It's eleven thirty. They're stuck behind a cab in West Hampstead and Feather is still replaying his conversation with Marcus Wain, thinking about Wain's lies and the schoolday connections. Mary's got the courtesy light on and is searching the A-Z. She tells Feather to take the third right. The taxi's in no hurry. Feather pulls them the wrong side of centre bollards and puts his foot down. The taxi speeds up and beats them to stay in front, but they're at the turning. Feather swings the wheels and loses him.

It's a street of terraces and mid market semis. They find a house with two cars on its tiny forecourt and a beat up Mazda on the road blocking them in. Parents' and kid's wheels. The vehicle jam says they're home despite the unanswered phone. They step out into the night and cross the pavement. Feather presses the doorbell. There's a delay. Mary steps forward and tries again. Holds the button. Lights come on and a guy in a dressing gown opens the door. Feather shows his brief and the guy confirms that his wife works at the bank. Feather says they need a word and the guy wastes a few seconds saying his wife's in bed, as if they're here on a damn social call.

'Bank business,' Feather says, meaning the guy isn't in the loop. He sees the way it is and invites them into their front lounge and heads up to rouse his wife. She comes down in her gown and Feather holds his card up again and asks about Marcus Wain. Andrea is wary. Yes, she knew Wain but she isn't authorised to talk. Same line as her manager. But this is urgent and this is face to face and when Feather asks Andrea whether she's followed the news about Kate Walker her eyes open in what looks like more than just surprise. Her face says she's making connections.

'We need to know about Wain,' Feather says. 'Right now.'

Andrea Oglethorpe thinks about it. She's a good looking woman in her mid forties, intelligent and sharp, even pulled from bed.

'This is unofficial,' Feather says. 'Nothing will be taken forward. If Mr Wain's involved we'll serve notice on the bank for information.'

'I'm still not sure what I should say.'

'Tell us,' Feather smiles, 'about your suspicion that Marcus Wain might be a stalker. Might be an abductor. We need anything you know right now. It could save Kate Walker's life. You can balance that against employee confidentiality.'

Andrea shakes her head.

'This is urgent,' Mary says.

Andrea looks at her. 'Let me talk to my manager,' she says.

'We already have. He'll tell you to keep quiet. But we've got a missing woman and time is running out. Wain's done something like this before, hasn't he?'

Andrea thinks again and folds her arms. Looks down and speaks.

'Marcus developed a fixation on a colleague. A married woman. He started showing up near her house and at pubs and shops she visited. Phoned her when her husband was out. And she once got a Valentine's at work that embarrassed her. She reported Marcus and he was cautioned. Things settled down for a while but then one evening he showed up at her house and scared her. She slammed the door and called the police. He had a story for them and they didn't take it further but the bank sacked him.' She looks up. 'I shouldn't

314

have told you this,' she says.

But she should. There's a woman missing and she knows it's entirely credible that Marcus Wain is the guy who has her.

They thank her and leave. Andrea isn't going to get much sleep tonight.

~~~~~

'It's him,' Mary says.

'We need to get into his flat,' Feather says. Andrea Oglethorpe's information confirms Wain as a credible suspect but doesn't give them a free ticket. They need a warrant. Mary calls and gets Crane working on the application but it's going to take ninety minutes minimum.

They climb into the Corsa and Feather cranks the heater. It's midnight and the street is dead and ninety minutes is an eternity. Feather's phone rings. It's Zav McGeary.

'He was watching her from across the road,' he says. 'There's a property for sale opposite her house.'

Feather already knows this. He pinches his nose and presses the phone to his ear. McGeary's still out there playing detective and he seems to be good at it. 'How do you know he used the property?' he says.

'I'm in here now,' McGeary says.

'You broke in?'

'Sue me,' McGeary says. 'But the abductor's been here. You need to get out of bed and find out who had access to this place.'

Feather's not in bed and he already knows who had access to the house and *fuck you*, McGeary. You think you're helping but all you're doing is muddying the waters. 'You can't break into properties,' he says.

'Sue me,' McGeary repeats. What Feather would like to do is kick him in the arse. If Wain's their man they'll need forensics from the house and McGeary's trampling about in there won't help that. Feather holds the pinch on his nose and tells McGeary to stay put and not touch anything. He kills the line and gives Mary the news. 'Tell Crane to get hold of the estate agent,' he says. 'She'll need to come out. And tell him to move with the warrant for Wain's place.'

315

Mary passes the message on as Feather turns the Corsa and drives back out, wondering if it's Wain's traces they'll find at the for sale property. They can take a look, anyhow. McGeary has reported a break-in – albeit his own – and it's their job to investigate. No warrant necessary. At the main road he waits for a cleaning truck to churn by then turns towards Maida Vale.

It's a quarter past midnight. Kate's street is dark. There's a shadow by the gate across from her house which materialises into McGeary. Feather parks the Corsa and he and Mary walk back and are just about to speak to him when an Audi pulls up and double-parks in front of the property. A tall, middle aged woman gets out. Feather fishes for his brief and the woman tells him she's Wendy Grey, here about the break-in. She goes ahead into the house with a loop of keys. McGeary follows.

Wendy switches on lights. The place is freezing.

'Where?' she asks, and McGeary gestures towards the back kitchen where he's smashed a pane. Wendy inspects the damage, unaware that the burglar is by her side. Feather's not interested in the door.

'Mind if we take a look?' he asks.

Wendy looks round the kitchen and tells Feather to go ahead and McGeary leads them upstairs to a bare bedroom. When the light is switched on it's clear that someone has been spending time here. There's a stool by the window taken from the kitchen breakfast bar and there's a plastic carrier bag on the floor with cans and wrappings inside. Wendy arrives and looks at the stool. 'That shouldn't be there,' she says. McGeary's watching Feather and sees that this place means something to him. Feather peers out of the window but sees only reflections. He turns to Wendy.

'You've got a guy called Marcus Wain works for you,' he says.

Wendy is caught by the assertion. Feather repeats it.

'Yes,' she says. 'Why do you ask?'

'He was using this property to keep watch on a house across the road.'

Wendy is open mouthed. She's been dragged out of bed for a break-in. Now they're talking about one of her work colleagues. And what's across the road anyway?

'Kate Walker's house,' Feather says and that's enough. Wendy reads the papers. She watches TV. 'Ohmygod,' she says.

'There'll be some officers coming round,' Feather says. 'Perhaps you'd wait for them.'

Wendy's hand clamps her mouth.

'Would Wain have access to this house?' Feather asks her.

Wendy nods. 'He'd just have to open the safe and sign out the keys.'

'And if there's no customer he wouldn't even need to sign for the keys because no one would notice they were missing.'

'Yes.'

'And if he copied the keys he'd be free to come and go.'

'You're saying he's involved with the missing solicitor?'

'Did you notice anything about Wain lately? Moods, anxiety, unusual activities?'

Wendy shakes her head. 'Marcus keeps himself to himself. We don't really talk...'

But there's something.

'The last few months?' Feather prompts. 'Last few days?'

This is one that Wendy can answer. 'He's been off sick this week,' she says.

'So you've not seen him since last week?'

Wendy looks at the stool and the window and the blackness beyond and her mouth is open but no words come.

'His behaviour?' Feather presses.

Wendy takes a breath.

'We've had some problems,' she says. 'Some account irregularities. Marcus has been called to Head Office.'

'He's been caught stealing?'

'I can't say exactly but we discovered some misappropriated payments.'

Feather nods. Turns to face the window again.

Gyminy Cricket. One of life's losers. Career in decline. Record of stalking and harassing women. Maybe not happy about life, maybe prepared to operate beyond the law. Wain in here, behind the window, watching Kate Walker's house. Now absent from work. But not sick: Gyminy was fine two hours ago.

Crane will be working through the warrant application form, ready to fax it. They'll have the thing in an hour.

But Gyminy knows they're coming.

They don't have an hour.
They'll go without the warrant.

53

The Corsa bucks and fishtails as Feather fights it across town with his foot to the floor. He checks the rearview and curses, and Mary turns to confirm that the Ducato's still on their tail. Go home! he'd told McGeary, but the bastard won't listen and he's on their tail like this is a Hollywood chase only this isn't Hollywood, this is an eighty-mile-per-hour dash along Marylebone with disaster threatening at every junction. The midnight streets are quiet but there are always traffic clusters, a rush of cabs across the lights, straggling cars, cleaning trucks, pedestrians, not all of them alert. If they meet the Teen Princesses again they're mincemeat. Feather bangs the gear and they jump reds at Great Portland and plunge into the underpass in a pulsing roar of tortured steel and rubber. A flare of brake lights, flashing concrete, then the black expands and they're out onto Euston with the Ducato hanging on their tail like a rutting barnacle, and if Feather even touches the brakes the van's going to total them. He curses again and spins the wheel and the rear wheels get away from him but he fights them straight with sheer fury and they're racing up York with the Corsa's exhaust blatting from the station walls and taxis swerving and venting horns. They cross the canal and jump endless reds. Then the bridge racks up and they dive below a disorientating streak of lights as a train sweeps across the sky. Mary's clutching the door and the dash and it's not a good ride with Feather gripping the wheel like a fighter pilot zooming high over the Channel. He pumps the brakes – sod the bloody Ducato – and tyres shriek and slide them into a street whose narrow perspective moves twice as fast. A cab is dropping off, blocking the street. Feather aims for the gap and squeezes through with a grunt. The grunt's for the Ducato. Get through there, you bastard! But it does, and Miracle Man McGeary's still with them. The guy's not thinking straight. The guy's going to kill himself and kill them, and Feather tastes McGeary's desperation, but it's too late, too fucking *late* my friend and you've got my sympathy, you lunatic bastard, because I used to have a woman the spitting image of Kate and I know what it's like to have that face smile at you, but you should have gone home and waited for the knock on the door because there's nothing you can do here but get us all killed. There's nothing you can do to make it *not* too late. Feather brakes, finally, hard, but overshoots Marcus Wain's corner building, and McGeary's headlights are almost in the back seat as the Corsa slides to a stop at an angle across the junction. The screech of the Ducato's tyres is in their ears as they open the doors.

Feather's out and striding across the pavement but before he gets to the step Mary's already thumbing the bell, holding the button and rap-rap-rapping the glass. McGeary arrives and he adds his fist to the door but there's no light in the glass and the front door's solid. They're not going to get through it unless McGeary attacks it with his head.

'Round the side,' McGeary says, and he's gone. Feather and Mary run round after him and find him kicking at a yard gate. The gate gives and they pile through into the stone-flagged yard and race to the back door. Back doors are never as sturdy, never as secure, and McGeary, the housebreaking expert, pulls a brick from an ornamental edging and puts it through the glass then finds a second brick to smash away the shards. If Wain is home and in bed he'll be jumping out of it. Bells you can ignore. Fists on the door will rouse you. But breaking glass demands action. Feather eases his arm through the broken pane and unlocks the door and tells McGeary to *stay there* then crunches in over glass with Mary behind him.

Feather opens a door and comes into a room that looks out onto the street. Wain has still not appeared. There are no lights, no footsteps except McGeary's, close behind them. Feather finds another door leading out into the hallway and strides towards it, holding up a hand for silence. They hear a thump. It came from somewhere on this level or maybe below. Feather opens the door and gropes for the switch and lights up the hall then gestures to Mary and runs across to open a door onto a dark bedroom and another onto a bathroom. Nothing. But beneath where the communal stairs angle up is another door. Feather eases it open and there are steps descending into near darkness and from down there they hear the sound of voices, a woman's sudden scream, a man's anger.

Feather plunges down. His feet barely fit the treads and threaten to pitch him down and he leaps the last three steps as his balance goes, landing shockingly hard on the cellar floor. He needs to visit that damn gym. He needs to lose that weight. He's just not built for dramatics. Feet are pounding down the steps behind him and he spins towards the back, a door in a dividing wall. The voices are coming from there. A woman's voice, sobbing. And Gyminy Cricket's voice. Marcus Wain. Angry. Then Feather is jolted aside as McGeary dives ahead.

'Stop,' Feather says.

But McGeary's already kicking the door open and the cellar floods with yellow light from the back room and instantly there are two bangs, then a third, and McGeary's thrown back, arms flailing, legs wheeling, and he crashes down at Feather's feet. Mary's alongside now and the two of them step right and left, clear of the line of sight as McGeary moans on the floor. Feather has no time to glance down. He finds cover to the left and from the angle he sees Marcus Wain standing with his back to a wall of photographs, aiming a pistol over the figure of Kate Walker who's down on a camp bed and turning with terrified eyes. When she sees McGeary she shrieks and scrambles over the bed, tumbling it, but she's only halfway through the door when the gun fires again and she goes down like she's been hit with a hammer.

Time slows. Time stops. Feather sweeps up a sheet metal firescreen and holds it ahead of him, angled to the ceiling and leaps over Kate's body. The firescreen is futile against even the smallest calibre bullet but it's a psychological shield and it's a diversion, it might induce Wain to fire clear of it, at what he can see, at Feather's lower limbs and arms. Might even, if Feather's lucky, deflect a bullet with it's angle. Even sheet metal can yield and deform and bounce a bullet away if it's hit at a shallow enough angle, but all the what-ifs and wherefores are irrelevant anyway because a second later Feather smashes into Marcus Wain and Wain's gun arm flies up to unleash a shot into the joists. Feather's momentum carries Wain back across a garden chair onto an old gramophone, sending junk flying all ways, and the chair shatters beneath them as they roll back off the unit and crash to the floor. Feather pushes himself up, grabbing for Wain's gun hand but the guy slips away and pulls up his arm and aims at Feather's ample target, then his feet catch the chain stretched taut by

Kate's prone body and he goes down against the piano. He lands hard but points the gun and grins a wild, hurting grin as he pulls the trigger, but before he finds the pressure he's hit in the face by a rusted iron billet, an old window counterweight Mary Charlton has hurled, and Wain's cheek blossoms red, but he still has the gun, which is a crappy little Walman semiautomatic, about a hundred years old, with one shot left in its magazine.

Feather's ears are ringing. He can barely hear McGeary's groans, nothing from Kate, and all that matters is that Mary gets the hell back through the door, but her ears must have gone too because she's not heeding him. Feather's yelling and waving her back and watching the nozzle of the gun but Mary's still there. She's all bad tactics. This isn't how you deal with an armed guy.

'Give it up,' Feather says, though maybe Wain can't hear. Wain's eyes are cold and scared and furious and his mouth grins in wonderment at what he's done, what this has come to, what it's always been coming to since those schooldays watching the girl who never saw him.

Sound returns.

'You bastard,' Kate's screaming. She's screaming at Wain as she tugs the chain to get at McGeary. 'You bastard! Do it!'

Wain grins.

'Do it!' she screams. 'Coward! Do it!'

Wain's eyes are on Kate and though he hears her he's listening to another conversation.

'Stay back,' Feather shouts. His arm rises to calm things down, to keep Wain's attention focused.

'Do it!' Kate Walker screams and her vehemence finally cracks Wain's calm. He looks at her from below the piano and illuminates her with his smile which is wide, a grin that splits his face and is more like a snarl, and Kate is yelling that this is what you wanted, you bastard, I can see you now, so what's stopping you, and Wain's smile splits to open his mouth and push the gun in. Feather leaps but it's too late.

~~~~~

It's a shit storm. The paramedics want McGeary on a stretcher but the steps are too steep and the bastard is cursing and saying he can get up them by himself, which is easy to say when you're lying on the floor. He's crawled towards the rear room where Kate is weeping softly as she holds him. She can't come out further until they get the chain off her. The bullet has done McGeary no great damage, more's the pity, but he'd bled profusely before the paramedics staunched it and Kate's hands are slippery. The shackle saved her life, whipped her off her feet and out of her own bullet's trajectory, and bar the one in McGeary's shoulder and the one Wain dealt himself there's little damage.

'Jesus Christ,' Clough is saying. He's in the front cellar with Feather and Andy Heldt and two CSIs waiting to go in. The paramedics are crowding Kate and McGeary. You can't move for people. Clough's told Feather ten times to go upstairs but Feather just keeps telling him to take it easy. He's watching a guy work on the chain beyond the paramedics. It's a slow job, a tiny hacksaw against tempered steel. It's going to take all night and McGeary will have bled to death long before he's through, but then Mary Charlton reappears down the stairs with a key that fits the hasp. It was on a peg in the hallway, she tells them. 'Jesus Christ,' Clough says and Heldt shakes his head and opens his mouth wide. 'I thought someone had checked. Why are the fuckers sawing it?'

Mary goes through and the hacksaw guy grins and Feather says take it easy, Guv. Clough tells him yet again to get the hell out of here and make some room in the place and Feather tells him he's going, any moment now. Then the CSIs squeeze past into the back room and stand looking at the photos whilst the paramedics get McGeary to his feet and moving towards the stairs. They bring him through, and Kate's now free and supporting him and the bastard's looking a little woozy now, though the bleeding has stopped. The party halts by Feather and Kate is speaking.

'He'd decided,' she says. 'He knew he was cornered. So he'd decided that neither of us would come out.' She's holding onto McGeary who's probably hurting like hell and needs to get up those stairs but the bastard pulls up a grin anyway.

'Close,' he says.

Feather has nothing to trump a comment of that calibre and isn't about to point out that if Wain knew how to shoot then none of them would be walking out of here. Five bullets are hard to waste in a confined space.

So yeah, it was close.

'Jesus Christ,' Clough says again. Heldt shakes his head.

'Did you find them?' Kate asks.

Feather looks at her. The paramedics tug at McGeary. They need to get him to hospital.

'The one who killed her.'

Donna Jordan.

Feather smiles. 'Her girlfriend,' he says. 'You met her.'

Kate's face drops, as if Donna's killer being someone who cared is worse than it being a stranger, which it probably is. Her shoulders sag but she grips McGeary's arm and turns him away and they make their slow way up, out of the cellar.

Feather waits until they're all clear then nods to Clough and Heldt and pulls his coat tight. Then he takes a deep breath and gets himself started up the steps.

THE END

ACKNOWLEDGEMENTS

I wrote this book to take a break from my PI Eddie Flynn series and start chipping away at the backlog of ideas awaiting development on my "Urban Thriller" shelf. There are a good few ideas stacked up there and I pulled this one out for no other reasons than that its subject matter offered the opportunity to try out a distinctive narrative style to match the immediacy of the subject. It was also convenient that the story could be tagged "thriller" as easily as "crime" and so perhaps reach a wider audience.

The book is not a legal thriller, but the heroine is a criminal solicitor, and various threads of the story have a distinctly legal background. It seemed important to me to get those details right. Assistance with this was provided by Kerry Davies who steered me clear of any major flaws whilst acknowledging, as a crime reader herself, that it's sometimes okay to colour reality for the purpose of entertainment. So any remaining errors and distortions related to the workings of the British lower court and the lives of criminal solicitors are not only mine but may even be deliberate.

I've consulted both my reference library and the internet for the information I needed, and in particular have found Mike Seabrook's advice from an old issue of Verbatim useful to help me avoid police jargon pitfalls, though I've no doubt a few general errors will be spotted by working coppers. Perhaps these also can be excused under the banner of "colour".

Thanks once again to my wife, Odette, who read the first draft and made suggestions, and with fond memories of our border collie Eric who took his last tea break with me during the writing.

BEHIND CLOSED DOORS
Michael Donovan

Family feuds, booze and bad company. Teenager Rebecca Slater's walk on the wild side has taken a downward spiral. And now she's disappeared.

But her family don't seem to have noticed. Wealthy, private, dysfunctional, the Slaters deny that their daughter is missing – even as they block all attempts by Rebecca's friends to contact her.

So the friends contact a private investigator.

Eddie Flynn is good at finding people. And he's good at spotting lies. It doesn't take him long to see through the Slaters' denials. So he digs around, and isn't too surprised when some unpleasant people come scuttling out of the cracks in the Slaters' perfect world.

But for these people the teenager's disappearance is part of a plan. One that's too important to be threatened by an investigator with more persistence than sense. So it's time for the investigator to disappear...

Winner of the **Northern Crime 2012** award, *Behind Closed Doors* has been acclaimed for its departure from the norm for British crime fiction...

'Donovan refreshingly breaks [the tradition] with remarkable success'
Cuckoo Review

'Eddie Flynn is part Philip Marlowe, part Eddie Gumshoe, a likeable wisecracking guy but with a temper when roused ... humour ... violent confrontations ... well recommended.'
eurocrime

www.michaeldonovancrime.com

THE DEVIL'S SNARE
Michael Donovan

They call them the "Killer Couple". Accused of killing their daughter the Barbers have been on the run from public opinion for two years.

But the Barbers are still fighting. And if their high profile campaign to clear their name and get their baby back has made them rich that was never their intention.

Meanwhile a failed prosecution hasn't dampened the media's hunger for revelations. Their investigators are on the job, moving towards an exposure that will spotlight the Barbers as the killers they are. And now a dangerous vigilante has joined the fray: if the system can't bring justice he'll mete out his own.

P.I. Eddie Flynn doesn't read the tabloids. Shuns limelight. Trusts only in facts. But can't resist challenges. When the Barbers come to him for help he pushes judgement aside and signs up. His mission: keep them safe and find their child.

Sounds like nice, solid detective work. Until Flynn realises that his clients are hiding something...

'A slick, dynamic mystery.'
Kirkus Reviews

'Escapism at its best'
Postcard Reviews

'... complicated ... wonderful ... brilliant. I recommend anyone ... to try this book. [It] will haunt your days and nights.'
Georgia Cuthbertson, Cuckoo Review

www.michaeldonovancrime.com

COLD CALL
Michael Donovan

In the black of night the intruder breaks into the victim's house armed with a knife and garrotte. Her body is found thirty hours later, a mass of stab wounds, a deadly laceration round her neck.

Is this the Diceman, killing again after seven years lying low? Or does London have a copycat killer?

P.I. Eddie Flynn has been out of that world since his failed hunt for the Diceman let the killer go free and cost him his job in the Metropolitan Police.

Now, with the new killer on the rampage a bizarre phone call from his dead victim drags Flynn right back to centre stage and a new hunt. But this killer – copycat or not – takes a P.I.'s interference personally.

So now he has a new focus for his madness.

www.michaeldonovancrime.com

Printed in Great Britain
by Amazon